DAVID EDDINGS

HIGH HUNT

HarperCollins*Publishers*

HarperCollins*Publishers*
77–85 Fulham Palace Road,
Hammersmith, London W6 8JB

Published by HarperCollins*Publishers* 1993
1 3 5 7 9 8 6 4 2

First published in the USA by
G. P. Putnam's Sons 1973

A catalogue record for this book
is available from the British Library

ISBN 0 00 224281 8

Set in Times

Printed in Great Britain by
HarperCollinsManufacturing Glasgow

HIGH HUNT

FOR JUFELEE

The more things change
The more they remain the same.

Prologue

WHEN we were boys, before we lost him and before my brother and I turned away from each other, my father once told us a story about our grandfather and a dog. We were living in Tacoma then, in one of the battered, sagging, rented houses that stretch back in my memory and mark the outlines of a childhood spent unknowingly on the bare upper edge of poverty. Jack and I knew that we weren't rich, but it didn't really bother us all that much. Dad worked in a lumber mill and just couldn't seem to get ahead of the bills. And, of course, Mom being the way she was didn't help much either.

It had been a raw, blustery Saturday, and Jack and I had spent the day outside. Mom was off someplace as usual, and Dad was supposed to be watching us. About all he'd done had been to feed us and tell us to stay the hell out of trouble or he'd bite off our ears. He always said stuff like that, but we were pretty sure he didn't really mean it.

The yard around our house was cluttered with a lot of old junk abandoned by previous tenants—rusty car bodies and discarded appliances and the like—but it was a good place to play. Jack and I were involved in one of the unending, structureless games of his invention that filled the days of our boyhood. My brother—even then thin, dark, quick, and nervous—was a natural ringleader who settled for directing my activities when he couldn't round up a gang of neighborhood kids. I went along with him most of the time—to some extent because he was older, but even more, I suppose, because even then I really didn't much give a damn, and I knew that he did.

After supper it was too dark to go back outside, and the radio was on the blink, so we started tearing around the house. We got to playing tag in the living room, ducking back and forth around the big old wood-burning heating stove, giggling and yelling, our feet clattering on the worn linoleum. The Old Man was trying to read the paper, squinting through the dime-store glasses that didn't seem to help much and made him look

3

like a total stranger—to me at least.

He'd glance up at us from time to time, scowling in irritation. "Keep it down, you two," he finally said. We looked quickly at him to see if he really meant it. Then we went on back out to the kitchen.

"Hey, Dan, I betcha I can hold my breath longer'n you can," Jack challenged me. So we tried that a while, but we both got dizzy, and pretty soon we were running and yelling again. The Old Man hollered at us a couple times and finally came out to the kitchen and gave us both a few whacks on the fanny to show us that he meant business. Jack wouldn't cry—he was ten. I was only eight, so I did. Then the Old Man made us go into the living room and sit on the couch. I kept sniffling loudly to make him feel sorry for me, but it didn't work.

"Use your handkerchief" was all he said.

I sat and counted the flowers on the stained wallpaper. There were twelve rows on the left side of the brown water-splotch that dribbled down the wall and seventeen on the right side.

Then I decided to try another tactic on the Old Man. "Dad, I have to go."

"You know where it is."

When I came back, I went over and leaned my head against his shoulder and looked at the newspaper with him to let him know I didn't hold any grudges. Jack fidgeted on the couch. Any kind of enforced nonactivity was sheer torture to Jack. He'd take ten spankings in preference to fifteen minutes of sitting in a corner. School was hell for Jack. The hours of sitting still were almost more than he could stand.

Finally, he couldn't take anymore. "Tell us a story, Dad."

The Old Man looked at him for a moment over the top of his newspaper. I don't think the Old Man really understood my brother and his desperate need for diversion. Jack lived with his veins, like Mom did. Dad just kind of did what he had to and let it go at that. He was pretty easygoing—I guess he had to be, married to Mom and all like he was. I never really figured out where I fit in. Maybe I didn't, even then.

"What kind of a story?" he finally asked.

"Cowboys?" I said hopefully.

"Naw," Jack vetoed, "that's kid stuff. Tell us about deer hunting or something."

"Couldn't you maybe put a couple cowboys in it?" I insisted, still not willing to give up.

Dad laid his newspaper aside and took off his glasses. "So

you want me to tell you a story, huh?"

"With cowboys," I said again. "Be sure you don't forget the cowboys."

"I don't know that you two been good enough today to rate a story." It was a kind of ritual.

"We'll be extra good tomorrow, won't we, Dan?" Jack promised quickly. Jack was always good at promising things. He probably meant them, too, at the time anyway.

"Yeah, Dad," I agreed, "extra, extra, special good."

"That'll be the day," the Old Man grunted.

"Come on, Dad," I coaxed. "You can tell stories better'n anybody." I climbed up into his lap. I was taking a chance, since I was still supposed to be sitting on the couch, but I figured it was worth the risk.

Dad smiled. It was the first time that day. He never smiled much, but I didn't find out why until later. He shifted me in his lap, leaned back in the battered old armchair, and put his feet upon the coffee table. The wind gusted and roared in the chimney and pushed against the windows while the Old Man thought a few minutes. I watched his weather-beaten face closely, noticing for the first time that he was getting gray hair around his ears. I felt a sudden clutch of panic. My Dad was getting old!

"I ever tell you about the time your granddad had to hunt enough meat to last the family all winter?" he asked us.

"Are there cowboys in it?"

"Shut up, Dan, for cripes' sakes!" Jack told me impatiently.

"I just want to be sure."

"You want to hear the story or not?" the Old Man threatened.

"Yeah," Jack said. "Shut up and listen, for cripes' sakes."

"It was back in the winter of 1893, I think it was," Dad started. "It was several years after the family came out from Missouri, and they were trying to make a go of it on a wheat ranch down in Adams County."

"Did Grandpa live on a real ranch?" I asked. "With cowboys and everything?"

The Old Man ignored the interruption. "Things were pretty skimpy the first few years. They tried to raise a few beef-cows, but it didn't work out too well, so when the winter came that year, they were clean out of meat. Things were so tough that my uncles, Art and Dolph, had to get jobs in town and stay at a boardinghouse. Uncle Beale was married and out on his own by then, and Uncle Tod had gone over to Seattle to work in

the lumber mills. That meant that there weren't any men on
the place except my dad and my granddad."

"He was our great-granddad," Jack told me importantly.

"I know that," I said. "I ain't that dumb." I leaned my head
back against Dad's chest so I could hear the rumble of his voice
inside my head again.

"Great-Granddad was in the Civil War," Jack said. "You
told us that one time."

"You want to tell this or you want me to?" the Old Man
asked him.

"Yeah," I said, not lifting my head, "shut up, Jack, for
cripes' sakes."

"Anyhow," the Old Man went on, "Granddad had to stay
and tend the place, so *he* couldn't go out and hunt. Dad
was only seventeen, but there wasn't anybody else to go.
Well, the nearest big deer herd was over around Coeur d'Alene
Lake, up in the timber country in Idaho. There weren't any
game laws back then—at least nobody paid any attention to
them if there were—so a man could take as much as he
needed."

The wind gusted against the house again, and the wood
shifted in the heating stove, sounding very loud. The Old Man
got up, lifting me easily in his big hands, and plumped me on
the couch beside Jack. Then he went over and put more wood
in the stove from the big linoleum-covered woodbox against
the wall that Jack and I were supposed to keep full. He slammed
the door shut with an iron bang, dusted off his hands, and sat
back down.

"It turned cold and started snowing early that year," he
continued. "Granddad had this old .45-70 single-shot he'd carried in the war, but they only had twenty-six cartridge cases
for it. He and Dad loaded up all those cases the night before
Dad left. They'd pulled the wheels off the wagon and put the
runners on as soon as the snow really set in good, so it was
all ready to go. After they'd finished loading the cartridges,
Granddad gave my dad an old pipe. Way he looked at it, if
Dad was old enough to be counted on to do a man's work, he
was old enough to have his own pipe. Dad hadn't ever smoked
before—except a couple times down in back of the schoolhouse
and once out behind the barn when he was a kid.

"Early the next morning, before daylight, they hitched up
the team—Old Dolly and Ned. They pitched the wagon-bed,

and they loaded up Dad's bedding and other gear. Then Dad called his dogs and got them in the wagon-bed, shook hands with Granddad, and started out."

"I'll betcha he was scared," I said.

"Grown men don't get scared," Jack said scornfully.

"That's where you're wrong, Jack," the Old Man told him. "Dad was plenty scared. That old road from the house wound around quite a bit before it dropped down on the other side of the hill, and Dad always said he didn't dare look back even once. He said that if he had, he'd have turned right around and gone back home. There's something wrong with a man who doesn't get scared now and then. It's how you handle it that counts."

I know that bothered Jack. He was always telling everybody that he wasn't scared—even when I knew he was lying about it. I think he believed that growing up just meant being afraid of fewer and fewer things. I was always sure that there was more to it than that. We used to argue about it a lot."

"You ain't scared of anything, are you, Dad?" Jack asked, an edge of concern in his voice. It was almost like an accusation.

Dad looked at him a long time without saying anything. "You want to hear the story, or do you want to ask a bunch of questions?" It hung in the air between them. I guess it was always there after that. I saw it getting bigger and bigger in the next few years. Jack was always too stubborn to change his mind, and the Old Man was always too bluntly honest to lie to him or even to let him believe a lie. And I was in the middle—like always. I went over and climbed back up in my father's lap.

The Old Man went on with the story as if nothing had happened. "So there's Dad in this wagon-bed sled—seventeen years old, all alone except for the horses and those two black and tan hounds of his."

"Why can't we have a dog?" I asked, without bothering to raise my head from his chest. I averaged about once a week on that question. I already knew the answer.

"Your mother won't go for it." They always called each other "your mother" and "your father." I can't think of more than two or three times while we were growing up that I heard either one of them use the other's name. Of course most of the time they were fighting or not speaking anyway.

"Well, Uncle Dolph had loaned Dad an old two-dollar mail-order pistol, .32 short. Dad said it broke open at the top like a kid's cap gun and wouldn't shoot worth a damn, but it was kinda comfortable to have it along. Uncle Dolph shot a Swede in the belly with it a couple years later—put him in the hospital for about six months."

"Wow!" I said. "What'd he shoot him for?"

"They were drinking in a saloon in Spokane and got into a fight over something or other. The Swede pulled a knife and Uncle Dolph had to shoot him."

"Gee!" This was a pretty good story after all.

"It took Dad all of three days to get up into the timber country around the lake. Old Dolly and Ned pulled that sled at a pretty steady trot, but it was a long ways. First they went on up out of the wheat country and then into the foothills. It was pretty lonely out there. He only passed two or three farms along the way, pretty broken-down and sad-looking. But most of the time there wasn't anything but the two shallow ruts of the wagon road with the yellow grass sticking up through the snow here and there on each side and now and then tracks where a wolf or a coyote had chased a rabbit across the road. The sky was all kind of gray most of the time, with the clouds kind of low and empty-looking. Once in a while there'd be a few flakes of snow skittering in the wind. Most generally it'd clear off about sundown, just in time to get icy cold at night.

"Come sundown he'd camp in the wagon, all rolled up in his blankets with a dog on each side. He'd listen to the wolves howling off in the distance and stare up at the stars and think about how faraway they were." The Old Man's voice kind of drifted off and his eyes got a kind of faraway look in them.

The wood in the stove popped, and I jumped a little.

"Well, it had gotten real cold early that year, and when he got to the lake, it was frozen over—ice so thick you coulda driven the team and wagon right out on it, and about an inch of snow on top of the ice. He scouted around until he found a place that had a lot of deer-sign and he made camp there."

"What's deer-sign, Dad?" I asked.

"Tracks, mostly. Droppings. Places where they've chewed off twigs and bark. Anyhow, he pulled up into this grove, you see—big, first-growth timber. Some of those trees were probably two hundred feet tall and fifteen feet at the butt, and there wasn't any of the underbrush you see in the woods around here. The only snow that got in under them was what had got blown in from out in the clearings and such, so the ground was pretty dry."

From where I sat with my head leaned against the Old Man's chest, I could see into the dark kitchen. I could just begin to build a dark pine grove lying beyond the doorway with my eyes. I dusted the linoleum-turned-pine-needle floor with a powder-sugar of snow made of the dim edge of a streetlight on the corner that shone in through the kitchen window. It looked about right, I decided, about the way Dad described it.

"He got the wagon set where he wanted it, unhitched the horses, and started to make camp."

"Did he build a fire?" I asked.

"One of the first things he did," the Old Man said.

That was easy. The glow of the pilot light on the stove reflected a small, flickering point on the refrigerator door. It was coming along just fine.

"Well, he boiled up some coffee in an old cast-iron pan, fried up some bacon, and set some of the biscuits Grandma'd packed for him on a rock near the fire to warm. He said that about that time he'd have given the pipe and being grown-up and all of it just to be back home, sitting down to supper in the big, warm, old kitchen, with the friendly light of the coal-oil lamps and Grandma's cooking, and the night coming down around the barn, and the shadows filling up the lines of foot-prints in the snow leading from the house to the outbuildings." Dad's voice got faraway again.

"But he ate his supper and called the dogs up close and checked his pistol when he heard the wolves start to howl off in the distance. There probably wasn't anybody within fifty miles. Nothing but trees and hills and snow all around.

"Well, after he'd finished up with all the things you have to do to get a camp in shape, he sat down on a log by the fire and tried not to think about how lonesome he was."

"He had those old dogs with him, didn't he, Dad?" I asked, "and the horses and all? That's not the same as being *all* alone, is it?" I had a thing about loneliness when I was a kid.

Dad thought it over for a minute. I could see Jack grinding his teeth in irritation out of the corner of my eye, but I didn't really look over at him. I had the deep-woods camp I'd built out in the kitchen just right, and I didn't want to lose it. "I don't know, Dan," the Old Man said finally, "maybe the dogs and the horses just weren't enough. It can get awful lonesome out there in the timber by yourself like that—awful lonesome."

I imagine some of the questions I used to ask when I was a kid must have driven him right up the wall, but he'd always try to answer them. Mom was usually too busy talking about herself or about the people who were picking on her, and Jack was too busy trying to act like a grown-up or getting people to pay attention to him to have much time for my questions. But Dad always took them seriously. I guess he figured that if they were important enough for me to ask, they were important enough for him to answer. He was like that, my Old Man.

The wood popped in the stove again, but I didn't jump this time. I just slipped the sound on around to the campfire in the kitchen.

"Well, he sat up by his fire all night, so he wouldn't sleep too late the next morning. He watched the moon shine down on the ice out on the lake and the shadows from his fire flickering on the big tree trunks around his camp. He was pretty tired, and he'd catch himself dozing off every now and then, but he'd just fill up that stubby old pipe and light it with a coal from the fire and think about how it would be when he got home with a wagon-load of deer meat. Maybe then his older brothers would stop treating him like a wet-behind-the-ears kid. Maybe they'd listen to what he had to say now and then. And he'd catch himself drifting off into the dream and slipping down into sleep, and he'd get up and walk around the camp, stamping his feet on the frosty ground. And he'd have another cup of coffee and sit back down between his dogs and dream some more. After a long, long time, it started to get just a little bit light way off along one edge of the sky."

The faint, pale edge of daylight was tricky, but I finally managed it.

"Now these two hounds Dad had with him were trained to hunt a certain way. They were Pete and Old Buell. Pete was a young dog with not too much sense, but he'd hunt all day and half the night, too, if you wanted him to. Buell was an old dog, and he was as smart as they come, but he was getting to the point where he'd a whole lot rather lay by the fire and have somebody bring him his supper than go out and work for it. The idea behind deer hunting in those days was to have your dogs circle around behind the deer and then start chasing them toward you. Then when the deer ran by, you were supposed to just sort of bushwhack the ones you wanted. It's not really very sporting, but in those days you hunted for the meat, not for the fun.

"Well, as soon as it started to get light, Dad sent them out. Pete took right off, but Old Buell hung back. Dad finally had to kick him in the tail to make him get away from the fire."

"That's mean," I objected. I had the shadowy shapes of *my* two dogs near my reflected-pilot-light fire, and I sure didn't want anybody mistreating *my* old dogs, not even my own grandfather.

"Dog had to do his share, too, in those days, Dan. People didn't keep dogs for pets back then. They kept them to work. Anyway, pretty soon Dad could hear the dogs baying, way back in the timber, and he took the old rifle and the twenty-six bullets and went down to the edge of the lake."

"He took his pistol, too, I'll bet," I said. Out in *my* camp in the forests of the kitchen, *I* took *my* pistol.

"I expect he did, Dan, I expect he did. Anyway, after a little bit, he caught a flicker of movement back up at camp, out of the corner of his eye. He looked back up the hill, and there was Old Buell slinking back to the fire with his tail between his legs. Dad looked real hard at him, but he didn't dare move or make any noise for fear of scaring off the deer. Old Buell just looked right straight back at him and kept on slinking toward the fire, one step at a time. He knew Dad couldn't do a thing about it. A dog can do that sometimes, if he's smart enough.

"Well, it seems that Old Pete was able to get the job done by himself, because pretty soon the deer started to come out on the ice. Well, Dad just held off, waiting for more of them, you see, and pretty soon there's near onto a hundred of them out there, all bunched up. You see, a deer can't run very good on ice, and he sure don't like being out in the open, so when they found themselves out there, they just kind of huddled up to see what's gonna happen."

I could see Jack leaning forward now, his eyes bright with excitement and his lips drawn back from his teeth a little. Of course, I couldn't look straight at him. I had to keep everything in place out on the other side of the doorway.

"So Dad just lays that long old rifle out across the log and touches her off. Then he started loading and firing as fast as he could so's he could get as many as possible before they got their sense back. Well, those old black-powder cartridges put out an awful cloud of smoke, and about half the time he was shooting blind, but he managed to knock down seventeen of them before the rest got themselves organized enough to run out of range."

"Wow! That's a lot of deer, huh, Dad?" I said.

"As soon as Old Pete heard the shooting, he knew his part of the job was over, so he went out to do a little hunting for himself. The dogs hadn't had anything to eat since the day before, so he was plenty hungry, but then, a dog hunts better if he's hungry—so does a man.

"Anyway, Dad got the team and skidded the deer on in to shore and commenced to gutting and skinning. Took him most of the rest of the day to finish up."

Jack started to fidget again. He'd gone for almost a half hour without saying hardly anything, and that was always about his limit.

"Is a deer very hard to skin, Dad?" he asked.

"Not if you know what you're doing."

"But how come he did it right away like that?" Jack demanded. "Eddie Selvridge's old man said you gotta leave the hide on a deer for at least a week or the meat'll spoil."

"I heard him say that, too, Dad," I agreed.

"Funny they don't leave the hide on a cow then when they butcher, isn't it?" the Old Man asked. "At the slaughterhouse they always skin 'em right away, don't they?"

"I never thought of that," I admitted.

Jack scowled silently. He hated not being right. I think he hated that more than anything else in the world.

"Along about noon or so," Dad continued, "here comes Pete back into camp with a full belly and blood on his muzzle. Old Buell went up to him and sniffed at him and then started casting back and forth until he picked up Pete's trail. Then he lined out backtracking Pete to his kill."

Jack howled with sudden laughter. "That sure was one smart old dog, huh, Dad?" he said. "Why work if you can get somebody else to do it for you?"

Dad ignored him. "Old Pete had probably killed a fawn and had eaten his fill. Anyway, my dad kinda watched the dogs for a few minutes and then went back to work skinning. After he got them all skinned out, he salted down the hides and rolled them in a bundle—sold the hides in town for enough to buy his own rifle that winter, and enough left over to get his mother some yard goods she'd wanted. Then he drug the carcasses back to camp through the snow and hung them all up to cool out.

"He cleaned up, washing his hands with snow, fed the team, and then boiled up another pan of coffee. He fried himself a big mess of deer liver and onions and heated up some more of the biscuits. After he ate, he sat on a log and lit his pipe."

"I'll bet he was tired," Jack said, just to be saying something. "Not being in bed all the night before and all that."

"He still had something left to tend to," Dad said. "It was almost dark when he spotted Old Buell slinking back toward camp. He was out on the open, coming back along the trail Pete had broken though the snow. His belly looked full, and his muzzle and ears were all bloody the same way Pete's had been."

"He found the other dog's deer, I'll betcha." Jack laughed. "You *said* he was a smart old dog."

Beyond the kitchen doorway, one of my shadowy dogs crept slowly toward the warmth of the pilot-light campfire, his eyes sad and friendly, like the eyes of the hound some kid up the block owned.

"Well, Dad watched him for a minute or two, and then he took his rifle, pulled back the hammer, and shot Old Buell right between the eyes."

The world beyond the doorway shattered like a broken mirror and fell apart back into the kitchen again. I jerked up and looked straight into my father's face. It was very grim, and his eyes were very intent on Jack, as if he were telling my brother something awfully important.

He went on without seeming to notice my startled jump. "Old Buell went end over end when that bullet hit him. Then he kicked a couple times and didn't move anymore. Dad didn't even go over to look at him. He just reloaded the rifle and set it where it was handy, and then he and Old Pete climbed up into the wagon and went to bed.

"The next morning, he hitched up the team, loaded up the deer carcasses, and started back home. It took him three days again to get back to the wheat ranch, and Granddad and Grandma were sure glad to see him." My father lifted me off his lap, leaned back and lit a cigarette.

"It took them a good two days to cut up the deer and put them down in pickling crocks. After they finished it all up and Dad and Granddad were sitting in the kitchen, smoking their pipes with their sock feet up on the open oven door, Granddad turned to my Dad and said, "Sam, whatever happened to Old Buell, anyway? Did he run off?"

"Well, Dad took a deep breath. He knew Granddad had been awful fond of that old hound. 'Had to shoot him,' he said. 'Wouldn't hunt—wouldn't even hunt his own food. Caught him feeding on Pete's kill.'

"Well, I guess Granddad thought about that for a while. Then he finally said, 'Only thing you could do, Sam, I guess. Kind of a shame, though. Old Buell was a good dog when he was younger. Had him a long time.'"

The wind in the chimney suddenly sounded very loud and cold and lonesome.

"But why'd he shoot him?" I finally protested.

"He just wasn't any good anymore," Dad said, "and when a dog wasn't any good in those days, they didn't want him around. Same way with people. If they're no good, why keep them around?" He looked straight at Jack when he said it.

"Well, I sure wouldn't shoot my own dog," I objected.

Dad shrugged. "It was different then. Maybe if things were still the way they were back then, the world would be a lot easier to live in."

That night when we were in bed in the cold bedroom upstairs, listening to Mom and the Old Man yelling at each other down in the living room, I said it again to Jack. "I sure wouldn't shoot my own dog."

"Aw, you're just a kid," he said. "That was just a story. Grandpa didn't *really* shoot any dog. Dad just said that."

"Dad doesn't tell lies," I said. "If you say that again, I'm gonna hit you."

Jack snorted with contempt.

"Or maybe I'll shoot you," I said extravagantly. "Maybe some day I'll just decide that *you're* no good, and I'll take my gun and shoot *you*. Bang! Just like that, and you'll be dead, and I'll betcha you wouldn't like that at all."

Jack snorted again and rolled over to go to sleep, or to wrestle with the problem of being grown-up and still being afraid, which was to worry at him for the rest of his life. But I lay awake for a long time staring into the darkness. And when I drifted into sleep, the forest in the kitchen echoed with the hollow roar of that old rifle, and my shadowy old dog with the sad, friendly eyes tumbled over and over in the snow.

In the years since that night I've had that same dream again and again—not every night, sometimes only once or twice a year—but it's the only thing I can think of that hasn't changed since I was a boy.

The Gathering

1

I guess that if it hadn't been for that poker game, I'd have never really gotten to know my brother. That puts the whole thing into the realm of pure chance right at the outset.

I'd been drafted into the Army after college. I sort of resented the whole thing but not enough to run off to Canada or to go to jail. Some of my buddies got kind of excited and made a lot of noise about "principle" and what-not, but I was the one staring down the mouth of that double-barrelled shotgun called either/or. When I asked them what the hell the difference was between the Establishment types who stood on the sidelines telling me to go to Nam and the Antiestablishment types who stood on the sidelines telling me to go to a federal penitentiary, they got decidedly huffy about the whole thing.

Sue, my girlfriend, who felt she had to call and check in with her mother if we were going to be five minutes late getting home from a movie, told me on the eve, as they used to say, of my departure that she'd run off to Canada with me if I *really* wanted her to. Since I didn't figure any job in Canada would earn me enough to pay the phone bill she'd run up calling Momma every time she had to go to the biffy, I nobly turned her down. She seemed awfully relieved.

I suppose that ultimately I went in without any fuss because it didn't really mean anything to me one way or the other. None of it did.

As it all turned out, I went to Germany instead of the Far East. So I soaked up *Kultur* and German beer and played nursemaid to an eight-inch howitzer for about eighteen months, holding off the red threat. I finished up my hitch in late July and came back on a troopship. That's where I got into the poker game.

Naturally, it was Benson who roped me into it. Benson and I had been inducted together in Seattle and had been in the same outfit in Germany. He was a nice enough kid, but he couldn't walk past a deck of cards or a pair of dice if his life

17

depended on it. He'd been at me a couple times and I'd brushed him off, but on the third day out from Bremerhaven he caught me in the chow line that wandered up and down the gray-painted corridors of the ship. He knew I had about twenty dollars I hadn't managed to spend before we were shipped out.

"Come on, Alders. What the hell? It's only for small change." His eyes were already red-rimmed from lack of sleep, but his fatigue pockets jingled a lot. He must have been winning for a change.

"Oh, horseshit, Benson," I told him. "I just don't get that much kick out of playing poker."

"What the fuck else is there to do?"

He had a point there. I'd gotten tired of looking at the North Atlantic after about twenty minutes. It's possibly the dullest stretch of ocean in the world—if you're lucky. Anyway, I know he'd be at me until I sat in for a while, and it really didn't make that much difference to me. Maybe that's why I started winning.

"All right, *Arsch-loch*." I gave in. "I'll take your goddamn money. It doesn't make a shit to me." So, after chow, I went and played poker.

The game was in the forward cargo hold. They'd restacked the five hundred or so duffle bags until there was a cleared-out place in the middle of the room. Then they'd rigged a table out of a dozen or so bags, a slab of cardboard, and a GI blanket. The light wasn't too good, and the placed smelled of the bilges, and after you've sat on some guy's extra pair of boots inside his duffle bag for about six hours, your ass feels like he's been walking on it, but we stuck it out. Like Benson said, what else was there to do?

The game was seven-card stud, seven players. No spit-in-the-ocean, or no-peek, or three-card-lowball. There were seven players—not always the same seven guys, but there were always seven players.

The first day I sat in the game most of the play was in coins. Even so, I came out about forty dollars ahead. I quit for the day about midnight and gave my seat to the Spec-4 who'd been drooling down my back for three hours. He was still there when I drifted back the next morning.

"I guess you want your seat back, huh?"

"No, go ahead and play, man."

"Naw, I'd better knock off and get some sleep. Besides, I ain't held a decent hand for the last two hours."

He got up and I sat back down and started winning again. The second day the paper money started to show. The pots got bigger, and I kept winning. I wondered how much longer my streak could go on. All the laws of probability were stacked against me by now. Nobody could keep winning forever. When I quit that night, I was better than two hundred ahead. I stood up and stretched. The cargo hold was full of guys, all sitting and watching, very quietly. Word gets around fast on a troopship.

On the morning of the third day, Benson finally went broke. He'd been giving up his place at the table for maybe two-hour stretches, and he'd grab quick catnaps back in one of the corners. He looked like the wrath of God, his blond, blankly young face stubbled and grimy-looking. The cards had gone sour for him late the night before—not completely sour, just sour enough so that he was pretty consistently holding the second-best hand at the table. That can get awfully damned expensive.

It was on the sixth card of a game that he tossed in his last three one-dollar bills. He had three cards to an ace-high straight showing. A fat guy at the end of the table was dealing, and he flipped out the down-cards to Benson, the Spec-4, and himself. The rest of us had folded. I could tell from Benson's face that he'd filled the straight. He might as well have had a billboard on the front of his head.

The Spec-4 folded.

"You're high," the fat dealer said, pointing at Benson's ace.

"I ain't got no money to bet," Benson answered.

"Tough titty."

"Come on, man. I got it, but I can't bet it."

"Bet, check, or fold, fella," the dealer said with a fat smirk.

Benson looked around desperately. There was a sort of house rule against borrowing at the table. "Wait a minute," he said. "How about this watch?" He held out his arm.

"I got a watch," the dealer said, but he looked interested.

"Come on, man. I got that watch when I graduated from high school. My folks give a hundred and a half for it. It'll sure as hell cover any bet in this chickenshit little poker game."

The fat guy held out his hand. Benson gave him the watch.

"Give you five bucks."

"Bull*shit*! That watch is worth a hundred and a half, I told you."

"Not to me, it ain't. Five bucks."

"Fuck you, Buster. You ain't gittin' *my* watch for no lousy five bucks."

"I guess you better throw in your hand then, huh?"

"Christ, man, gimme a break."

"Come on, fella," the fat guy said, "you're holdin' up the game. Five bucks. Take it or leave it."

I could see the agony of indecision in Benson's face. Five dollars was the current bet limit. "All right," he said finally.

He bet two. The dealer raised him three. Benson called and rolled over his hole cards. He had his straight. His face was jubilant. He looked more like a kid than ever.

The fat guy had a flush.

Benson watched numbly, rubbing his bare left wrist, as the chortling fat man raked in the money. Finally he got up and went quickly out of the cargo hold.

"Hey, man," the fat dealer called after him, "I'll give you a buck apiece for your boots." He howled with laughter.

Another player took Benson's place.

"That was kinda hard," a master sergeant named Riker drawled mildly from the other end of the table.

"That's how we play the game where I come from, Sarge," the fat man said.

It took me two days to get him, but I finally nailed him right to the wall. The pots were occasionally getting up to forty or fifty dollars by then, and the fat man was on a losing streak.

He had two low pair showing, and he was betting hard, hoping to get even. It was pretty obvious that he had a full house, seven and threes. I had two queens, a nine and the joker showing. My hand looked like a pat straight, but I had two aces in the hole. My aces and queens would stomp hell out of his sevens and threes.

Except that on the last round I picked up another ace.

He bet ten dollars. I raised him twenty-five.

"I ain't got that much," he said.

"Tough titty."

"I got you beat."

"You better call the bet then."

"You can't just *buy* the fuckin' pot!"

"Call or fold, friend." I was enjoying it.

"Come *on*, man. You can't just *buy* the fuckin' pot!"

"You already said that. How much you got?"

"I got twelve bucks." He thought I was going to reduce my bet so he could call me. His face relaxed a little.

"You got a watch?" I asked him quietly.

He caught on then. "You bastard!" He glared at me. He sure wanted to keep Benson's watch. "You ain't gettin' this watch *that* way, fella."

I shrugged and reached for the pot.

"What the hell you doin'?" he squawked.

"If you're not gonna call—"

"All right, all right, you bastard!" He peeled off Benson's watch and threw it in the pot. "There, you're called."

"That makes seventeen," I said. "You're still eight bucks light."

"Fuck you, fella! That goddamn watch is worth a hundred and fifty bucks!"

"I saw you buy it, friend. The price was five. That's what you paid for it, so I guess that's what it's worth. You got another watch?"

"You ain't gettin' *my* watch."

I reached for the pot again.

"Wait a minute! Wait a minute!" He pulled off his own watch.

"That's twenty-two," I said. "You're still light."

"Come on, man. My watch is worth more than five bucks."

"A Timex? Don't be stupid. I'm giving you a break letting you have five on it." I reached for the pot again.

"I ain't got nothin else."

"Tell you what, sport. I'll give you a buck apiece for your boots."

"What the fuck you want my fuckin' boots for?"

"You gonna call?"

"All right. My fuckin' boots are in."

"Put 'em on the table, sport."

He scowled at me and started unlacing his boots. "There," he snapped, plunking them down on the table, "you're called."

"You're still a buck light." I knew I was being a prick about it, but I didn't give a damn. I get that way sometimes.

He stared at me, not saying anything.

I waited, letting him sweat. Then I dropped in on him very quietly. "Your pants ought to cover it." Some guy laughed.

"My *pants*!" he almost screamed.

"On the table," I said, pointing, "or I take the pot."

"Fuck ya!"

I reached for the pot again.

"Wait a minute! Wait a minute!" His voice was desperate.

He stood up, emptied his pockets, and yanked off his pants. He wasn't wearing any shorts and his nudity was grossly obscene. He threw the pants at me, but I deflected them into the center of the table. "All right, you son of a bitch!" he said, not sitting down. "Let's see your pissy little straight beat a full-fuckin' house!" He rolled over his third seven.

"I haven't got a straight, friend."

"Then I win, huh?"

I shook my head. "You lose." I pulled the joker away from the queens and the nine and slowly started turning up my buried aces. "One. Two. Three. And four. Is that enough, friend?" I asked him.

"Je-sus Christ!" some guy said reverently.

The fat man stood looking at the aces for a long time. Then he stumbled away from the table and almost ran out of the cargo hold, his fat behind jiggling with every step.

"I *still* say it's a mighty hard way to play poker," Sergeant Riker said softly as I hauled in the merchandise.

"I figured he had it coming," I said shortly.

"Maybe so, son, maybe so, but that still don't make it right, does it?"

And that finished my winning streak. Riker proceeded to give me a series of very expensive poker lessons. By the time I quit that night, I was back down to four hundred dollars. I sent the fat guy's watch, boots, and pants back to him with one of his buddies, and went up on deck to get some air. The engine pounded in the steel deck plates, and the wake was streaming out behind us, white against the black water.

"Smoke, son?" It was Riker. He leaned against the rail beside me and held out his pack.

"Thanks," I said. "I ran out about an hour ago."

"Nice night, ain't it?" His voice was soft and pleasant. I couldn't really pin down his drawl. It was sort of Southern.

I looked up at the stars. "Yeah," I said. "I've been down at that poker table for so long I'd almost forgotten what the stars looked like."

The ship took a larger wave at a diagonal and rolled with an odd, lurching kind of motion.

"You still ahead of the game, son?" he asked me, his voice serious.

"A little bit," I said cautiously.

"If it was me," he said, "I wouldn't go back no more. You've won yourself a little money, and you got your buddy's watch back for him. If it was me, I'd just call 'er quits."

"I was doing pretty well there for a while," I objected. "I think I was about fifteen hundred dollars to the good before I started losing. I'll win that back in just a few hours, the way the pots have been running."

"You broke your string, son," Riker said softly, looking out over the water. "You been losin' 'cause you was ashamed of yourself for what you done to that heavyset boy."

"I still think he had it coming to him," I insisted.

"I ain't arguin' that," Riker said. "Like as not he did. What I'm sayin', son, is that you're ashamed of yourself for bein' the one that come down on him like you done. I been watchin' you, and you ain't set easy since that hand. Funny thing about luck—it won't never come to a man who don't think he's got it comin'. Do yourself a favor and stay out of the game. You're only gonna lose from here on out."

I was going to argue with him, but I had the sudden cold certainty that he was right. I looked out at the dark ocean. "I guess maybe the bit about the pants *was* going a little too far," I admitted.

"Yeah," he said, "your buddy's watch woulda been plenty."

"Maybe I will stay out of the game," I said. "I'm about all pokered out anyway."

"Yeah," he said, "we'll be gettin' home pretty quick anyway."

"Couple, three days, I guess."

"Well," he said, "I'm gonna turn in. Been nice talkin' to you, son." He turned and walked off down the deck.

"Good night, Sergeant Riker," I called after him.

He waved his hand without looking back.

So I quit playing poker. I guess I've always been a sucker for fatherly advice. Somehow I knew that Riker was right though. Whatever the reason, I'd lost the feeling I'd had that the cards were going to fall my way no matter what anybody tried to do to stop them. If I'd have gone back the next day, they'd have cleaned me out. So the next day I watched the ocean, or read, and I didn't think about poker.

Two days later we slid into New York Harbor. It was early morning and foggy. We passed the Statue and then stacked up out in the bay, waiting for a tug to drag us the rest of the way in. We all stood out on deck watching the sun stumble up out of the thick banks of smoke to blearily light up the buildings on Manhattan Island.

It's a funny feeling, coming home when you don't really have anything to come home to. I leaned back against a bulkhead, watching all the other guys leaning over the rail. I think I hated every last one of them right then.

Two grubby tugboats finally came and nudged us across the bay to a pier over in Brooklyn. Early as it was, there must have been a thousand people waiting. There was a lot of waving and shouting back and forth, and then they all settled down to wait. The Army's good at that kind of thing.

Benson dragged his duffle bag up to where I was and plunked it down on the deck. I still hadn't told him I had his watch. I didn't want him selling it again so he could get back in the game.

"Hey, Alders," he puffed, "I been lookin' for you all over this fuckin' tub."

"I've been right here, kid."

"Feels good, gettin' home, huh?" he said.

"It's still a long way to Seattle," I told him. His enthusiasm irritated hell out of me.

"You know what I mean."

"Sure."

"You think maybe they might fly us out to the West Coast?"

"I doubt it," I said. "I expect a nice long train ride."

"Shit!" He sounded disgusted. "You're probably right though. The way my luck's been goin' lately, they'll probably make *me* walk."

"You're just feeling picked on."

Eventually, they started unloading us. Those of us bound for West-Coast and Midwest separation centers were loaded on buses and then we sat there.

I watched the mass family reunion taking place in the dim gloom under the high roof of the pier. There was a lot of crying and hugging and so forth, but we weren't involved in any of that. I wished to hell we could get going.

After about a half hour the buses started and we pulled away from the festivities. I slouched low in the seat and watched the city slide by. Several of the guys were pretty boisterous, and the bus driver had to tell them to quiet down several times.

"Look," Benson said, nudging me in the ribs. *"Eine amerikanische Fräulein."*

"Quit showing off," I said, not bothering to look.

"What the hell's buggin' you?" he demanded.

"I'm tired, Benson."

"You been tired all your life. Wake up, man. You're home."

"Big goddamn deal."

He looked hurt, but he quit pestering me.

After they'd wandered around for a while, the guys who were driving the buses finally found a train station. There was a sergeant there, and he called roll, got us on the train, and then hung around to make sure none of us bugged out. That's Army logic for you. You couldn't have gotten most of those guys off that train with a machine gun.

After they got permission from the White House or someplace, the train started to move. I gave the sergeant standing on the platform the finger by way of farewell. I was in a foul humor.

First there was more city, and then we were out in the country.

"We in Pennsylvania yet?" Benson asked.

"I think so."

"How many states we gonna go through before we get back to Washington?"

"Ten or twelve. I'm not sure."

"Shit! That'll take *weeks*."

"It'll just seem like it," I told him.

"I'm dyin' for a drink."

"You're too young to drink."

"Oh, bullshit. Trouble is, I'm broke."

"Don't worry about it, Kid. I'll buy you a drink when they open the club car."

"Thanks," he said. "That game cleaned me out."

"I know."

We watched Pennsylvania slide by outside.

"Different, huh?" Benson said.

"Yeah," I agreed. "More than just a little bit."

"But it's home, man. It's all part of the same country."

"Sure, Kid," I said flatly.

"You don't give a shit about anything, do you, Alders?" Sometimes Benson could be pretty sharp. "Being in Germany, winning all that money in the game, coming home—none of it really means anything to you, does it?"

"Don't worry about it, Kid." I looked back out the window.

He was right though. At first I'd thought I was just cool— that I'd finally achieved a level of indifference to the material world that's supposed to be the prelude to peace of mind or whatever the hell you call it. The last day or so, though, I'd begun to suspect that it was more just plain, old-fashioned alienation than anything else—and *that's* a prelude to a vacation at the funny-farm. So I looked out at the farmland and the grubby backsides of little towns and really tried to feel something. It didn't work.

A couple guys came by with a deck of cards, trying to get up a game. They had me figured for a big winner from the boat, and they wanted a shot at my ass. I was used up on poker though. I'd thought about what Riker had told me, and I decided that I wasn't really a gambler. I was a bad winner. At least I could have let that poor bastard keep his pants, for Christ's sake. The two guys with the cards got a little snotty about the whole thing, but I ignored them and they finally went away.

"You oughta get in," Benson said, his eyes lighting up.

"I've *had* poker," I told him.

"I don't suppose you'd want to loan me a few dollars?" he asked wistfully.

"Not to gamble with," I told him.

"I didn't think so."

"Come on, Kid. I'll buy you a drink."

"Sure," he said.

The two of us walked on down the swaying aisles to the club car. I got myself about half in the basket, and I felt better.

In Chicago there was another mob of relatives waiting, and there was a general repetition of the scene on the dock back in New York. Once we changed trains though, we highballed right on through.

I spent a lot of time in the club car with my heels hooked over the rung of a bar stool, telling lies and war stories to a slightly cross-eyed Wave with an unlimited capacity for Budweiser and a pair of tightly crossed legs. At odd moments, when I got sick of listening to her high-pitched giggle and raucous voice, I'd ease back up the train to my seat and sit staring at North Dakota and Montana sliding by outside. The prairie country was burned yellow-brown and looked like the ass-end of no place. After a while we climbed up into the mountains and the timber. I felt better then.

I had a few wild daydreams about maybe looking up the guy Sue had told me about in her last letter and kicking out a few of his teeth, but I finally decided it wouldn't be worth the effort. He was probably some poor creep her mother had picked out for her. Then I thought about blousing her mother's eye, and that was a lot more satisfying. It's hard to hate somebody you've never met, but I could work up a pretty good head of steam about Susan's mother.

I generally wound up back at the club car. I'd peel my cock-eyed Wave of whomever she'd promoted to beer-buyer first class and go back to pouring Budweiser into her and trying to convince her that we were both adults with adult needs.

Anyhow, they dropped us off in Tacoma about five thirty in the morning on the fourth day after we'd landed in New York. My uniform was rumpled, my head was throbbing, and my stomach felt like it had a blowtorch inside. The familiar OD trucks from Fort Lewis were waiting, and it only took about an hour to deliver us back to the drab, two-story yellow barracks and bare drill fields I'd seen on a half dozen posts from Fort Ord to Camp Kilmer.

They fed us, issued us bedding, assigned us space in the transient barracks, and then fell us out into a formation in the company street. While they were telling us about all the silly-ass games we were going to play, my eyes drifted on out across the parade ground to the inevitable, blue-white mound of Mount Ranier, looming up out of the hazy foothills. I was dirty, rumpled, hung over, and generally sick of the whole damned world. The mountain was still the same corny, picture-postcard thing it had always been—a ready-made tourist attraction, needing only a beer sign on the summit to make it complete. I'd made bad jokes about its ostentatious vulgarity all the way through college, but that morning after having been away for so damned long, I swear I got a lump in my throat just looking at it. It was the first time I'd really felt anything for a long time.

Maybe I was human after all.

2

THEY weren't ready to start processing us yet, so they filled in the rest of the day with the usual Mickey-Mouse crap that the Army always comes up with to occupy a man's spare time. At four-thirty, after frequent warnings that we were still in the Army and subject to court-martial, they gave us passes and told us to keep our noses clean. They really didn't sound too hopeful about it.

I walked on past the mob-scene in the parking lot—parents, wives, girlfriends, and the like, crying and hugging and shaking hands and backslapping—and headed toward the bus stop. I'd had enough of all that stuff.

"Hey, Alders," someone yelled. "You want a lift into town?" It was Benson naturally. He'd been embarrassingly grateful when I'd given him back the watch, and I guess he wanted to do something for me. His folks were with him, a tall, sunburned man and a little woman in a flowered dress who was hanging onto Benson's arm like grim death. I could see that they weren't really wild about having a stranger along on their reunion.

"No thanks," I said, waving him off. "See you tomorrow." I hurried on so he wouldn't have time to insist. Benson was a nice enough kid, but he could be an awful pain in the ass sometimes.

The bus crawled slowly toward Tacoma, through a sea of traffic. By the time I got downtown, I'd worked up a real thirst. I hit one of the Pacific Avenue bars and poured down three beers, one after another. After German beer, the stuff still tasted just a wee bit like stud horsepiss with the foam blown off even with the acclimating I'd done on the train. I sat in the bar for about an hour until the place started to fill up. They kept turning the jukebox up until it got to the pain level. That's when I left.

The sun was just going down when I came back out on the street. The sides of all the buildings were washed with a coppery kind of light, and everybody's face was bright red in the reflected glow.

I loitered on down the sidewalk for a while, trying to think of something to do and watching the assorted GI's, Airmen, and swab jockeys drifting up and down the Avenue in twos and threes. They seemed to be trying very hard to convince each other that they were having a good time. I walked slowly up one side of the street, stopping to look in the pawnshop windows with their clutter of overpriced junk and ignoring repeated invitations of sweaty little men to "come on in and look around, Soljer."

I stuck my nose into a couple of the penny arcades. I watched a pinball addict carry on his misdirected love affair with a seductively blinking nickle-grabber. I even poked a few dimes into a peep-show machine and watched without much interest while a rather unpretty girl on scratchy film took off her clothes.

Up the street a couple girls from one of the local colleges were handing out "literature." They both had straight hair and baggy-looking clothes, and it appeared that they were doing their level best to look as ugly as possible, even though they were both not really that bad. I knew the type. Most of the GI's were ignoring them, and the two kids looked a little desperate.

"Here, soldier," the short one said, mistaking my look of sympathy for interest. She thrust a leaflet into my hand. I glanced at it. It informed me that I was engaged in an immoral war and that decent people looked upon me as a swaggering bully with bloody hands. Further, it told me that if I wanted to desert, there were people who were willing to help me get out of the country.

"Interesting," I said, handing it back to her.

"What's the matter?" she sneered. "Afraid an MP might catch you with it?"

"Not particularly," I said.

"Forget him Clydine," the other one said. That stopped me.

"Is that *really* your name?" I asked the little one.

"So what?"

"I've just never met anybody named Clydine before."

"Is anything wrong with it?" she demanded. She was very short, and she glared up at me belligerently. "I'm not here for a pickup, fella."

"Neither am I, girlie," I told her. I dislike being called "fella." I always have.

"Then you *approve* of what the government's doing in Vietnam?" She got right to the point, old Clydine. No sidetracks for her.

"They didn't ask me."

"Why don't you desert then?"

Her chum pitched in, too. "Don't you *want* to get out of the country?"

"I've just *been* out of the country," I objected.

"We're just wasting our time on this one, Joan," Clydine said. "He isn't even politically aware."

"It's been real," I told them. "I'll always remember you both fondly."

They turned their backs on me and went on handing out pamphlets.

Farther up the street another young lady stopped me, but she wasn't offering politics. She was surprisingly direct about what she *was* offering.

Next a dirty-looking little guy wanted to give me a "real artistic" tattoo. I turned him down, too.

Farther along, a GI with wasted-looking eyeballs tried to sell me a lid of grass.

I went into another bar—a fairly quiet one—and mulled it around over a beer. I decided that I must have had the look of somebody who wanted something. I couldn't really make up my mind why.

I went back on down the street. It was a sad, grubby street with sad, grubby people on it, all hysterically afraid that some GI with money on him might get past them.

That thought stopped me. The four hundred I'd won was in my blouse pocket, and I sure didn't want to get rolled. It was close enough after payday to make a lone GI a pretty good target, so I decided that I'd better get off Pacific Avenue.

But what the hell does a guy do with himself on his first night back in the States? I ticked off the possibilities. I could get drunk, get laid, get rolled, or go to a movie. None of those sounded very interesting. I could walk around, but my feet hurt. I could pick a fight with somebody and get thrown in jail—that one didn't sound like much fun at all. Maybe I could get a hamburger-to-go and jump off a bridge.

Most of the guys I'd come back with were hip-deep in family by now, but I hadn't even bothered to let my Old Lady know I was coming back. The less I saw of her, the better we'd both feel. That left Jack. I finally got around to him. Probably it was inevitable. I suppose it had been in the back of my mind all along.

I knew that Jack was probably still in Tacoma someplace. He always came back here. It was his home base. He and I hadn't been particularly close since we'd been kids, and I'd only seen him about three times since the Old Man died. But this was family night, and he was it. Ordinarily, I wouldn't have driven a mile out of my way to see him.

"Piss on it," I said and went into a drugstore to use the phone.

"Hello?" His voice sounded the same as I remembered.

"Jack? This is Dan."

"Dan? Dan who?"

Now there's a great start for you. Gives you a real warm glow right in the gut. I almost hung up.

"Your brother. Remember?" I said dryly.

"Dan? Really? I thought you were in the Army—in England or someplace."

"Germany," I said. "I just got back today."

"You stationed out here at the Fort now?"

"Yeah, I'm at the separation center."

"You finishing up already? Oh, that's right, you were only in for two years, weren't you?"

"Yeah, only two," I said.

"It's my brother," he said to someone, "the one that's been in the Army. How the hell should I know?—Dan, where are you? Out at the Fort?"

"No, I'm downtown."

"Pitchin' yourself a liberty, huh?"

"Not really," I said. "I've only got three more days till I get out, and I think I'll keep my nose clean."

"Good idea—hey, you got anything on for tonight? I mean any chickie or anything?"

"No," I said, "just kicking around. I thought I'd just give you a call and let you know I was still alive, is all."

"Why don't you grab a bus and bag on out? I'd come and pick you up, but Margaret's workin' tonight, and she's got the car."

"Your wife?"

"Yeah—and I've got to watch the kids. I've got some beer in the fridge. We can pop open a few and talk old times."

"All right," I said. "How do I find the place?"

"I'm out on South Tacoma Way. You know which bus to take?"

"I think I can remember."

"Get off at Seventy-eighth Street and come down the right hand side. It's the Green Lodge Trailer Court. I'm in number seventeen—a blue and white Kenwood."

"OK," I told him. "I'll be out in a half hour or so."

"I'll be lookin' for you."

I slowly hung up. This was going to be a mistake. Jack and I hadn't had anything in common for years now. I pictured an evening with the both of us desperately trying to think of something to say.

"Might as well get it over with," I muttered. I stopped by a liquor store and picked up a pint of bourbon. Maybe with enough anesthetic, neither one of us would suffer *too* much.

I sat on the bus reading the ads pasted above the windows and watching people get off and on. They were mostly old ladies. There's something about old ladies on buses—have you ever noticed? I've never been able to put my finger on it, but whatever it is, it makes me want to vomit. How's that for an inscription on a tombstone? "Here Lies Daniel Alders—Old Ladies on Buses Made Him Want to Puke."

Then I sat watching the streets and houses go by. I still couldn't really accept any of it as actuality. It all had an almost dreamlike quality—like coming in in the middle of a movie. Everybody else is all wrapped up in the story, but *you* can't even tell the good guys from the bad guys. Maybe that's the best way to put it.

The bus dropped me off at Seventy-eighth, and I saw the sickly green neon GREEN LODGE TRAILER COURT sign flickering down the block. I popped the seal on the pint and took a good belt. Then I walked on down to the entrance.

It was one of those "just-twenty-minutes-from-Fort Lewis" kind of places, with graveled streets sprinkled with chuckholes. Each trailer had its tired little patch of lawn surrounded by a chicken-wire fence to keep the kids out of the streets. Assorted broken-down old cars moldered on flat tires here and there. What few trees there were looked pretty discouraged.

It took me a while to find number seventeen. I stood outside for a few minutes, watching. I could see my brother putzing around inside—thin, dark, moving jerkily. Jack had always been like that—nervous, fast with his hands. He'd always had a quick grin that he'd turn on when he wanted something. His success with women was phenomenal. He moved from job to job, always landing on his feet, always trying to work a deal, never quite making it. If he hadn't been my brother, I'd have called him a small-time hustler.

I stood outside long enough to get used to his face again. I wanted to get past that strangeness stage when you say all kinds of silly-ass things because most of your attention is concentrated on the other person's physical appearance. I think that's why reunions of any sort go sour—people are so busy looking at each other that they can't think of anything to say.

Finally I went up and knocked.

"Dan," he called, "is that you? Come on in."

I opened the screen door and stepped inside.

"Hey there, little brother, you're lookin' pretty good," he said, grinning broadly at me. He was wearing a T-shirt, and I could see the tattoos on his arms. They had always bothered me, and I always tried not to look at them.

"Hello, Jack," I said, shaking his hand. I tried to come on real cool.

"God damn," he said, still grinning and hanging onto my hand. "I haven't seen you in three or four years now. Last time was when I came back from California that time, wasn't it? I think you were still in college, weren't you?"

"Yeah, I think so," I said.

"You've put on some beef since then, huh?" He playfully punched me in the shoulder. "What are you now? About a hundred and ninety?"

"One-eighty," I said. "A lot of it's German beer." I slapped my belly.

"You're lookin' better. You were pretty scrawny last time I seen you. Sit down, sit down, for Chrissake. Here gimme your jacket. It's too fuckin' hot for that thing anyway. Don't you guys get summer uniforms?"

"Mine are all rolled up in the bottom of my duffle bag," I told him, pulling off the jacket. I saw him briefly glance at the pint I had tucked in my belt. I wasn't trying to hide it.

He hung my blouse over a kitchen chair. "How about a beer?"

"Sure." I put the brown-sacked pint on the coffee table and sat down on the slighly battered couch. He was fumbling around in the refrigerator. I think he was a little nervous. I got a kick out of that for some reason.

I looked around. The trailer was like any other—factory-

made, filled with the usual cheap furniture that was guaranteed
to look real plush for about six weeks. It had the peculiar smell
trailers always have and that odd sense of transience. Somehow
it suited Jack. I think he'd been gravitating toward a trailer all
his life. At least he fit in someplace. I wondered what I was
gravitating toward.

"Here we go," he said, coming back in with a couple caps
of beer. "I just put the kids to bed, so we've got the place to
ourselves." He gave me one of the cans and sat in the armchair.

"How many kids have you got?" I asked him.

"Two—Marlene and Patsy. Marlene's two and a half, and
Patsy's one."

"Good deal," I said. What the hell else can you say? I pushed
the pint over to him. "Here, have a belt of bourbon."

"Drinkin' whiskey," he said approvingly.

We both had a belt and sat looking at each other.

"Well, " I said inanely, "what are you up to?" I fished out
a cigarette to give myself something to do.

"Oh, not a helluva lot really, Dan. I've been workin' down
the block at the trailer sales place and helping Sloane at his
pawnshop now and then. You remember him, don't you? It's
a real good deal for me because I can take what he owes me
out in merchandise, and it don't show up on my income tax.
Margaret's workin' in a dime store, and the trailer's paid for,
so we're in pretty good shape."

"How's the Old Lady? You heard from her lately?" It had
to get around to her sooner or later. I figured I'd get it out of
the way.

"Mom? She's in Portland. I hear from her once in a while.
She's back on the sauce again, you know."

"Oh, boy," I said with disgust. That was really the last
damned straw. My mother had written me this long, tearjerker
letter while I was in Germany about how she had seen the light
and was going to give up drinking. I hadn't answered the
damned thing because I really didn't give a shit one way or
the other, but I'd kind of hoped she could make it. I hadn't
seen her completely sober since I was about twelve, and I
thought it might be kind of a switch.

"You and her had a beef, didn't you?" Jack asked, lighting
a cigarette.

"Not really a beef," I said. "It just all kind of built up. You
weren't around after Dad died."

"Naw. I saw things goin' sour long before that. Man, I was

in Navy boot camp three days after my seventeenth birthday. I barely made it back for the funeral." He jittered the cigarette around in his hands.

"Yeah, I remember. After you left, she just got worse and worse. The Old Man hung on, but it finally just wore him down. His insurance kind of set us up for a while, but it only took her a year or so to piss that away. She was sure Mrs. High Society for a while though. And then, of course, all the boy-friends started to show up—like about a week after the funeral. Slimy bastards, every one of them. I tried to tell her they were just after the insurance money, but you never could talk to her. She knew it all."

"She hasn't got too much upstairs," Jack agreed, "even when she's sober."

"Anyway, about every month, one of her barroom Romeos would break it off in her for a couple of hundred and split out on her. She'd cry and blubber and threaten to turn on the gas or some damned thing. Then after a day or so she'd get all gussied up in one of those whorehouse dresses she's partial to and go out and find true love again."

"Sounds like a real bad scene."

"A bummer. A two-year bummer. I cut out right after high school—knocked around for a year or so and then wound up in college. It's a good place to hide out."

"You seen her since you split?"

"Couple times," I said. "Once I had to bail her out of jail, and once she came to where I was staying to mooch some money for booze. Gave me that 'After all, I *am* your mother' routine. I told her to stick it in her ear. I think that kind of withered things."

"She hardly ever mentions you when I see her," Jack said.

"Maybe if I'm lucky she'll forget me altogether," I said. "I need her about like I need leprosy."

"You know something, little brother?" Jack said, grinning at me, "you can be an awful cold-blooded bastard when you want to be."

"Comes from my gentle upbringing," I told him. "Have another belt." I waved at the whiskey bottle.

"I don't want to drink up *all* your booze," Jack said, taking the pint. "Remember, I *know* how much a GI makes."

"Go ahead, man," I said. "Take a goddamn drink. I hit it big in a stud-poker game on the troopship. I'm fat city." I knew that would impress him.

"Won yourself a bundle, huh?"

"Shit. I was fifteen hundred ahead for a while, but there was this old master sergeant in the game—Riker his name was—and he gave me poker lessons till who laid the last chunk."

"How much you come out with?"

"Couple hundred," I said cautiously. I didn't want to encourage the idea that I was rich.

"Walkin' around money anyway," he said, taking a drink from the pint. He passed it back to me, and I noticed that his hands weren't really clean. Jack had always wanted a job where his hands wouldn't get dirty, but I saw that he hadn't made it yet. I suddenly felt sorry for him. He was smart and worked hard and tried his damnedest to make it, but things always turned to shit on him. I could see him twenty years from now, still hustling, still scurrying around trying to hit just the right deal.

"You got a girl?" he asked.

"Had one," I said. "She sent me one of those letters about six months ago."

"Rough."

I shrugged. "It wouldn't have worked out anyway." I got a little twinge when I said it. I thought I'd pretty well drowned that particular cat, but it still managed to get a claw in my guts now and then. I'd catch myself remembering things or wondering what she was doing. I took a quick blast of bourbon.

"Lotsa women," Jack said, emptying his beer. "Just like streetcars."

"Sure," I said. I looked around. The furniture was a bit kid-scarred, and the TV set was small and fluttered a lot, but it was someplace. I hadn't had any place for so long that I'd forgotten how it felt. From where I was sitting, I could see a mirror hanging at a slant on the wall of the little passage leading back to the bedrooms. The angle was just right, and I could see the rumpled, unmade bed where I assumed he and his wife slept. I thought of telling him that he might be making a public spectacle of his love life, but I decided that was his business.

"What'd you take in college anyway?" Jack demanded. "I never could get the straight of it out of the Old Lady."

"English, mostly," I said. "Literature."

"English, for Chrissake! Nouns and verbs and all that shit?"

"Literature, Stud," I corrected him. "Shakespeare and Hemingway, and all *that* shit. I figured this would be the issue that would blow the whole reunion bit. As soon as he gave me the "What the hell good is that shit?" routine, he and I would part company, fast. I'd about had a gutful of that reaction in the Army.

He surprised me. "Oh," he said, "that's different. You always did read a lot—even when you were a kid." "It gives me a substitute for my own slightly screwed-up life."

"You gonna teach?"

"Not right away. I'm going back to school first."

"I thought the Old Lady told me you graduated."

"Yeah," I said, "but I'm going on to graduate school."

"No shit?" He looked impressed. "I hear that's pretty rough."

"I think I can hack it."

"You always were the smart one in the connection."

"How's your beer holding out?" I asked him, shaking my empty can. I was starting to relax. We'd gotten past all the touchy issues. I lit another cigarette.

"No sweat," he said, getting up to get two more. "If I run out, the gal next door has a case stashed away. We'll have to replace it before her old man gets home, but Marg ought to be here before long, and then I'll have wheels."

"Hey," I called after him. "I meant to ask you about that. I thought your wife's name was Bonnie."

"Bonnie? Hell, I dumped her three years ago."

"Didn't you have a little girl there, too?"

"Yeah. Joanne." He came back with the beer. I noticed that the trailer swayed a little when anyone walked round. "But Bonnie married some goof over at the Navy Yard, and he adopted Joanne. They moved down to L.A."

"And before that it was—"

"Bernice. She was just a kid, and she got homesick for Mommie."

"You use up wives at a helluva rate, old buddy."

"Just want to spread all that happiness around as much as I can." He laughed.

I decided that I liked my brother. That's a helluva thing to discover all of a sudden.

3

A car pulled up outside, and Jack turned his head to listen. "I think that's the Mama Cat," he said. "Sounds like my old bucket." He got up and looked out the window. "Yeah, it's her." He scooped up the empty beer cans from the coffee table and dumped them in the garbage sack under the sink. Then he hustled outside.

They came in a minute or so later, Jack rather ostentatiously carrying two bags of groceries. I got the impression that if I hadn't been there, he wouldn't have bothered. My current sister-in-law was a girl of average height with pale brown hair and a slightly sullen look on her face. I imagine all Jack's women got that look sooner or later. At any rate Margaret didn't seem just exactly wild about having a strange GI brother-in-law turn up.

"Well, sweetie," Jack said with an overdone joviality, "what do you think of him?"

I stood up. "Hello, Margaret," I said, smiling at her as winningly as I could.

"I'm very happy to meet you, Dan," she said, a brief, automatic smile flickering over her face. She was sizing me up carefully. I don't imagine the pint and the half-full beer can on the coffee table made very many points. "Are you stationed out here at the Fort now?" I could tell that she had visions of my moving in on them as a semipermanent houseguest.

"Well," I said, "not really what you'd call stationed here. I'm being discharged here is all. As soon as they cut me loose, I'll be moving back up to Seattle." I wanted to reassure her without being too obvious.

She got the message. "Well, let me get this stuff put away and then we can talk." She pulled off the light coat she was wearing and draped it over one of the kitchen chairs.

I blinked. She had the largest pair of breasts I've ever seen.

38

I knew Jack liked his women that way, but Margaret was simply unbelievable.

"Isn't she something?" Jack said, leering at me as he wrapped a proprietary arm about her shoulders. The remark sounded innocent enough, but all three of us knew what he meant.

"Come on, Jack," she said, pushing him off. "I want to get all this put away so I can sit down." She began bustling around the kitchen, opening cupboards and drawers. The kitchen area was separated from the living room by a waist-high divider, so we could talk without yelling.

"Dan just got back today," Jack said, coming back and plunking himself on the couch. "He's been in Germany for a couple of years."

"Oh?" she said. "I'll bet that was interesting, wasn't it, Dan?"

"It's got Southeast Asia beat all to heck," I said.

"Did they let you travel around any—I mean visit any of the other countries over there?"

"Oh, yeah. I visited a few places."

"Did you get to London at all? I'd sure like to go there." Her voice sounded a little wistful.

"I was there for about ten days on leave," I told her.

"I never made it up there," Jack said. "When I was with the Sixth Fleet, we stayed pretty much in the Mediterranean."

"Did you get to see any of the groups while you were in London?" Margaret persisted. She really wanted to know; she wasn't just asking to have something to say.

"No," I said. I didn't want to tell her that groups weren't particularly my thing. She might think I was trying to put her down.

"My wife's a group-nut," Jack said tolerantly. "That one cabinet there is stacked full of albums. Must be twenty of the damn things in there."

"I dig them," she said without apologizing. "Oh, Jack, did you get the kids to bed OK?"

"All fed, bathed, and tucked in," he told her. "You know you can trust me to take care of things."

"Patsy's been getting a little stubborn about going to bed," she said. "She's at that age, I guess."

"I didn't have no problems," Jack said.

"Are you guys hungry?" she asked suddenly. Woman's eternal answer to any social situation—feed 'em. It's in the blood, I guess.

"I could eat," Jack said. "How about you, Dan?"

"Well—"

"Sure you can," he insisted. "Why don't you whip up a pizza, Mama Cat? One of those big ones."

"It'll take a while," she said, opening herself a beer. She turned on the overhead light in the kitchen. She looked tired.

"That's OK," he said. "Well, Dan, what are you going to do with yourself now that you're out?" He said it as if he expected me to say something important, something that would impress hell out of Margaret.

"I'll be starting in at the U in October," I told him. "I got all the papers processed and got accepted and all by mail. I'd have rather gone someplace else, but they were going to bring me back here for separation anyway, so what the hell?"

"Boy, you sure run rampant on this college stuff, don't you?" He still tried to use words he didn't know.

"Keeps me off the streets at night." I shrugged.

"Dan," Margaret said. "Do you like sausage or cheese?" She was rummaging around among the pots and pans.

"Either one, Margaret," I said. "Whichever you folks like."

"Make the sausage, sweetie," Jack said. He turned to me. "We get this frozen sausage pizza down at the market. It's the best yet, and only eighty-nine cents."

"Sounds fine," I said.

"You ever get pizza in Germany?" Margaret asked.

"No, not in Germany," I said. "I had a few in Italy though. I went down there on leave once."

"Did you get to Naples?" Jack asked. "We hauled in there once when I was with the Sixth Fleet."

"Just for a day," I said. "I was running a little low on cash, and I didn't have time to really see much of it."

"We really pitched a liberty in Naples," he said. "I got absolutely *crazed* with alcohol." We drifted off into reminiscing about how we'd won various wars and assorted small skirmishes. We finished the pint and had a few more beers with the leathery pizza. Margaret relaxed a little more, and I began to feel comfortable with them.

"Look, Dan," Jack said, "you've got a month and a half or so before you start back to school, right? Why don't you bunk in here till you get squared away? We can move the two curtain-climbers into one room. This trailer has three bedrooms, and you'd be real comfortable."

"Hell, Jack," I said, "I couldn't do that. I'd be underfoot
and all."

"No trouble at all," he said. "Right, Marg?"

"It wouldn't really be any trouble," she said a little uncertainly. She was considerably less than enthusiastic.

"No," I said. "It just wouldn't work out. I'd be keeping odd
hours and—"

"I get it." Jack laughed knowingly. "You've got some tomato
lined up, huh? You want privacy." I don't know if I'd ever
heard anyone say "tomato" for real before. It sounded odd.
"Well, that's no sweat. We can—"

"Jack, how about that little trailer down the street at number
twenty-nine?" Margaret suggested. "Doesn't Clem want to rent
that one out?"

He snapped his fingers. "Just the thing," he said. "It's a
little forty-foot eight-wide—kind of a junker really—but it's
a place to flop. He wants fifty a month for it, but seeing as
you're my brother, I'll be able to beat him down some. It'll
be just the thing for you." He seemed really excited about it.

"Well—" I said doubtfully. I wasn't really sure I wanted to
be that close to my brother.

"It'll give you a base of operations and you'll be right here
close. We'll be able to get together for some elbow-bendin'
now and then."

"OK," I said, laughing. "Who do I talk to?" It was easier
than arguing with him. I hadn't really made any plans anyway.
It was almost as if we were kids again, Jack making the arrangements and me going along with him because I really didn't
care one way or the other. It felt kind of good.

"You just leave everything to me," Jack said importantly.
He'd always liked to take over—to manage things for people—
and he'd always make a big deal out of everything. He hadn't
really changed at all. "I'll check it over from stem to stern and
make old Clem give you some decent furniture from the lot—
He owns the place where I work as well as this court. We've
got a whole warehouse full of furniture. We'll put in a good
bed and a halfway decent couch—we might even be able to
scrounge up a TV set from someplace."

"Look, Jack," I said, "it's only going to be a month or so.
Don't go to any special trouble." I didn't want to owe him too
much. Owing people is a bum trip.

"Trouble? Hell, it's no special trouble. After all, you're my
brother, ain't you. No brother of *mine* is going to live in some

broken-down junker. Besides, if you've got some tomato lined up, you'll want to make a favorable impression. That counts for a lot, doesn't it, Marg?"

"You really will want some new stuff in there," she agreed. "Nelsons lived in there before, and Eileen wasn't the neatest person in the world." Now that I wasn't going to move in with them Margaret seemed to think better of me. I could see her point though.

"Neat?" Jack snorted, lighting a cigarette. "She was a slob. Not only was she a boozer, she was the court punchboard besides. Old Nels used to slap her around every night just on general principles—he figured she probably laid three guys a day just to keep in practice, and usually he was guessin' on the low side."

"How would you know about that, *Mister* Alders?" Margaret demanded.

"Just hearsay, sweetie, just hearsay. You know me."

"That's just it," she said, "I *do* know you."

"Now, sweetie—"

There was a heavy pounding on the side of the trailer. I jumped. "OK, in there," a voice bellowed from outside, "this is a raid."

"Hey," Jack said, "that's Sloane." He raised his voice. "You'll never take us alive, Copper!" It sounded like a game that had been going on for a long time.

A huge, balding man of about forty came in, laughing in a high-pitched giggle. His face was red, and he wore a slightly rumpled suit. He looked heavy, but it wasn't really fat. He seemed to fill up the whole trailer. His grin sprawled all over his face and he seemed to be just a little drunk. He had a half-case of beer under one arm.

"Hi, Margaret, honey," he said, putting down the beer and folding her in a bear hug. "How's my girlfriend?"

"Sloane, you drunken son of a bitch," Jack said, grinning, "quit pawin' my wife and shake hands with my brother Dan. Dan, Cal Sloane."

"Dan?" Sloane asked, turning to me. "Aren't you Alders' college-man brother?"

"He went in the Army after he got out of college," Jack said. "He's out at the separation center now."

"You on leave?" Sloane asked, shaking my hand.

"I told you, Cal," Jack said, "he's at the *separation center.*

He's gettin' out. Why don't you listen, you dumb shit?" The insults had the ring of an established ritual, so I didn't butt in.

"Hey, that's a reason for a party, isn't it?" Sloane said.

"Isn't everything reason enough for you?" Jack demanded, still grinning.

"Not *everything*. I didn't drink more than a case or two at my Old Lady's funeral."

"Dan here's been drinkin' German beer," Jack boasted. "He can put you under the table without even settlin' the dust in his throat."

"Didn't we meet a couple times a few years back?" Sloane asked me, pulling off his coat and settling down in a chair.

"I think so," I said.

"Sure we did. It was when Alders here was still married to Bonnie." He loosened his tie.

"Yeah," I said, "I believe it was."

We talked for about an hour, kidding back and forth. At first Sloane seemed a little simple—that giggle and all—but after a while I realized that he was really pretty sharp. I began to be very glad that I'd called Jack and come on out here to his place. It began to look like I had some family to come home to after all.

About eleven or so we ran out of beer, and Sloane suggested that we slip out for a couple glasses of draft. Margaret pouted a little, but Jack took her back into the hallway and talked with her for a few minutes, and when they came back she seemed convinced. Jack pulled on a sport shirt and a jacket, and Sloane and I got ourselves squared away. We went outside.

"I'll be seeing you, Margaret," I said to her as she stood in the doorway to watch us leave.

"Now you know the way," she said in a sort of offhand invitation.

"Be back in an hour or so, sweetie," Jack told her.

She went back inside without answering.

We took Jack's car, a slightly battered Plymouth with a lot of miles on it.

"I won't ride with Sloane when he's been drinking," Jack said, explaining why we'd left Sloane's Cadillac. "The son of a bitch has totalled five cars in the last two years."

"I have a helluva time gettin' insurance." Sloane giggled.

We swung on out of the trailer court and started off down South Tacoma Way, past the car lots and parts houses.

"Go on out to the Hideout Tavern," Sloane said. He was sprawled in the back seat, his hat pushed down over his nose.

"Right," Jack said.

"I hear that a man can do some pretty serious drinking in Germany," Sloane said to me.

"Calvin, you got a beer bottle for a brain," Jack told him, turning a corner.

"Just interested, that's all. That's the way to find out things—ask somebody who knows."

"A man can stay pretty drunk if he wants to," I said. "Lots of strange booze over there."

"Like what?" Sloane asked. He seemed really interested.

"Well, there's this one—Steinhäger, it's called—tastes kind of like a cross between gin and kerosene."

"Oh, God"—Jack gagged—"it sounds awful."

"Yeah," I admitted, "it's moderately awful, all right. They put it up in stone bottles—probably because it would eat its way out of glass. Screws your head up something fierce."

We wheeled into the parking lot of a beer joint and went inside, still talking. We ordered pitchers of draft and sat in a booth drinking and talking about liquor and women and the service. The tavern was one of those usual kind of places with lighted beer signs all along the top of the mirror behind the bar. It had the usual jukebox and the usual pinball machine. It had the uneven dance floor that the bartender had to walk across to deliver pitchers of beer to the guys sitting in the booths along the far wall. There were the solitary drinkers hunched at the bar, staring into their own reflections in the mirror or down into the foam on their beer; and there was the usual group of dice players at the bar, rolling for drinks. I've been in a hundred joints like it up and down the coast.

I realized that I was enjoying myself. Sloane seemed to be honestly having a good time; and Jack, in spite of the fact that he was trying his damnedest to impress me, seemed to really get a kick out of seeing me again. That unholy dead feeling I'd been fighting for the last months or so was gone.

"We got to get Dan some civilian clothes," Cal was saying. "He can't run around in a uniform. That's the kiss of death as far as women are concerned."

"I've got some civvies coming in," I said. "I shipped them here a month ago—parcel post. They're probably at the General Delivery window downtown right now."

"I've got to run downtown tomorrow," Jack said. "I'll stop by and pick them up for you."

"Don't I have to get them myself?" I asked. "I mean, don't they ask for ID or anything?"

"Hell, no," Jack scoffed. "You can get anybody's mail you want at the General Delivery window."

"Kinda shakes a guy's faith in the Hew Hess Government," I said. "I mean, if you can't trust the goddamn Post Office Department—say, maybe we ought to take our business to somebody else."

"Who you got in mind?" Sloane asked.

"I don't know, maybe we could advertise—'Deliver mail for fun and profit'—something like that."

"I'm almost sure they'd find some way to send you to Leavenworth for it," Jack said.

"Probably," I agreed. "They're awfully touchy about some things. I'd sure appreciate it if you could pick those things up for me though. If you can, dump them off at a cleaner's someplace. I imagine they're pretty wrinkled by now." I emptied my beer.

"Another round, Charlie," Sloane called to the barman. "Put your money away," he told me as I reached for my wallet. "This is my party."

About a half hour later, a kind of hard-faced brunette came in. She hurried across to the booth and sat down beside Cal. She glanced back at the door several times and seemed to be a little nervous. "Hi, Daddy," she said. She made it sound dirty.

"Hello there, baby," he said. "This is Alders' brother, Dan. Dan, this is Helen."

"Hi," she said, nodding briefly at me. "Hi, Jack."

I looked carefully at her. She had makeup plastered on about an inch thick. It was hard to see any expression under all that gunk. Maybe she didn't have any expression.

She turned back to Sloane with an urgent note in her voice. "Baby's got a problem, Daddy." It still sounded dirty. I decided that I didn't like her.

"Well, tell Daddy." Sloane giggled self-consciously.

She leaned over and whispered in his ear for a moment. His face turned a little grim.

"OK," he said shortly, "wait in the car—drive it around in back."

She got up and went out quickly.

"Dumb bitch!" Sloane muttered. "She's been gettin' careless

and her Old Man's suspicious. I'd better get her a room some-place until he cools off."

"Is he pretty steamed?" Jack asked. "You've got to watch yourself with that husband of hers, Cal. I hear he's a real *mean* mother."

"He just wants to clout her around a little," Sloane said. "See if he can shake a few answers out of her. I'd better get her out of sight. I'll have her swing me by your trailer lot, and I'll pick up my car. Then we'll ditch hers on a back street. I know a place where she can hole up." He stood up and put a five-dollar bill on the table. "Hate to be a party-poop but—" He shrugged. "I'll probably see you guys tomorrow. Drink this up on me, OK?" He hurried across the dance floor and on out, his hat pulled down low like a gangster in a third-rate movie.

"That dumb bastard's gonna get himself all shot up one of these days," Jack said grimly.

"He cat around a lot?"

"All the time. He's got a deal with his wife. He brings in the money and doesn't pester her in bed, and she doesn't ask him where he goes nights."

"Home cookin' and outside lovin'?" I said. "Sounds great."

Jack shrugged. "It costs him a fortune. Of course, he's got it, I guess. He's got the pawnshop, and a used car lot, and he owns a piece of two or three taverns. He's got a big chunk of this joint, you know."

"No kidding?"

Jack nodded. "You wouldn't think so to look at him, but he can buy and sell most of the guys up and down the Avenue just out of his front pockets. You ought to see the house he lives in. Real plush."

"Nice to have rich friends," I said.

"And don't let that dumb face fool you," Jack told me. "Don't ever do business with Cal unless I'm there to keep an eye on him for you. He'll gyp you out of your fillings—friend or no friend."

"Sure wouldn't guess it to look at him."

"Lots of guys think that. Just be sure to count your fingers after you shake hands with him."

"What's the deal with this—baby—whatever her name is?"

"Helen? She's married to some Air Force guy out at McChord Field—Johnson, his name is. He's away a lot and she likes her nookie. Sloane's had her on the string for a couple of months now. I tried her and then passed her on. Her Old Man's a real mean bastard. He kicked the livin' shit out of one guy he caught messin' with her. Put the boots to him and broke both his arms. She's real wild in the sack, but she's got a foul mouth and she likes it dirty—you know. Also, she's a shade on the stupid side. I just didn't like the smell of it, so I dumped her in Sloane's lap."

"You're a real friends," I said.

"Sloane can handle it," Jack said. He looked warily around the bar and then at the door several times. "Hey, let's cut out. That Johnson guy might come in here, and I'd rather not be out in plain sight in case he's one or two guys behind in his information. I think I could handle him, but the stupid bastard might have a gun on him. I heard that he's that kind."

"I ought to be getting back out to the Fort, anyway."

"I'll buzz you on out," Jack said, pocketing Sloane's five.

We walked on out to the parking lot and climbed into Jack's Plymouth. We were mostly quiet on the way out to the Fort. I was a little high, and it was kind of pleasant just to sit back and watch the lights go past. But I was a little less sure about the arrangement than I had been earlier in the evening. There was an awful lot going on that I didn't know about. There was no way I could back out gracefully now though. Like it or not, I was going to get reacquainted with my brother. I almost began to wish I'd skipped the whole thing.

4

THE following Saturday I got out of the Army. Naturally, they had to have a little ceremony. Institutions always feel they have to have a little ceremony. I've never been able to figure out why really. I'm sure nobody really give a rat's ass about all that nonsense. In this case, we walked in a line through a room; and a little warrant officer, who must have screwed up horribly somewhere to get stuck with the detail, handed each of us a little brown envelope with the piece of paper in it. Then he shook hands with us. I took the envelope, briefly fondled his sweaty hand, walked out, and it was all over.

"You sure you got my address, Alders?" Benson asked as we fished around in the pile for our duffle bags.

"Yeah, kid, I got it," I told him.

"*Les-ter*," a woman's voice yodeled from the parking lot.

"That's my mom," Benson said. "I gotta go now."

"Take care, kid," I told him, shaking his hand.

"Be sure and write me, huh? I mean it. Let's keep in touch."

"*Les-ter!* Over here."

"I gotta run. So long, Dan." It was the only time in two years he'd ever used my first name.

"Bye, Les," I said.

He took off, weighted way off-balance by his duffle bag. I watched him go.

I stood looking at the parking lot until I located Jack's Plymouth. I slung the duffle bag by the strap from my left shoulder and headed toward my brother's car. It's funny, but I almost felt a little sad. I even saluted a passing captain, just to see if it felt any different. It did.

Jack was leaning against the side of his car. "Hey, man, you sure throw a sharp highball." He grinned as I came up. "Why didn't you just thumb your nose at the bastard?"

I shrugged. "He's still in and I'm out. Why should I bug him?"

"You all ready? I mean have you got any more bullshit to go through?"

"All finished," I said. "I just done been civilianized. I got my divorce papers right here." I waved the envelope at him.

"Let's cut out, then. I've got your civvies in the back seat."

I looked around once. The early afternoon sun blasted down on the parking lot, and the yellow barracks shimmered in the heat. It looked strange already. "Let's go," I said and climbed into the back seat.

There was a guy sitting in the front seat. I didn't know him.

"Oh," Jack said, "this is Lou McKlearey, a buddy of mine. Works for Sloane."

McKlearey was lean and sort of blond. I'd have guessed him at about thirty. His eyes were a very cold blue and had a funny look to them. He stuck out his hand, and when we shook hands, he seemed to be trying to squeeze the juice out of my fingers.

"Hi, Dogface," he said in a raspy voice. He gave me a funny

feeling—almost like being in the vicinity of a fused bomb. Some guys are like that.

"Ignore him," Jack said. "Lou's an ex-Marine gunnery sergeant. He just ain't had time to get civilized yet."

"Let's get out of here, huh?" Suddenly I couldn't stand being on Army ground anymore.

Jack fired up the car and wheeled out of the lot. We barreled on down to the gate and eased out into the real world.

"Man," I said "it's like getting out of jail."

"Anyhow, Jackie," McKlearey said, apparently continuing what he'd been talking about before I got to the car, "we unloaded that crippled Caddy on a Nigger sergeant from McChord Field for a flat grand. You know them fuckin' Niggers; you can paint 'Cadillac' on a baby buggy, and they'll buy it."

"Couldn't he tell that the block was cracked?" Jack asked him.

"Shit! That dumb spade barely knew where the gas pedal was. So we upped the price on the Buick to four hundred over book, backed the speedometer to forty-seven thousand, put in new floor mats, and dumped it on a red-neck corporal from Georgia. He traded us a '57 Chevy stick that was all gutted out. We gave him two hundred trade-in. Found out later that the crooked son of a bitch had packed sawdust in the transmission—oldest stunt in the book. You just can't trust a reb. They're so goddamn stupid that they'll try stuff you think nobody's dumb enough to try anymore, so you don't even bother to check it out.

"Well, we flushed out the fuckin' sawdust and packed the box with heavy grease and then sold that pig for two and a quarter to some smart-ass high school kid who thought he knew all about cars. Shit! I could sell a three-wheel '57 Chevy to the smartest fuckin' kid in the world. They're all hung up on that dog—Niggers and Caddies; kids and '57 Chevies—it's all the same.

"So, by the end of the week, we'd moved around eight cars, made a flat fifteen hundred clear profit, and didn't have a damn thing left on the lot that hadn't been there on Monday morning."

"Christ"—Jack laughed—"no wonder Sloane throws money around like a drunken sailor."

"That lot of his is a fuckin' gold mine," McKlearey said. "It's like havin' a license to steal. Of course, the fact that he's

so crooked he has to screw himself out of bed in the morning
doesn't hurt either."

"Man, that's the goddamn truth," Jack agreed. "How you
doin' back there, Dan?"

"I'm still with you," I said.

"Here," he said. He fumbled under the seat and came out
with a brown-bagged bottle. He poked it back at me. "Celebrate
your newfound freedom."

"Amen, old buddy," I said fervently. I unscrewed the top
and took a long pull at the bottle, fumbling with my necktie
at the same time.

"You want me to haul into a gas station so you can change?"
he asked me.

"I can manage back here, I think," I told him. "Two hundred
guys got out this morning. Every gas station for thirty miles
has got a line outside the men's room by now."

"You're probably right," Jack agreed. "Just don't get us
arrested for indecent exposure."

It took me a mile or two to change clothes. I desperately
wanted to get out of that uniform. After I changed though, I
rolled my GI clothes very carefully and tucked them away in
my duffle bag. I didn't ever want to wear them again—or even
look at them—but I didn't want them wrinkled up.

"Well," I said when I'd finished. "I may not be too neat,
but I'm a civilian again. Have a drink." I passed the bottle on
up to the front seat.

Jack took a belt and handed the jug to McKlearey. He took
a drink and passed the bottle back to me. "Have another rip,"
he said.

"Let's stop and have a couple beers," I suggested. I suddenly
wanted to go into a bar—a place where there were other people.
I think I wanted to see if I would fit in. I wasn't a GI anymore.
I wanted to really see if I was a civilian.

"Mama Cat's got some chow waitin'," Jack said, "but I
guess we've got time for a couple."

"Any place'll do," I said.

"I know just how he feels, Jackie," Lou said. "After a hitch,
a man needs to unwind a bit. When I got out the last time in
Dago, I hit this joint right outside the gate and didn't leave for
a week. Haul in at the Patio—it's just up the street."

"Yeah," Jack agreed, "seems to me I got all juiced up when
I got out of the Navy, too. Hey, ain't that funny? Army, Navy,

Marines—all of us in here at once." It was the kind of thing
Jack would notice.

"Maybe we can find a fly-boy someplace and have a summit
conference," I said.

Jack turned off into the dusty, graveled parking lot of a
somewhat overly modern beer joint.

"I'm buying," I said.

"OK, little brother," Jack said. "Let's go suck up some
suds." We piled out of the car and walked in the bright sunlight
toward the tavern.

"This is a new one, isn't it?" I asked.

"Not really," Jack told me, "it's been here for about a year
now."

We went inside. It was cool and dim, and the lighted beer
signs behind the bar ran to the type thet sprinkled the walls
with endlessly varying patterns of different colored lights.
Tasteful beer signs, for Chrissake! I laid a twenty on the polished bar and ordered three beers.

The beer was good and cold, and it felt fine just to sit and
hold the chilled glass. Jack started telling the bartender that
I'd just got out, and that I was his brother. Somehow, whenever
Jack told anybody anything, it was always in relation to himself.
If he'd been telling someone about a flood, it would be in terms
of how wet *he'd* gotten. I guess I hadn't remembered that about
him.

Lou sat with us for a while and then bought a roll of nickels
and went over to the pinball machine. Like every jarhead I've
ever known, he walked at a stiff brace, shoulders pulled way
back and his gut sucked in. Marine basic must be a real bitch-
kitty. He started feeding nickels into the machine, still standing
at attention. I emptied my beer and ordered another round.

"Easy man," Jack said. "You've got a helluva lot of drinkin'
to do before the day's over, and I'd hate to see you get all
kicked out of shape about halfway through. We've got a party
on for tonight, and you're the guest of honor."

"You shouldn't have done that, Jack," I said. What I'd really
meant to say was that I wished to hell he hadn't.

"Look," he said, "my brother doesn't get out of the Army
every day, and it's worth a blowout." I knew there was no
point arguing with him.

"Is Marg really waiting?" I asked.

"Sure," he said. "She's got steak and all the trimmings on.
I'm supposed to call her and let her know we're on the way."

"Well," I said, "we shouldn't keep her waiting. Hey, Jack, who's this McKlearey guy anyway?" I thumbed over my shoulder at Lou.

"He works at Sloane's used car lot. I knew him when I was in the Navy. We met in Yokosuka one time and pitched a liberty together. He's got ten years in the Corps—went in at seventeen, you know the type—washed out on a medical—malaria, I think. Probably picked it up in Nam."

"Bad scene," I said. "He seems a little—tight—keyed-up or something."

"Oh, Lou's OK, but kind of watch him. He's a ruthless son of a bitch. And for God's sake don't lend him any money— you'll never see it again. And don't cross him if you can help it—I mean *really* cross him. He's a real combat Marine—you know, natural-born killer and all that shit. He was a guard in a Navy brig one time, and some poor bastard made a break for the fence. McKlearey waited until the guy was up against the wire so he couldn't fall down and then blasted him seven times between the shoulder blades with a .45. I knew a guy who was in there, and he said that McKlearey unloaded so fast it sounded like a machine gun. Walked 'em right up the middle of the guy's back."

"Kill him?"

"Blew him all to pieces. They had to pick him up in a sack."

"Little extreme," I said.

"That's a Gyrene for you. Sometimes they get kill-happy."

I finished my beer. "Well," I said, "if you're done with that beer, I think I'm ready to face the world again. Besides, I'm coming down with a bad case of the hungries."

"Right," he said, draining his glass. "Hey, Lou, let's go."

"Sure thing," McKlearey said, concentrating on the machine. "Just a minute—goddamn it!" The machine lit TILT, and all the other lights went out. "I just barely touched the bastard," he complained.

"We got to go, anyway," Jack said. "You guys go on ahead, and I'll give Marg a quick buzz."

Lou and I went back on out in the sunlight to Jack's Plymouth and had another belt from the bottle.

"I'd just hit the rollover," Lou said, "and I had a real good chance at two in the blue." His eyes had the unfocused look of a man who's just been in the presence of the object of his obsession.

"That pay pretty good?" I asked.

"Hundred and sixty games," he said. "Eight bucks. God-damn machines get real touchy when you've got half a chance to win something."

"I prefer slots," I said. "There was this one over in Germany I could hit three times out of four. It was all in how you pulled the handle."

He grunted. Slots weren't his thing. He wasn't interested.

"She's puttin' the steaks on right now," Jack said as he came across the parking lot. He climbed in behind the wheel. "They'll be almost ready by the time we get there." He spun us out of the nearly empty lot and pointed the nose of the car back down the highway.

We pulled in beside his trailer about ten minutes later and went on in. Margaret came over and gave me a quick kiss on the cheek. She seemed a little self-conscious about it. I got the feeling that the "cousinly" kiss or whatever wasn't just exactly natural to her. "Hi, Civilian," she said.

"That's the nicest thing anybody ever said to me," I told her, trying to keep my eyes off the front of her blouse.

We all had another drink—whiskey and water this time—while Marg finished fixing dinner. Then we sat down to the steaks. I was hungry and the food was good. Once in a while I'd catch myself looking at McKlearey. I still didn't have him figured out, and I wasn't really sure I liked him. To me, he looked like a whole pile of bad trouble, just looking for some-place to happen. Some guys are like that. Anyway, just being around him made me feel uncomfortable. Jack and Margaret seemed to like him though, so I thought maybe I was just having a touch of the "first day out of the Army squirrelies."

After dinner Marg got the kids up from their naps, and I played with them a little. They were both pretty young, and most of the playing consisted of tickling and giggles, but it was kind of fun. Maybe it was the booze, but I don't think so. The kids weren't really talking yet, and you don't have to put anything on with a kid that age. All they care about is if you like them and pay attention to them. That hour or so straight-ened me out more than anything that happened the rest of the day. We flopped around on the floor, grabbing at each other and laughing.

"Hey, Civilian," Jack said. "Let's dump your gear over at your trailer. I want you to see how we got it fixed up."

"Sure," I said. "Uncle Dan's gotta go now, kids," I told the girls. Marlene, the oldest—about two—gave me a big, wet kiss, and Patsy, the baby, pouted and began to cry. I held her until she quit and then handed her to Marg. I went to the door where Jack was waiting.

"You guys go ahead," Lou said. "I got my shoes off. Besides, I want to watch the ballgame."

I glanced at the flickering TV set. A smeary-looking baseball game was going on, but I'd swear he hadn't been watching it. I caught a quick glance between him and Margaret, but I didn't pay much attention.

"You guys going to be down there long?" Margaret asked.

"We ought to unpack him and all," Jack said. "Why?"

"Why don't you put the girls out in the play yard then— so I can get the place cleaned up?"

"Sure," Jack said. "Dust McKlearey, too—since he's a permanent part of that couch now."

Lou laughed and settled in a little deeper.

"We'll take the jug," Jack said.

"Sure," Lou answered. "I want to rest up for tonight anyway."

Jack and I put the little girls out in the little fenced-in yard and drove his Plymouth down the street to the trailer I'd rented. We hauled my duffle bag out of the back seat and went in.

It was hot and stuffy inside, and we opened all the windows. The trailer was small and dingy, with big waterstains on the wood paneling and cracked linoleum on the floor. Jack had been able to scrounge up a nearly new couch and a good bed, as well as a few other odds and ends of furniture, a small TV set, dishes, and bedding. It was kind of a trap, but like he said, it was a place to flop. What the hell?

"Pretty good, huh?" he said proudly. "A real bachelor pad." He showed me around with a proprietary attitude.

"It's great," I said as convincingly as I could. "I sure do appreciate all you've done in here, Jack."

"Oh, hell, it's nothing," he said, but I could see that he was pleased.

"No, I mean it—cleaning up the place and all."

"Margaret did that," he said. "All I did was put the arm on Clem for the furniture and stuff."

"Let's have a drink," I said. "Christen the place."

"Right." He poured some whiskey in the bottom of two mismatched glasses and we drank. My ears were getting a little hot, and I knew I'd have to ease up a bit or I'd be smashed before the sun went down. It had been a real strange day. It had started at six that morning in a mothball-smelling barracks, and now I'd left all of that for good. Soon I'd be going back to the musty book-smell and the interminable discussions of art and reality and the meaning of truth. This was a kind of never-never land in between. Maybe it was a necessary transition, something real between two unrealities—always assuming, of course, that this was real.

We hauled my duffle bag and my civvies back to the tiny little bedroom and began hanging things up in the little two-by-four closet and stashing them in the battered dresser.

"You gonna buy a set of wheels?" he asked.

"I guess I'd better. Nothing fancy, just good and dependable."

"Let's see what we can finagle out of Sloane tonight."

"Look, Jack," I said, "I don't want to cash in on—"

"He can afford it," Jack interrupted. "You go to one of these two-by-four lots on the Avenue, and they'll screw you right into the wall. Me and Lou and Sloane will put you into something dependable for under two hundred. It may not look too pure, but it'll go. I'll see to it that they don't fuck over you."

I shrugged. Why fight a guy when he's trying to do you a favor? "OK," I said, "but for a straight deal—I want to pay for what I get."

"Don't worry," Jack said.

"Where's the big blowout tonight?" I asked him.

"Over at Sloane's place. Man, wait'll you see his house. It's a goddamn mansion."

"McKlearey going to be there?"

"Oh, sure. Lou'll show up anywhere there's free booze."

"He's an odd one."

"Lou's OK. You just gotta get used to him is all."

"Well," I said, depositing my folded duffle bag in the bottom of the closet, "I think that's about got it."

"Pretty good little pad, huh?" he said again.

"It'll work out just fine," I said. "Hey, you want to run me to a store for a minute? I'd better pick up some supplies. I guess I can't just run down to the friendly neighborhood mess hall anymore."

"Not hardly." He laughed. "But, hell, you could eat over at my place tomorrow."

"Oh, no. I'm not fit to live with until about noon. Marg and I get along fairly well, and I sure don't want to mildew the sheets right off the bat."

"What all you gonna need?"

"Just staples—coffee, beer, aspirin—you know."

"Get-well stuff." He laughed again.

We went out and climbed into his car.

"Hadn't you better let Marg know where we're going?" I asked him as he backed out into the street.

"Man, it's sure easy to see *you've* never been married. That's the first and worst mistake a guy usually makes. You start checkin' in with the wife, and pretty soon she starts expectin' you to check in every five minutes. Man, you just go when you want to. It doesn't take her long to get the point. Then she starts expectin' you when she sees you."

The grocery store was large and crowded. It took me quite a while to get everything. I wasn't familiar with the layout, and it was kind of nice just to mingle with the crowd. Actually, I wound up getting a lot more than I'd intended to. Jack kept coming across things he thought I really ought to have on hand.

"Now you'll be able to survive for a few days," he told me as we piled the sacks in the back seat of his car.

We drove back to my trailer, unloaded the groceries, and put the stuff that needed to be kept cold in the noisy little refrig beside the stove. Jack picked up the whiskey bottle, and we drove his car back up to his trailer. We got out and went up to the door. The screen was latched.

"Hey," Jack yelled, rattling the door, "open the gate."

Lou got up from the couch, looking a little drowsy and mussed. "Keep your pants on," he said, unlocking the door.

"Why in hell'd you lock it?" Jack asked him.

"I didn't lock it," Lou answered. "I dropped off to sleep."

"Where's Marg?"

"I think I just heard her in the can."

"Marg," Jack yelled, "what the hell'd you lock the front door for?"

"Was it locked?" Her voice was muffled.

"No, hell, it wasn't locked. I'm just askin' because I like the sound of my own voice."

"I don't know," her voice came back. "Maybe it's getting loose and slipped down by itself."

He snapped the latch up and down several times. It seemed quite stiff. "It couldn't have," he yelled back at her, "it's tighter'n hell."

"Well, I don't know. Maybe I latched it myself from force

of habit." The toilet flushed, and she came out. "So why don't you beat me?"

"I just wanted to know why the door was latched, that's all."

"Lou and I were having a mad, passionate affair," she snapped, "and we didn't want to be interrupted. Satisfied?"

"Oh," Jack said, "that's different. How was it, Lou?"

"Just dandy," Lou said, laughing uneasily.

"Let's see now," Jack said, "am I supposed to shoot you, or her, or both of you?"

"Why not shoot yourself?" Margaret suggested. "That would be the best bet—you *have* got your insurance all paid up, haven't you?"

Jack laughed and Margaret seemed to relax.

"Where'd you guys take off to in the car?" she asked me.

"We made a grocery run," Jack said. "Had to lay in a few essentials for him—you know, beer, aspirin, Alka-Seltzer—staples."

"We saw you take off," she said. "We kinda wondered what you were up to."

"Hey, Alders," Lou said, "what time are we supposed to be at Sloane's?"

"Jesus," Jack said. "you're right. We better get cranked up. We've got to pick up Carter."

"Who's he?" I asked.

"Another guy. Works for the city. You'll like him."

"We'll have to stop by a liquor store, too, won't we?" I said.

"What for? Sloane's buying."

"Sloane always *buys*," McKlearey said, putting on his shoes. "He'd be insulted if anybody showed up at one of his parties with their own liquor."

"Sure, Dan," Jack said. "It's one of the ways he gets his kicks. When you got as much money as old Calvin's got, you've already bought everything you want for yourself so about the only kick you get out of it is spendin' it where other guys can watch you."

"Conspicuous consumption," I said.

"Sloane's conspicuous enough, all right," Jack agreed.

"And he can consume about twice as much as any three other guys in town." Lou laughed.

"We'll probably be late," Jack told Margaret.

"No kidding," she said dryly.

"Come on, you guys," Jack said, ignoring her. We went out of the trailer into the slanting late-afternoon sun.

"I'll take my own car," McKlearey said. "Why don't you guys pick up Carter? I've got to swing by the car lot for a minute."

"OK, Lou," Jack said. "See you at Sloane's place." He and I piled into his Plymouth and followed McKlearey on out to the street. I knew that my brother wasn't stupid. He *had* to know what was going on with Margaret. Maybe he just didn't care. I began not to like the feel of the whole situation. I began to wish I'd stayed the hell out of that damned poker game.

5

MIKE Carter and Betty, his wife, lived in a development out by Spanaway Lake, and it took Jack and me about three-quarters of an hour to get there.

We pulled into the driveway of one of those square, boxy houses that looked like every other one on the block. A heavyset guy with black, curly hair came out into the little square block of concrete that served as a front porch.

"Where in hell have you bastards been?" he called as Jack cut the motor.

"Don't get all worked up," Jack yelled back as we got out of the car. "This is my brother, Dan." He turned his face toward me. "That lard-ass up there is Carter—Tacoma's answer to King Kong."

Mike glanced around quickly to make sure no one was watching and then gave Jack the finger, *"Wie geht's?"* he said to me grinning.

"Es geht mir gut," I answered, almost without thinking. Then I threw some more at him to see if he really knew any German. *"Und wie geht's Ihnen heute?"*

"Mit dieses und jenes," he said, pointing at his legs and repeating that weary joke that all Germans seem to think is so hysterically funny.

"Es freut mich," I said dryly.

"How long were you in Germany?" he asked, coming down the steps.

"Eighteen months."

"Where were you stationed?"

"Kitzingen. Then later in Wertheim."

"Ach so? Ich war zwei Jahren in München."

"Die Haupstadt von die Welt? Ganz glücklich!"

Jack chortled gleefully. "See, Mike, I told you he'd be able to *sprechen* that shit as well as you."

"He's been at me all week to talk German to you when he brought you over," Mike said.

"Man"—Jack laughed—"you two sounded like a couple of real Krauts. Too bad you don't know any Japanese like I do. Then we could *all* talk that foreign shit. Bug hell out of Sloane." Very slowly, mouthing the words with exaggerated care, he spoke a sentence or two in Japanese. "Know what that means?"

"One-two-three-four-five?" Mike asked.

"Come on, man. I said, 'How are you? Isn't this a fine day?'" He repeated it in Japanese again.

"Couldn't prove it by me," I said, letting him have his small triumph.

He grinned at both of us, obviously very proud of himself. "Hey, Mike, how's that boat comin'?" he asked. "Is it gonna be ready by duck season?"

"Shit!" Mike snorted. "Come on out back and look at the damn thing."

We trooped on around to the back of the house. He had a fourteen-foot boat overturned on a pair of sawhorses out by the garage. It was surrounded by a litter of paint-scrapings which powdered the burned-out grass.

"Look at that son of a bitch," Mike said. "I've counted twelve coats of paint already, and I'm still not down to bare wood. It feels pretty spongy in a couple places, too—probably rotten underneath. I'm afraid to take off any more paint— probably all that's holding it together."

Jack laughed. "That's what you get for doin' business with Thorwaldsen. He slipped you the Royal Swedish Weenie. I could have told you that."

"That sure won't do me much good right now," Mike said gloomily.

We went into the house long enough for me to meet Betty. She was a big, pleasant girl with a sweet face. I liked her, too.

Then the three of us went out and piled into Jack's car. Betty stood on the little porch and waved as we pulled out of the driveway.

Jack drove on out to the highway, and we headed back toward town through the blood-colored light of the sunset.

"You have yourself a steady *Schatzie* in Germany?" Mike asked me.

"Last few months I did," I told him. "Up until then I was being faithful to my 'One and Only' back here in the States. Of course 'One and Only' had a different outlook on life."

"Got yourself one of those letters, huh?"

"Eight pages long," I said. "By the end of the fourth page, it was all my fault. At the end of the last page, I was eighteen kinds of an unreasonable son of a bitch—you know the type."

"Oh, *gosh*, yes." Mike laughed. "We used to tack ours up on a bulletin board. So then you found yourself a *Schatzie?*"

I nodded. "Girl named Heidi. Pretty good kid, really."

"I got myself tied up with a nympho in a town just outside Munich," Mike said. "She even had her own *house*, for God's sake. Her folks were loaded. I spent every weekend and all my leave-time over at her place. Exhausting!" He rolled his eyes back in his head. "I was absolutely *used* when I came back to the States."

I laughed. "She had it pretty well made then. At least you probably didn't get that 'Marry me Chee-Eye, und take me to der land uf der big P-X' routine."

"No chance. I said good-bye over the telephone five minutes before the train left."

"That's the smart way. I figured I knew this girl of mine pretty well—hell, I'd done everything but hit her over the head to make her realize that we weren't a permanent thing. I guess none of it sunk in. She must have had visions of a vine-covered cottage in Pismo Beach or some damned thing. Anyway, when I told her I had my orders and it was *Auf Wiedersehen*, she just flat flipped out. Started to scream bloody murder and then tried to carve out my liver and lights with a butcher knife."

They both laughed.

"You guys think it's funny?" I said indignantly. "You ever try to take an eighteen-inch butcher knife away from a hysterical woman without hurting her or getting castrated in the process?"

They howled with laughter.

I quite suddenly felt very shitty. Heidi had been a sweet, trusting kid. In spite of everything I'd told her, she'd gone on dreaming. Everybody's entitled to dream once in a while. And if it hadn't been for her, God knows how I'd have gotten through the first few months after that letter. Now I was treating her like she was a dirty joke. What makes a guy do that anyway?

"I had a little Jap girl try to knife me in Tokyo once," Jack said, stopping for a traffic light. "I just kicked her in the stomach. Didn't get a scratch. I think she was on some kinda dope— most of them gooks are. Anyway she just went wild for no reason and started wavin' this harakari knife and screamin' at me in Japanese. Both of us bare-assed naked, too."

The light changed and we moved on.

"How'd you get the knife away from the German girl?" Mike asked.

I didn't really want to talk about it anymore. "Got hold of her wrist," I said shortly. "Twisted her arm a little. After she dropped it, I kicked it under the bed and ran like hell. One of the neighbor women beaned me with a pot on my way downstairs. The whole afternoon was just an absolute waste."

They laughed again, and we drifted off into a new round of war stories. I was glad we'd gotten off the subject. I was still a little ashamed of myself.

It took us a good hour to get to Sloane's house out in Ruston. The sun had gone down, and the streets were filled with the pale twilight. People were still out in their yards, guys cutting their lawns and kids playing on the fresh-cut grass and the like. Suddenly, for no particular reason, it turned into a very special kind of evening for me.

Ruston perches up on the side of the hill that rises steeply up from both sides of Point Defiance. The plush part, where Sloane lived, overlooks the Narrows, a long neck of salt water that runs down another thirty miles to Olympia. The Narrows Bridge lies off to the south, the towers spearing into the sky and the bridge itself arching in one long step across the mile or so of open water. The ridge that rises sharply from the beach over on the peninsula is thick with dark fir trees, and the evening sky is almost always spectacular. It may just be one of the most beautiful places in the whole damned world. At least I've always thought so.

Sloane's house was one of the older places on the hill— easily distinguishable from the newer places because the shrubs and trees were full grown.

We pulled up behind McKlearey's car in the deepening twilight and got out. Jack's Plymouth and McKlearey's beat-up old Chevy looked badly out of place—sort of like a mobile poverty area.

"Pretty plush, huh?" Jack said, his voice a little louder than necessary. The automatic impulse up here was to lower your voice. Jack resisted it.

"I smell money," I answered.

"It's all over the neighborhood," Mike said. "They gotta have guys come in with special rakes to keep it from littering the streets."

"Unsightly stuff," I agreed as we went up Sloane's brick front walkway.

Jack rang the doorbell, and I could hear it chime way back in the house.

A small woman in a dark suit opened the door. "Hello, Jack—Mike," she said. She had the deepest voice I've ever heard come out of a woman. "And you must be Dan," she said. "I've heard so much about you." She held her hand out to me with a grace that you've got to be born with. I'm just enough of a slob myself to appreciate good breeding. I straightened up and took her hand.

"It's a pleasure to meet you, Mrs. Sloane," I said.

"Claudia," she said, smiling. "Please call me Claudia."

"Claudia," I said, smiling back at her.

We went on into the house. The layout was a bit odd, but I could see the reason for it. The house faced the street with its back to the view—at least that's how it looked from outside. Actually, the front door simply opened onto a long hallway that ran on through to the back where the living room, dining room, and kitchen were. The carpets were deep, and the paneling was rich.

"You have a lovely home," I said. I guess that's what you're supposed to say.

"Why, thank you, Dan," she said. She seemed genuinely pleased.

The living room was huge, and the west wall was all glass. Over beyond the dark upswell of the peninsula, the sky was slowly darkening. Down on the water, a small boat that looked like a lighted toy from up there bucked the tide, moving very slowly and kicking up a lot of wake.

"How on earth do you ever get anything done?" I asked. "I'd never be able to get away from the window."

She laughed, her deep voice making the sound musical. "I pull the drapes," she said. She looked up at me. She couldn't have been much over five feet tall. Her dark hair was very smooth—almost sleek. I quickly looked back out the window to cover my confusion. This was one helluva lot of woman.

There was a patio out back, and I could see Sloane man-handling a beer keg across the flagstones. McKlearey sprawled in a lawn chair, and it didn't look as if he was planning to offer any help. Sloane glanced, red-faced, up at the window.

"Hey, you drunks, get the hell on out here!" he bellowed.

"We're set up on the patio," Claudia said.

"Thinkin' ahead, eh, Claude?" Jack said boisterously. "If somebody gets sick, you don't have to get the rug cleaned."

I cringed.

"Well," she said, laughing, "it's cooler out there."

"Which one of you bastards can tap a keg?" Sloane screamed. "I'm afraid to touch the goddamn thing."

"Help is on the way," Mike called. We went on through the dining room and the kitchen and on out to the patio through the sliding French doors.

"I'm sure you fellows can manage now," Claudia said, pick-ing up a pair of black gloves from the kitchen table and coming over to stand in the open doorway. "I have to run, so just make yourselves at home." She raised her voice slightly, obviously talking to Sloane. "Just remember to keep the screens closed on the French doors. I don't want a house full of bugs."

"Yes, ma'am," Sloane yelped, coming to attention and throwing her a mock salute.

"Clown," she said, smiling. She started to pull on the gloves, smoothing each finger carefully. "Oh, Calvin, I finished with the books for the car lot and the pawnshop. Be sure to put them where you can find them Monday morning—*before* you swandive into that beer keg."

"Have we got any money?" Cal asked.

"We'll get by," she said. "Be sure and remind Charlie and Mel out at the Hideout that I'll be by to check their books on Tuesday."

"Right," he said. He turned to us. "My wife, the IBM machine."

"Somebody has to do the books," she said placidly, still working on the gloves, "and after I watched this great financier add two and two and get five about nine times out of ten, I decided that it was going to be up to me to keep us out of bankruptcy court." She smiled sweetly at him, and he made a face.

"I'm so glad to have met you, Dan," she said, holding her hand out to me again. Her deep musical voice sent a shiver up my back. "I'm sure I'll be seeing you again."

"I'd hate to think we were driving you out of your own house," I said sincerely.

"No, no. I have a meeting downtown, and then I'm running over to Yakima to visit an aunt. I'd just be in the way here anyway. You boys have fun." She raised her voice again. "I'll see you Monday evening, Calvin."

He waved a brusque farewell and turned his attention back to the beer keg.

She looked at him for a moment, sighed, and went smoothly on back into the house. I suddenly wanted very much to go down to the patio and give Sloane a good solid shot to the mouth. A kiss on the cheek by way of good-bye wouldn't have inconvenienced him all that much, and it would have spared her the humiliation of that public brush-off.

I went slowly down the three steps to the patio, staring out over the Narrows and the dark timber on the other side.

There was a sudden burst of spray from the keg and a solid "klunk" as Mike set the tap home. "There you go, men," he said. "The beer-drinking lamp is lit."

"Well, ahoy there, matey," Jack said, putting it on a bit too much.

The first pitcher was foam, and Sloane dumped it in the fishpond. "Drink, you little bastards." He giggled.

Somebody, Claudia probably, had set a trayful of beer mugs up on a permanently anchored picnic table under one of the trees. I got one of them and filled it at the keg and drifted over to the edge of the patio where the hill broke sharply away, running down to the tangled Scotch-broom and madrona thicket below.

I could hear the others horsing around back at the keg, but I ignored them for the moment, concentrating on the fading line of daylight along the top of the hills across the Narrows.

"Pretty, huh?"

It was Sloane. He stood with a mug of beer, looking out over the water. "I used to come up here when I was a kid and just look at it. Weren't many houses or anything up here then."

Somehow I couldn't picture Sloane as a kid.

"I made up my mind then that someday I was gonna live up here," he went on. "Took me a long time, but I made it."

"Was it worth it?" I couldn't resist asking him. I didn't like him much right then.

"Every lousy, scratching, money-grubbing, fuckin' minute of it," he said with a strange intensity. "Sometimes I sit up here lookin' out at it, and I just break out laughing at all the shit I had to crawl through to get here."

"We all do funny things," I said. Now he had me confused.

"I'd have never made it without Claudia," he said. "She's really something, isn't she?"

"She's a real lady," I said.

"She was hoppin' tables in a beer bar when I met her," he said. "She had it even then. I can meet guys and swing deals and all, but she's the one who puts it all together and makes it go. She's one in a million, Dan."

"I can tell that," I said. How the hell do you figure a guy like Sloane?

"Hey, you bastards," Jack called to us, "this is a *party*, not a private little conflab. Come on back here."

"Just showin' off my scenery," Cal said. The two of us went back to the keg.

Sloane went over and pawed around under one of the shrubs. "As soon as you guys get all squared away," he said, "I've got a little goodie here for you." He pulled out a half-gallon jug of clear liquid.

"Oh, shit!" Jack said. "Auburn tanglefoot. Goddamn Sloane and his pop-skull moonshine."

"Guaranteed to have been aged at least two hours." Sloane giggled.

"I thought the government men had busted up all those stills years ago," Mike said.

"No way," Jack said. "Auburn'd blow away if it wasn't anchored down by all those pot stills."

McKlearey got up and took the jug from Sloane. He opened it and sniffed suspiciously. "You sure this stuff is all right?"

"Pure, one-hundred-per-cent rotgut," Sloane said.

"I mean, they don't spike it with wood alcohol, do they?" There was a note of worry in Lou's voice. "Sometimes they do that. Makes a guy go blind. His eyes fall out."

"What's the sense of poisoning your customers?" Sloane asked. "You ain't gonna get much repeat business that way."

"I've heard that they do it sometimes, is all," McKlearey said. "They spike it with wood alcohol, or they use an old car radiator instead of that copper coil—then the booze gets tainted with all that gunk off the solder. Either way it makes a guy go blind. Fuckin' eyes fall right out."

"Bounce around on the floor like marbles, huh, Lou?" Jack said. "I can see it now. McKlearey's eyes bouncin' off across the patio with him chasin' 'em." He laughed harshly. He knew about Lou and Margaret, all right. There was no question about that now.

"I don't think I want any," McKlearey said, handing the jug back to Sloane.

"Old Lou's worried about his baby-blue eyeballs," Jack said, rubbing it in.

"I just don't want any. OK, Alders?"

"Well, I'm gonna have some," Mike said, reaching for the jug. "I cut my teeth on Auburn moonshine. My eyes might get a little loose now and then, but they sure as hell don't fall out." He rolled the jug back over his arm professionally and took a long belt.

"Now, there's an old moonshine drinker," Jack said. "Notice the way he handles that jug."

We passed the jug around, and each of us tried to emulate Mike's technique. Frankly, the stuff wasn't much good—I've gotten a better taste siphoning gas. But we all smacked our lips appreciatively, said some silly-ass thing like "damn good whiskey," and had a quick beer to flush out the taste.

McKlearey still refused to touch the stuff. He went back to his lawn chair, scowling.

"Hey, man," Jack said, "I think my eyes are gettin' loose." He pressed his fingers to his eyelids.

"Fuck you, Alders," Lou said.

"Yeah," Jack said. "They're definitely gettin' loose—oops! There goes one now." He squinted one eye shut and started pawing around on the flagstones. "Come back here, you little bastard!"

"Aw, go fuck yourself, Alders!" Lou snapped. "You're so goddamn fuckin' funny!"

"Oh, Mother," Jack cried, "help me find my fuckin' eyeball." He was grinding Lou for all he was worth.

Lou was starting to get pretty hot, and I figured another crack or two from my brother ought to do it. I knew I should say something to cool it down, but I figured that Jack knew what he was doing. If he wanted a piece of McKlearey, that was his business.

"Hey, you guys," Mike said, inspecting Sloane's substantial

outside fireplace, "let's build a fire." It was a smooth way to handle the situation.

"Why?" Sloane demanded. "You cold or something, for Chrissake?"

"No, but a fire's kinda nice, isn't it? I mean, what the hell?"

"Shit, I don't care," Cal said. "Come on. There's a woodpile over behind the garage."

The four of us left McKlearey sulking in his lawn chair and trooped on over to the woodpile.

It took us a while to get the fire going. We wound up going through the usual business of squatting down and blowing on it to make it catch. Finally, it took hold, and we stood around looking at it with a beery sense of having really done something worthwhile.

Then we all hauled up lawn chairs and moved the keg over handy. Even Lou pulled himself in to join the group. By then it was getting pretty dark.

Sloane had a stereo in his living room, and outside speakers as well. He was piping out a sort of standard, light music, so it was pleasant. I discovered that a shot of that rotten homemade whiskey in a glass of beer made a pretty acceptable drink, and I sat with the others drinking and telling lies.

I guess it was Jack who raised the whole damned thing. He was talking about some broad he'd laid while he was on his way down to Willapa Bay to hunt geese.

"... anyhow," he was saying, "I went on down to Willapa— got there about four thirty or five—and put out my dekes. Colder'n a bastard, and me still about half blind with alcohol. About five thirty the geese came in—only by then my drunk had worn off, and my head felt like a goddamn balloon. Man, you want to see an act of raw courage? Just watch some poor bastard with a screamin' hangover touch off a 12 gauge with three-inch magnum shells at a high-flyin' goose. Man, I still hurt when I think about it."

"Get any geese?" I asked.

"Filled out before seven," he said. "Even filled on mallards before I started back—a real carnage. I picked up my dekes, chucked all the birds in the trunk, and headed on back up the pike. I hauled off the road in Chehalis again and went into the same bar to get well. Damned if she wasn't right there on the first stool again."

And that started the hunting stories. Have you ever noticed how when a bunch of guys are sitting around, the stories kind of run in cycles? First the drinking stories—"Boy did we get plastered"—then the war stories—"Funny thing happened when I was in the Army"—and then the hunting stories, or the dog stories, or the snake stories. It's almost like a ritual, but very relaxed. Nobody's trying to outdo anybody else. It's just sort of easy and enjoyable. Even McKlearey and Jack called a truce on the eyeball business.

I guess maybe the fire had something to do with it. You get a bunch of guys around an open fire at night, and nine times out of ten they'll get around to talking about hunting sooner or later. It's almost inevitable. It's funny some anthropologist hasn't noticed it and made a big thing out of it.

We all sifted back through our memories, lifting out the things we'd done or stories we'd heard from others. We hunted pheasant and quail, ducks and geese, rabbits and squirrels, deer and bear, elk and mountain lions. We talked guns and ammunition, equipment, camping techniques—all of it. A kind of excitement—an urge, if you want to call it that—began to build up. The faint, barely remembered smells of the woods and of gun-oil came back with a sharpness that was almost real. Unconsciously, we all pulled our chairs in closer to the fire, tightening the circle. It was a warm night, so it wasn't that we needed the heat of the fire.

"You know," Jack was saying, "it's a damn shame there's no season open right now. We could have a real ball huntin' together—just the bunch of us."

"Too goddamn hot," Lou said, pouring himself another beer.

"Not up in the mountains, it's not," Mike said.

"When does deer season open?" Sloane asked.

"Middle of October," Jack said. "Of course we could go after bear. They're predators on this side of the mountains, and the season's always open."

"Stick that bear hunting in your ear," Mike said. "First you've got to have dogs; and second, you never know when one of those big hairy bastards is gonna come out of the brush at about ten feet. You got time for about one shot before he's chewin' on your head and scatterin' your bowels around like so much confetti."

"Yuk!" Sloane gagged. "There's a graphic picture for you."

"No shit, man," Mike said. "I won't go anywhere near a goddamn bear. I shot one just once. Never again. I had an old .303 British—ten shots, and it took every goddamn one of them. That son of a bitch just kept comin'. Soaked up lead like a blotter. The guys that hunt those babies all carry .44 magnum pistols for close work."

"Hell, man," McKlearey said, "you can stop a *tank* with a .44 mag."

Mike looked at him. "One guy I talked to jumped a bear once and hit him twice in the chest with a .300 Weatherbee and then went to the pistol. Hit him four times at point-blank range with a .44 mag before he went down. Just literally blew him to pieces, and the damned bear was still trying to get at him. I talked to the guy three years later, and his hands were still shakin'. No bears for this little black duck!"

"Would a .45 stop one?" I asked.

"Naw, the military bullet's got a hard jacket," Mike said. "Just goes right through."

"No, I mean the long Colt. It's a 250-grain soft lead bullet."

"That oughta do it," Jack said. "Just carryin' the weight would slow him down enough for a guy to make a run for it."

"I've got an old Colt frontier-style stored with my clothes and books in Seattle," I said, leaning over and refilling my beer mug.

"No kiddin'?" Jack said. "What the hell did you get a cannon like that for?"

"Guy I knew needed money. I lent him twenty, and he gave me the gun as security—never saw him again. The gun may be hot for all I know."

"Ah-ha!" Sloane said. "Pawnbroking without a license!" He giggled.

"It's got a holster and belt—the whole bit," I said. "I'm going to have to pick up all that junk anyway. I'll bring it on down."

"I'd like to see it," Jack said, "and Sloane here knows about guns—he takes in a lot of them in pawn—he ought to be able to tell you what it's worth."

"Sure," Sloane said, "bring it in. Maybe we can dicker."

"Hey!" Mike shouted suddenly. "Shut up, you guys. I just thought of something." He leaned forward, his slightly round face suddenly excited. "How about the High Hunt?"

"Are you kiddin'?" Jack demanded. "You really want to try the 'Great White Hunter' bit?"

"What the goddamn hell is the High Hunt?" McKlearey demanded harshly.

"Early high Cascade Mountains deer season," Mike said, his eyes gleaming in the firelight.

"—In some of the roughest, emptiest, steepest, highest country in the whole fuckin' world," Jack finished for him.

"It's not *that* bad," Mike said.

"Aw, bullshit!" Jack snorted. "The damned boundaries start right where the roads all end. And do you know why the roads end there? Because there's not a fuckin' thing back up in there, that's why. Man, most of that country's above the timberline."

"All alpine meadow," Mike said almost dreamily. "It gets snowed in so early that nobody ever got a chance to hunt it before they opened this special season. Some of the biggest deer in the state are up there. One guy got a nine-pointer that when four hundred pounds."

"Eastern count, I'll bet," Jack said.

"Eastern count my ass. Full Western count—the number of points on the smallest side not counting brow tines. Eastern count would have gone twenty—maybe twenty-one points. That was one helluva big deer."

"And the guy got a hernia gettin' it out of the woods." Sloane giggled.

"No—hell, they had horses."

". . . and guides," Sloane went on, "and a wrangler, and a camp cook, and a bartender. Probably didn't cost more than a thousand a week for two guys."

"It's not all *that* much," Mike said tentatively. "I know a guy—a rancher—who'll take out a fair-sized party real reasonable. You could get by for fifty bucks apiece for a week— ten days. Food extra, of course. He's tryin' to get into the business, so he's keepin' his rates down for the first couple years." Mike's voice was serious; he wasn't just talking. He was actually proposing it to us as a real possibility. His face had a kind of hunger on it that you don't see very often. Mike wanted this to go, and he wanted it badly.

"Who the fuck wants to pay to go up in the boonies for ten days?" McKlearey demanded harshly, putting it down.

It hung there, almost like it was balanced on something. I knew that if I left it alone, McKlearey's raspy vote for inertia would tip it. At that moment I wasn't really sure if I wanted to go up into the high country, but I *was* sure of one thing; I didn't much like McKlearey, and I did like Mike Carter.

"It's what we've been talking about for the last hour," I said, lighting a cigarette. "All you guys were so hot to trot, and now Mike comes up with something solid—a real chance to do some real hunting, not just a little Sunday-morning poaching with a twenty-two out of a car window—and everybody gets tongue-tied all of a sudden."

"Didn't you get enough of maneuvers and bivouac and shit like that in the Army?" McKlearey demanded, his eyes narrowing. I remembered what Jack had told me about crossing him.

"I did my share of field-soldiering," I told him, "but this is hunting, and that's different."

"Are *you* gonna pay to go out and run around in the brush?" He was getting hot again. God, he was a touchy bastard.

"If the price is like Mike said it was, and if we can work out the details, you're goddamn right I will." A guy will make up his mind to do something for the damnedest reasons sometimes.

"You're outa your fuckin' skull," McKlearey said, his voice angry and his face getting kind of pinched in.

"Nobody's twistin' your arm, Lou," Jack said. "You don't have to go no place."

"I suppose *you'd* go along, too, huh, Alders?" For some reason, McKlearey was getting madder by the minute. He was twisting around in his chair like a worm on a hot rock.

"You damn betcha," Jack said. "Just give me ten minutes to pack up my gear, and I'll be gone, buddy—long gone."

"Shit!" McKlearey said. "You guys are just blowin' smoke outa your fuckin' ears. You ain't even got a rifle, Alders. You sure as shit can't go deer huntin' with a fuckin' shotgun."

"I could lend you guys rifles from the pawnshop," Sloane said very quietly. He was leaning back, and I couldn't see his face.

Mike swallowed. I think the hope that it would go had been a very faint one for him. Now, a strange combination of things had laid it right in his lap. "I'd better get a piece of paper and figure out a few things," he said.

"The bugs are about to get me anyway," Sloane said. "Let's take the keg into the kitchen."

We carted it inside and sat down around the table in the breakfast nook to watch Mike write down a long list with figures opposite each item.

McKlearey straddled a chair over in the corner, scowling at us.

Mike finally leaned back and took a long drink of beer. "I think that's it," he said. "Figure fifty for the horses and the guide—that's for a week or ten days. Food—probably twenty-five. License, ammunition, stuff like that—another twenty-five. Most of us probably already have the right kind of clothes and a guy can always borrow a sleeping bag if he don't already have one. I figure a guy can get by for a hundred."

We sat in the brightly lighted kitchen with the layer of cigarette smoke hovering over our heads and stared at the sheet of paper in front of Mike.

I glanced out the window at the rusty glow of the dying fire. The hills over on the peninsula loomed up against the stars.

"I'm in," I said shortly.

Mike scratched his cheek and nodded. "A man owes himself one good hunt in his life," he said. "It may start a small war in the Carter house, but what the hell?" He wrote his name and mine on the bottom of the paper. "Jack?" he asked my brother.

"Why not?" Jack said. "I'll probably have to come along to keep you guys from shooting yourself in the foot."

Mike put Jack's name down on the list.

"God damn!" Cal said regretfully. "If I didn't have the shop and the lot and—" He paused. "Bullshit!" he said angrily. "I own *them*; they don't own *me*. Put my name down. I'm goin' huntin'. Piss on it!" He giggled suddenly.

Mike squinted at the list. "I'm not sure if Miller—that's this guy I know—will go along with only four guys. We might have to scrounge up a few more bodies, but that shouldn't be too tough. You guys might think about it a little though. I'll call Miller on Monday and see if we can't get together on the price of the horses and the guide."

"Guide?" Jack yelped. "Who the hell needs a goddamn baby-sitter? If you can't find your own damn game, you're not much of a hunter."

"It's a package deal, shithead," Mike said. "No guy is just gonna rent you a horse and then point you off into the big lonely. He may not give two hoots in hell about you, but he wants that horse back."

Jack grumbled a bit, but there wasn't much he could do about it. It was going to go; it was really going to go.

Mike called a guy he knew and found out that the season opened on September 11, just about a month away. "At least that'll give us time to get our affairs in order." Mike laughed. "You know, quit our jobs, divorce our wives, and the like."

We all laughed.

Suddenly McKlearey stood up. He'd been sitting in the corner, nursing his beer. "Where's that fuckin' paper?" he demanded.

Mike blinked and pulled it out of his shirt pocket.

McKlearey jerked it out of his hand, picked up the pencil Mike had been using, and laboriously wrote along the bottom.

"Louis R. McKlearey," he wrote.

"What the hell—" Jack said, stunned.

"Fuck ya!" Lou snapped. Then he leaned back his head and began to laugh. The laugh went on and on, and pretty soon the rest of us were doing it too.

"Why you sneaky son of a bitch!" Jack howled. "You bad-mouthed the whole idea just to get us all hooked. You sneaky, connivin' bastard!"

Lou laughed even harder. Maybe the others accepted Jack's easy answer, but I wasn't buying it. Not by a damn sight, I wasn't.

After that, things got noisy. We all got to hitting the keg pretty hard, and it turned out to be a pretty good party after all.

I guess it was almost three in the morning by the time we got Mike home.

"I was gonna take you by to see Sandy," Jack said as we drove back to the trailer court, "but it's pretty late now." His voice was a little slurred.

"Sandy? Who's that?"

"Little something I've got on the side. She's a real fine-lookin' head. Tends bar at one of the joints. You'll get a chance to meet her later."

I grunted and settled down in the seat. I realized that I didn't know this brother of mine at all. I couldn't understand him. A certain amount of casual infidelity was to be expected, I guess, but it seemed to him to be a way of life. Like his jobs and his wives, he just seemed to drift from woman to woman, always landing on his feet, always making out, always on the lookout for something new. Maybe that's why he wasn't so worked up about Lou and Margaret. I guess the word I was looking for was "temporary." Everything about him and his life seemed temporary, almost like he wasn't real, like nothing really touched him.

I drifted off to thinking about the hunt. Maybe I was kind of temporary myself. I didn't have a family, I didn't have a girl, and I didn't have a job. I guess maybe the only difference between Jack and me was that he liked it that way, and I didn't. To him the hunt was just another thing to do. To me it already seemed more important. Maybe I could find out something about myself out in the brush, something I'd sure as hell never find out on a sidewalk. So I sat musing as the headlights bored on into the dark ahead of us.

6

IT wasn't until Thursday that we finished up the deal on the car I was buying from Sloane's lot. I guess I got a pretty good deal on it. It was a ten-year-old Dodge, and I got it for a hundred and fifty. One of the fenders was a little wrinkled, and the paint wasn't too pure, but otherwise it seemed OK. Jack assured me that I wouldn't have been able to touch it for under three hundred anywhere else on the Avenue.

It was cloudy that day, one of those days when the weather just seems to be turned off—not hot, not cold, not raining, not sunny—just "off." I kind of wandered around the car lot, kicking tires and so forth while McKlearey finished up the paper work in the cluttered little shack that served as an office. I hate waiting around like that, I get to the point where I want to run amok or something. It wasn't that I had anything to do really. I just hated the standing around.

Finally Lou finished up and I took the paper and the keys from him.

"Be sure to keep an eye on the oil," he told me.

"Right."

"And watch the pressure in the right rear tire."

"Sure thing." I climbed in and fired it up. Lou waved as I drove off the lot. I didn't wave back.

There's something about having your own car—even if it's only four wheels and a set of pedals. You aren't tied down any more. You're not always in the position of asking people for a lift or waiting for buses.

I drove around for an hour or so through the shadowless

light, getting the feel of the car. It was still fairly early—maybe then thirty or eleven in the morning—and finally it dawned on me that I didn't have anyplace to go really. Jack was busy at the trailer lot, and I hate to stand around and watch somebody else work.

I thought about taking a run up to Seattle, but I really didn't want to do that. None of the people I'd known would still be around. Maxwell had taken off and Larkin, too, probably. I sure as hell didn't want to look up my old girlfriend; that was one thing I knew for sure.

Larkin. I hadn't really been thinking at all. Last time I'd heard from him, he'd been teaching high school here in Tacoma someplace. I guess I'd just associated Tacoma with guys like my brother and McKlearey and Carter—beer-drinking, broad-chasing types. Stan Larkin just didn't fit in with that kind of picture.

Stan and I had roomed together for a year at the university. We didn't really have much in common, but I kind of liked him. There are two ways a guy can go if he's a liberal arts major—provided, of course, that he doesn't freak out altogether. He can assume the pose of the cultured man, polished, urbane, with good taste and all that goes with it. Or he can play the role of the "diamond in the rough," coarse, even vulgar, but supposedly intelligent in spite of it all—the Hemingway tactic, more or less. Larkin was the first type—I obviously wasn't.

I think liberal arts majors are all automatically defensive about it, probably because we're oversensitive. The dum-dums in PE with their brains in their jockstraps, the goof-offs in Business Administration, the weird types in the hard sciences, and the campus politicians in the social sciences, have all seen fit at one time or another to question the masculinity of any guy in liberal arts. So we get defensive. We rise above them, like Stan does, or we compensate, like I do. It kind of goes with the territory.

Anyway, Stan had spent a year picking up my dirty sox and dusting my books, and then he'd given up and moved back to the dorm. Even our literary interests hadn't coincided. He was involved with Dickens, Tennyson, Wordsworth, and Pope, while I was hung up on Blake, Donne, Faulkner, and Hardy. It's a wonder we didn't wind up killing each other.

I'd dropped him an occasional postcard from Europe, and he'd responded with the beautifully written letters that seemed, to me at least, almost like my picture of Stan himself—neat, florid, and somehow totally empty of any meaning.

At least he'd be somebody to talk to.

I wheeled into a tavern parking lot, went in and ordered a beer. I borrowed a phone book from the bartender and leafed through the *L*'s. He was there all right: *Larkin, Stanley*, and right above it was *Larkin, Monica*. Same address, same number. I remembered that he'd mentioned a girl named Monica something or other in a couple of his letters, but I hadn't paid much attention. Now it looked like he was married. I don't know why, but he'd never seemed to be the type. I jotted down the number and the address and pushed the phone book back to the bartender.

I finished my beer and had another, still debating with myself, kind of working myself up to calling him. I have to do that sometimes.

"Hey, buddy, you got a pay phone?" I finally asked the bartender.

He pointed back toward the can. I saw it hanging on the wall.

"Thanks," I said and went on back. I thumbed in a dime and dialed the number.

"Hello?" It still sounded like him.

"Stan? I didn't really think I'd catch you at home. This is Dan—Dan Alders."

"Dan? I thought you were in the Army."

"Just got out last weekend. I'm staying here in town, and I thought I'd better look you up."

"I guess *so*. It's good to hear your voice again. Where are you?" His enthusiasm seemed well-tempered.

"Close as I can figure, about eighty-seven blocks from your place."

"That's about a fifteen-minute drive. You have a car?"

"Just got one. I think it'll make it that far."

"Well then, come on over."

"You sure I won't be interrupting anything?"

"Oh, of course not. Come on, Dan, we know each other better than that."

"OK, Stan." I laughed. "I'll see you in about fifteen minutes then."

"I'll be waiting for you."

I went back to the bar and had another beer. I wasn't sure this was going to work out. I wouldn't mind seeing Stan again, but we hadn't really had a helluva lot in common to begin with, and now he was married, and that along with a couple of years can change a guy quite a bit.

The more I thought about it, the less I liked it. I went out and climbed in my car. I pulled out of the lot and headed off toward his house, dodging dogs and kids on bicycles, and swearing all the way. It had all the makings of a real bust.

Oddly enough, it wasn't. Stan had aged a little. He was a bit heavier, and his forehead was getting higher. He was combing his hair differently to cover it. He was still neat to the point of fussiness. His slacks and sport shirt were flawlessly pressed, and even his shoe-soles were clean. But he seemed genuinely glad to see me, and I relaxed a bit. He showed me around a house that was like a little glass case in a museum, making frequent references to Monica, his wife. The house was small, but everything in it was perfect. I could almost feel the oppressive presence of his bride. The place was so neat that it made me wonder where I could dump my cigarette butt. Stan gracefully provided me with an ashtray—an oversized one, I noticed. He obviously hadn't forgotten my slobby habits. He had changed in more ways than just his appearance. He seemed to be nervous—even jumpy. He acted like somebody who's got a body in the cellar or a naked girl in the bedroom. I couldn't quite put my finger on it.

We sat down in the living room.

"How's Susan?" he asked me.

My stomach rolled over. "I wouldn't know really," I answered in as neutral a tone as possible.

"But I thought you and she—"

"So did I, Stan. But apparently she shopped around a bit while I was in Germany. She must have found somebody more acceptable to her mother—you know, some guy who thought that the Old Lady was a cross between the Virgin Mary, Joan of Arc, and Eleanor Roosevelt."

"I'm sorry, Dan. I really am." He meant it.

"Those are the breaks, old buddy," I said. "It's probably all for the best anyway. Her Old Lady and I probably would have been at each other's throats most of the time anyway. About the first time I told her to stick those chest pains in her ear, the proverbial shit would have hit the proverbial fan."

"Did she have a bad heart?"

"She had a *useful* heart. It may have been rotten to the core, but it was as sound as the Chase Manhattan Bank—how's that for mixing metaphors?"

"Scrambling them might be a little more precise."

"Anyway, the old bag would get this pained look on her face, and the old hand would start clutching at the maternal bosom anytime Sue and I were about to leave the house. One of the great weapons of motherhood, the fluttery ticker. My Old Lady never tried it. I don't think she was ever sober enough."

"You still haven't much use for motherhood, have you, Dan?" he asked me, an amused look on his face.

"As an institution, it ranks just downstream of San Quentin," I said sourly.

Stan laughed. I think that's one of the reasons he and I had gotten along. With him I could be as outrageous as I liked, and he was always amused. I'd never really offended him.

"Could you drink a glass of wine?" he asked suddenly. The perfect host.

"I can always drink—anything," I told him.

"Alders, you're a boozer, you know that?"

"It's part of my charm." I grinned at him.

He went out to the kitchen and came back a minute later with two glasses of pink wine. "This is a fairly good little domestic rosé," he said handing me one of the glasses.

"Thank you," I said. "Your manners, charm, and impeccable good taste are exceeded only by your unspeakable good looks."

"Steady on," he said. He glanced at his watch. I seemed to catch that edginess again. Maybe I was imagining things.

"How's your gun eye?" I asked him. Oddly enough—or maybe not, when you think about it—Stan was a spectacular shotgunner. He'd started out on skeet and trap—gentlemanly, but not very nourishing in terms of meat in the pot—and had moved on up to birds. I'd actually seen him triple on ducks once—one mallard coming in high, another on a low pass right out in front of the blind, and a widgeon going away like a bat out of hell. He'd just raised up and very methodically dumped all three of them, one after another.

"Probably a little rusty," he said. "I've only been out to the range a few times this summer."

"You'd better get on it, old buddy," I told him. "The season's coming on, you know."

"I don't know if I'll get the chance to go out much this year," he said regretfully. "Monica and I are pretty busy."

I got another flash of that nervousness from him. Something

was definitely wrong. I decided to let it drop. I didn't want to be grinding on any open sores.

"Say," I said suddenly, "do you ever hear from Maxwell?"

"He was in California last I heard," Stan said. Maxwell had been a sometime visitor when we had roomed together. He was a nut, but we'd both liked him.

"Did he really burn his draft card that time?" I asked.

"Of course not," Stan snorted. "He was just trying to make a big impression on a girl who had an acute case of politics. He told me later that he just pulled out one of those printed ID cards—you know, the kind that comes with the wallet— and set fire to it before anyone could see what it was. The real joke was that he was really 4-F or whatever they call it."

"You're kidding. A hulk like that?"

"He had a kidney removed when he was eleven. The military wouldn't touch him."

"Man"—I laughed—"what a con artist. Did he ever make it with the girl?"

"I suppose," Stan said. "He usually did, didn't he?"

"That's why he flunked out of school. If he'd spent half as much time on his classes as he did on those elaborate campaigns of seduction, he'd have chewed up the department." I took a belt of his wine.

"Alders, you know, you're a beer drinker at heart. You drink a fine rosé like you would a glass of draft beer in a tavern two minutes before closing time."

"Baby, I've had the best. Liebfraumilch, Lacrima Christi, Piper Heidsieck—you name it, I've swilled it."

He winced. "What a word—swilled. All right, now that we've gotten past the amenities, tell me, how was Paris?" I should have known that was coming. Paris is always the favorite city of anybody who hasn't been to Europe.

"It's a dirty town, Stan," I said sadly, telling him the truth. "I think that all my life I've wanted it to be great, but it's just another dirty town with a lot of dirty people trying to stick their hands in your pockets. Berlin was wild, very sad; Florence was lovely—but the flood—" I shrugged. "Venice is a crumbling slum in the middle of a sewer; Naples is still in rubble; Rome is—well, it's Rome—a monument. If you can get clear of the tourist traps, it's fine. London is dignified, honorably scarred, and—where the action is supposed to be at—cheap. The plays are good, but the eating and drinking are rotten. You

want my vote, try Vienna—or Heidelberg—or Zürich. And
that completes the Cook's toenail tour."

"Germanophile," he snorted.

"No," I said seriously. "The others are out to make a buck,
any way they can. Most of them would sell you their little
brother if their little sister or their mother wasn't to your taste.
The Germans don't give a shit if you like them or not, and
God knows they don't need your money. Benson—this guy I
knew—and I used to ride bicycles across a small mountain to
a little farming village—a kind of no-name sort of place with
only a church, a *Gasthaus*, a few other shops, and a dozen or
two houses, maybe two-three hundred people all together. We
were the only Americans in the whole damned town. We rode
through one afternoon and stopped for a beer. We just kept
going back. The people there really got to like us, and we liked
them. They had a big party for the oldest guy in town—everybody knocked off work for the whole day. The old boy was
about ninety-seven or so. Benson and I were the only two
outsiders invited to that blast. Not just the only two Americans—the only *outsiders*. It was absolutely great."

"Ah, the pleasures of rural life," he said. "Swains and maid-
ens in the first flower of youth."

"Larkin," I said, "you're a phony bastard, you know that?"

"I know," he said, and I think he was serious. He had a
habit of going into those "I'm not really real" depressions. As
I recall, that's one of the reasons we parted company. Too much
of that stuff can get on a guy's nerves.

Then Monica came in. I vaguely remembered seeing her
around school when I'd still been there. She was a sleek brunette; and, I don't know—polished is the word, I guess——or
maybe brittle. I'd seen a couple of girls like her in Germany—
the hundred-marks-a-night sort of girl. At first she treated me
like a piece of garbage on the floor, but when she learned that
I'd been to *Europe*, her attitude changed. She started poking
the usual bright questions at me, trying to make sure I'd really
been there—though how in hell she'd know is beyond me. She
wanted to talk about Paris, naturally, and mentioned a lot of
names I remembered only as the tourist-trappy kind of places
to stay away from. About the only thing we agreed on was the
Rodin Museum, but I think it was for different reasons. It began
to sound as if she'd been there and I hadn't. I think she was
a little peeved that I didn't fake it for her as others I knew did
so often, gushing about places they really couldn't stand, sim-

ply because it was the "thing to do." I listened to her chatter
politely. There was something sort of odd here, but I couldn't
quite get hold of it.

"Stanley," she said, turning to him. "Did you run those
things through the washer that I asked you to this morning?"
There was a threat in her tone, a kind of "You'd better have,
if you know what's good for you" sort of thing.

"Yes, dear," he said meekly.

That was it then. The whole thing fell into place. She had
the big stick, and he knew it—and he'd been ashamed to let
me find out. Married not more than a couple of years on the
very outside, and he was pussy-whipped already. Poor Stan.

"Good," she said. She turned back to me and smiled briefly—
like switching on a light in an empty room and then switching
it off again. Click-click. "I'd *love* to stay and talk with you,
Dan, but I've really *got* to run. We're trying to set up a little
drama group, and there are a *million* details. You know how
it is." Click-click went the smile again. That room was still
empty.

"Oh, Stanley," she said, "don't forget that we're going over
to the Jamisons' for dinner this evening." That was obviously
for my benefit. She didn't want me hanging around the house.
"Wear the blue suit. You know how conservatively Mr. Jamison
dresses, and we do need their support if this little theater group
is going to go anywhere."

He nodded. Stan needed instructions on how to dress like
I needed instructions on opening beer bottles. It was just a little
dig to keep him in line.

"I'll be back about fourish," she went on, "and I'll be in
the mood for a Manhattan by then. You *will* be a good boy
and mix up a small pitcher, won't you?"

Click-click went the smile again. What a phony bitch!

"Of course," he said. She was humiliating him, and she
damned well knew it. I guess he wasn't allowed to have any
friends that she hadn't passed on first.

"I've really *got* to run," she said. "It's been *lovely* meeting
you, Dan."

We all stood up, and she left. We sat down again.

"Well, Dan," Stan said, rather quickly, I thought, "what are
you going to do now that you're a civilian again?"

"Graduate school, I guess," I said.

"Up at the U?"

I nodded.

"Going into Education?"

I shook my head. "Straight English. Education courses are a waste of time."

"Oh, I don't know. I went on and took *my* MS."

"Hey, Stan, that's really fine," I said, ignoring the defensive tone in his voice. "I didn't know whether you'd finished or not."

"Oh, yes," he said, "about a year ago. I'm teaching high school now, but after I get a little more experience, I'm going to apply at several colleges. Monica's working on her master's, too, and we'll be in excellent shape as soon as she finishes."

"That's fine, buddy," I said. "I'm glad to hear it."

"We should get together a few times before you go back up to Seattle," he said.

"We'll do that, Stan. I'm a little tied up right now. We're getting ready to go hunting in early September."

"Hunting?" Stan said with sudden interest. "I didn't know there were any seasons open this early."

"We're going up on the High Hunt—high Cascade deer season—way to hell and gone back up in the mountains. We've got a guide and horses all lined up. We're going up to the Methow River into the country on the back side of Glacier Peak. We'll be in there for about ten days."

"God," he said, "I'd really love to do something like that." He meant it. I must have hit a nerve. "It must be pretty expensive though."

"Not bad—fifty skins apiece for the whole deal—food extra. There are five of us going altogether."

"That would be just great," he said longingly. "I'd been hoping to get a chance to get away this year, but it doesn't look like I'll be able to make it even for birds. Monica's going to be pretty tied up during the regular season this year—her drama group and all—so I'll have to manage the house." He hesitated a moment. "I imagine your plans and arrangements are all made."

"No. We're pretty fluid."

"You know, I've been working pretty hard for the last few years—getting my degree and then getting the house here and setting everything up just the way Monica and I want it. I haven't had much of a chance to really take a look at myself—you know, stop and really see where I am."

"That happens to all of us now and then, Stan," I said.

"Something like this, you know—getting away for a while,

going way back up into the mountains away from all the rush
and pressure. It would give a man a chance to really think
things through."

"That's why I'm going," I said seriously. I lit another cigarette. "I'm at loose ends—kind of in between the Army and
school. It's a good time to do some thinking."

"That's it exactly," he said. "And the hunting is something
just thrown in extra really. It's the getting away from things
that counts—oh, not Monica, of course—but the other things,
the pressure and all."

"You ever been out for deer?" I asked him, trying to cover
it over a little so I wouldn't have to see the naked trapped look
in his eyes.

"Just once," he said, "a few years ago. It was just absolutely
great, even though I didn't even see any. I certainly envy you,
Dan."

"You could probably come along, if you feel like it," I said.
I think I really threw it out to see if he'd bite at it. I didn't
really expect him to go for it.

"Oh, I couldn't do that," he said. "I'm sure the others
wouldn't want a stranger horning in." But he was hooked.
Suddenly I wanted to do him a favor. Stan and I might not
have agreed about much, but I figured he deserved a better
break than he'd gotten. Maybe if he got away from her for a
while he could get his balance again.

"I doubt if these guys would give a damn about that. It's
just a bunch my brother knows, and we just decided to take
off and go."

"I'm sure I couldn't get away at the school!"—he paused
thoughtfully—"although I *have* got some sick leave accumu-
lated, and in a way it would be for health reasons, wouldn't
you say?"

"You're doing the talking." I laughed.

He sat back, smiling sheepishly. "I guess I do sound like
I'm trying to talk myself into something," he said.

"I don't think the deal with our guide is really very firm
yet," I told him, "and it could just be that another guy would
help swing it. I'll talk with the others and see what they say,
if you want me to."

"Well," he started, "don't make it too definite. I'll have to
give it some thought and talk it over with Monica—not that I
have to—" He left it hanging, but I understood. He went on
quickly. "Well, we *do* kind of like to talk things over. We make

better decisions as a team. We feel that marriages work better that way, don't you agree?"

"Makes sense," I said. "I'll sound out the other guys and let you know."

"I'd appreciate it," he said. "But mind, nothing definite yet."

"Sure, Stan," I said. "I understand."

We kicked it around for another hour or so before I finally made an excuse to get away. Stan was all right, but the house was so damned neat it gave me the creeps. I guess I'm just a natural-born slob.

7

ON Friday morning I went up to Seattle and picked up my stuff from the place where I'd had it stored. I kind of putzed around a little but I couldn't find anybody I knew, so I drove on back to Tacoma.

I spent most of the afternoon unpacking the stuff. I wound up with books all over the place. After I got it all squared away, it dawned on me that I was just going to have to pack it all up again anyway in a little while, but what the hell? I like having my books and things out where I can lay my hands on them. It was a little crowded though. My stereo alone took up a sizable chunk of the living room.

That evening I went across town to the "art movie" theater to catch an Italian flick I'd been wanting to see for three or four years.

"I don't see why you want to see that silly thing anyway," Jack said when I asked him if he wanted to go along. "I know a guy who seen it Tuesday. He said it was a real loser. Nothin' happens at all."

"Maybe he just looked too fast," I said. "You want to come along or not?"

"Naw, I don't think so, Dan," he said. "I really don't get much out of foreign movies."

"Just thought I'd ask," I told him. It kind of bugs me when somebody puts something down that I'm really enthusiastic about. Probably everybody's the same way really.

The "art theater" was like all the others I've been to—a grubby, rattletrappy, converted neighborhood showhouse with maybe a hundred and fifty uncomfortable seats. The lobby was painted a nauseating shade—something like a cross between pea-soup green and antique egg-yolk yellow—and the walls were cluttered with poster art and smeary abstracts. The popcorn counter had been replaced by card tables covered with paper cups full of synthetic espresso.

The movie itself was preceded by a couple of incomprehensible short subjects, an artsy cartoon, and about two years' worth of coming attractions. Then there was the intermission, and everybody went out to gag down some of that rotten coffee and stand around making polite conversation.

I choked on a mouthful of the lukewarm ink and drifted over to lean against the wall and watch the animals.

Across the lobby I spotted Stan Larkin and Monica, she looking very bright and very chic and he hovering over her like a man with a brand-new car he's afraid someone's going to scratch. They chatted back and forth with bright, cultured expressions on their faces, drawing a fairly obvious wall around themselves, keeping the college kids and the freaks who thought all foreign movies were dirty at arm's length. With that attitude, it was pretty unlikely that either of them would notice me, but I turned my head away from them anyway. A little bit of Monica went a long way.

When I turned my head, I caught a familiar face. Where in hell had I seen that little girl before? I was sure I didn't know any of the local college kids, and with the straight hair, bare feet, granny glasses, jeans, and sweatshirt, she had to be a college girl.

Then Joan came out of the women's john, and I snapped to it. It was Clydine, the little Pacific Avenue pamphleteer I'd met on my first night back in Tacoma. It was an impulse, but I needed some protective covering in case Stan spotted me. I pushed my way through toward them.

"Clydine!" I said in simulated surprise. "Joan! How *are* you girls anyway?"

They looked at me blankly for an instant, not having the faintest notion who I was. "Uh—just fine," Clydine said, covering up beautifully. "We haven't seen you in—" She left it hanging, hoping I'd give her a clue. Joan was still looking at me doubtfully, her eyes flickering to my haircut. While it wasn't exactly GI, it was still too short to put me in their crowd.

"Let's see," I said, "it must have been just before I got sent to Leavenworth."

Their eyes bulged slightly.

"I'll bet you didn't even recognize me with this haircut and without my beard," I said, "but they keep you clipped pretty short in the Big House." It was a little thick, but they bought it.

"How long have you been—out?" Joan asked sympathetically, the suspicion fading from her face.

"About a week now."

"Was it—I mean—well—" Clydine's eyes were brimming, and her hand had moved to touch my arm comfortingly. I was a martyr to the cause. She wasn't sure exactly what cause yet, but whatever it was, she was with me all the way. Some girls are like that.

I carefully arranged my face into what I hoped was an expression of suffering nobility. "Anything," I said in a voice thick with emotion, "anything is better than participating in an immoral war." That ought to narrow it down for them.

Clydine embraced me impulsively. For a moment I thought she was going to plant ceremonial kisses on each of my cheeks. As soon as Clydine let go, Joan gave me a quick squeeze. I began to feel a little shitty about it. The kids were pretty obviously sincere about the whole thing.

"Come on, girls," I said, trying to cool it a little. In about a minute one of them would have made a speech. "It wasn't really that bad. It's gonna take a whole lot more than a year and a half in a federal joint to get old Dan down." I thought I'd better give them a name to hang on me.

The lobby lights blinked twice, letting us know that the projectionist was ready if we were. I was about to ease away gracefully.

"We'd better go find our seats," Clydine said, glomming onto my arm like grim death. Joan caught the other one, and I was led down the aisle like a reluctant bridegroom.

I'd overplayed it, and now I was stuck with them. All I'd really wanted was someone to hold Stan off with, but they weren't about to let a bona fide hero of the revolution get away. I was hauled bodily into the midst of a gaggle of college types and plunked down into a seat between Joan and Clydine. I could hear a ripple of whispers circling out from where I sat, and I slouched lower in my seat, wishing the floor would open under me.

The movie was good—not as good as I'd expected, but then they never really are—and I enjoyed it despite the need to keep up my little masquerade.

After it was over, one hairy young cat suggested we all go up to his pad and blow some grass. I saw an easy out for myself. I took Clydine aside out in the lobby.

"Uh—look, Clydine," I said in a slightly embarrassed undertone, "I don't want to crimp the party, but my parole officer and the local office of the FBI are staying awfully close to me. They're just waiting for the chance to bust me back into the big joint, and if they caught me at a pot party, well—I'll just split out and—"

Her eyes flashed indignantly. She had gorgeous eyes, very large. "Stay right here," she ordered me. "Don't you dare move." She circled off through the crowd with her long dark hair streaming out behind her, and her little fanny twitching interestingly in her tight jeans. She was back in about a minute and a half.

"It's all fixed, Danny," she told me. "We're all going to the Blue Goose for beer instead." She grabbed my arm again. I felt Joan move in on the other side. Trapped.

The Blue Goose was a beer joint near the campus, and by the time we got there the place was packed to the rafters. Word had leaked out.

Clydine and Joan brought me in like the head of John the Baptist. All they needed was a plate—and maybe an ax.

"Danny," Clydine said in an undertone, "I hate to say this, but I've forgotten your last name, and if I'm going to introduce you—"

"No last names," I muttered to her quickly. "The FBI—" I left it hanging again.

Her eyes narrowed, and she nodded conspiratorially. "I understand," she said, "leave everything to me."

"I won't be able to stay long," I said. "I think I've shaken off my tail but—"

The rest of the evening was like something out of a very bad spy movie or one of those Russian novels of the late nineteenth century. I said as little as possible, concentrating on drinking the beer that everybody in the place seemed intent on buying for me.

A number of girls insisted on kissing me soundly, if indiscriminately, about the head. Even one guy with a beard slipped up behind me and planted one on my cheek. He called it the "kiss of brotherhood," but if he carries on like that with his brothers, his family has serious problems. Still, it *was* the first time I'd ever been kissed by anybody with a beard. I can't really say that I recommend it, all things considered.

After a couple hours I was getting a little bent out of shape from all the beer. Most of the time the place was deadly quiet. Everybody just sat there, watching me guzzle down the suds. Now I know how the girl feels who provides the entertainment at stag parties.

Most of the conversation consisted of half-spoken questions and cryptic answers, followed by long intervals of silence while they digested the information. "Was it—?" one young guy with a mustache asked.

"Yeah," I said, "pretty much."

They thought about that.

"Is there any kind of—well, you know—among the resisters, I mean?" another one asked.

"I don't think I should—well—the guys still inside—you know."

They kicked that around for a while.

"Do the other inmates—?"

"Some do. Some don't."

That shook them.

"Do you think a guy really ought to—? Instead of—well, you know."

"That's something everybody's got to decide for himself," I said. I could say that with a straight face, because I really believed it. "When the time comes, *you're* the one with your head in the meat grinder. After all the speeches and slogans—from all possible sides—you're still the one who has to decide which button you're going to push because it's *your* head that's going to get turned into hamburger."

That really got to them.

"I'd better split now," I said, lurching to my feet. I walked heavily toward the door, feeling just a little like James Bond—or maybe Lenin—or just possibly like Baron Munchausen. I turned at the doorway and gave them the peace sign—they'd earned it. Look at all the beer they'd bought me.

"Keep the faith," I said in a choked-up voice. Then I went on out.

The patter of little bare feet behind me told me that I hadn't really escaped after all.

"You'd better go on back to your friends, Clydine," I said, not bothering to look around.

Glom! She had me by the arm again. She pulled me to a halt beside my car.

"Danny," she said, looking up at me. "I think you're just the most—well—" She climbed up my arm hand over hand and pulled my face down to hers.

Despite some bad experiences, I'm not a woman-hater. On the whole, I think the idea of two sexes is way out front of any possible alternatives. I responded to Clydine's kiss with a certain enthusiasm.

After a while she pulled her face clear and looked at me, her big eyes two pools of compassion behind those gogglelike granny glasses.

"How long has it been, Danny?" she whispered.

As a matter of fact it *had* been a little better than a month.

"Too long," I said brokenly, "too long."

She let go of me, opened the door of my car, and got in.

"Will there be any problem at the place where you live?" she asked matter-of-factly.

"No," I told her, starting the car.

We drove across town to the trailer park in silence. Clydine nestled against my shoulder. In spite of the shabby clothes which she wore as a sort of uniform, she smelled clean. That's a pretty common misconception about girls like Clydine. I've never met one yet who wasn't pretty clean most of the time.

As a matter of fact, the first thing she did when we got to my trailer was to go into the bathroom and wash her bare feet.

"I wouldn't want to get your sheets all filthy," she said. She stopped suddenly, her hand flying to her mouth. Silently she mouthed the words "Is this place bugged?" at me. Too many movies.

Motioning her to silence, I picked up my FM transistor from the coffee table and stuffed the earplug into the side of my head. I turned it on, picking up a fairly good Beethoven piano sonata—which she, of course, couldn't hear. I made a pretense of checking out the trailer.

"It's clean," I told her, switching it off.

"How does that—"

"It's a little modification," I said. "An old con in the joint showed me how. You get anywhere near a microphone with it

and you pick up a feedback—you know, a high-pitched whistle."
I jerked the plug and switched the piano sonata back on. "And
that'll blank out any directional mike from outside." I moved
carefully to all the windows, looking out and then pulling the
drapes. Then I locked the door. I go to movies, too.

"We're all secure now," I said.

"Do you want to talk about it?" she asked.

I shook my head.

"I understand, Danny. Maybe after."

I wished to hell she wouldn't be so cold-blooded about it.
"You want a drink?" I asked. I always get nervous. I always
have.

"Well, maybe a little one."

I mixed us a couple, hitting hers a little hard with bourbon.
I didn't want her to get away.

We sat on the couch drinking silently. I just sipped at mine.
I didn't want to booze myself out of action.

She took off the granny glasses and laid them on the table.
Without the damned things, she had a cute little face. She was
one of those short, perky little girls who used to get elected
cheerleaders before all this other stuff came along. Then, without so much as turning a hair, she shucked off the sweatshirt.
She wasn't wearing a bra.

My faint worry about the booze turned out to be pretty
irrelevant.

She stood up, her frontage coming to attention like two pink
little soldiers. "Let's go to bed now, shall we?" she said and
walked on back down the narrow hallway to the bedroom.

I put down my drink and turned out the lamp in the living
room.

"Don't forget to bring in the transistor," she reminded me.

I picked it up and went on back.

She had finished undressing, and she was lying on the bed.
My hands began to shake. She had a crazy build on her—real
wall-to-wall girl. I started to take off my shirt.

"Do you have to leave it on that station?" she asked, pointing
at the transistor. "I mean is that the only frequency that—"

"That's the one," I said. "I'd have to take it all apart
to—"

"It's OK," she said. "It's just that I've never done it with
that kind of music on before. Groups most of the time or folk
rock—never Beethoven."

At least she recognized it.

I was having a helluva time with my shirt.

"Here," she said, sitting up, "let me." She pushed my hands out of the way and finished unbuttoning my shirt. "Do you like having the light on?"

"It's a little bright, isn't it?" I asked, squinting at it.

"Some men do, that's all—that's why I asked."

"Oh."

"Do you like to be on top, or do you want me to—"

I reached down and gently lifted her chin. "Clydine, love, it's not just exactly as if we were about to run a quarterback sneak off-tackle. We don't have to get it all planned out in the huddle, do we? Let's just improvise, make it up as we go along."

She smiled up at me, almost shyly. "I just want it to be good for you, is all," she said softly.

"Quit worrying about it," I told her. I sat down on the bed and reached for her. "One thing though," I said, cupping one of the little pink soldiers.

"What's that?" she asked, nuzzling my neck.

"How in the hell did you ever get a name like Clydine?"

She told me, but I promised never to tell anybody else.

8

"WHAT'S this doing here?" Clydine was standing over me the next morning, stark naked, with my Army blouse clutched in her little fist. She shook it at me. "What's this doing here?" she demanded again.

"You're wrinkling it," I said. "Don't wrinkle it."

"You're a GI, aren't you?" she said, her voice shaking with fury. "A no-good, lousy, son-of-a-bitching, mother-fucking GI!"

"Clydine!" I was actually shocked. I'd never heard a girl use that kind of language before.

"You bastard!"

"Calm down," I told her, sitting up in bed.

"Motherfucker!"

"Clydine, please don't use that kind of language. It sounds very ugly coming from a girl your age."

"Motherfucker, motherfucker, motherfucker!" she yelled, stamping her foot. Then she threw the blouse on the floor and collapsed on the bed, sobbing bitterly.

I got up, hung the blouse back up in the closet, and padded barefoot on out to the kitchen. I got myself a beer. I had a bit of a headache. Then I went on back to the bedroom. She was still crying.

"Are you about through?" I asked her.

"Son-of-a-bitching motherfucker!" she said, her voice muffled.

"I'm getting a little tired of that," I told her.

"Bite my ass!"

I reached over and got a good grip on her arm so she couldn't get a swing at me, then I leaned down and bit her on the fanny, hard.

"Dan! Stop that! Ouch, goddammit! Stop that!"

I let go. I'd left a pretty good set of teethmarks on her can. "Any more suggestions?" I asked her.

"Of all the—" She rubbed at her bottom tenderly. "Goddammit, that *hurt*!"

"It was *your* idea," I said, taking a pull at the beer bottle.

"Can I have some?" she asked me after a minute or so. She sounded like a little girl.

"If you promise not to throw it at me."

"I'll be good."

I gave her the bottle, and she took a drink. "Oh, Danny, how *could* you? All that beautiful story about letting them put you in prison for a principle. It was all a *lie*, wasn't it?"

"Are you ready to listen now?"

"I *believed* in you, Danny."

"You want to hear this?"

"I really *believed* in you."

I got up and walked on out to the living room.

After a minute she came padding out, still rubbing at her bare fanny. Her little soldiers were still at attention. She was just as cute as hell.

"All right. Let's hear it," she said.

"First off," I said, plunking myself on the couch. "I'm not a GI—not anymore anyway."

"You've *deserted*!" she squealed, sitting down beside me.

"No, dear. I was discharged—honorably."

"You mean you didn't even—"

"Hush," I said, "I was drafted. I thought it all over, and I went ahead and went in. I spent eighteen months in Germany."

"Germany!"

I kissed her—hard. Our teeth clacked together. "Now I'm going to do that every time you interrupt me," I told her.

"But—"

I did it again. It was kind of fun.

"I did *not* run off to Canada. I did *not* go to Leavenworth. I did *not* go to Nam. I didn't kill anybody. I didn't help anybody kill anybody. I drank a lot of German beer. I looked at a lot of castles and museums. Then I came home."

"But how—"

I kissed her again.

"Not so hard—" she said, her fingertips touching her mouth tenderly.

"All right. Now, on my first night back from the land of Wiener schnitzels, you and Joan braced me down on Pacific Avenue with a fistful of pamphlets—we chatted a minute or two. That's how I came to know your names."

She looked at me, her eyes widening suddenly.

"At the theater last night," I went on, "there were some people I didn't want to talk to, so when I saw you and Joan, I just moved in on you with the first silly-ass story that came into my head. After that, things just got out of hand. I *did* try to get away several times. You'll have to admit that."

"Can I talk?" she asked.

"Go ahead," I told her. "End of explanation."

"Once we got away from the others—I mean, once we got here, why didn't you tell me?"

"Because, little one, you are an extremely good-looking, well-constructed, female-type person. You are also, and I hope you'll forgive my saying this, just a wee bit hooked on things political. I wasn't about to take a chance on losing the old ballgame just for the sake of clearing up a few minor misconceptions. I'm probably as honest as the next guy, but I'm not a nut about it."

"Danny?"

"Yes?"

"Do you really think I'm—what you said—good-looking?"

I laughed and gathered her into my arms. I kissed her vigorously about the head and neck. "You're a doll," I told her.

Later, back in bed, she nudged me with her elbow.

"Hmmm?"

"Danny, if you ever tell Joan that you haven't been in prison, I'll *kill* you. I'll just *kill* you."

"Watch that, my little nasturtium of nonviolence. That kind of talk could get you chucked out of the Peace Movement right on your pretty, pink patootie."

"Piss on the Peace Movement!" she said bluntly. "This is serious. Don't ever *dare* tell Joan. I'd be the laughingstock of the whole campus. Do you know that I turned down a date with the *captain* of the football team because I thought he was politically immature? I've got a reputation to maintain on campus, so you keep your goddamn mouth shut!"

I howled with laughter. "We've got to do something about your vocabulary," I told her.

"To hell with my vocabulary! Now I want you to promise."

"All right, all right. Put the gun away. My lips are sealed. Whenever I'm around Joan I'll be an ex-con. I'll flout my prison record in everybody's face. But it's gonna cost you, kid."

"Well, it's the *only* way I'll be able to hold up my head," she explained.

After I drove her back to the campus and made a date for that night, I went on downtown to buy myself some clothes. A lot of my old things that I'd picked up the day before were too tight now—and probably a little out of date, though I really didn't much give a damn about that. I didn't want to go overboard on clothes, but I did need a few things.

I had a fair amount of cash, the four hundred from the poker game, three hundred in mustering-out pay, and I'd religiously saved twenty-five a month while I was in the Army—about six hundred dollars there when I got out. I had maybe thirteen hundred altogether. The car and the rent and my share of the hunt and some walking-around money took me down to under a grand, but I figured I was still OK.

It was kind of nice to go into the stores and try on the new-smelling clothes. I got a couple pair of slacks and a sport jacket, some shirts and ties and a couple pair of shoes—nothing really fancy.

About one o'clock, I bagged on back out to the Avenue and dropped into Sloane's pawnshop. Sloane had a lot of new stuff in it as well as the usual sad, secondhand junk. I thought I could see the influence of Claudia there. I kind of halfway hoped she'd be there so I could see her again.

"Hey, Dan," Sloane said, "be right with you." He turned back to the skinny, horse-faced guy he'd been talking to. "I'm sure sorry, friend," he said, "but five dollars is as high as I can go. You saw the window—I've got wristwatches coming out my ears."

"But I aint tryin' to *sell* it," the man objected with a distinct, whining Southern drawl. "I'd be in here first thing on payday to get it back. I jus' gotta have ten anyway. Y'see, m'car broke down and I had a feller fix it fer me, and now he won't give it back to me 'lessen I give 'im at least part of the money. That's why I just *gotta* have ten for the watch anyway."

"I'm just as sorry as I can be, friend, but I just can't do a thing for you on that watch."

"I noticed the prices you got on them watches in the window," the man said accusingly. "I didn't see no five-dollar watches out there."

Suddenly I remembered another five-dollar watch not too long ago.

"I'm really sorry, friend," Sloane said, "But I just don't think you and I can do business today."

"That there's a semdy-fi'-dollar watch," the man said holding it out at Sloane and shaking it vigorously, "an' all I want is for you to borrow me ten fuckin' dollars on it for about ten measly little ol' days. Now I think that's mighty damn reasonable."

"It could very well be, friend, but I just can't do 'er."

"Well, mister, I'm agonna tell you som'thin'. They's just a whole lotta these here pawnshops in this here little ol' town. I think I'll jus' go out and find me one where they don't try to screw a feller right into the damn ground."

"It's a free country, friend," Sloane said calmly.

"You just ain't about to get no semdy-fi'-dollar watch off'n *me* for no five measly fuckin' dollars. I'll tell you that right now. And I can shore tell you one thing—you ain't gonna get no more o' *my* business. And I'm shore gonna tell all the fellers in my outfit not to give you none o' their business neither. It'll be a cold day in hell when anybody from the Hunnerd-and-Semdy-First Ree-con Platoon comes into *this* stingy little ol' place!"

"I'm sorry you feel that way, friend."

"Sonnabitch!" the man growled and stomped out of the shop.

Sloane looked at me and giggled. "I get sonofabitched and motherfuckered more than any eight other businessmen on the block," he said. "Stupid damned rebels! If that shit kicker paid more than fifteen for that piece of junk, then he *really* got screwed right into the ground."

"Why didn't you tell him?"

"Doesn't do any good. They'd a helluva lot rather believe that I'm trying to cheat them than that somebody else already has. That way *they're* smart, and *I'm* the one who's stupid."

"That's a GI for you."

"Yeah. He's got all the makings of a thirty-year man. Chip on his shoulder instead of a head. What can I do for you?"

"I thought I'd look over your guns."

"Sure—right over there in the rack behind the counter. Gonna decide which one to take on the hunt, huh?"

"No, I thought I might buy one, if we can get together."

"Well, now. A real cash customer." He hustled on ahead of me to the rack. "Here's a good-looking .270," he said, handing me a well-polished, scope-mounted job.

"Little rich," I said, looking at the price tag.

"I can knock fifteen off that," he said.

'No. Thanks all the same, Cal, but what I've really got in mind is an old Springfield .30-06 military. That's a good cartridge, and I've got a little time to do some backyard gunsmithing."

"Just a minute," he said, scratching his chin. "I think I might have just the thing." He led me back into the storage room and pulled a beat-up-looking rifle down off the top shelf. He looked at the tag attached to the trigger guard and then ripped it off. "I thought so," he said. "It's two weeks past due. That bastard won't be back." He handed me the gun. "I'll let you have that one for thirty-five dollars. It's a real pig the way it sits, but if you want to take a little time to fix it up, you'll have a good weapon."

I took it out into the shop where the light was better and checked the bore. It looked clean, no corrosion. The stock was a mess. Some guy had cut down the military stock and then had painted it with brown enamel. The barrel still had the lathe marks on it. I glanced at the receiver and saw that it had been tapped and drilled for a scope. The bolt and safety had been modified.

"All right," I said, "I'll take it."

Sloane had been following my eyes, and his smile was a little sick. He hadn't noticed the modifications before he'd quoted me the price. I wrote him a check and tucked the gun under my arm. "Pleasure doing business with you, Calvin," I said.

"I think I just got screwed," he said ruefully.

"Win a few, lose a few, Cal baby," I said, patting his cheek. "See you around. Don't take any semdy-fi'-dollar watches."

A man creates a certain amount of stir walking up the street with a rifle under his arm, but I kind of enjoyed it. I put the gun on the floor in the back seat of my car and went on down a couple blocks to the gunsmith's shop. I bought a walnut stock blank, scope mounts, sling-swivels, a sling, a used four-power scope, some do-it-yourself bluing, and a jar of stock finish. Altogether, it cost me another forty dollars. I figured I'd done a good day's business, so I went into a tavern and had a beer.

About an hour or so later the phone rang and the bartender answered it. He looked up and down the bar. "I don't know him," he said, "just a minute." He raised his voice. "Is Dan Alders here?"

It always gives me a cold chill to be paged in a public place—I don't know why. It took me a moment to answer. "Yeah," I said, "that's me."

It was Jack. "You gonna be there a while?" he asked.

"I suppose."

"Sit tight then. I'll be there in about twenty minutes. I got somebody I want you to meet, OK?"

"Sure," I said. "How'd you find me?"

"I called Sloane. He said he could see your car, so I figured you might be at a water hole. I just called all the joints on the Avenue."

"Figures," I said.

"Say," he said, his voice sounding guarded, "didn't you have a tomato over at your pad last night?"

"Yeah."

"Pick her up at that foreign flick?"

"Sure," I said. I thought I'd rub him a little. "There was one there for you, too—a blonde, about five eight, thirty-six, twenty-four, thirty-six, I'd say. I threw her back."

"You son of a bitch!" he moaned. "Don't *waste* 'em, for Chrissake."

"You're the one who doesn't like foreign flicks," I told him.

"Not a word about any other women when I get there with this girl, OK?"

"Sure."

About half an hour later, Jack came in with a tall, very

attractive brunette. He waved me over to a booth and ordered a pitcher and three glasses.

"Dan," he said, "this is Sandy. You remember—I told you about her. Sandy, this is my long-lost brother, Dan."

"Hello, Dan," she said quietly, not really looking at me. She seemed frozen, somehow indifferent to everything around her. She concentrated on her cigarette.

"Hey," Jack said, "I hear you broke it off in Sloane."

"He quoted the price," I said a little smugly, "I didn't."

"He claims he could have got fifty bucks for that gun."

"I doubt it," I said. "It's a pretty butchered-up piece."

"What do you want it for if it's such a junker?"

"I'm going to rework it. New stock, dress down the barrel, and so forth, and it should be a pretty fair-looking rifle."

"Sounds like a lot of work to me," he said dubiously.

"I've got lots of time." I shrugged.

We went on talking about guns and the hunt. Sandy didn't say much. I glanced at her from time to time. She seemed withdrawn and seldom looked up. She was quite a nice-looking girl. I wondered how she'd gotten tangled up with a son of a bitch like my brother. Her hair was very dark and quite long— almost as long as Clydine's, but neater. She had long lashes which made her eyes seem huge. She seemed to smoke a helluva lot, I noticed. Other than lighting cigarettes, she hardly moved. There was an odd quality of frozen motion about her— as if she had just stopped. She bugged me. When I looked at her, it was like looking into an empty closet. There wasn't anything there. It was like she was already dead.

"Hey," Jack said, "did you pick up that pistol the other day in Seattle?"

"Yeah, it's over at the trailer."

"You know," he said, "I've been thinking maybe I ought to take along a handgun, too. There *are* bears up there, and you know what Mike was saying."

So we kicked that idea around for a while. We had another pitcher of beer.

Sandy kept smoking, but she still didn't say much.

9

I worked—off and on—at the gun all the next week, and by Saturday it was beginning to take shape. I did most of the work over at Mike's since he had a vise and a workbench in his garage. Also, it was a good place to get away from Clydine's three-hour-long telephone calls. I began to wish that classes would start so she'd have something to keep her busy.

I had the shape of the rifle stock pretty well roughed in, and I was working on the metal. I'd filed off the front sight, and now I was taking the lathe marks off the barrel with emery cloth—a very long and tedious job.

Betty was feeling punk, and I was checking in on her now and then to see if she was OK. She had a recurrent kidney problem that had Mike pretty worried. She'd had to spend a week in the hospital with it that spring, and he was afraid it might crop up again.

I was about ready to start polishing on the barrel with fine-grade emery cloth when Betty called me from the back door. I made it in about two seconds flat.

"Are you OK?" I demanded breathlessly.

"Oh, it's not me"—she laughed—"I'm fine."

"Please," I said, "don't do that anymore. I like to had a coronary."

"You've got a phone call."

"Oh, for God's sake! How did she find the number?" I grabbed up the phone. "Now look, you little clothhead, I'm busy. I can't spend all day—"

"Hey." It was Jack. "What's got you so frazzled?"

"Oh. Sorry, Jack, I thought it was that dizzy little broad again. I swear she spends at least six hours a day on the horn. I'm starting to get a cauliflower ear just listening to her."

"Why don't you do something about it?"

"I am," I said, "I'm hiding."

He laughed. "Could you do me a favor?"

"I suppose. What?"

"I'm over here at Sloane's pawnshop sittin' in for him. He said he was going to be back, but he just called and said he was tied up. I've got some stuff at the cleaners on Thirty-eighth Street—you know the place. They close at noon today, and if I don't get that stuff outta there, I'll be shit out of luck until Monday. You think you could make it over there before they close?"

"Yeah, I think so. I'm about due to take a beer break anyway. Will you be at the shop?"

"Yeah, I'll stick around till you get here. Sloane ought to be back before then, but you can't depend on him."

"OK," I said, "I'll crank up and bag on over there—on Thirty-eighth Street?"

"Yeah—you know the place. Right across from that beer joint with the shuffleboard."

"Oh. OK."

"Thanks a lot, buddy. You saved my bacon."

"Sure. See you in a bit."

I made sure that Betty was feeling OK and then took off. My hands were getting a little sore anyway.

The weather had begun to break, and it was one of those cloudy, windy days we get so often in Tacoma. It's the kind of day I really like—cool, dry, windy, with a kind of pale light and no shadows. I made it to the cleaners in plenty of time and then swung over onto South Tacoma Way.

Sloane still hadn't shown up, and Jack was puttering around in the shop. "Thanks a million, Dan," he said when I came in with his cleaning. "How much was it?"

I told him and he paid me.

"How you comin' with that gun?" he asked me.

"I'm about down to the polishing stage on the barrel," I told him. "I've still got to dress off the receiver and trigger guard. A couple more days and I can blue it. Then I'll finish up the stock."

"You get a kick out of that stuff, don't you?"

"It's kind of fun," I said. "Gives me something to do besides drink beer."

"Let me show you the gun I'm takin'," he said.

We went on into the back of the shop. He took a converted military weapon out of one of the cubbyholes.

"Eight-mm German Mauser," he said.

"Good cartridge," I told him. I looked the piece over. Somebody'd done a half-assed job of conversion on it, but it had all the essentials. "It'll do the job for you, Jack."

"Oh, hey, look at this." He reached back into another bin and came out with his hand full of .45 automatic. The damned thing looked like a cannon. He stood there grinning, pointing that monster right at my belly. I don't like having people point guns at me—even as a joke. The goddamn things weren't made to play with. I was still holding the Mauser, but I was being careful with the muzzle.

"Let's see it," I said, holding out my left hand.

He pulled back the hammer with the muzzle still pointed at me. His face got a little funny.

Slowly, with just my right hand, I raised the Mauser until it was pointing at him. I thumbed off the safety. It was like being in a dream.

"All right, Jack," I said softly, "let's count to three and then find out which one of these bastards Sloane forgot to unload."

"Christ, Danny," he said, quickly turning the .45 away from me. "I never thought of that."

I lowered the Mauser and slipped the safety back on. Jack hadn't called me Danny since we were very little kids.

"You ain't mad, are you?" he asked, sounding embarrassed.

"Hell, no." I laughed. Even to me it sounded a little hollow.

We checked both guns. They were empty. Still, I think it all took some of the fun out of Jack's day. We put the guns away and went back out into the pawnshop.

"Where the hell *is* that damned Sloane anyway?" he said to cover the moment.

"Probably visiting Helen What's-her-name," I said. I'd run into Sloane and Helen a few times, and I didn't like her. Maybe it was because of Claudia.

"I wouldn't doubt it a goddamn bit. Say, that reminds me, you want to go on a party?"

"I'm almost *always* available for a party," I said with more enthusiasm than I really felt. I wanted to get past that moment in the back room as badly as he did.

"It's Sloane's idea really. That's why I kind of wanted to wait for him to show up, but piss on him. He owns this house out in Milton that he rents out—furnished. The people who were livin' there just moved out, and the new people aren't due in until the first of the month—Wednesday."

"What's all this real estate business got to do with a party?" I asked.

"I'm gettin' to it. Anyway, the place needs cleanin'—you know, sweep, mop, vacuum, mow the lawn—that sort of shit."

"*That's* your idea of a party?"

"Keep your pants on. Now, Sloane'll provide the beer and the booze and some steaks and other stuff."

"And brooms, and mops, and lawnmowers, too, I hope," I said.

"All right, smart ass. Here's where the party comes in. We each bring a tomato—Sloane'll bring Helen, I'll bring Sandy, and you can bring What's-her-name. We'll bag on over there tomorrow afternoon about four, hit the place a lick or two— the girls can get the inside, and we'll do the outside—and then it's party-time. Give me and Sloane a perfect excuse to get away from the wives."

I shrugged. "I'm not sure Clydine would go for the domestic scene," I said. "That's not exactly her bag."

"Ask her," Jack said. "I bet she goes for it. Where else can you stir up a party on Sunday afternoon?"

"I'll ask her," I said. It was easier than arguing with him. "But I'm not making any promises."

"I'll bet she goes for it," he said.

"We'll see."

We batted it around for about half an hour, and then Sloane called. He was still tied up. Jack grumbled a bit but promised to hang on. I wanted to swing on by the trailer court to check my mail, and he asked me to drop the cleaning off at his trailer so Marg could hang it up before it got wrinkled. I took his clothes on out to my car again and drove on up the Avenue toward the court.

That whole business with the guns had been just spooky as hell. *"Maybe someday I'll just decide that you're no good, and I'll take my gun and shoot you. Bang! just like that, and you'll be dead, and I'll betcha you wouldn't like that at all."* When had I said that to Jack? Somewhere back in the long, shabby morning of our childhood. The words came echoing down to me, along with a picture of a dog rolling over and over in the snow. I tried to shrug it off.

I saw McKlearey's car in the lot at the Green Lantern Tavern about two blocks from the court, and I decided that if he was still there when I came back, I'd haul in and buy him a beer. If we were going to go hunting together, I was going to have to make some kind of effort to get along with him. I still didn't much like him though.

When I drove past Jack's trailer, I saw the two little girls out in their play-yard, and I waved at them. I parked at my place and checked my mail—nothing, as usual. Then I slung Jack's cleaning over my shoulder and hiked on up to his trailer. Maybe I could promote some lunch out of Marg if she didn't have a whole trailerful of gossiping neighbors the way she usually did.

As I came up to the trailer, I glanced through the front window. I saw that mirror back in the hallway I'd noticed the first time I'd visited. I'd meant to tell Jack about it, but I'd forgotten. The angle from where I was standing gave me a view of part of the bedroom. I had visions of Margaret unveiling her monumental breasts to the scrutiny of casual passersby. I straightened up and craned my neck to see just how much of the bedroom you could really see.

Margaret was on the bed with McKlearey. They were both bare-ass naked, and their hands were awfully busy.

I have my faults, God knows, but being a Peeping Tom is not one of them. I think I was actually frozen to the spot. You hear about that, and I've always thought it was pure nonsense, but I honestly couldn't move. Even as I watched, Lou raised up over her and came down between her widely spread thighs. Her huge, dark nippled breasts began to bob rhythmically in a kind of counterpoint to Lou's bouncing, hairy buttocks. Her head rolled back and forth, her face contorted into that expression that is not beautiful unless you are the one who is causing it. I don't think I'd ever fully realized how ugly the mating of humans can look to someone who isn't involved in it. Even dogs manage to bring it off with more dignity.

I turned around and walked on back to my trailer, suppressing a strong urge to vomit. I went inside and closed the door. I laid Jack's clothes carefully on the couch, went to the kitchen and poured myself a stiff blast of whiskey. Then, holding the glass in my hand, I took a good belt out of the bottle. I put the bottle down and drank from the glass. It didn't even burn going down.

The phone rang. It was Clydine.

"I've been trying to get you all morning," she said accusingly. "Where have you been?"

"I was busy," I said shortly.

She started to tell me about some article she'd just read in some New Left journal she was always talking about. I grunted in appropriate places, leaning over the sink to watch Jack's trailer out of the kitchen window. Even from here, I could see the whole damn thing rocking. I'll bet you could walk through any trailer court in town and tell who was going at it at any given moment. Old Lou had staying power though—I had to admit that.

"Are you listening to me?" Clydine demanded.

"Sure, kid," I said. "I was just thinking."

"About what?"

"We've been invited to a party."

"What kind of a party?"

"Probably a sex orgy," I told her bluntly. "My brother and another guy and their girlfriends—it's in a house."

"I thought your brother was married."

"So's the other guy," I said. I told her the details.

"No swapping?" It sounded like a question—or maybe an ultimatum, I don't know.

"I doubt it. I've met the girls—one of them would probably dig that sort of stuff, but I'm pretty sure the other one wouldn't. You want to go?"

"Why not? I've never been to an orgy."

"Come on, Clydine," I said. "It's like being spit on. They're not inviting you to meet their *wives*—just their mistresses."

"So? I'm *your* mistress, aren't I? Temporarily at least."

"It's different. I'm not married."

"Danny, honestly. Sometimes you can be the squarest guy in the world. I think I might get a kick out of it. Maybe I can catch some of the vibrations from their sneaky, guilty, sordid, little affairs."

"You're a nut, do you know that? This thing tomorrow has all the makings of a sight-seeing trip through a sewer."

"Boy, you're sure in a foul humor," she said. "What's got you bum-tripped now?"

"My brother pulled a gun on me."

"He *what*?"

"Just a bad joke. Forget it. Are you sure you want to go on this thing tomorrow?"

"Why not?"

"That may just be the world's *stupidest* reason for doing anything," I told her. "Hey, let's go to a drive-in movie tonight."

"What the hell for?"

"I want to neck," I said. "No hanky-panky. I just want to sit in the car and eat popcorn and drink root beer and neck— like we were both maybe sixteen or something."

"*That's* a switch. Well, why not?—I mean, sure." She paused, then said rather tentatively, "you want me to get all gussied up—like it was a real—well—*date* or something?" She sounded embarrassed to say the word.

"Yeah, why don't you do that? Wear a dress. I'll even put on a tie."

"Far out," she said.

"And wear your contacts. Leave those hideous goggles at home."

"Are you sure we aren't going to—well—I mean, I wouldn't want to lose my contacts." I'd asked her before why she didn't wear contact lenses. She told me she had them but didn't wear them because they popped out when she made love. "I don't know why," she'd said, "they just pop out." I'd laughed for ten minutes, and she'd gotten mad at me.

"They're perfectly safe," I said. "Hang up now so I can call my brother and tell him you want to go to his little clambake tomorrow."

"Bye now." She hung up, then she called right back.

"What time tonight?"

I told her.

I opened myself a beer and sat down at the kitchen table. What in the hell was I mixed up in anyhow? This whole damned situation had all the makings of a real messy blow-up. Christ Almighty, you needed a damned scoreboard just to keep track of who was screwing who—whom. When they all caught up with each other, it could wind up like World War III with bells on it, and I was going out in the woods with these guys— every one of them armed to the teeth. Shit O'Deare!

I didn't belong in this crowd. But then I didn't belong with a guy like Stan either, with the chic little gatherings and the little drama groups. Nor probably with my little Bolshevik sweetheart with her posters and pamphlets and free love. Nor with the phony artsy crowd with the paste-on beards and the Latvian folk-music records. Maybe for guys like me there just aren't any people to really be with. Maybe if they were really honest, everybody would admit the same—that all this buddy-buddy crap or "interaction" shit was just a dodge to cover up the fact that they're all absolutely alone. Maybe nobody's got anybody, and maybe that's what we're all trying to hide from. Now there's an ugly little possibility to face up to in the middle of a cool day in August.

Finally Lou left. I waited a while longer and then took the

cleaning up to Jack's trailer. Marg pulled a real bland face. She'd be a tiger in a poker game. We talked a few minutes, and then I drove back over to Mike's place and went back to work on the rifle. At least that was something I could get my hands on.

10

I picked up Clydine about three thirty the next afternoon, and we drove on out to Milton for the combination GI-party-sex-orgy Sloane had cooked up. I was still a little soured on the whole thing, but Clydine seemed to think it would be a kind of campy gas to watch a couple of Establishment types and what she persisted in calling "their sordid little affairs."

"You're beginning to sound like T. S. Eliot," I told her.

She ignored that.

"What kind of a cat is your brother?" she asked me. "Is he anything like you?"

"Jack? Hell no," I snorted. "He's a couple years older than I am. He was in trouble a lot when he was a kid. Then six years in the Navy right after high school. Married three times. Works in a trailer lot—part-time sales and general flunky. Drinks beer most of the time because he can't afford whiskey. Chases women. Screws a lot. He can charm the birds right out of the trees when he wants to. Something of an egomaniac. I guess that covers it."

"Typical Hard Hat, huh?" she said grimly.

"Look, my little daffodil of the downtrodden, one of the things you'll learn as you grow older is that group labels don't work. You say Hard Hat, and you get a certain picture. Then you close your mind. But you scream bloody murder when some fortyish guy in a suit looks at you and says 'Hippie' and then closes *his* mind. These goddamn labels and slogans are just a cop-out for people who are too lazy to think or don't have the equipment. Your labels won't work on my brother. He's completely nonpolitical."

"You know," she said quietly, "I wouldn't take that from anybody but you. I think it's because I know you don't care. Sometimes it gives me goose bumps all over—how much you don't care."

"Come on," I said, "don't get dramatic about it. I'm just at loose ends right now, that's all."

"You'd make a terrific revolutionary," she said. "With that attitude of yours, you could do anything. But that's inconsistent, isn't it? To be a revolutionary, you'd have to care about something. Oh, dear." She sighed mightily.

I laughed at her. Sometimes she could be almost adorable.

"I'm *serious*," she said. "What about the other guys?"

"Sloane? A hustler, *Petit-bourgeois* type."

"That's a label, too, isn't it?" she demanded.

"Now you're learning. Calvin Sloane is a very complex person. He was probably fat, unloved, and poor as a child. He went right to the root of things—money. He's a pawnbroker, a used-car dealer, a part-owner of several taverns, and God knows what else. Anything that'll turn a buck. He's got it made. He uses his money the way a pretty girl uses her body. As long as Sloane's buying, everything's OK. Maybe he's accepted the fact that nobody's really going to like him unless he pays them for it. He can't accept honest, free friendship or affection—not even from his wife. That's why he takes up with these floozies. They're bought and paid for. He understands them. He can't really accept any other kind of relationship. Don't ever tell him this, but I like him anyway—in spite of his money."

"You sure make it hard to hate the enemy," she said.

"Walt Kelly once said, 'We have met the enemy, and he is us.'"

"Who's Walt Kelly?"

"The guy who draws *Pogo*."

"Oh. I prefer *Peanuts*."

"That's because you're politically immature," I told her.

She socked me on the shoulder. I think our popcorn-root-beer-drive-in-movie date the night before had caused us both to revert to adolescence. She'd been almost breathtaking in a skirt, sweater, and ponytail, and without those damned glasses; but I'd stuck to my guns—we'd only necked. Both of us had gone home so worked-up we'd been about ready to climb the walls. She'd made some pretty pointed threats about what she was going to do to me at the orgy.

"What about the women?" she asked. "The concubines?"

"Helen—that Sloane's trollop—is a pig. She's got a mind like a sewer and a mouth to match. Even in the circles she moves in, she's considered stupid since she does all of her thinking, I'm told, between her legs. Her husband's in the Air Force, and he's maniacally jealous, but she cheats on him anyway. I think she cheats just for the sake of cheating. I've about halfway got a hunch that this little blowout today was her idea. She likes her sex down and dirty, and probably she's been thrilled by orgies in some of the pornography she's always reading—undoubtedly moving her lips while she does—and she figures diddling in groups has just got to be dirtier than doing it in pairs. Maybe she figures to get a bunch-punch out of the deal."

"Bunch-punch?"

"Multiple intercourse—gang-bang."

"Oh. What about the other one?"

"Sandy? You got me, kid. She's good-looking, but she never says anything. You think *I'm* cool? She's so cool, she's just barely alive—or just recently dead, I haven't decided which. If you can figure her out, let me know."

We drove on across the Puyallup River bridge and on out toward Fife and Milton.

The house Sloane had out in Milton was a little surprising. I'd half-expected one of those run-down rabbit hutches that are described euphemistically as "rental properties"—not good enough to live in yourself, but good enough to house former sharecroppers or ex-galley-slaves—always provided that they can come up with the hundred and a quarter a month.

Sloane's house, on the other hand, was damned nice. It was an older frame place with one of those deep porches all across the front, and it nestled up to its eaves in big, old shrubbery. There was about a half acre of lawn in front and probably more in back. A long driveway went up to the house and along one side of it to the garage behind the house. On the other side of the driveway was a garden plot that had pretty much gone to weeds.

I ran my car on up the driveway and pulled up just behind Sloane's Cadillac.

"Nice place," Clydine said, looking out at the white-picket-fence-enclosed backyard.

"Well, well, well," Jack said, bustling out of the house with a bottle of beer in his hand. "What have we here?"

Clydine and I got out of the car.

"My"—Jack grinned, coming through the gate—"she's a *little* one, isn't she?" He was giving her the full benefit of the dazzling Jack Alders' smile, guaranteed to melt glaciers and peel paint at a hundred yards.

"Jack," I said, "this is Clydine."

"*Clydine*? How the hell'd you ever get a name like that, sweetie?"

"I won it in a raffle," she said with a perfectly straight face.

"She won it in a raffle!" Jack chortled with a forced glee. "That's pretty sharp, pretty sharp. Come on in the house, kids. Fuel up." He waved the beer bottle at us and led the way toward the house.

"Far out," Clydine murmured to me.

"Hey, gang," Jack announced as we went in the back door, "you all know my brother Dan, and this is his current steady, *Clydine*. Isn't that a handle for you?" He pointed to each of the others standing around in the kitchen and repeated their names. "Tell you what, sweetie," he said to Clydine, "I'm never gonna be able to manage that name of yours, so I'm just gonna call you *Clyde*." He winked broadly at the rest of us.

She smiled sweetly at him, and then said very pleasantly but very distinctly, "If you do, I'll kick you right square in the balls."

Sloane shrieked with laughter, almost collapsing on the floor. Jack looked stunned but covered it well, laughing a little hollowly with the rest of us. His jaws tightened up some though.

We had a couple of beers, got the girls organized, and then Jack, Sloane, and I went outside to tackle the yardwork.

I fell heir to a scythe and the chore of leveling the jungle that had been a garden. Once I got into it, I discovered that in spite of the weeds, there was a pretty fair amount of salvageable produce there. By the time I got through, I'd laid a couple bushels of assorted vegetables over on the grass strip between the garden and the driveway—radishes, carrots, lettuce, onions, cucumbers, and so forth. I hauled great armloads of weeds and junk back to a brush pile behind the garage. The place looked a lot better when I was done.

I washed off my produce at an outside faucet and put it on the back porch. Then I grabbed another beer and went to see how Jack and Cal were doing. I found them sitting on the front porch, staring down at the half-mowed lawn.

"Takin' a beer break, hey, Dan?" Sloane said.

"No. I finished up."

"No shit?"

They had to come out and inspect the job. Then they looked at my haul on the back porch, and then we went back to the front porch to sit and stare at the lawnmower some more.

Sloane sighed. "Well," he said, "I guess it's my turn in the barrel." He walked heavily down the front stairs and cranked up the mower.

"That tomato of yours has got kind of a smart mouth, hasn't she?" Jack said sourly, lighting a cigarette.

"She just says what she thinks," I told him.

"If she was with me, I'd slap a few manners into her." He was still stinging from the put-down.

"You'd get your balls kicked off, too," I told him. "She meant what she said about that."

"A tough one, huh?" he said. "Where'd you latch onto her anyway?"

"She's the one I met at that Italian movie, remember?"

"Oh, *that* one. You sure got a weird taste in women, is all I can say."

"She's a human being," I said, "not just a stray piece of tail. As long as you treat her like a human being, fine. It's when you come on like she was a cocker spaniel that you run into trouble." I knew there wasn't much point in talking to him about it. He wasn't likely to change.

"I'd still slap some manners into her if it was me," he said.

"I don't hit women much," I said, looking out toward the sunset.

He grunted and went down to spell Sloane on the mower.

Sloane came back up the steps, puffing and sweating like a pig. "Man," he gasped, "am I ever out of shape. I'm gonna have to start jogging or something before we go up into the high country."

"You said a mouthful there, buddy," I said. "We probably all should. Otherwise one of us is going to blow a coronary."

"Hey"—he giggled—"I like that little girl of yours. She's cute as a button, isn't she?"

"She's a boot in the butt," I agreed.

"Boy, did she ever get the drop on old Jack. I thought he was gonna fall right on his ear when she threatened to bust his balls for him."

"I think he's still a little sore about it."

"He isn't used to havin' women react that way to his line."

"She just doesn't buy the glad-hand routine," I said, "and Jack doesn't know any other approach."

"How'd you manage to latch onto her?"

"You'd never believe it," I said.

"Try me."

I told him about it.

"No kidding?" he said, laughing. Then a thought flickered across his face. "Say, she isn't a user, is she? I mean, a lot of those kids are. She hasn't got any stuff with her, has she? I can square the beef if the cops come in here because we're makin' too much noise or something, but if they come in and find her stoned out of her mind on something, that could get a little sticky."

"No," I told him. "No sweat—oh, she blows a little grass now and then, but I've told her that I don't particularly care for the stuff, and I don't get much kick out of talking to people when they're stoned. It's like talking into a wet mop. She stays away from it when she's with me. We've got a deal; I tell all her friends I'm an ex-con, and she stays off the grass when I'm around. What she does on her own time is her business."

"Sounds like you two have quite an arrangement going."

"For the most part, we don't try to tell each other what to do, that's all. We get along pretty good that way."

"There, you lazy bastards!" Jack yelled, killing the lawn-mower. "It's all done."

"You do nice work," Sloane said. "Let's go get cleaned up. I brought towels and soap and stuff. I get firsties on the shower."

The girls had finished the inside cleanup and had already bathed and changed clothes. Sloane, Jack, and I all showered and changed while they cooked up the steaks and whipped up a salad out of some of my produce. We all had mixed drinks with dinner and a couple more afterward. Along about sundown things started to loosen up a bit.

"Hey," Helen said, her hard, plastered-on face brightening, "let's play strip poker."

"I didn't bring any cards," Sloane said.

"Oh, darn," she pouted. "How about you, Jack? Dan? Haven't one of you guys maybe got a deck of cards in your car?"

We both shook our heads.

"Maybe the people who lived here—" She jumped to her feet and ran into the kitchen to start rummaging through the various drawers.

"Je-sus *Christ*!" Clydine said, "if she wants to take her clothes off so goddamn bad, why doesn't she just go ahead and take her clothes off?"

Sandy smiled slightly. It was the first time I'd ever seen her do it.

"Come on, you guys," Helen called, "help me look."

"We cleaned out all those drawers this afternoon," Sandy said, her voice seeming very far away.

"Damn it all, anyway," Helen complained, coming back into the living room. She plunked herself back down on the couch beside Sloane, sulking.

The orgy wasn't getting off the ground too well.

"Jeeze," Helen said, "you'd think somebody'd have a deck of cards. Myron *always* has a deck of cards with him. All the sergeants do. They play cards all the time."

"At least when they're playing cards, they're not dropping napalm on little kids," Clydine said acidly.

Helen's eyes narrowed. "I don't know about some people, but I think we ought to back up our servicemen all the way."

"So do I," Clydine said. I blinked at her. What the hell? "I think we ought to back them up as far as Hawaii, at least," she finished.

It took Helen a minute or two to figure that one out.

"I'm *proud* to be the wife of a serviceman," she said finally, not realizing how that remark sounded under the circumstances.

"Let it lay," I muttered to Clydine.

"But—"

"Don't stomp a cripple. It's not sporting."

"Hey," Jack said, moving in quickly to avert a brawl, "I meant to ask you, Cal, are we gonna take pistols with us, too? On the hunt, I mean?"

"Sure," Sloane said. "Why not? If we don't get any deer, we can always sit around and plink beer cans." He giggled.

"You got anything definite out of that other guy yet, Dan?" Jack was pretty obviously dragging things in by the heels to keep Helen and Clydine away from each other's throats. A beef between the women could queer the whole party.

"Carter says the whole deal could hang on him goin'. You better nudge him a little."

"He's gotta make up his own mind," I said. "I can't do it for him."

We kicked that around for a while. We had another drink. I imagine we were all starting to feel them a little, even though we'd been pretty carefully spacing them out. Even Sandy started to get loosened up a bit.

Then we started telling jokes, and they began to get raunchier and raunchier—which isn't unusual, considering what this party was supposed to be. In all of her jokes, Helen kept referring to the male organ as a wiener, which, for some reason, just irritated hell out of me.

I went on out to the kitchen to get a beer, figuring to back off on the whiskey a little to keep from getting completely pie-eyed. I heard the padding of bare feet behind me. Clydine had her shoes off again.

She caught me at the refrigerator. "*This* is an *orgy?*" she said. "I don't think these people know *how*. They're like a bunch of kids sitting around trying to get up nerve enough to play spin the bottle."

"You want some action?" I leered at her.

"Well, after that popcorn and purity routine last night, I'm pretty well primed. When does something happen?"

"Hey, in there," Helen called, "no sneaking off into dark corners. If you're gonna do something, you gotta do it out here where we can all watch." She giggled coarsely.

"That does it!" Clydine said. She grabbed my arm. "Let's go screw—right in the middle of the goddamn rug!"

"Cool it," I said, "I'll get things moving."

"Well, somebody's going to have to. This is worse than a goddamn Girl Scout camp."

I rummaged around until I found a large glass. Then I got a couple more bottles of beer and went back to the living room.

"I'll bet he was copping a feel." Helen snickered. "How was it, honey?"

I ignored that, but Clydine glowered at her.

"I just remembered a game," I announced. "The Germans play it in the beer halls."

"What kinda game?" Helen demanded a little blearily.

"It's a kind of drinking game," I said, pouring beer into the large glass.

"A *drinking* game," she objected. "That's no goddamn fun. How about a *sex* game?"

"Just hang tough," I said. "The point of this game is that the person who takes the *next* to the last drink out of his glass— not the last one, but the *next* to the last one—has to pay a penalty of some kind."

"What kind of penalty?" Sloane asked.

"Any penalty we decide. Everybody gets to kick him in the butt, or he has to go outside and bay at the moon, or he—or she—has to take off one piece of clothing or—"

"Hey," Helen said, "I like that last one." Some how I *knew* she would. "That sounds like a swell game."

"That's a pretty big glass," Jack objected.

"That's the point," I explained. "Nobody can just chug-a-lug it down. You can take a big drink or a little one, but remember if the next player finishes it off, you gotta peel off one item of clothing—a sock, your pants, a bra, or whatever."

We haggled a bit about the rules, but finally everybody agreed to them. We all discarded our shoes to get that out of the way. I caught a glimpse of Sandy's face. It seemed completely indifferent. We pulled our seats into a kind of circle and began passing the glass around.

Sloane, of course, polished off the first glass, and Helen, with a great deal of giggling and ostentatious display of leg, peeled off a stocking. I think that mentally she was still at the "You show me yours, and I'll show you mine" stage of development. Then Jack caught Sandy, and she mutely followed Helen's example.

It went several rounds, with Sloane, Jack, and me pretty well able to control it—simply because we could take bigger drinks. I hadn't dropped it on Clydine yet.

"Come on, crumb," she hissed at me. "I'm beginning to feel like a virgin." Helen was down to her panties and bra, and Sandy was in her slip. I'd lost one sock and both Jack and Sloane were down to their slacks and shorts. I was trying not to look at Jack's tattoos.

"How much have you got on under that?" I asked Clydine. She had on a dark jersey and a pair of slacks. No sox.

"Just panties," she said. "I want to beat that dim-witted exhibitionist down to skin." Her competitive spirit was up. It was a silly game, but we were all drunk enough to start taking it a little seriously.

So the next time around, I emptied the glass, Clydine stood up and slowly pulled off the jersey. Her little soldiers snapped to attention. I heard a sharp intake of breath from Jack. Clydine took a deep breath, and Sloane choked a little.

"Come on, come on," Helen snapped, "let's get on with the game. That's not the only set of boobs in the room." What a pig!

Sandy lost her slip, and then Helen's bra went. She thrust

her breasts out as far as she could, but they were pretty sorry-looking in comparison to my two little friends. It's a funny thing about nudity. Helen looked vulgar, but Clydine didn't. My little Bolshevik was completely natural about the whole thing. After the first shock wore off, her nude breasts were almost an extension of her face—pretty but not vulgar. Helen's face stopped at her neck with the sharp line where her makeup left off. Below that she was obscene.

I lost my other sock, Jack lost his pants, and Sandy's bra went. There was a sort of simplicity, almost a purity in the way she numbly exposed herself.

"Break-time," Sloane giggled. "My kidneys are awash." He hustled on back to the can with Jack right behind him. Clydine wandered around a little, looking at the furniture, and Helen sat sulking. She was obviously outclassed; Sandy had a great shape, and Clydine, of course, was out of sight.

"It's not much of a game really," I said apologetically to Sandy.

She lit a cigarette, seemingly oblivious of her own nakedness. "It doesn't matter," she said. "It's only for a little while, so it doesn't make any difference." I was suddenly disgusted with myself for having come up with the whole silly idea. Why does a guy do things like that?

"I'm not being nosey," I said, lying in my teeth, "but why do you hang around with Jack anyway? You know there's no future in it for you."

"Oh, Jack's all right," she said. "If it wasn't him, it would just be somebody else. It's only for a little while anyway."

She kept on saying that. Nobody was *that* cool. Maybe it was just a way of keeping things from getting to her.

"I like your little friend," she said, suddenly flashing a quick smile toward Clydine. The smile made her face suddenly come alive, and there was something just under the surface that made me look away.

Sloane and Jack came back, and the rest of us trekked back one at a time to use the facilities.

The game continued in a fairly predictable way, with all the girls winding up totally nude, and Sloane, Jack, and me in just our shorts. Despite some fairly obvious suggestions from Helen about where the final penalty should be paid, each couple retired to a separate bedroom for the last stages of the party.

As I said before, Clydine and I had both gotten pretty well worked-up the preceding night, and we went at each other pretty hot and heavy the first time. The booze, however, took its well-known and pretty obvious toll. I wasn't really making much headway the second time around, just sort of trying to entertain a friend, so to speak.

"It's not working, Danny," she said softly. "We're both too tipsy. Let's talk."

I started to roll over.

"No," she said, locking her legs around me, "just stay there. It's kind of nice, and this way I'm sure I've got your attention."

"Oh, *gosh*, yes," I said, mimicking Carter. "This may add an entirely new dimension to the art of conversation."

"Just relax," she told me. She pulled me down.

"We're not for keeps, Danny," she said after a moment. "You know that, don't you? I'm saying this because I keep having this awful impulse to tell you that I love you."

I started to say something, but she squeezed me sharply with her legs.

"Let me finish," she said, "while I've still got the courage. I know you think it's silly, all this—well—political stuff I'm involved in, but it's awfully important to me. I believe in it. I wish you did, too. Sometimes I just wish you'd believe in *something—anything*, but you don't."

I started to say something again, and she gave her pelvis a vicious little twist that damned near emasculated me.

"I'm going to do that every time you interrupt me," she said. She had a long memory. I don't think I've ever been so completely helpless before or since. She had me—as they say—at her mercy.

"In about a month," she went on, "you're going back up to the U, and I'll be starting to go to class here in a couple of weeks. You're going to be gone for ten days on this hunting expedition of yours. Between now and the first of October— less than ten days—is all we've really got. Am I getting maudlin?"

I didn't dare answer.

"If you've gone to sleep, damn you, I'll cripple you."

"I'm here," I said, "don't get carried away."

"Have I made any sense?" she asked.

"I'm tempted to argue," I said, "but I think you're probably right. If we try to keep it going after I get to Seattle, it'll just die on us anyway, and we'd both feel guilty about it. It's easy to say that it's only thirty miles, but the distance between Seattle and Tacoma is a lot more than that really."

"It's a damned shame," she said. She rocked her hips a few times under me, gently. "When it comes to this, you're just clear out of sight, but that's not really enough, is it?"

"Not in the end, it isn't," I said sadly. "At first it is."

"Let's give it another try," she said. "I want to say something silly, and I want you to be too distracted to hear me."

This time we made it, and just as we did she said, "I love you," very softly in my ear.

I whispered it back to her, and then she cried.

I held her for a long while, and then we got up and got dressed.

Sandy was standing at the kitchen sink with a cigarette and a glass of whiskey, still nude, looking out the window at the moonlight.

"We have to run, Sandy," I told her softly. "Tell Jack, OK?"

She nodded to me and smiled vaguely at Clydine. "He's asleep now," she said. "He always goes to sleep. Sometimes I'd like to talk, but he always goes to sleep. They all do." She took a drink of whiskey.

"It'll be all right," I said inanely.

"Of course," she said, her voice slurring a bit. "In just a little while."

Clydine and I went on out and got in the car. I backed on out to the road and drove on down toward Fife.

"She kept saying that all night," I said. " 'It's only for a little while.' What the hell is that supposed to mean?"

"You're not as smart as I thought you were," Clydine said to me. "It's as plain as the nose on your face."

"What?"

"She's going to kill herself."

"Oh, come on," I said.

"She'll be dead before Christmas."

I thought about it. Somehow it fit. "I'd better tell Jack," I said.

"Mind your own business," she told me. "It hasn't got anything to do with him."

"But—"

"Just stay out of it. You couldn't stop it anyway. It's something that happened to her a long time ago. She's just waiting for the right time. Leave her alone."

Women!

"Let's go back to your place," she said. "I want us both to

take a good hot bath, and then I want to sleep with you—just sleep. OK?"

"Why not?" I said.

"Seems to me you said that was the worst reason in the world for doing anything."

"I'm always saying things like that," I told her.

11

THE following Wednesday, the first of September, we were all going to get together out at Carter's to make sure we had everything all set for the hunt. We were going to be leaving on the ninth, and so we were kind of moving up on it.

Stan had finally committed himself to going along, which surprised me since I figured that Monica would just flat veto the idea. I guess maybe she figured that that would be too obvious—or maybe she'd tried all the tricks in her bag, first the nagging, then the icicles, then crossing her legs, and none of them had worked. Stan was pretty easygoing most of the time, but he could get his back up if the occasion came along. I'd gotten a vague hint or two about the kind of pressure she was putting on him, but he was hanging in there. Then, quite suddenly, she seemed to give in. She got real nice to everybody, and that *really* worried me.

The other guys had decided to bring their wives on out to Carter's to kind of quiet down the rumblings of discontent which were beginning to crop up as a result of our frequent all-male gatherings and planning sessions. I'd asked Clydine, but there was a meeting of some kind she wanted to attend. Besides which, she told me, she'd about *had* the establishment types and their antics. I'd wanted her to meet Claudia; but, all things considered, it was probably for the best that she didn't come. Jack and Cal would have been as jumpy as cats with her around after the little orgy on Sunday. I knew she could keep her mouth shut, but they wouldn't have been so sure.

Anyhow I was over at Mike's that afternoon finishing up

the rifle. Maybe it was just luck, but the thing was coming out beautifully. I hadn't really taken pride in anything for a long time, and I was really getting a kick out of it. Mike came out when he got home from work and sat on the edge of the workbench with a quart of beer while I put the last coat of stock-finish on the wood. I'd finished bluing the action the day before. All that was left was a last rubdown on the wood, mounting the sling swivels and assembling the gun.

"Man," he said admiringly, "that's gonna be one fine-looking weapon. How much you say you've got into it?"

"About seventy-five bucks altogether," I said, "and about thirty-forty hours of work."

"Beautiful job," he said, handing me the quart. I took a guzzle and gave it back.

"Now I just hope the son of a bitch shoots straight, " I said. "I never fired it before I started on this."

"Oh, I wouldn't worry," he said. "That old Springfield was always a pretty dependable piece of machinery. As long as you can poke one up the spout, she'll shoot."

"I sure hope you're right," I said, carefully leaning the stock against the garage wall to dry. I scoured my hands off with turpentine and began working at them with some paste hand-cleaner.

"Betty says you're staying to dinner." He finished the quart and pitched it into a box in the corner.

"Yeah," I said. "I'll have to start paying board here pretty quick." I *had* been eating with them pretty often.

"Glad to have you," he said, grinning. "It gives me some-body to swap war stories with." Mike and I got along well.

"Hey," he said. "I hear that was quite a party Sunday."

"It was an orgy," I said. "You ever met Helen—that pig of Sloane's?"

"Once or twice."

"Then you've probably got a pretty good idea of how things went."

"Oh, *gosh*, yes." He chuckled. "Jack was telling me that little girl you brought has got quite a shape on her."

"You can tell that she's a girl."

"He said he didn't much care for her though."

I laughed about that, and then I told Mike about the little confrontation.

"No kidding?" He laughed. "I'd sure love to have been able to see the expression on his face."

"What face?" I laughed. "It fell right off."

"Was Sandy What's-her-name there with Jack?" he asked.

"Yeah. Quiet as ever."

"She's a strange one, isn't she?"

"Clydine—that's my little girl-chum—says that Sandy's gonna kill herself pretty quick." I probably shouldn't have said anything, but I knew Mike had sense enough to keep his mouth shut.

"What makes her think so?"

"I don't know for sure—maybe they talked or maybe my little agitator is relying on the well-known, but seldom reliable, intuition women are supposed to have."

"Maybe so," Mike said thoughtfully, "but I've heard that girl say awfully weird things sometimes. If that's what she's got in mind, it would sure explain a helluva lot. You tell Jack?"

I shook my head. "He wouldn't believe it in the first place, and what could he do about it?"

"That's true," Mike admitted. He slid down off the bench and looked ruefully at his belly. "Sure is gonna get tiresome carryin' this thing up and down mountains. God damn, a man can get out of shape in a hurry." I think we both wanted to get off the subject of Sandy.

"Beer and home cookin'," I said. "Do it to you every time."

I washed my hands at the outside faucet, dried them on my pants, and got my clean clothes out of my car. We went inside, and I changed clothes in the bathroom. After we ate, Mike and I had a couple beers and watched TV while Betty cleaned up in the kitchen. She sang while she was working, and her voice was clear and high, and she hit the notes right on. There's nothing so nice as a woman singing in the kitchen.

Jack and Marg showed up about seven with a case of beer, and we all sat around talking. Marg looked like she'd gotten a head start on the drinking. She was a little glassy-eyed.

"How'd you get tangled up with this Larkin guy, Dan?" Jack asked me. "He seemed a little standoffish when I met him the other day."

"Oh, Stan's OK," I said. "He's just a little formal till he gets to know you. He'll loosen up."

"I sure hope so."

"We shared an apartment for a while when I was up at the U," I said. "We got along pretty well."

"He done much hunting?" Mike asked.

"Birds, mostly," I said. "I've been duck hunting with him

a few times. He's awfully damned good with a shotgun." I told them about Stan's triple on ducks.

"That's pretty good, but I'll bet I could still teach him a thing or two about shotgun shootin'," Jack boasted.

"Here we go," Margaret said disgustedly, "the mighty hunter bit." Her words were a little slurred.

"I'm good, sweetie," Jack said. "Why should I lie about it? I am probably one of the world's finest wing shots. Every time I go out, you can count on pure carnage."

"You know what's so damned disgusting about it?" Mike said. "The big-mouth son of a bitch can probably make it stick. I saw him bust four out of five thrown beer bottles one time with a twenty-two rifle."

"Never could figure out how I missed that last one," Jack said. "Must have been a defective cartridge."

"You're impossible." Betty laughed. Nothing bothered Betty.

"Just good," he said, "that's all. Class will tell." Jack smirked at us all.

"When you guys get him out in the woods," Margaret said dryly, "why don't you do the world a favor and shoot him?"

We drank some more beer and sopped up dip with potato chips. Mike and Betty had a comfortable little house with furniture that was nice but not so new as to make you afraid to relax. It was a pleasant place to talk.

Sloane and Claudia drifted in about eight with some more beer and Sloane's ever-present jug of whiskey.

"Hey"—he giggled—"is this where the action is?" He bulked large in the doorway, the case of beer under one arm and his hat shoved onto the back of his head. Claudia pushed him on into the room. They looked odd together. She was so tiny, and he was so goddamn gross. It dawned on me that she was even smaller than my little radical cutie. I wondered how in the hell she'd ever gotten tangled up with Sloane.

With him at the party, of course, any hope of quiet conversation went down the drain. He was a good-natured bastard though.

"Wait till you see what Dan's done with the rifle you unloaded on him," Mike said.

"Get it done, old buddy?" Sloane asked me.

"Not quite," I said.

"Bring it around when you get done with it," he said. "I might just buy it back."

"I believe I'll hang onto this one," I told him.

Stan and Monica came a little later, and I could see the icicles on her face. She clicked that smile on and off rapidly as I introduced them to everybody. Stan seemed ill at ease, and I knew she'd been at him pretty hard again.

"I thought Stanley said there were going to be *six* of you on this little expedition," she said brightly. "Somebody must be missing."

"McKlearey," Jack said. "He's pretty undependable. Likely he's in jail, drunk, or in bed with somebody's wife—maybe all three."

"Really?" she said with a slightly raised eyebrow. She looked around the room. "What a charming *little* house," she said, and I saw Betty's eyes narrow slightly at the tone in the voice.

So *that* was her new gimmick. She was going to put us down as a bunch of slum-type slobs and make Stan feel shitty for having anything to do with us.

"It's a lot more comfortable than the trailer the 'great provider' here has me cooped up in," Marg said, playing right into her hands.

"Oh, do you live in one of *those*?" Monica asked. "That must be nice—so *convenient* and everything."

I ground my teeth together. There was nothing I could do to stop her.

"Sometimes I wish *we* lived in one," Claudia's low voice purred. "When your husband needs a living room the size of a basketball court to keep from knocking things over, you get a bit tired just keeping the clutter picked up."

I knew damned well Claudia wouldn't be caught dead in a trailer, but she wasn't about to let this bitch badmouth Betty and Marg.

"Oh," Monica said, "you have a *large* house?"

"Like a barn." Sloane giggled.

"I just adore big, *old* houses," Monica said. "It's such a shame that the neighborhoods where you find them deteriorate so fast."

Jack laughed. "Sloane's neighborhood up in Ruston isn't likely to deteriorate much. He's got two bank presidents, a mill owner, and a retired admiral on his block. The whole street just reeks of money."

Monica faltered. Certain parts of Ruston were about as high class as you were going to get around Tacoma.

Sloane giggled again. "Costs a fortune to live there. They *inhale* me every year just for taxes."

"Oh, Calvin," Claudia said suavely, "it's not that bad, and the neighbors are nice. they don't feel they have to 'keep up' or put each other down. They don't have this 'status' thing." Monica's face froze, but that put an end to it. Claudia had real class, the one thing Monica couldn't compete with. The little exchange had backfired, and *she* was the one who came out looking like a slob. She hadn't figured on Claudia.

Then Lou showed up. He was a little drunk but seemed to be in a good humor. "Hide your women and your liquor," he announced in that raspy voice of his. "I'm here at last." A kind of tension came into the room very suddenly. McKlearey still seemed to carry that air of suppressed violence with him. Maybe it was that stiff Gyrene brace he stood in all the time.

Why in hell couldn't he relax? I still hadn't really bought that quick changeover of his on the night when we'd first started talking about the High Hunt. I'd figured it was a grandstand play and he'd back out, but so far he hadn't. One thing I knew for sure—I'd have sure felt a lot better if he and Jack weren't going up into the woods together. Both of them could get pretty irrational, and there were going to be a lot of guns around.

"Where in hell have you been McKlearey?" Jack demanded. "You're an hour late."

"I got tied up," Lou said.

"Yeah? What's her name?"

"Who bothers with names?" McKlearey jeered.

I saw Margaret glance sharply at Lou, but his face was blank. She was actually jealous of that creepy son of a bitch, for Chrissake!

"Let's all have a belt," Sloane suggested. He hustled into the kitchen and began mixing drinks.

I sat back, relaxing a bit now that all the little interpersonal crises were over for the moment. I think that's why I've always been kind of a loner. When people get at each other and the little tensions start to build, I get just uncomfortable as hell. It's like having your finger in a light socket knowing some guy behind you has his hand on the switch. You're pretty sure he won't really turn it on, but it still makes you jumpy.

I glanced over at Claudia. I liked her more and more. I wished to hell I didn't know about Sloane and his outside hobbies.

Stan caught my eye with a look of strained apology. He, of course, had been on to Monica's little performance even more than I had. I shrugged to him slightly. Hell, it wasn't *his* fault.

Sloane distributed the drinks and then stood in the archway leading to Mike's dining room. "And now," he announced, "if you ladies will excuse us, we'll adjourn to the dining room here and discuss the forthcoming slaughter." He giggled.

"Right," Jack said, getting up. "We got plans to make." He was a little unsteady on his feet, but I didn't pay much attention just then.

The rest of us got up, and we trooped into the dining room. I saw Monica's face tighten as Stan got up. She didn't want him out of sight, not even for a minute.

"Now," Mike said after we'd pulled up the chairs and sat around the table, "I've made the deal with this guy named Miller in Twisp, so that's all settled."

"Where in hell is Twisp, for Chrissake?" Lou demanded.

Mike got a map, and we located Twisp, a small town in the Methow Valley.

"How'd you get to know a guy way to hell and gone up there?" Sloane asked.

"I've got a cousin who lives up there," Mike said. "He introduced me to Miller when I was up there a year ago."

"What kind of guy is he?" Jack asked.

"Rough, man. He tells you to do something, you damn well better do it."

"He better not try givin' *me* a bad time," Lou said belligerently.

"He'd have *you* for breakfast, Lou," Mike said. "I've seen him, and you can take it from me, he's *bad*."

"Yeah?" Lou said, his jaw tightening.

"Knock it off, McKlearey," Sloane said; he wasn't smiling. Lou grumbled a bit, but he shut up.

"Anyway, this is the deal," Mike went on. "It's fifty bucks each for ten days. He'll buy the food, and we'll pay him for it when we get there. He figures about thirty bucks a man. It would usually be a helluva lot more, but, like I told you, he's just getting into the business, and so he doesn't want to charge full price yet."

"How the hell is he gonna feed us on three bucks a day each?" Jack demanded, taking a straight belt of whiskey from Sloane's bottle.

"We'll eat beans mostly, I expect," Mike said. "I told him we weren't exactly rolling in money, and not to get fancy on the chow. He said we could get by with a little camp meat to tide us over."

"Camp meat? What the hell's that?" Lou asked. He was being deliberately dense.

"He'll knock over a doe once we get up into the high country," Mike explained. "We'll eat that up before we come out. All the guides up there do it. I guess the game wardens don't much care as long as you don't bring any of the meat out— or if they do, there's not a helluva lot they can do about it."

"Good deal," I said, lighting a cigarette.

"Now," Mike went on, "he said we'll each need a rifle, one box of shells, a pair of good boots, a good warm coat, several pair of heavy sox, a couple changes of clothes, and a good sleeping bag. Oh, one other thing—he wants us to put our clothes and stuff in some kind of sack so we can hang them here and there on the packhorses."

"Hell," Lou said, "why don't we just roll 'em up in our sleeping bags?"

"Then what do you do with them at night, you dumb shit?" Jack demanded.

"Hang 'em on a fuckin' tree," Lou said.

"They'd be soaking wet by morning," I told him.

"Can everybody get all the stuff I just read off together?" Mike asked.

"Shouldn't be much trick to that," Jack said. "The clothes shouldn't be any problem, and Cal's bringin' most of the guns. Sleeping bag's about the only big thing, if a guy can't borrow one." He took another drink of whiskey.

"Miller says it's colder'n hell up there in the high country," Mike said, "and we damn well better be ready for it. I wouldn't recommend skimping on the sleeping bag. He says he's got the tents and cookware, so we won't have to worry about that."

"Oh, hey," I said, "I was down at that surplus store downtown. I got a pretty good bag—army job—for about ten bucks. Some of you guys might want to check them out."

"That sure beats the twenty or thirty they cost at the department stores," Jack said. His voice sounded a little thick. He'd been hitting the jug pretty hard.

"I'd have to take a look at them," Lou said, his voice surly. By God! He was *still* fighting this thing, even now. If he didn't want to go, why the hell didn't he just say so and quit bugging the rest of us?

"I guess that's about everything then," Mike said, looking at the list. "We get together at Sloane's on the evening of the eighth for a final check-through on all the gear, and then we leave at midnight on the ninth."

"One thing," Jack said. "Are we gonna take pistols or not?"

"What did Miller say about it?" I asked Mike. I hoped to hell that he'd vetoed the idea. A guy might stop and think with a rifle, but a damned pistol is just too easy to use.

"He didn't say, one way or the other," Mike said.

"Well," Jack persisted, "are we gonna take 'em or not?" He'd been pushing the handgun business from the very start, but he'd never told me way.

"All right," Sloane said, "let's take 'em." There went my last hope. Most of the guns that were going were Sloane's, from the pawnshop. If he'd said no, that would have been it.

"I'll take that .45 automatic," Jack said. The gun he'd pulled on me that day. That just brightened hell out of my whole evening.

"Say," Stan said, coming into the conversation for the first time, "while you're all here maybe I can get a question answered. I've shot a lot of birds, but I've never shot at a big animal. This may sound a little silly, but where exactly are you supposed to aim for?" Stan was trying to be one of the guys, but he still seemed a little stiff.

"Right through the neck," Lou said, poking at Stan's windpipe with his finger. It was supposed to look like a demonstration, but like always, Lou poked a little harder than necessary.

"Depends on how far away you are," I said. "I wouldn't try for a neck shot at two hundred and fifty yards. Best bet all around is right behind the front shoulder."

"Right through the boiler factory," Jack agreed. "I'll go along with Dan on that. You've got heart, lungs, and liver all in the same place. You're bound to hit something fatal." He sounded drunk.

"And you don't spoil much meat," I said. "A few spareribs is about all."

"But for God's sake, don't gut-shoot," Mike said. "A gut-shot deer can run five miles back into the brush. You've got to track for hours to find him."

Stan shook his head. "I don't know," he said. "When it gets right down to it, I wonder if I could really pull the trigger. I went out once after deer, but I didn't see anything. I thought about it that time, too. A bird is one thing, but a deer is— well, a lot more like we are. It might be a little hard to shoot if you think about it too much." Oh, God, I thought, the Bambi syndrome.

"Shit!" McKlearey exploded. "You make more fuss about a damn deer than I ever did about shootin' *people*! It's the same thing—just point and pull and down they go." McKlearey had taken an instant dislike to Stan—just like I had to *him*.

Stan looked at him. "I guess it's what you're used to," he said. These two were about as far apart as two guys are likely to get.

"If you feel that way about it, why are you comin' along?" Lou said belligerently.

"Lou, why don't you shut up?" Mike said. "You're getting obnoxious."

"Well, he gives me a pain."

Stan stood up. His face was set. He looked like he was getting ready to paste McKlearey in the mouth. I was a little surprised to see him take offense so easily—maybe Monica's chipping was putting him on edge.

"Sit down, Stan," I said. "He's drunk."

"What if I am?" Lou said. "What if I am?"

"That's enough, Lou," Sloane said. His voice was rather quiet, but you could tell he meant what he said. Sloane could surprise you. He was such a clown most of the time that you forgot sometimes just how much weight he could swing. Not only was he big enough to dismantle Lou with one hand, but he could fire him when he got done.

Lou sat back and shut up.

We talked about it a little more, and then went back into the living room with the girls. I had a couple more beers and sat back on the couch, watching. Margaret seemed to be pretty well loaded. Her voice was loud, and she seemed to be hanging around McKlearey. I thought that she'd have had better sense. I hadn't been counting drinks on her, but she was flying high.

Claudia came over and sat beside me. "You boys get everything all squared away in there?" she asked, her deep, soft voice sending the usual shiver up my back.

I nodded. "I think everything's all lined up."

"Sounded like there might have been a bit of an argument."

"McKlearey," I said. "I wish to hell he'd show up someplace sober some time."

"He's rotten when he's drunk," she agreed, "but he's not much better sober."

"He's a real creep," I said.

"I wish Calvin would get rid of him," she said. "I just hate to have him around." She paused for a moment. "Dan," she said finally, "what's the problem with Mrs. Larkin? She had no reason to talk to Margaret and Betty the way she did."

"I don't know, Claudia. I think what it boils down to is that she doesn't want Stan to go on this trip, and she's doing her level best to make things miserable for him."

"Oh, that's sad," she said. "Is she that unsure of herself with him?"

"I thought it was the other way around," I said. "She seems to have him on a pretty short leash."

"That's what I mean," she said. "A woman doesn't do that unless she's not sure of herself."

"Never thought of it that way," I said. Suddenly it all clicked into place. Claudia knew about her husband and his affairs, and it wasn't that she didn't care—as Jack had said that first night. She probably cared a great deal, but she knew Cal and the squirming insecurity that kept driving him back to the gutter for reassurance. She could live with it—maybe not accept it entirely—but live with it. But why Sloane, for God's sake?

"Oh-oh," Claudia said, "trouble." She nodded her head toward the dining room. I saw Jack and Margaret standing in there talking to each other intensely. Margaret's face was flushed, and she looked mad as hell. They were both drunk.

Her voice rose a little higher. "I'll drink as much as I damn well please, *Mister* Alders," she said.

"You're gettin' bombed, stupid," Jack said. Loaded with charm, my brother.

"So what?" she demanded.

"You're makin' a damn fool of yourself," he said, his voice mushy. "You been crawlin' all over Lou like a bitch in heat."

"What if I have?" she said. "What's it to you?"

"Grow up," Jack said.

"He doesn't seem to mind," she said.

"He's just bein' polite."

"That's all you know, Mister Big Shot!" Margaret said, her voice getting shrill.

"Shut up," he told her.

"Don't tell me to shut up, Big Mouth," she said loudly. "There's a few things you don't know, and maybe it's time I wised you up."

"Oh, boy," I muttered, "here we go." I glanced over at Lou and saw him easing toward the door. I shifted, getting ready to move. If anybody was going to get a piece of McKlearey, it was going to be me. If this blew, I'd stack him up in a corner if I could possibly manage it.

"Will you shut your goddamn stupid mouth?" Jack demanded.

"No, I won't," she said. "I'm gonna tell you something, and you're gonna—"

Then he hit her. It was an open-handed slap across the face but a good solid shot, not just a pat. She rocked back, her eyes a little glazed. I came up moving fast and got hold of him. Claudia and Betty got Margaret and led her off toward the bathroom. She seemed a little wobbly, and she hadn't started hollering yet.

"Let's get some air, buddy," I said to Jack and took him on out through the kitchen door into the backyard.

"That stupid big-mouth bitch!" he said when I got him outside. "She was gonna blab it all over the whole damn room about her and McKlearey. I shoulda had my head examined when I married her."

He knew about it. He'd known about it all along.

"That was a pretty hefty clout you gave her, wasn't it?" I said.

"Only way to get her attention," he said, trying to focus his eyes on me. "Got to hit her hard enough to shut her up."

"Maybe," I said. There's no point in arguing with a drunk.

"Sure. Only way to handle 'em. Couldn't let her shoot her mouth off like that in front of everybody, could I?"

I could sure see why he didn't stay married for very long at a time. I took his car keys out of his pocket and sat him on Mike's lawn couch. I didn't want him getting any wild ideas about trying to drive anyplace.

"Why don't you cool off a bit?" I suggested.

"Good idea," he said, leaning back. "It was gettin' pretty hot in there."

"Yeah."

"God damn, I'm glad you came back home, little brother," he said. "You're OK, you know that?" He patted my arm clumsily. "Never knew how good it'd be to have you around." His eyes weren't focusing at all now.

I stood there for a few minutes, and then I heard a snore. I decided it was warm enough. I'd pour him in the back seat of my car later. I went back inside.

"Really? That sounds *terribly* exciting," Monica was saying. She was sitting on the couch with Lou, and he was telling her war stories. She was up to something else now, and I thought I knew what. Lou, of course, was just stupid enough to go along with her. Somebody was going to have to shoot that son of a bitch yet.

I glanced at Stan, and his face made me want to hide. "Or maybe her," I said to myself. Her little tactic was pretty obvious. Mike came over to me. "Jack OK?" he asked quietly.

"He's asleep on that couch thing in the backyard," I said. "We'll have to wring him out to get him home."

"Yeah," Mike said, "he gets drunk pretty easy sometimes." He stopped a minute. "Come on out in the kitchen," he said, jerking his head. I followed him. "Dan," he said hesitantly, "is something going on between Margaret and Lou?" I looked quickly at him. I'd thought that he was about half in the bag. He was a shrewd bastard and no more drunk than I was.

"Yeah," I said shortly. Again I knew I could trust him. "Jack knows about it, too," I added.

He whistled. "Son of a bitch! This could get a little intense. And the way that Larkin broad is throwin' her ass at him, Lou's likely to get a piece of her before too long, too. You know, Dan, this has the makings of a real fun trip."

"You know it, buddy," I said. "We may have to haul that Jarhead son of a bitch out of the woods in a sack."

"He's pure trouble. I wish to hell he was out of this little hunt."

"You and me both," I agreed. "Mike, you're not screwing anybody's wife, are you? I don't think my nerves could take any more of this crap."

He laughed. "Betty would castrate me," he said. "You got no more worries."

"God"—I chuckled—"what a relief." I looked on into the living room. Monica was really snuggling up to old Lou, and he was lapping it up. "We'd better get McKlearey away from her before he throws the blocks to her right there on the couch," I said. "She doesn't know what she's messing with, I don't think. Or maybe she does—anyway, she can diddle with King Kong for all of me, but I'd rather not have Stan watching."

"Right," he said. "I'll get him to help me with Jack. You want us to put him in your car?"

"Yeah," I said, "you'd better. Here are the keys. Why don't you drive him on over and take McKlearey and Sloane with you? I'll bring Marg along in Jack's car when the girls get her straightened out. Then I can run you guys back here. That ought to break up the action a little."

"We can hope," Mike said and went to get McKlearey and Cal.

This whole damned thing was getting wormier and wormier. We'd be damn lucky if *any* of us got out of the woods alive. I went on back to the bedroom to see how the girls were doing with Margaret.

12

BY the next Saturday we were all getting things pretty well in shape. I had decided that I could find enough clothing in my duffle bag to keep me warm and dry in the woods. All I needed was a good warm jacket and a red hat. There was no trick to locating those.

It took a little more scrounging, but I found a guy—a GI out at the Fort, I think—who sold me a whole bucketful of .30-06 military ammunition at five cents a round. I suspect that he'd stolen it, but I didn't ask.

That morning I took my guns to the police range and began the tedious business of sighting in the rifle. It was cool and cloudy, with no wind—a perfect day for shooting. I finally got it honed into a good tight group about an inch high at two hundred yards and decided that would do it. Then I went over to the pistol range and pumped a few through that old single action .45. I came to the conclusion that if I ever had to shoot anything with it, I'd better be pretty damn close.

I was supposed to pick up Clydine about three thirty, but I still had plenty of time, so I swung on by Stan's place on the way back from the range. I knew he was having a real bad time, and he needed all the support he could get. Monica was making life miserable for him, if her behavior at the party was any indication. For some reason this hunt had become a major issue between them. I figured that if he could just win this one, it might change the whole picture.

"How's it going, old buddy?" I asked with false cheerfulness when he answered the door. The place was still uncomfortably neat.

"Not too well," he said with a gloomy face. "Sometimes I think this was all a mistake."

"Oh, come on now," I said. "You've just got the pre-season jitters."

"No. Monica isn't really very happy about my going. She said some pretty nasty things about you and the others when we got home Wednesday."

"I'll bet," I said. "Wednesday night was kind of a bummer anyway. Don't let it shake you—her being against it, I mean."

"Still," he said dubiously, "it's the first really serious disagreement we've ever had. I don't know if it's worth it." She just about had him on the ropes. I was goddamned if I'd let her win now.

"Look, Stan," I said, "no woman has ever been that excited about her man's wanting to hunt and fish. It's in the blood—you know, basic functions, cave-keeping and bringing home the meat. Modern women have got us cave-broken, and they hate to see us reverting. But a man needs to bust out now and then. Give him a chance to get dirty and smelly and unhouse-broke. It's good for the soul. Deep down, women really don't mind all that much. Oh, they put up a fight, but they don't really mind. It puts things back in perspective for them." It was crackpot anthropology, but he bought it. I kind of thought he would. He wanted to win this one, too.

"Are you sure?" he asked, wanting to believe.

"Of course," I told him, "you're dealing with primitive instincts, Stan. Monica doesn't even know why she's fighting it. You can be damn sure, though, that she really wants you to stand up to her. She's *testing* you, that's all." *That* ought to throw some reverse English on the ball.

"Maybe you're right," he said.

"Sure," I told him, "that's what hunting is really all about. God knows we don't need the meat. You can buy better meat a helluva lot cheaper at the supermarket. Deer meat is going to average about five dollars a pound—that's for something that tastes like rancid mutton." I was laying it on pretty thick, and he was buying every bit of it. He really wanted to go, and convincing him wasn't all that hard.

"You get that rifle you were going to borrow?" I asked him, wanting to change the subject before he caught me up a tree.

I'd planted enough, though, I thought. At least he wouldn't roll over and play dead for her.

"Yes," he said, "I picked it up this morning. It belongs to a fellow at the school, but he had a heart attack and can't hunt anymore. He said that if I like the way it shoots on this trip, he'll sell it to me."

He fetched the gun, and I looked it over. It was one of those Remington pumps in .30-06 caliber, scope-mounted and with a sissy-pad on the butt. I felt my shoulder gingerly. Maybe a recoil pad *would* be a good investment if a man planned to do a lot of shooting.

"Good-looking piece," I said. "You sighted it in yet?"

"The fellow said that it was right on at two hundred yards."

"Probably wouldn't hurt to poke a few through it just to make sure," I told him. "Sometimes they get knocked around a little and won't hit where you're aiming. I'll give you a fistful of military rounds so you can make sure." I told him where the police range was, but he already knew. So I showed him how to adjust the sights, gave him about fifteen rounds and took off. I didn't want to be around if Monica came back. He'd told me she'd been gone since early that morning on some kind of errand, and he didn't expect her back until evening, but I didn't want to take any chances. I might just have trouble being civil to her.

I wanted to swing on by Sloane's pawnshop to see how things were shaping up with the other guys, so I buzzed right on over there. My ears were still ringing and I could have used a beer, but I figured that could wait.

Sloane was in the place alone when I got there.

"Hey, Dan," he said, "how'd it shoot?"

"Dead on at two hundred," I said.

"Good deal. Say, you hear about Betty?"

"What? No. What's up?"

"That damned kidney of hers went sour again. Mike had to put her in the hospital again last night."

"Oh, no," I said, "that's a damned shame."

"Yeah. I'm afraid Mike won't be able to go with us, poor bastard. He wouldn't dare leave now."

"Christ, Cal," I said, "that'll wash out the whole deal then, won't it?" I felt sick.

"No, I don't think so," Sloane said. "I called Miller this morning as soon as I heard about it. He wasn't any too happy, but he'll still take us. It's too late for him to get another party."

"It's still a damn shame," I said. "Poor Betty was just getting back on her feet from last spring, and Mike's really been counting on this trip. I was looking forward to getting out with him."

"It's a lousy break," Sloane said. "It's a good thing we included Larkin in. Miller wouldn't have held still for just four guys."

"I had to give Stan a shot of high life just a little while ago," I said. "His wife's giving him a whole bunch of crap about the trip."

"She's a real bitch, isn't she?"

"They'd have been ahead to have drowned her and raised a puppy," I agreed.

"She was really out to raise hell last Wednesday," Sloane said. "Hey, could you use a blast? I've got a jug in the back, and it's about time for my early afternoon vitamin shot."

"Oh, I guess I could choke some down," I said. "Might take some of the sting out of my shoulder."

"That old aught-six steps back pretty hard, doesn't it?" he said, leading me into the back room.

"You know she's there when you touch 'er off," I agreed.

He took a fifth of good bourbon down from one of the shelves. "I stick it up high," he said, "so Claudia doesn't find it. She's sudden death on drinking on the job. I wouldn't want to get fired." He giggled.

"Hadn't you better sit where you can keep an eye out front?" I asked.

"What the hell for? On the fourth of the month the GI's are fat city—rollin' in money. Everybody's already redeemed last month's pawns, and nobody looks for pawnshop bargains on Saturday afternoon. Their neighbors might see them and think they were hurting for money. Here." He passed me the jug.

I took a long pull. "Good whiskey," I said as soon as I got my breath.

"Fair," he agreed, taking a drink. "Oh, hey. I wanted to show you the pistol I'm taking along." He rummaged around and came up with a .357 Ruger, frontier style.

"Christ, Sloane," I said, "isn't that a little beefy?"

"It shoots .38 special as well," he said. "I'll probably take those."

"It's got a good helf to it," I said, holding the pistol.

"Got a holster too," he said, pulling a fancy Western-type cartridge belt and holster out of one of his bins.

"Man," I said, "Pancho Villa rides again. We're going to

go into the woods with more armament than a light infantry platoon."

"Jack's got that Army .45 auto, and McKlearey's taking a Smith and Wesson .38 Military and Police," he said.

"I don't know if Stan's got a handgun," I said. "When you get right down to it, they're not really necessary." I wanted to say something more about that, but I figured it was too late now.

"It just kind of goes with the trip," Sloane said, almost apologetically. "If it's the kind of thing you only do once, you might as well go all the way."

"Sure, Cal," I said, looking at my watch. "Say, I've got to run."

"O.K. Here, have one for the road." He handed me the jug again. I took another belt, and we walked on back out into the shop again.

"Keep in touch," he said.

"Right." I waved and went on out to the street. Goddamn Sloane was just a big kid. I began to understand Claudia even a little better now. God knows he needed somebody to take care of him.

I dropped the guns and clothes off at the trailer and buzzed on out to the Patio for a few beers. I still had a couple hours before I was supposed to pick up Clydine. It was still cloudy, but no rain. It was the kind of day that's always made me feel good. Even the news about Betty hadn't been able to change that. I parked the car and went inside whistling.

McKlearey was there at the pinball machine—as usual—still standing at attention. He saw me before I could back out.

"Hey, Danny," he said, "come have a beer." I hate having people I don't like call me Danny. My day went sour right about then.

"Sure," I said. I followed him to the bar and ordered a draft.

"Hey, old buddy," he said, slapping me on the shoulder with a false joviality that stuck out like a sore thumb. "How you fixed for cash money?"

"Oh," I said cautiously, "I've still got a couple bucks."

"Can you see your way clear to loan me five till payday?"

I couldn't think up an excuse in a hurry. I reached for my wallet before I even stopped to think. You get that reflex in the Army, I don't know why.

"I get paid on Wednesday," he said, watching me, "and I'll get it right back to you then."

I pulled out a five and handed it to him.

"Got to pick up some stuff, Lou," I said. "I don't think I'd better cut it any tighter."

"Sure," he said, "that's OK. This'll get me by. I'll be sure to get it right back to you on Wednesday."

"No sweat, Lou," I said.

"No," he said, "a guy ought to stay on top of his obligations."

There was five bucks down the tube.

"You hear about Carter's wife?" he asked, settling back down at the bar.

"Yeah," I said, "I just stopped by the pawnshop. Sloane told me."

"Damn shame," he said indifferently. "Oh, well, there's enough of us to make the trip OK." He seemed almost glad that Mike wasn't going. He was a rotten son of a bitch.

"Sure," I said, "we'll be able to swing it."

"I just got here a few minutes ago," he said. "You was lucky to catch me. I just had a real high-class broad in the sack at my place."

"Oh?" I had a picture of what he'd call a "high-class broad."

"Yeah. I only met her a few days ago, but it don't take a guy long to make out if he knows the score. You know her, but I ain't gonna tell you who she is. Nice set of jugs on her and a real wild ass."

McKlearey was about as subtle as a brick. What in hell was Monica up to? If she wanted a little strange stuff, she sure as hell could have done better than this creep.

McKlearey chuckled obscenely. "You should have seen it, Danny boy. She comes to my fuckin' pad about ten this morning, see. Some dumb routine about something she'd 'misplaced' at a party we was both at, and had I seen it. At first I thought she was tryin to say I'd stole it, see, so I was a little hot about it—you know, cut her right off. Well, she hung around and hung around, smilin' and givin' me the glad eye and stickin' her tits out at me, see, so I ask her if she wants a beer, see. She says she don't mind, and we have a beer and start to get friendly."

I could just picture Monica gagging down a beer at ten in the morning.

"Well, I make my move, see," he went on, "and all of a sudden she gets cold feet, see. Comes on with this 'I don't know what you *think* I came here for, but it certainly wasn't *that*!'" He mimicked her voice fairly well. "But I know women, see, and she was just pantin' for it. I figure she wanted it rough, see—them high-class broads always like it like that—so I says, 'Come here, you bitch,' and I yanks off her clothes and throws her on the bed, and I poke it to her, right up to the hilt. At first she kind of half-ass tries to fight me off, but pretty soon she gets with it, see. Wild piece of tail, man!" He chuckled again and ordered another beer.

I began to hope he'd get hit by a truck before we ever went into the woods. This was going to be a bum trip, and now I was out five bucks. I told him I had to run, and I took off. The whole business with Monica had me a little confused though. Why McKlearey, for Chrissake?

I asked Clydine about it that evening at my place, explaining the situation and describing the people and what had happened.

"Now, why in God's name would she want to have anything to do with that creepy Jarhead?" I asked her.

Clydine sighed and shook her head. "Oh, Danny," she said in a long-suffering tone. "You're so smart about some things and so hopeless when it comes to women."

"I manage to get by," I said, slipping my hand up under her sweatshirt and grinning at her.

"Do you want to play or do you want to listen?" she asked tartly. "Somehow I've never been able to believe a man's seriously listening to what I'm saying if he's fondling me at the same time."

I pulled my hand out. "OK," I said, "all serious now. No fondling. Shoot."

"All right. One: Wifey doesn't want Hubby to go out and shoot Bambi—right?"

"No—Wifey doesn't want Hubby to get off the leash."

"Whatever. Two: Hubby is jealous of Wifey's good-looking round bottom, right?"

"OK," I said.

"Three: Wifey knows there's bad blood between Hubby and Creepy Jarhead, right?"

"Go on."

"Four: Wifey figures that if Creepy Jarhead makes big pass at Wifey's good-looking round bottom, Hubby will blow his cool, punch Creepy Jarhead in the snot-locker and stay home and hold Wifey's hand instead of going out with the bad old hairy-chested types to dry-gulch poor little Bambi, right?"

"Wrong," I said. "Creepy Jarhead did *not* just make pass.

Creepy Jarhead threw the blocks to Wifey's little round bottom. It shoots your theory all to hell."

She shook her head stubbornly. "Not at all," she said. "Wifey moves in those circles where when a lady says no, the men are polite enough to stop. Poor little Wifey underestimated the Creepy Jarhead, and that's why she got blocks in her bottom."

I blinked. By God, she had it! "You are an absolute doll," I told her. "Now tell me, since this went gunnysack on her, what position is Wifey in now?"

"Little Wifey's got her tit in the wringer," Clydine said sweetly. "She can't scream rape—it's too late for that, and besides, Hubby might go to the Fuzz and then the Creepy Jarhead would spill his guts about her being the one who made the first move. She is, if she's a normal Establishment woman, feeling guilty as hell about now for having committed adultery with a man she doesn't even like. I'd say she screwed herself right out of action—literally. Hubby can go out and exterminate the whole deer population and she won't be able to raise a finger. End of analysis. Satisfied?"

"It all fits together perfectly," I said. "You know, my little pansy of the proletariat, you are absolutely beautiful."

"I'm glad you noticed," she said, snuggling up to me. "Now you may fondle, if you like."

13

ON Tuesday night we gathered at Sloane's with all our gear. Jack and I got there a little late, and the others were already sitting around the kitchen waiting for us. Stan's face looked grim, and McKlearey was already a little drunk. Sloane seemed relieved to see us, so I imagine things had been getting a bit strained.

"There they are," Sloane said as we walked in. "Where in hell have you guys been?"

"I had to get cleaned up," Jack said. "I've been crawlin' around under a fuckin' trailer down at the lot all day."

"Have a beer, men," Sloane said, diving into the refrigerator. He came up with a fistful of beer cans and began popping tops. "You guys bring your gear?"

"Yeah," I said, "it's out in the car."

"Why don't you go ahead and bring it on in," he said. "I've got the list of all the stuff we'll each need, so I'll check everybody off." It was sort of funny really. Sloane was such a clown most of the time that you hardly took him seriously, but when Mike had dropped out, he'd taken charge, and nobody questioned him about it.

"What we'll do," he went on, "is get everything all packed up, and then we'll store it all here. That way nobody forgets anything, OK?"

We all agreed to that.

"Then tomorrow night, we all take off from here. Stan is going to ride with me, right Stan?"

Stan nodded.

"We can swap off driving that way," Sloane said. "Dan, you and Jack are going in his car, right?"

"Yeah."

"And Lou wants to take his own car, I guess. Damned if I know why, Lou. There'd be plenty of room in either of the other cars."

"I just want to take my own car," Lou said. "Does anybody have any objections to me takin' my own fuckin' car?" He was sitting off by himself like he had that first night, and his eyes looked a little odd. I thought maybe he was drunker than I'd figured at first.

"It just seems a little unnecessary, that's all," Sloane said placatingly.

"Does anybody have any objections to me takin' my own fuckin' car?" Lou repeated. He really had a bag on.

"Take the motherfucker," Jack said. "Nobody gives a shit."

"All right, then," Lou said. "All right, then." His voice was a little shrill.

"All right, calm down, you guys," Sloane said. "If we start chipping at each other, we'll never get done here." Everybody seemed to be in a foul humor.

Jack and I went back out to the car to pick up our gear. "That fuckin' McKlearey is gettin' to be a big pain in the ass," Jack said as he hauled out his sack. "I wish to Christ we'd included him out."

"We needed the extra guy to make the deal with Miller," I said.

"We could have found a dozen buys that would have been better."

"He's a first-class shitheel, all right," I agreed, lifting out my rifle. "He tapped me for five bucks the other day."

"Oh, no shit?" Jack said. "Didn't I warn you about that? Well, you can kiss that five good-bye."

We went on inside with the gear.

"Let's take it all into the living room," Sloane said. "We've got room to spread out in there, but for Chrissake don't spill any beer on Claudia's carpet! She'll hang all our scalps to the lodge-pole if somebody messes up."

"We're all housebroke," Jack said. "Quit worryin' about the goddamn carpeting." He was in a particularly lousy mood tonight for some reason.

"OK, you guys, spread out and dump out your gear," Sloane said. For some reason he reminded me of a scoutmaster with a bunch of city kids.

"Sleeping bag," Sloane said.

Each of us pushed his sleeping bag forward.

"Gear-bag—or clothes bag, or whatever the hell you want to call it." He looked around. We each held up a sack of some kind. Looky, gang, Daddy's going to take me camping. "OK, now as we check off the items of clothing and what-not, stow them in your sack, OK?"

He went down through the list of items—clothing, soap, towels, everything.

"OK," he said, "that takes care of all that shit. You'll each be wearing your jackets and boots and all that crap, so we're all set there. Now, have you all got your licenses and deer-tags?"

"I'll pick up mine tomorrow," Lou said.

"McKlearey," Jack said angrily, "can't you do one fuckin' thing right? We were all supposed to have that taken care of by now."

"Don't worry about me," Lou said. "Just don't worry about me, Alders. I'll have the fuckin' license and tag."

"But why in hell didn't you take care of it before now, you dumb shit?" Jack shouted. "You've had as much time as the rest of us."

"All right," I said. "It's no big deal. So he forgot. Let's not make a federal case out of it."

"Dan's right," Sloane said. "You guys are touchy as hell tonight. If we start off this way, the whole thing's gonna be a bust." He could feel it, too.

"Let's get on with this," Stan said. "I've got to get home before too late."

"Keepin' tabs on that high-class wife of yours, huh?" Lou snickered.

"I don't really see where that's any of your business," Stan said with surprising heat. I guess that McKlearey had been at him before Jack and I got there.

"McKlearey," I said, trying to keep my cool and keep the whole thing from blowing up, "you're about half in the bag. You'd be way out in front to back off a little, don't you think?"

"You countin' my fuckin' drinks?" he demanded. "First your shithead brother, and now you, huh? Well, I can get my own fuckin' license, and I sure as hell don't need nobody to count my fuckin' drinks for me."

"That's enough," Sloane said sharply, and he wasn't smiling. "You guys all got your rifles with you?"

We hauled out the hardware. Sloane had the .270 he'd tried to sell me, Stan had the Remington, Jack had that Mauser, Lou had a converted Springfield, and I had the gun I'd been working on. All the rifles had scopes.

"Two boxes of ammunition?" Sloane asked. We each piled up the boxes beside our rifles.

"Hunting knives?"

We waved our cutlery at him.

"I guess that's about it then."

"Say," Jack said, "how about the handguns?"

"God damn"—Sloane giggled—"I almost forgot. I've got them in the closet. Let's see. Dan, you and Stan each have your own, don't you?"

Stan nodded. "I have," he said quietly. He reached into one end of his rolled sleeping bag and after some effort took out a snub-nosed revolver. He fished in again and came out with a belt holster and a box of shells. Somehow the gun seemed completely out of character. I could see Stan with a target pistol maybe, but not a people-eater like that. And he handled it like he knew what he was doing.

"Christ," I said, "that's an ugly-looking little bastard."

"We had a burglar scare last year," he said, seeming a little embarrassed.

"What the hell can you hit with that fuckin' little popgun?"
Lou sneered.

"It's a .38 special," Stan said levelly. "That's hardly a popgun. And I've had it out to the range a few times, and I can
hit what I shoot at." He gave Lou a hard look that was even
more out of character.

Lou grunted, but he looked at Stan with an odd expression.
Maybe the son of a bitch was thinking about how close he'd
come to getting a gutful of soft lead bullets for playing silly
games with Monica. I hoped he'd get a few nervous minutes
out of it.

"You got yours, haven't you, Dan?" Sloane asked.

I nodded. I'd rolled up the gun belt, holster, and pistol and
brought them over in a paper sack. I pulled the rig out and laid
it across the sleeping bag. The curve of the butt and the flare
of the hammer protruding from the black leather holster looked
a little dramatic, but what the hell?

"Jesus," Sloane said, almost reverently, "look at that big
bastard."

Nothing would do but to pass the guns around and let everybody fondle them.

"You got ours here, Cal?" Jack asked. He sure seemed jumpy
about it—like he wasn't going to relax until he got his hands
on that pistol.

Sloane got up and went out of the room for a minute. He
came back with three belts and holsters. The .357 Ruger of
his was almost a carbon copy of my old .45, a little heavier
in the frame maybe. His holster and belt were fancier, but the
leather was new and squeaked a lot. McKlearey's .38 M & P
had a fairly conventional police holster and belt, but Jack's .45
auto was in a real odd lash-up. It looked like somebody had
rigged up a quick-draw outfit for that pig. I don't know how
anyone could figure to get an Army .45 into operation in under
five minutes, but there it was.

We sat around in a circle, passing the guns back and forth.
My .30-06 got a lot of attention. Sloane particularly seemed
quite taken with it.

"I'll give you a hundred and a half for it," he said suddenly.

"Come on, Cal," I said. "You can get a brand-new gun,
scope and all, for that. You couldn't get more than a hundred
and a quarter for that piece of mine, even if you were selling
it to a halfwit."

"I don't want to sell it," he said. "I just like the gun." He swung the piece to his shoulder a couple more times. "Damn, that's a sweet gun," he said.

Stan took the gun from him. "You did a nice job, Dan," he said.

"Poor Calvin figures he got royally screwed on that deal," Jack said, laughing.

"No," Sloane said, "it was my business to look at the merchandise before I set the price. I screwed myself, so I've got no bitch coming."

Lou went out and got another beer.

Jack held up his rifle. "This thing's a pig, but it shoots where you aim it, so what the hell?"

"That's all that counts," Stan said.

McKlearey came back.

"We're all pretty well set up," I said. "I was about half afraid somebody'd show up with a .30-30. That beast's got the ballistic pattern of a tossed brick. About all it's good for is heavy brush. Out past a hundred yards, you might as well throw rocks."

"And we're not likely to be in brush," Jack said. "You get up around the timberline and it opens up to where you're gettin' two- and three-hundred-yard shots."

"Miller says we'll be camping just below the timberline," Sloane said, "and we'll be riding on up to where we'll hunt, so it'll likely be pretty soon."

"Good deal," Lou grunted. "I've about had a gutful of fuckin' jungle."

"Air gets pretty skimpy up there, doesn't it?" Jack asked.

"At six to eight thousand feet?" Sloane giggled. "You damn betcha. Some of you flatlanders'll probably turn pretty blue for the first couple days."

We carried the gear into Sloane's utility room and piled it all in a corner and then went back into the breakfast room just off the kitchen. Sloane opened another round of beers, and we sat looking at a map, tracing out our route.

"We'll go on up to Everett and then across Stevens Pass," Sloane said. "Then, just this side of Wenatchee, we'll swing north on up past Lake Chelan and up into the Methow Valley to Twisp."

"I thought that was *Mee-thow*," Lou said.

"No," Sloane answered. "Miller calls it *Met*-how."

Lou shrugged.

"Anyhow," Cal went on, "if we leave here at midnight, we

ought to be able to get over there by eight thirty or nine. Some of those roads ain't too pure, so we'll have to take it easy."

"We'll be leaving for camp as soon as we get to Miller's?" Stan asked.

"Right. He said he'd feed us breakfast and then we'd hit the trail."

"Gonna be a little thin on sleep," I said.

"I'm gonna sack out for a few hours after work," Jack said.

"Probably wouldn't be a bad idea for all of us," Sloane agreed.

We had a few more beers and began to feel pretty good. The grouchy snapping at each other eased off. It even seemed like the hunt might turn out OK after all. We sat in the brightly lighted kitchen in a clutter of beer cans and maps with a fog of cigarette smoke around us and talked about it.

"Hey, Danny," Lou said suddenly, "you pretty fast with that old .45?"

"Oh, I played with it some when I first got it," I said. "I guess everybody wants to be Wyatt Earp once in his life."

"How fast are you?" he insisted.

"God, Lou, I don't know. I never had any way to time it. I could beat that guy on *Gunsmoke*—Matt Dillon—you know how he used to draw at the start of the program? I'd let him reach first, and then I'd beat him."

"Pretty fast," he said, "pretty fast. Let's see you draw." He wasn't going to let it go.

"Aw, hell, Lou, I haven't handled that thing for two years. I probably couldn't even find the gun butt."

"Go ahead, Dan," Jack said. "Show us how it's done. You a gun-fanner?"

I shook my head. "I tried fanning just once—out at the range—and I splattered lead all over the country. That might be all right across a card table, but at any kind of range, forget it."

"Let's see you draw," Lou said again, prodding me with his elbow. Once again it was a little harder than necessary.

"Sure, Dan," Sloane said, "let's see the old pro in action."

Now don't ask me, for Chrissake, why I gave in. I don't know why. The whole idea of having pistols along had spooked me right from the start, and the more that things had built up between these guys, the less I liked it. In the second place, I don't like to see a bunch of guys messing around with guns. It's too easy for somebody to get hurt. What makes it

even worse is that this quick-draw shit starts too many people's
minds working in the wrong direction. All things considered,
the whole damned business may just have been one of the
stupidest things I've ever done in my life. I suppose when you
get right down to it, it was because that goddamn McKlearey
rubbed me the wrong way. He acted like he didn't believe I
knew how to handle the damned gun. The fact that I didn't
like McKlearey was pushing me into a whole lot of decisions
lately, it occurred to me.

Anyway, I got up and went back into the utility room and
got my gun belt. I pulled the wide belt around my waist and
buckled it. I was a notch bigger around the belly than I'd been
before I went in the Army. Too much beer. I tied the rawhide
thong at the bottom of the holster around my thigh and checked
the position of the holster. I made a couple of quick passes to
be sure I could still find the hammer with my thumb. It seemed
to be where I'd left it. I took the gun out of the holster and
went back out to the kitchen.

"Hey," Jack said, "there's the gunfighter. God damn, that
gun belt sure looks evil strapped on like that." Jack was getting
a little high again.

"If you start with the gun already out of the holster," Lou
said, "I can see how you could beat Matt Dillon."

"You want to take a chance on my having forgotten to unload
this thing?" I asked him flatly.

"God, no," Sloane yelped. "For Chrissake don't shoot out
my French doors."

I opened the loading gate, slipped the hammer and rolled
the cylinder along my arm at eye level, checking it carefully.
I figured I might as well give them the whole show. I snapped
the gate shut and spun the gun experimentally a couple times
to get the feel of the weight again. Frankly, I felt a little silly.

"Fancy," Sloane said.

"Just limbering up," I told him.

"Let's see how it's done," Lou insisted.

I slipped the pistol into the holster and positioned my hand
on the belt buckle.

"Draw!" Lou barked suddenly.

As luck would have it, I was ready, and I found the hammer
with my thumb on the first grab. The gun cleared smoothly,
and I snapped it about waist high and a little out. It was a fair
draw.

"Jesus!" Sloane said blinking.

"God damn!" Jack said. "Just like a strikin' snake." He was getting a kick out of it.

"Lucky," I said.

Even Lou looked impressed. Stan grinned. He'd seen this before. God knows how many hours he'd watched me practice when we'd been roommates.

"Do that again," Jack demanded.

"Why don't I quit while I'm ahead," I said. "Next time I might not even be able to find the damn thing."

"No," he insisted, "I mean do it slow, so we can see how it's done."

I holstered. "Look," I said. "You spread out your hand and come back, see? You catch the curve of the hammer on the neck of your thumb, like this. As soon as you hit it, you close in your hand—you cock the gun and grab onto the butt at the same time. Then you pull up and out, putting your trigger finger inside the guard as the gun comes out. You're ready to shoot when it comes up on line. The idea is to make it all one motion." Silly as it sounds, I was getting a kick out of it. The sullen scowl on McKlearey's face made it all worthwhile.

"You did all *that* just now?" Jack said incredulously. "Shit, if a man was to blink, he'd miss the whole thing."

"It took a few hours to get it down pat," I said, doing the tie-down. I'd grabbed a little hard, and my thumb was stinging like hell. I could feel it clear to the elbow. I'd done it OK though, so I figured it was a good time to quit. No point in making a *complete* ass of myself.

"Here," Sloane said, getting up, "give me some lessons." He went into the utility room and came out with the Ruger and the new belt and holster. He cinched the belt around his middle.

"Lower," I said, sitting back down.

He pushed down on the belt. "Won't go no lower," he complained.

"Loosen it."

He backed it off a couple of notches. "That's the last hole," he said.

"It'll do."

"He looks like a sack of potatoes tied in the middle." Jack laughed.

"Just keep mouthin' off, Alders," Sloane threatened, "and I'll drill you before you can blink." He took on a menacing stance, his hand over the gun butt.

"OK," I said, "tie it down."

He grunted as he bent over and lashed the thong around his leg.

"Let's see the gun," I said. He handed it to me and I opened the loading gate. The pale twinkle of brass stared back at me. I felt a sudden cold hand twist in the pit of my stomach. He must have reloaded it when he put it back in the utility room after we'd been looking them over out in the living room. I should have known this was a mistake. I tipped up the gun, slipped the hammer, and dropped the shells out of the cylinder onto the table, one by one, slowly. They sounded very loud as they hit the table and bounced.

"Shit, man!" Lou said in a strangled whisper.

I picked up one of the shells and looked at the base, ".357 magnum," I observed in a voice as calm and mild as I could make it. "You could blow the refrigerator right through the wall with one of these."

Sloane blushed, I swear he did. "I forgot," he mumbled.

"Or you could knock McKlearey's head halfway down to the bay—beer can and all."

"All right, I forgot. Don't make a federal case out of it." Sloane was getting pissed off.

"Well, that's lesson number one," I said, handing him back the gun. He holstered it.

"Lesson number two. Don't trust anybody when he says a gun is empty. Always check it yourself." I palmed the shell I was holding.

"But I saw you unload it," he protested.

"How many bullets on the table?"

He counted and his eyes bulged. He snatched out the gun and checked the cylinder. I dropped the last one on the table.

"Smart ass!" He snorted.

"Never hurts to be sure. Guns are made to kill with. If you're going to play with them, you damn well better be sure they understand. A gun's got a real limited mentality, so *you've* got to do most of the thinking." Maybe if I could shake them up a little, they'd stop and give the whole business a little thought.

"All right, don't rub it in. What do I do now?"

"Hold your hand about waist high and spread out your fingers."

"You started from over here," he objected putting his hand on his belly.

"You can get fancy once you get the hang of it," I told him.

I talked him through the draw a couple of times. Then he tried it fast and naturally he dropped it on his foot.

"God damn!" he bellowed, hopping around holding the foot.

"Heavy, aren't they?" I asked him pleasantly. "And somehow they always seem to land on your foot."

He gingerly put his weight on his foot and limped heavily around the room.

"That's called gunfighter's gimp," I told the others. "Next to the Dodge City Complaint, that's the most common ailment in the business."

"What's the Dodge City Complaint, for God's sake?" Sloane demanded.

"That's when you start practicing with a loaded gun and blow off your own kneecap."

"Bull*shit*, too!" He winced. "Not this little black duck." He started unstrapping the belt. "I'll stick to Indian wrestling. These goddamn things are just as dangerous from the back as from the front." That's what I'd been trying to tell them.

"Let's see that fuckin' thing," Lou demanded, getting up. He strapped it on. It hung a little low, but it looked a lot more businesslike on him than it had on Sloane. He went through it slowly a couple times and then began to pick up speed. He was pretty good and not quite as drunk as I'd thought.

"Come on, Alders," he said to Jack, "I'll take you." He snapped the gun at Jack's head.

God *damn* it, I hate to see somebody do that!

"Come on, shithead," Jack told him, waving his hand. "Don't point that fuckin' thing at me."

"Strap on your iron, hen-shit," Lou said.

"Give me your gun, Dan," Jack said suddenly. He was about half-drunk, too.

I saw that there was no point in trying to talk them out of it. I stood up, stripped off the belt and handed it to Jack. He strapped it on and tied it down.

"You've got to give me a couple minutes to practice," he said.

"Sure," Lou said. "Take as long as you want."

Jack hooked and drew a few times. He picked it up fairly fast, but I knew he was no match for McKlearey. As I watched him, I noticed for the first time how small my brother's hands were. That .45 looked like a cannon when he pulled it.

"All right, you big-mouth son of a bitch," he said to Lou. "Somebody call it."

They squared off about ten feet apart.

"On three," I said. It might as well be me. I was hoping Jack would win by some fluke. That might quiet things down.

I counted it off, and Lou won by a considerable margin.

"Now I guess we know who's the best man." He laughed.

"Big deal," Jack said disgustedly.

Lou snapped the gun at him again. "Back in the old days, you'd be buzzard-bait right now, Alders," he said. "Well, who's next? Who wants to take on the fastest fuckin' gun in Tacoma?" He stood at a stiff brace, his face fixed in a belligerent leer.

Jack dropped the gun belt back on the table. He was grinding his teeth together. He was really pissed. I knew I should have just let it die, but I couldn't let that bastard get away with it. Goddamn McKlearey rubbed me the wrong way, and I didn't like the way he'd put down my brother. I figured it was time he learned that he wasn't King Shit. I stood up and strapped on the gun.

"Well, well," he said, "the last of the Alders. I beat you and I'm top gun, huh?"

"That'll be the day," Stan said quietly.

"You don't think I can?" Lou demanded.

I finished tying down the gun.

"Who's gonna count?" Lou said.

"Never mind the count," I said. "Just go ahead when you're ready." I wanted to rub his face in it, and I'd noticed that Lou always squinted when he started to draw. I figured that was about all the edge I'd need.

It was. I had him cold before he got the gun clear. I didn't snap the trigger but just held the gun leveled at his face. He froze and gawked at the awful hole in the muzzle of that .45. I guess Lou'd had enough guns pointed at him for real to know what it was all about. I waited about ten seconds and then slowly squeezed the trigger. The snap of the hammer was very loud.

I spun the gun back into the holster, grinding him a little more. He was still standing there, frozen in the same place. He was actually sweating, and his eyes had a weird look in them.

"And that about takes care of the fastest gun in Tacoma," I said, and I took off my gun belt.

Lou tried to get Sloane or Stan to draw with him, but they weren't having any. Sloane and I put our guns away, and I figured we'd gotten past *that* little shit-pile. These guys weren't

kidding, empty guns or no. I think we were *all* starting to slip
a few gears.

"I can still outhunt you bastards," Lou said, his voice getting
shrill again.

"You'll have to prove that, too," Jack said.

"Don't worry, I'll prove it," Lou said. "Any bet you want.
First deer, biggest deer, longest shot. You name it, and I'll beat
you at it." He was pissed off now. He'd been put down, and
no Marine can ever take that. What was worse, he knew I could
do it again, any time I felt like it. Even that might help keep
things under control. If he knew I'd be there and I could take
him if I had to, it might just keep his mind off the goddamn
guns.

"Hey, there's an idea," Sloane said. "Best deer—using *Boone
and Crockett* points—the other guys pitch in and buy him a
fifth of his favorite booze."

"Why not a jug from each guy?" Lou said. "I can drink one
jug in an afternoon."

"All right," Jack said. "One jug of Black Label from each
guy, OK?"

"Why not?" Stan said.

"Sure," I agreed.

Sloane shrugged. Money didn't mean that much to him.

"And a little side bet, too," Jack said. "Just between you
and me, Lou. Ten bucks says I get a better deer than you do."
I don't think he'd have made the bet if he'd been sober.

"You got it," Lou said. "Anybody else want a piece of the
action?" He looked around.

"I'll cover you," Stan said. I looked at him quickly. His
face was expressionless. "Ten dollars. Same bet." What the
hell was this? I suddenly didn't like the smell of it. Stan didn't
make bets—ever. How much did he know anyhow?

"You got it," Lou said. "Anybody else." He looked at me.
I looked back at him and didn't say anything. I didn't have
anything to prove—I didn't have a wife.

Sloane opened another round of beer, and we drifted off
into talking about the trip and hunting in general.

"I think I'd better go," Stan said. "I've got classes tomorrow,
and it's going to be a long night tomorrow night."

"You got a point, Stan," Jack said.

"Don't forget our fuckin' bet, Larkin," Lou said. He went
into the utility room and came back with that M & P .38
strapped on. He stood in the kitchen, snatching the gun out of

the holster and putting it back. "Take that, you motherfucker," he muttered, jerking out the pistol and snapping it. I had a vague feeling it was me he was talking to.

Sloane, Jack, and I went with Stan to the front door.

"That McKlearey and I don't get along too well," he said as he went out.

"Don't feel like the Lone Ranger, Stan," Jack said. "I got a gutful of that bastard already, and we ain't even left yet."

"Maybe we can push him off a cliff," I said.

"*After* he's paid his share of the guide fee." Sloane giggled.

Stan went on out to his car, and the rest of us went back into the house.

"Son of a *bitch!*" Lou's voice came from the kitchen. We trooped in, and he stood there with blood dripping onto the tiles from a gash in his left hand. The stupid bastard had been trying to *fan* that double-action .38.

Hot-diggety-damn, this was going to be a fun trip!

14

It rained all the next day. The sky sagged and dripped, and the trailer court was gloomy and sad. I tried sleeping, but after about eleven or so it was useless. I visited with Margaret, but she was drying clothes on a rack in the living room, and the place was steamy and smelled of wet clothes so badly that it made me even more miserable. Then a couple of her coffee-drinking friends came in and started the usual woman talk. There was nothing after that but to go to a tavern and drink beer. Clydine was busy registering for classes until about three or so.

The inside of my car felt damp and clammy as I fired it up, and the windshield fogged over immediately. I drove up the street to the Patio, listening to the hiss of my tires on the wet pavement. The parking lot was sodden and full of puddles. I ran inside to get out of the rain as quickly as possible, and sat

down on a stool at the bar and ordered a beer. There were four
other guys in the place, all about as dispirited as I was.

I sat at the bar, hunched over, watching the cars whoosh by
with the spray flying and the windshield wipers slapping back
and forth. By three I was so goddamn depressed I couldn't
stand myself. I called Mike from the bar and found out that
Betty was better. He sounded pretty bitter about not being able
to go with us as well as half-sick with worry over Betty, so I
cut it pretty short.

I was still depressed when I got to Clydine's place. She
lived in a shabby little second-floor apartment with Joan—the
usual stuff—old sofa cushions on the floor to sit on, posters
on the wall, bricks and boards for bookcases. Joan had gone
home right after she'd finished registering, probably to keep
on the good side of her folks, so Clydine and I had the place
to ourselves.

She'd been standing around in the rain, and her hair was
soaked. She looked very young, sitting cross-legged on a sofa
cushion as she dried her hair with a big towel—very young
and very vulnerable.

"What's the matter, Danny?" she asked me, looking up. I
was slouched in their ruptured armchair with a sour look on
my face, looking out the steamy window.

"The rain, I guess," I said shortly.

"You're living in the wrong part of the country if the rain
bothers you that much," she said.

"I don't know, Clydine," I said, "maybe it's not really the
rain."

"You're worried about this trip, aren't you?" she said.

"I suppose that's it," I said. "Things got a little hairy last
night." I told her about it.

"Wow!" she said. "It sounds like a bad Western."

"Maybe that's the point," I said glumly. "The only way a
bad Western can end is with a big shoot-out. You ever seen a
Western yet that didn't have a shoot-out?"

"Why don't you just back out?" she asked.

I shook my head. "It's too late for that. Besides, I really
want to go; I really do."

She shivered.

"Are you cold?" I asked her.

"I'll warm up in a little," she said.

"You little clobberhead," I said. I went over, knelt down

beside her, and felt her bare foot. It was like a dead fish. I ran my hand up her leg. Her Levis were soaked.

"Watch it," she murmured.

I ignored that and slid my hand up under her sweatshirt. The little soldiers were clammy. "You knucklehead," I said angrily. "You're going to get pneumonia."

"I'll be all right," she said, shivering again. "You're just a worrier."

I stood up and went into her dinky little bathroom. I dumped all the dirty clothes out of the bathtub and started to fill it with hot water. I went back into the living room and snapped my fingers at her. "Up," I said.

"What?"

"Up. Up. On your feet." I wasn't about to take any crap from her about it. She grumbled a bit but she got up. "Now march," I ordered, pointing at the bathroom.

"This is *silly*," she said.

I swatted her on the fanny. Not too hard.

"But the bathroom is such a *mess*," she wailed.

I pushed her on inside. The tub was almost full. I turned it off and checked it out. It was hot but not scalding.

"Strip," I said.

"What?"

"Strip! Peel. Take it off."

"Danny!" She sounded horribly shocked.

"Oh, for Christ's sake! Look, Rosebud, you've been running around my place wearing nothing but your sunny smile for weeks now. This is no time to come down with a case of false modesty."

"But not in the *bathroom!*" she objected, still in that shocked tone of voice.

Women! I reached out and very firmly pulled off her sweatshirt.

"Danny," she said plaintively, "please." She crossed her arms in front of her breasts. She was blushing furiously. I sat down on the toilet seat and hauled off her soggy Levis.

"Danny." Her complaining voice was very small.

Then I took off her panties. They were wet, too. She went into the "September Morn" crouch.

"All right," I said, "in the tub."

"But—"

"In the tub!"

"Turn your head," she insisted.

"Oh, for God's sake!" I turned my head.

"Well," she said defensively, "it's in the *bathroom*. Ouch! That's *hot*!"

I looked at her quickly.

"You turn your goddamn head back where it was, you goddamn Peeping Tom!"

I looked away again.

"All right," she said finally in that small voice, "I'm in now." She was all scrunched up in the tub, hiding all her vital areas.

"Sit tight," I told her. "I'll be back in a minute."

"Where are you going?" she yelled after me as I hurried out. I didn't answer. I clumped on down the steps and went out in the rain to my car. I had a pint of whiskey in the glove compartment, and it was about half full. I got it and went on back up to her apartment.

"Is that you?" she called.

"No, it's me," I said. Let her figure that one out. It'd give her something to do. "Not in the *bathroom*"—for Chrissake! I heard a lot of splashing.

"Stay in the damn tub!" I yelled in to her.

"I *am*," she yelled back. "I don't know why you got so bossy all of a sudden."

I mixed her a good stiff hot toddy. As an afterthought, I mixed myself one as well. I carried them into the bathroom.

She'd poured about a quart of bubble bath in the water and had stirred it all up. She was in suds up to her chin.

"Well," she said in that same defensive tone, "if you're going to insist on this 'Big Brother is washing you' business, at least I'm going to be *decent*." She sounded outraged.

"Drink this," I said, handing her one of the cups.

"What is it?"

"Medicine. Drink it." I sat back down on the john.

"Boy, are *you* ever a bear," she said, sipping at the toddy. "Hey, I like this. What is it?"

I told her.

Somehow in the interim she'd tied her hair up into a damp tumble on top of her head. She looked so damned appealing that I got a sudden sharp ache in the pit of my stomach just looking at her.

We sat in silence, drinking our toddies.

"Oooo," she finally said with a long, shuddering sigh, "I *was* cold."

"I don't know why you gave me so much static about it,"
I said.

"But, Danny," she said, "it's the *bathroom*. Don't you
understand?"

"Never in a million years." I laughed. "And don't try to
explain it to me. It would just give me a headache."

We sat in silence again.

"Danny," she said tentatively, studying the sudsy toe she'd
thrust up out of the water.

"Yes, Blossom?"

"What we were talking about before—this hunting thing.
You said you really wanted to go."

"Yeah," I said, "I really do."

"It just doesn't fit," she said. "You aren't the type. I mean,
you're not some fat forty out to assert his manhood by killing
things." She'd never talked about it before, but I guess it had
been bothering her.

"You're labeling again," I said. "Oh sure, I've seen the
type you're talking about— probably more of them than you
have, but that's not the only kind of guy who hunts. For one
thing, I eat everything I kill. That kind either gives it away
or throws it in the garbage can. I don't give game away
either. If I don't like the taste of an animal, I won't hunt
it—I won't butcher for somebody else. And I don't collect
trophies—not even horns. People who do that are disgusting.
They have contempt for the animal they kill. They want a
stuffed head around to prove to their friends that they're
smarter than the deer was. Well, big goddamn deal!" Suddenly
I was pretty hot about it.

"Well, don't get mad at *me*," she said.

"I'm not mad at you, kid," I said. "It's just that it burns me
to think about it. The beery blowhard with the broad ass and
the big mouth is the picture everybody's got of the guy who
hunts—probably because he's so obnoxious. He's the shithead
who litters the woods with beer cans and poaches a big buck
before shooting time, and wastes game, and hangs mounted
heads all over his wall, and pays his dues to the NRA, and
calls himself a 'sportsman,' for God's sake—like hunting was
some kind of far-out football game."

"And he probably belongs to the John Birch Society, too,"
she added.

I let that go by.

"Well, I *know* why he's trying to be a mighty hunter," she

said, splashing her feet under the slowly dissolving suds, "but you still haven't told me why *you* are."

I shrugged. "I have to," I said. "It's something I have to do. That's the thing the Bambi-lovers can't understand. They simper about 'immaturity,' and 'man doesn't need violence toward his fellow creatures,' and 'let's have a reverence for life and keep our forests and wild life just to look at—as nature intended.' I get so goddamn sick of the intentional fallacy. Whatever the hell some half wit decides is right is automatically what nature or God intended. Bullshit! Preserve the pheasant from the bad old hunter so that the fox can tear him to pieces with his teeth. Preserve the cute little bunny so the hawk can fly him up about a thousand feet and drop him screaming to the ground. You ever hear a rabbit scream? He sounds just like a baby. Preserve the pretty deer—Bambi—so he càn over-multiply, overgraze, and then starve to death—or get so weak that the coyotes can run him down and start eating on his guts while he's still alive and bleating.

"Nature isn't some well-trimmed little park, Flower Child. It's very savage. These idiots get all mushy and sentimental about our little furry friends, and they get upset when a grizzly in the Yellowstone chews up a couple kids."

"You sound like you hate animals," she said. "Is that it?"

"I love animals," I said. "Nobody who hates animals hunts. But I respect the animal for what he is—wild. I don't try to make a pet out of him. When I go into the woods, I'm going into his territory. I respect his rights. Am I making any sense?"

"I'm not sure," she said. "But you still haven't told me why you like to go out and kill things."

I shrugged again. "It's something I have to do—every so often I have to go out. It's not the killing—that's really a very small part of it. It's the woods, and being alone, and—well— the hunting. That word gets misused. Actually, it's going out, finding the animal you want in his own territory, and then getting close enough to him to do a clean job. He deserves that much from you. Call it respect, if you like. Anybody who gets all his kicks out of the killing has got some loose marbles."

"I don't understand," she objected, "I don't understand it at all."

"You're not a hunter," I said. "Very few people really are."

"Of course not," she said sarcastically, "after *all*, I'm a *woman*."

"I've met women who were hunters," I said, "and damn good ones, too."

"Is it—well—now don't get mad—sexual?"

"You've been reading too much Hemingway." I laughed. "People use sexual terms to describe it because that's about as close as you can get to it in everyday language that nonhunters would understand. Hemingway knew the difference, and he knew other hunters would, too, and he knew they'd excuse him."

"You make it all sound awfully exotic," she said doubtfully.

"It's not," I said, "actually, it's very simple. You just can't explain it to people, that's all."

"Are you a good hunter?" she asked.

"I try," I said, "and I keep on learning. I guess that's about all any guy can do."

"You know," she said, looking straight at me. "I don't think this conversation is really happening. It's surrealistic—me in the bathtub and you sitting on the john trying to eff the ineffable to me."

"What makes it even more psychedelic"—I grinned at her—"is the fact that you're convinced that you're concealed up to the neck when in reality your suds melted about five minutes ago."

She blinked and looked down at herself. Then she squealed, suddenly contorting herself into a knot. She glared at me, her face flaming. "You get out of here!" she said. "You get out of my bathroom, right now!"

I laughed and went on out to the living room. I could hear her perking and grumbling like a small pot behind me. I mixed myself another drink. I felt better. She made me feel good just being around her. I sat down in the chair and looked out at the soggy tail end of the afternoon in a much better humor.

"Hey, *you!*" She was standing in the doorway. Her hair was still tucked on top of her head. Except for the hair ribbon she was stark naked. She pitched her damp towel back through the bathroom door and snapped her fingers at me. "Up!" she said. "On your feet, Buster!"

I got up. "Now, what—"

"March," she said, pointing imperiously at the bedroom.

"I don't think you ought to get too overheated," I started. "I mean, you got a bad chill and—"

"Bullshit! Nobody—and I mean *nobody*—is going to yank

my panties off like you did just now and then tip his hat and walk away. Now you get into that bedroom!"

I went into the bedroom.

After she finished her revenge, or whatever you want to call it, we talked some more. About ten o'clock that evening I kissed her good-bye and went out to my car. "Not in the *bathroom*!" For Christ's own private sake! I laughed all the way back across town.

I took a shower, dressed in my hunting clothes, and then clumped on up to Jack's trailer, wincing as the rain spotted my Army boots. I'd spent a lot of hours polishing them.

Jack was a little groggy from his nap, but he dressed quickly, and we drove on over to Sloane's house through the rain-swept streets. We didn't say much except to complain about the weather.

"Sure as hell hope it isn't rainin' on the other side of the mountains," Jack said. I grunted agreement. We stopped by a liquor store and each bought a fifth of bourbon.

"God knows if we'd be able to find a store open later on," Jack said.

We got to Sloane's place about a quarter to twelve and sat down and had a beer with Calvin after we'd stowed our gear in the car. Stan and Lou both showed up about five to twelve, and they loaded up. All of us had a good stiff belt of Cal's whiskey, and we took off.

We stopped at a roadhouse tavern just before we got to Seattle and laid in a supply of beer, about a case in each car. It was one of those overchromed joints, all fancy and new. The only guy in there besides the bartender was a drunk in the back booth, snoring for all he was worth. The bartender had a solitaire game laid out on the bar. Real swinging joint. We bought our beer, pried Lou away from the pinball machine, and took off again, blasting along in the wake of Sloane's Cadillac. We didn't get to Everett until almost two, and we stopped for gas. Once we got past Snohomish, we were about the only cars on the road. The flat farmland of the Snohomish River Valley stretched on back into the mist and darkness on either side of us, and the fences with the bottom strand of wire snarled in weeds sprayed out on either hand as we passed. Now and then we'd see a house and barn—all dark—near the road. Once in a while a car would pass, going the other way like a bat out of hell and spraying muddy water on the windshield.

Jack and I switched off, and I drove for a while. There's

something about driving late at night in the rain. It's almost as if the world has stopped. The rain sheets down in tatters, and the road unrolls out in front of your headlights. We went up through the small silent, mountain towns, always climbing. Each town seemed emptier than the last, with the rain washing the fronts of the dark old buildings, and the streetlights swinging in the wind. We kept the radio going, and neither one of us said much until we got on past Gold Bar, the last town before we really started to climb. Once we got up into the mountains, the radio faded, and after about ten miles of static, I switched it off.

"Bust me open another beer, Jack," I said, breaking the silence.

"Sure." He cracked one and handed it to me.

"Damn. I hope this weather breaks at the summit," I said.

"Didn't you hear that last weather report?" he asked. "It's pretty much all on this side."

"That's a break."

"Yeah." We lapsed into silence again, watching the headlights spear on out in front of the car and the windshield wipers flopping back and forth. I turned up the heater.

"God damn," he said suddenly, "I wish to hell Mike could have made it. It's a damn shame, you know that? He's been tryin' to get away for the High Hunt for the last four years now, and some damn thing always comes up so he can't make it."

"Yeah," I said, "and Mike's a good head. He'd have been fun to have along."

Jack nodded gloomily. "You want a belt?" he said suddenly.

I wasn't really sure I did, but I saw that he needed one. "Why not?"

He fished his bottle out from under the seat and cracked the seal. He took a long pull and handed it to me. I took a short blast and handed it back.

"I guess we'd better go easy on this stuff," he said. "We show up drunk and Miller's liable to send us back down the mountain." He put the jug away.

"Right."

"You know, Dan," he said after a while. "I'm damn glad we got the chance to do this together. We never got to know each other much when we were kids, what with one damn thing and another—the Old Lady and all. Maybe it's time we got acquainted."

"I've had a pretty good time the last few weeks," I said.

"I'm not sorry I got in touch with you." It was more or less true.

"It'd all be great if it wasn't for that son-of-a-bitchin' McKlearey," he said bitterly.

"Yeah. What the hell's got him off on the prod so bad, anyway?"

"Aw shit! He was the big-ass gunnery sergeant in the Corps—you know, a hundred guys jumped every time he farted. He was a big shot. Now he's low man on the totem pole at Sloane's used-car lot—a big plate of fried ratshit. He's not in charge anymore. Some guys just can't hack that."

"Institutional mentality," I said.

"What the hell's that?"

"It's like the ex-con who gets busted for sticking up a police station two days after he gets out of the pen. He really wants to go back. They take care of him, do his thinking for him. He's safe inside. Guys in the military get the same way."

"Maybe that's it, Jack said. "When I knew him in the service, he was a different guy. Now he's drunk all the time and shacked-up with a half dozen women and a real first-class prick. I wouldn't be surprised if he's been throwin' the wood to Marg every time my back's turned."

I was suddenly very wide awake. Christ, had he been so drunk that night he couldn't remember what he'd said? "Oh?" I said carefully.

"It wouldn't be the first time she's played around. Maybe I've given her reason enough. She was pretty young and simple when I married her, and I'm not one to pass up some occasional strange stuff. Maybe she figures she's entitled. I don't give a shit. Me and her are about ready to split the sheets anyway." He slumped lower in the seat and lit a cigarette.

"Sorry to hear that," I said. I meant it.

"I've been through it a couple of times already. I know the signs. I don't really give a rat's ass; I'm about ready to go the single route myself anyway. Marriage is fine for a while—steady ass and home cookin'—but it gets to be a drag."

"I'm still sorry to hear it."

"But no matter what, I'm a blue-balls son of a bitch if I want to get cut out by that fuckin' McKlearey while I'm still payin' the bills. That's one of the reasons I'm gonna outhunt that motherfucker if it kills me. Maybe if I rub his nose in it hard enough, he'll get the idea and move on." Jack's voice was harsh.

"I don't know," I said. "As stupid as he is, getting an idea through his head might take some doing."

"I suppose I could always shoot the bastard."

"Not worth it." I was about half-afraid he meant it.

"I suppose not, but he could sure use shootin'."

"You know it, buddy."

"Another beer?"

"Sure."

The moon was slipping in and out of the clouds as we climbed higher, and the drops that hit the windshield were getting smaller. The rain was slacking off. The big fir trees at the side of the road caught briefly in our headlights had their trunks wreathed in tendrils of mist. I leaned forward and looked up through the windshield at the slowly emerging stars.

"Looks like it's going to quit," I said.

"That's what I told you," he said.

The High Hunt

15

SLOANE'S Cadillac was still leading, and at the summit he signaled for a left.

"Where the hell's he going?" I asked. "Off into the timber?"

"Naw. He probably wants to use the can. McKlearey's been droppin' back for the last ten miles anyway, so we better let the son of a bitch catch up."

I turned Jack's car into the lot at the summit behind Sloane, stopping beside his car and switching off the engine.

Sloane stuck his head out the window on the driver's side and yelled, "Piss call!" The echoes bounced off down the gorge we'd just come up.

"Christ, Sloane," Jack hissed, "keep it down. There's people livin' over in the lodge there."

"Oooops," Sloane said. He and Jack hotfooted it over to the rest room while Stan and I stood out in the sprinkling rain waiting to flag down McKlearey. It was so quiet you could hear the pattering drops back in the timber.

"Pretty chilly up here," Stan said. His voice was hushed, and his breath steamed. He had his hands jammed down into the pockets of his new bright-orange hunting jacket. The jacket clashed horribly with his old red duck-hunting cap.

"It's damned high," I said.

"What time is it?"

"About three thirty," I said.

"You think Lou's car has broken down?"

"About right now I wouldn't give a damn if that bastard had driven off into the gorge somewhere. I've had a gutful of him, and a steering post through the belly might civilize him some."

"I've met people I've liked a lot more," Stan agreed. That's Stan for you. Never say what you mean.

"How are you and Sloane getting along?"

"Just fine. He's a strange one, you know? He plays the fool, but he's really very serious. He was telling me that he hates that pawnshop and all the sad little people who come in wanting just a couple of dollars for a piece of worthless trash—they know it's not worth anything, but it's all they have—but he can't get his money back out of the place right now, so he has to stay there."

"Yeah," I said, "Sloane's a really odd duck."

"And he's really very intelligent—well-read, aware of what's going on in the world—all of this foolishness is just an act."

"I wouldn't want to try to outsmart him," I agreed.

Cal and Jack came back. "Hasn't that shithead made it yet?" Jack demanded. "Oh, hell, yes," he imitated McKlearey's voice, "I'm gonna drive *my* car. It's a real goin' machine. Cost me sixty-five bucks. I'd feel perfectly safe drivin' from here to the end of the block in that car."

"I think that's his car now," Stan said. He pointed far off down the mountain we'd just climbed. We saw a flash of headlights sweeping out across the gorge, flaring out in a sudden bright swipe through the mist.

Stan and I went to the rest room, came back, and joined the others watching Lou's old car labor up the highway.

"Is this the fuckin' top?" he demanded as he pulled up alongside, his radiator hissing ominously.

"This is her," Sloane said. "Car heat up on you?"

"Aw, this cripple," Lou said in disgust. "Is there any water here?"

"Over by the latrine," I said, pointing.

He pulled over to the side of the rest-room building and popped the hood. He got out and threw a beer bottle off into the trees. The bandage on his left hand gleamed whitely in the darkness. He eased off the radiator cap, and the steam boiled out, drifting pale and low downwind. He poured water into the radiator, and pretty soon it stopped steaming. Then he fished out a can of oil from the trunk and punched holes in the top with an old beer opener. He dumped the oil into the engine and then threw the can after the beer bottle. He slammed the hood, unzipped his pants, and pissed on the front tire.

"Christ, McKlearey!" Jack said, "there's the latrine right there."

"Fuck it!" Lou said. "What time is it?"

"Nearly four," I told him.

"Let's go huntin', men," he said and climbed back in his car. The rest of us went to our cars, and we started down the other side.

Jack was driving again, and I slumped down in the seat.
The sky was clear on this side, and the stars were very bright.
I picked one out and watched it as we drifted down the moun-
tain.

What in the goddamn hell was I doing here anyway? I was
running off into the high mountains with a bunch of guys I
didn't really know, to do something I didn't really know all
that much about, despite what I'd told Clydine. Maybe I was
still running and this was just someplace else to run to. But I
had a strange feeling that whatever I'd been running after—
or away from—was going to be up there. Maybe Stan was
right. When you strip it all away, and it's just you and the big
lonely out there, you can get down to what counts.

Maybe it was more than that, too. Up until Dad died, I'd
heard hunting stories—about him and Uncle Charles, about
Granddad and Great-Uncle Beale—all of them. And I'd started
going out as soon as I was old enough—alone most of the
time. It was something where you couldn't work the angles or
unload a quick snow job or any of the crap I'd somehow gotten
so good at in the last few years. There was no way to fake it;
it had to be real. If you didn't kill the damned deer, he wouldn't
fall down. You couldn't talk to him and tell him that he was
statistically dead and convince him to take a dive. He had too
much integrity. He knew what it was all about, and if you
didn't really nail him down, he'd go over the nearest mountain
before you could get off a second shot. He knew he was real.
It was up to you to find out if you were.

"Hey, Jack," I said.

"Yeah?"

"You remember Dad?"

"Sure."

"He liked to hunt, didn't he?"

"Whenever he could. The Old Lady was pretty much down
on it. About all he could do by the time you were growin' up
was to go out for ducks now and then. He used to sneak out
of the house in the morning before she woke up. She wouldn't
let him go out for deer anymore."

"Whatever happened to that old .45-70 Granddad left him?"

"She sold it. Spent the money on booze."

"Shit! You know, I've got a hunch we'd have been raised
better by a bitch wolf."

"You're just bitter," he said.

"You're goddamn right I am," I said. "I wouldn't walk across the street for her if she was dying."

"She calls once in a while," he said. "I try to keep her away from the kids. You never know when she's gonna show up drunk."

"How's she paying her way?"

"Who knows? Workin' in a whorehouse for all I know."

"I wonder why the Old Man didn't kick her ass out into the street."

"You and me, that's why," my brother said.

"Yeah, there's that, too, I suppose."

We passed through Cashmere about five and swung north toward Lake Chelan. The sky began to get pale off to the east.

"God damn, that's nice, isn't it?" Jack said, pointing at the sky.

"Dawn the rosy-fingered," I said, misquoting Homer, "caressing the hair of night."

"Say, that's pretty good. You make it up?"

I shook my head.

"You read too goddamn much, you know that? When I say something, you can be pretty goddamn sure it's right out of my own head." He belched.

We drove on, watching the sky grow lighter and lighter. As the light grew stronger, the poplar leaves began to emerge in all their brilliant yellow along the river bottoms. The pines swelled black behind them.

"Pretty country," Jack said.

"Hey," I said, "look at that."

A doe with twin fawns was standing hock-deep in a clear stream, drinking, the ripples sliding downstream from where she stood. She raised her head, her ears flicking nervously as we passed.

"Pretty, isn't she?" he said.

We got to Twisp about eight and hauled into a gas station. Sloane went in and called Miller while we got our gas tanks filled.

"He's got everything all ready," he said when he came back out. "He told me how to get there."

"How far is it?" Lou asked. "This bucket is gettin' pretty fuckin' tuckered." He slapped the fender of his car with his bandaged hand.

"About fifteen miles," Sloane said. "Road's good all the way."

We paid for the gas and drove on out of town. Twisp is one of those places with one paved street and the rest dirt. It squats in the valley with the mountains hulking over it threateningly, green-black rising to blue-black, and then the looming white summits.

The road out to Miller's wasn't the best, but we managed. The sun was up now, and the poplar leaves gleamed pure gold. The morning air was so clear that every rock and limb and leaf stood out. The fences were straight lines along the road and on out across the mowed hayfields. The mountains swelled up out of the poplar-gold bottoms. It was so pretty it made your throat ache. I felt good, really good, maybe for the first time in years.

Sloane slowed up, then went on, then slowed again. He was reading mailboxes. Finaly he signaled, the blinker on his Caddy looking very ostentatious out here.

We wheeled into a long driveway and drove on up toward a group of white painted buildings and log fences. A young colt galloped along beside us as we drove to the house. He was all sleek, and his muscles rolled under his skin as he ran. He acted like he was running just for the fun of it.

"Little bastard's going to outrun us," Jack said, laughing.

We pulled up in the yard in front of the barn and parked where a stumpy little old guy with white hair and a two-week stubble directed us to. He was wearing cowboy boots and a beat-up old cowboy hat, and he walked like his legs had been broken a half dozen times. If that was Miller, I was damn sure going to be disappointed.

It wasn't.

Miller came out of the house, and I swear he had a face like a hunk of rock. With that big, old-fashioned white mustache, he looked just a little bit like God himself. He wore cowboy boots and had a big hat like the little white-haired man, and neither of them looked out of place in that kind of gear. Some guides dress up for the customers, but you could tell that these two were for real. I took a good look at Miller and decided that I'd go way out of my way to keep from crossing him. He was far and away the meanest-looking man I've ever seen in my life. I understood what Mike had meant about him.

We turned off the motors, and the silence seemed suddenly very solid. We got out, and he looked at us—hard—sizing each one of us up.

"Men," he said. It was a sort of greeting, I guess—or maybe

a question. His voice was deep and very quiet—no louder than it absolutely had to be.

Even Sloane's exuberance was a little dampened. He stepped forward. "Mr. Miller," he said, "I'm Cal Sloane." They shook hands.

"I'll get to know the rest of you in good time," he said. "Right now breakfast's ready. Give Clint there your personal gear and sleepin' bags, and we'll go in and eat." I never learned Clint's last name or Miller's first one.

We unloaded the cars and then followed Miller on up to the house. He led us through a linoleumed kitchen with small windows and an old-fashioned sink and wood stove, and on into the dining room, where we sat down at the table. The room had dark wood paneling and the china was very old, white with a fine-line blue Japanese print on it. The room smelled musty, and I suspected it wasn't used much. There was a wood-burning heating stove in the corner that popped now and then. Miller came back out of the kitchen with a huge enameled coffee pot and filled all our cups.

The coffee was hot and black and strong enough to eat the fillings out of your teeth. The stumpy little guy came in and started carting food out of the kitchen. First he brought out a platter of steaks.

"Venison," Miller said. "Figured we'd better clean up what's left over from last winter."

Then there were biscuits and honey, then eggs and fried potatoes. There were several pitchers of milk on the table. We all ate everything Miller ate; I think we were afraid not to.

But when the little guy hauled out a couple of pies, I had to call a halt.

"Sorry," I said. "I'll have to admit that you guys can outeat me." I pushed myself back from the table.

"The Kid just can't keep up." Jack laughed.

"Well, you don't have to eat it all," Miller said. "We just figured you might be a little hungry."

"Hungry, yes," I said, grinning, "but I couldn't eat all that if I was starving."

"Better eat," the man Miller had called Clint growled. "Be four hours in the saddle before you feed again."

"I think I'm good for twelve," I said. I lit a cigarette and poured myself another cup of coffee.

"After a few hours in the high country," Clint warned, "your

belly's gonna think your th'oat's been cut." He sounded like
he meant it.

The others finished eating, and Clint poured more coffee
all around. Miller fished out a sheet of paper from one of his
shirt pockets and a pair of gold-rimmed glasses out of another.

"Guess we might as well get all this settled right now," he
said, putting on the glasses. "That way we won't have it hangin'
fire."

We all took out our wallets. Clint went out and came back
with a beat-up old green metal box. Miller opened it and took
out a receipt book.

"Ten days," Miller said, "fifty dollars a man." We all started
counting money out on the table. He looked around and nodded
in approval. He started filling out receipts laboriously, licking
the stub of the pencil now and then. He asked each of us our
names and filled them in on the receipts. Clint took our money
and put it away in the tin box.

"Now," Miller said, squinting at the paper, "the grub come
to a hundred and fifty dollars. I got a list here and the price
of ever-thing if you want to check it. I already took off for me
and Clint. Your share come to a hundred and fifty and a few
odd dollars, but call it a hundred and fifty. I figured it out, and
it's thirty dollars a man. You can check my figures if you want.
I kept it down as much as I could. We won't eat fancy, but
it'll stick with us." He looked around, offering the paper. We
all shook our heads.

"I'll give you the hundred and a half," Sloane said. "The
others can settle up with me." The receipt-writing had obviously
bugged him.

"Thanks anyway," Miller said, "but if it's all the same to
you men, I'd a whole lot rather get it from each man myself.
Then I know it's right, and there's no arguments later."

Sloane shrugged, and we each counted out another thirty
dollars. Miller struggled through another five receipts and then
took off his glasses. I noticed the sweat running down the outer
edges of his mustache.

"There," he said with obvious relief. "Well, men, this ain't
gettin' us up into the high country. Let's go pick out some
horses and get 'em loaded up in the truck. We got a ways to
drive before we get to the horse trail."

We all got up and followed him on out of the house. Clint
began picking up the dishes as we left. It was still chilly outside,
and the morning sun was very bright. Miller stopped out in the

yard and waited for us all to gather around. He looked up into the mountains and cleared his throat.

"Just a few more things I want to get straight before we leave, men," he said, and I could see that he'd have preferred not to say it. "I've been known to take a drink now and then myself, but you men are goin' to be up there with loaded guns, and it's damn high where you'll be huntin'. You might be able to drink like a fish down here, but two drinks up there and you'll be fallin' over your own feet. I know you've got liquor with you, and I'll probably take a bottle along myself, but I don't want any of us takin' a drink before the sun goes down and the guns are all hung up. I sure don't want nobody shootin' hisself—or me. OK?"

We all nodded again. He wasn't the kind of man you argued with.

"And if any of you got any quarrels with each other, leave 'em down here. Any trouble up there, and we'll all come out, and no refunds. We all straight on that?" He looked around at us, and his face was stern.

We all nodded again.

"Good," he said, and he looked relieved. "Last thing. I know that country up there and you men don't. If I tell you to do somethin', you'd better do 'er. I ain't gonna be tellin' you 'cause I like bossin' men around. I'll have a damn good reason, so don't give me no hard times about it. OK, now I've said my piece, all right?"

We nodded again. What else could we do?

"Well then, I guess that takes care of all the unpleasantness. Let's go on down to the corral and pick out some horses. Sooner we get that done, the sooner we can go hunt deer." He started off, and we fell in behind him. He took damn big steps.

I began to feel better about this. Miller knew his business, and there wouldn't be any horseshit nonsense with him around. I looked up at the mountains, blue in the morning light.

God damn, it might just be a good trip after all.

16

It took us the better part of an hour to cut out horses from the herd in the corral down by the big log barn. Miller and Clint leaned across the top rail, pointing out this horse, then that one, calling them by name and telling us their good points—almost like they were selling them. I picked a big gray they called Ned. He looked pretty good at first, but then I caught a glimpse of his other eye and wasn't so sure. We herded them up into the back of a big stock-truck along with some pack-horses and then began hauling saddles out to a battered pickup.

"Some of you men'll have to ride in the back of the pickup," Miller said, squinting into the tangle of saddles, straps, and ropes we'd piled in there. "Might be a bit uncomfortable, but it ain't too far."

"I'll take my car," Lou said shortly.

"Here we go again," Jack muttered to me disgustedly, yanking his red baseball cap down over his forehead.

"Road's pretty rough," Clint warned.

Miller shrugged, "Suit yourself," he said. "Couple of you can go with me in the pickup, then, and one of you with Clint in the stock-truck, and one other man in the car with this man here, all right?"

We all nodded and started pitching the sleeping bags and clothing sacks that Clint had hauled down here earlier into the back of the pickup.

"I'll go with McKlearey," Sloane told the rest of us, "and we can pile the guns in his back seat." Sloane was thinking ahead. He was probably the only one of us who could ride five miles with Lou without getting into a fight.

"Good idea," Miller said. "Guns could get banged around some in the pickup." He turned to Clint. "You lock up?" he asked.

"Right, Cap," Clint said, "and I got it all squared away with

173

Matthews. His oldest boy's comin' by to feed the stock while
we're gone."

"Good," Miller said. "Well, men, let's get goin'." He led
the way over to the trucks. I hung back a little, letting Jack
and Stan go ahead. They both got into the pickup with Miller,
so I climbed up into the cab of the stock-truck with Clint.
Sloane and McKlearey rode along with us, hanging onto the
outside of the cab as far as the main yard where our cars were
parked. Then we all got out, put our guns in the back seat of
McKlearey's car, and climbed back in.

We drove on out of the yard and on down the long driveway,
the pickup leading, then McKlearey's weary Chevy, and Clint
and I bringing up the rear in the stock-truck. The colt ran along
beside us again as we drove on down to the highway.

"Little fella sure likes to run, doesn't he?" I ventured to
Clint.

"Young horse ain't got much damn sense," Clint growled.
"Just like a damn kid. About all he wants to do is run and play.
Older horse rests ever' chance he gets."

"Looks like he's going to be pretty fast," I said.

"Sure as hell ought to be," Clint said, "considerin' what ol'
Cap paid for stud fee. We got this quarter-horse mare—that's
her standin' over there in the shade. Got good blood-lines, so
he goes all out on gettin' her bred." He cranked the wheel
around, swinging wide out onto the highway. I could hear a
thump or two from the back as the horses stumbled around
with the sudden shift in direction.

"Sure as hell hope that fella can keep up with ol' Cap's
pickup," Clint said, thrusting his stubbled chin toward the blue
fog coming out of the tailpipe of McKlearey's car.

"I wouldn't bet on it," I said sourly. "He's been lagging
behind all night. That car of his is a cripple. We have any big
hills to climb?"

"Nothin' too bad," Clint said, "and we got good gravel all
the way after we turn off the tar."

"That's a break," I said.

"What'd he do to his hand?" he asked. I'd seen both him
and Miller eyeing McKlearey's bandage.

"He cut it. It isn't bad."

"That's good."

We drove on up the highway for a few miles.

"I didn't catch your name," he said finally.

"Dan," I said, "Dan Alders."

He stuck out a knobby hand without looking away from the road, and we shook. "Just call me Clint," he said. "Ever'body else does."

"Right, Clint," I said.

We wound along the paved road that hugged the bottom of the valley, crossing the narrow bridges that stepped back and forth across the twisting little stream that sparkled in the mid-morning sun. I suddenly wished that Clydine were along so that she could see this.

"Many fish in here, Clint?" I asked, looking down into the water.

"I can usually pick up a few," he said. "I got a hole I work pretty often. Some pretty nice cutthroat in there."

I glanced down at the water as we crossed the stream again. "Looks pretty shallow," I said, watching the clear water slide over the smooth brown pebbles.

"It backs up behind rocks and downed trees," he told me. "Fish'll hole up in there. Hit 'em with a small spoon or bait, and they'll go for it ever' time."

"Any size?" I asked.

"Lifted a three-pounder this spring," he said.

"That could get pretty wild and woolly in that fast water," I said.

"It was sorta fun." He grinned. "You fish much?"

"When I get the chance," I said.

He grunted approvingly, and we drove on a ways in silence.

I slid a little lower in the sea, sliding my tail to the edge of the cushion. "Getting a little butt-sprung," I said, explaining.

"Wait'll later," he said, grinning again. "That car seat's soft compared to a saddle."

"I don't suppose anybody's ever figured out a way to ride standing up."

"Not so's you'd notice it."

"Oh, well," I said.

"You done much ridin'?" he asked me tentatively after a long pause.

"I know which end of the horse is which is about all."

He scratched his stubbled chin. "I'd kinda watch old Ned then if I was you." He squinted into the morning sunlight as we swung off the pavement onto a graveled road. "He ain't been rode for a few weeks, and he's had time to build up a good head of steam. He could be pretty green, so you might have to iron a few of the kinks out of him."

My stomach lurched. "You figure he'll buck?" I asked nervously.

"Oh, nothin' fancy. He'll probably rear a couple times and maybe hump up a little. Just be ready for him. Keep kinda loose, is all, and haul him up tight. That's the main thing—don't let him get his head down between his front legs. If he gets too persnickety, just slap him across the ears with the end of the reins. That'll bring him around."

"I'd hate to start off the trip getting dumped on my butt in the gravel," I said.

He chuckled. "I didn't mean to spook you none. You'll be OK if you're ready for him."

"I sure hope so," I said doubtfully.

We had begun to climb up out of the valley. The white trunks and golden leaves of the poplar trees that had bordered the little stream gave way to dark pines. The gravel road was splotched with alternate patches of shadow and bright sunlight. It looked cool and damp back in under the trees. Every so often a red squirrel scampered across the road in front of us, his tail flirting arrogantly.

"Pushy little guys, aren't they?" I said to Clint.

"I think they do that just for the fun of it," he agreed.

We came around a corner, and I could suddenly see all the way up to the summit of the surrounding mountains. The sun sparkled on the snowfields outlined against the deep blue of the sky.

"God damn!" I said, almost reverently.

"Pretty, ain't it?" Clint agreed.

"Are we going up there?" I asked, pointing up toward the snow.

"Not quite," he said. "Pretty close, though."

We drove on, twisting up along the gravel road. There's a kind of bluish color to the woods in the morning that makes things look unreal. An eagle or hawk of some kind turned big wide circles way up, hunting, or just flying for the hell of it.

"Where 'bouts is it you work?" Clint asked after another mile or so.

"I just got out of the service," I told him. "I'll be going back to school pretty soon."

"Which branch you in?" he asked.

"Army."

"Me and Cap was in the Horse-Marines when we was younger."

"Oh? Lou up there—guy who's driving his own car—was a Marine."

"I kinda figured he mighta been. Tell by the way he walks."

We drove on up the gravel road for about an hour, climbing gradually but steadily. The road grew narrower and narrower but was still in pretty good shape. It was close to ten thirty when Miller pulled out into a wide place beside the road. The rest of us pulled off and stopped.

"This is where we saddle up," Clint said, pulling on the hand brake. "Road goes on about another hundred yards and then gives up."

We climbed down from the truck and went over to where the others had gathered at the back of the pickup. It was quite a bit colder up here than it had been in the valley. Lou's radiator was steaming again.

"We'll unload the horses one at a time," Miller said. "They stay calmer that way."

Clint and I went to the back of the stock-truck and pulled out the unloading ramp.

"Packhorses first, Clint," Miller said.

Clint grunted and went up the ramp. He unhooked the gate and swung it back. There was a thumping and several snorts as he disappeared inside the truck. He came to the door leading a somewhat discouraged-looking horse by the halter. Miller passed him up the snap-end of a lead-rope, and he fastened it to the halter. Then Miller pulled, and Clint slapped the horse sharply on the rump. The horse laid back his ears and carefully stepped down the ramp. Clint hopped out and closed the gate again.

They led the horse over to the pickup and put a cumbersome-looking packsaddle on him. Then they tied him to a sapling and went back to the stock-truck. They unloaded three more packhorses, one by one.

"We could get by with just a couple," Miller explained, "but we'll need this many to bring out the deer."

Then they began bringing out the saddle horses. Jack's horse came out first. After he'd been saddled and bridled, Miller told Jack to mount and walk him up and down the road a ways to loosen him up. I could see that Jack was getting a kick out of it. That baseball cap of his made him look like a kid.

McKlearey's horse was next, and Lou took off at a gallop.

"Hey!" Miller said sharply as Lou came back up the road. "I said to walk him! That horse plays out on you, and you're gonna be afoot." Lou reined in and did as he was told. I thought that was a good sign. I began to have hopes that Miller might just be able to keep McKlearey in line.

They brought out Ned next, and my stomach tightened up. He looked meaner than ever. I particularly didn't like the way he kind of set himself when Clint threw the saddle on him. I walked up to the horse slowly. He laid his ears back and watched me. I pulled off my quilted red jacket and red felt hat. No point in messing up my hunting gear. Skin heals. Clothes don't.

Clint held the stirrup for me while Miller held the horse's head. They hadn't done that for anybody else, and that sure didn't help my nerves any. I got up into the saddle and got my feet arranged in the stirrups.

"You all set?" Miller asked, with the faintest hint of a smile under his mustache.

"I guess."

Miller nodded sharply, and both he and Clint jumped back out of the way. Now, that *really* makes you feel good. Ned stood perfectly still for a minute. I could feel him wound up like a spring under me.

"Give 'im a boot in the ribs," Miller said. I nudged the horse gently with my heels. Nothing happened. I looked around for a soft place to land.

"Kick 'im," Miller said, grinning openly now.

I gritted my teeth and really socked the horse in the ribs. His front feet came up off the ground. If old Clint hadn't warned me, I think I'd have been dumped right then. That big gray horse pranced around on his hind feet for a minute, fighting to get some slack in the reins so he could get his head down. Then he dropped down again, still fighting. I was hanging onto the reins with one hand and the saddle horn with the other. He jumped a couple times and spun around.

"Kick 'im again, Dan!" Clint shouted, laughing. "Stay with 'im, boy!" I kicked the horse in the ribs again, and he reared just as he had the first time. This time I wasn't so surprised, so I let go of the saddle horn and swung the reins at his ears the way Clint had told me to. Then he twisted around and tried to bite my leg. I whacked him in the nose with the reins, and that seemed to settle him a little. He humped a couple more times, shivered, and took off down the road at a trot.

"Better run that horse a little," Miller called. "Others don't need it, but Old Ned's a bit frisky."

"Right," I said, and nudged the horse into a lope. I kicked him a little harder. "The man says run," I explained to horse.

McKlearey scowled at me as I barreled on past him.

The wind whistled by my ears, and I could feel the easy roll of Ned's muscles as he ran. I slowed him up and turned him about a half mile down the road. Then I opened him up to a dead run. I was laughing out loud when I pulled up by the trucks. I couldn't help it. I hadn't had so much fun in years. Ned pranced around a little, blowing and tossing his head. I think he was getting a kick out of it, too.

"Hey, cowboy," Jack yelled, "where'd you learn to ride like that?"

"Beginner's luck," I said. I looked over to where Miller and Clint were saddling Stan's horse. "OK to walk him now?" I asked.

"Yeah, he looks to be settled a bit," Miller said, still grinning.

I pulled Ned in beside Jack's horse, and the two of us rode on back down the road.

"You looked pretty fancy there, little brother," he said.

"I picked the wrong horse," I told him. "That little exhibition back there was all his idea."

"How the hell'd you manage to stay on?"

"Clint warned me about this knothead in the truck on the way up. I was ready for him. You might not have noticed, but I had a pretty firm grip on this saddlehorn."

Jack laughed. "You two didn't slow down long enough for me to see that part of it."

I gingerly felt my rump. "I sure hope he doesn't feel he has to go through this every time we start out."

Jack laughed again, and we plodded down the road.

"How's this Miller strike *you*?" I asked him.

"I don't think I'd want to cross him."

"Amen to that, buddy," I agreed.

"'He sure as hell acts like he knows what he's doin'," my brother said.

"He's an old-time Marine," I said. "Him and Clint both."

"McKlearey'll cash in on that," Jack said, unbuttoning his quilted hunting vest.

"Wouldn't doubt it."

"How's Clint? He seemed pretty grouchy back at the house."

"That's mostly bark," I said. "We talked quite a bit on the way up. Like I told you, he was the one that warned me about this horse and his little habits."

"Yeah," Jack said. "I noticed that he was callin' you by name when you guys got down from the truck."

We turned around and rode back on up to the others. Stan and Sloane were mounted now and were starting off down the road. Sloane seemed to be puffing pretty hard. Maybe his horse had him a little spooked, or maybe his down-filled parka was a little too warm.

Jack and I got down and helped Miller and Clint load up the packhorses. Then Miller called in the others.

"Now here's how we'll go," he said after they had dismounted. "I'll lead out and Clint'll bring up the rear with the packhorses. Don't try nothin' fancy along the trail. Let the horse do all the work and most of the thinkin'. Just set easy and watch the scenery go by. The horses know what they're doin', so trust 'em."

He showed us how to tie our rifles to the saddle where they'd be out of the way. His own gun case was lashed to the back of one of the packhorses, and Clint's .30-30 was tucked in beside it.

I think we all saw the quick glance that passed between Miller and Clint when we hauled our pistol belts out of McKlearey's car.

"Bears," Sloane explained, almost apologetically.

"Bears!" Clint snorted. "Ain't no damn bears up that high."

"Oh," Sloane said meekly. "We thought there might be."

Miller scratched his mustache dubiously. "Can't leave 'em here," he said finally. "Somebody might come along and steal 'em. I guess you'll have to bring the damn things along. They might be some good for signalin' and the like." He shook his head and walked off a ways by himself, his fists jammed down into the pockets of his sheepskin coat and that big hat pulled down low over his eyes.

We all looked at each other shamefacedly and slowly strapped on our hardware.

"Looks like the goddamn Tijuana National Guard," Clint muttered in disgust.

We stood around like a bunch of kids who'd been caught stealing apples until Miller came back.

"All right," he said shortly, "get on your horses and let's get goin'."

We climbed on our horses—Ned didn't even twitch this time—and followed Miller on up to the end of the road and onto the saddle trail that took off from there. The trail moved up along the side of a ridge. Once we got up a ways, the pines thinned out and we could see out for miles across the heavily timbered foothills. The horizon ahead of us was a ragged line of snow-covered peaks; to the east, behind us, it faded off into blue, hazy distance. The grass up here was yellow and knee-high, waving gently in the slight wind that followed us up the ridge. I could see little swirls and patterns on top of the grass as gusts brushed here and there.

It was absolutely quiet, except for the horses and the sound of the wind. I felt good—I felt damned good.

At the top of the ridge we stopped.

"Better let the horses blow a bit," Miller said. "Always a good idea to let 'em settle into it easy." He seemed to have gotten his temper back.

"Do we have quite a bit farther to go?" Sloane asked, breathing deeply. He looked pretty rough. I guessed that he was feeling the lack of sleep.

"We're just gettin' started," Miller said. "We'll cut on up across that saddleback there and then down into the next valley. We stay to the valley a piece and then go up to the top of the other ridge. Then on into the next hollow. 'Bout another twelve miles or so."

Sloane shook his head and took another deep breath. "I think I've got this damned belt too tight," he said. He opened the parka, undid his gun belt, looped it a couple times around the saddle horn and buckled it. He eased off on his pants belt a couple notches. "That's better," he said.

"I told you your beer-drinkin' habit would catch up to you someday, Calvin," Jack said laughing.

"Doe!" Miller said suddenly, pointing up the ridge at a deer that had stopped about a quarter of a mile away and was watching us nervously.

Sloane pulled a pair of small binoculars out of his coat pocket and glassed the ridge. "Where?" he demanded.

"See that big pine off to the left of that patch of gray rock?"

"Back in the shade a bit," I said.

"I don't—oh, yeah, now I see her."

We watched the doe step delicately on over the ridge and go down into the brush on the other side.

"There's a big game trail up there," Miller said. "I followed it down last winter during the big snow. It was the only place I could be sure of the footing."

"On horseback?" Stan asked.

"I was leadin' 'im," Miller said. "He'd gone lame on me up the ridge a ways. I had to hunker down under a ledge for two days till the snow eased up."

Stan shook his head. "That would scare me into convulsions," he admitted. "Did you ever think you weren't going to make it?"

"Oh, it give me a few nervous minutes," Miller said. A stray gust of wind ruffled that white mustache of his. He squinted up the ridge, his face more like rock than ever.

McKlearey came up. He'd been hanging back, riding about halfway between the rest of us and Clint, who was a ways back with the packhorses. Maybe he was ashamed of himself because Miller'd had to speak to him about running the horse. He reined in a little way from the rest of us and sat waiting, watching us and rubbing at his bandaged hand.

"It's good country up here," Miller was saying. "Ain't nobody around, and things are nice and simple. Air's clean, and a man can see a ways. Good country."

I reached out and scratched Ned's ears. He seemed to like it. My eyes were a little sandy from lack of sleep, but Miller was right—you could see a ways up here—a long ways.

17

ABOUT three thirty that afternoon we crossed the second ridge and dropped down into a little basin on the far side. There were several small springs in the bottom, all feeding into a little creek that had been dammed a couple times by beavers. There were several old corrals down there—poles lashed to trees with baling wire—and a half dozen or so tent frames back under the trees. You wouldn't have expected to find a place like this up on the mountainside.

"Old sheep camp," Miller said as we rode down into the basin. "Herders are all down now, so I figured it'd be about right."

"Looks good," Jack said.

"Got water, shelter, and firewood—and the corrals, of course," Miller said. "And the deer huntin' up on that ridge is about as good as any you'll find." He nodded to a ridge that swelled on up out of the scrubby timber into the open meadows between us and the rockfalls just below the snow line.

We reined up in the camp area and climbed down off the horses. My legs ached, and I was a little unsteady on my feet. We tied our horses to the top rail on one of the corrals and walked around a bit, looking it over.

The six tent frames were in a kind of semicircle at the edge of the trees, facing a large stone fire pit and looking out over the grassy floor of the basin and the largest of the beaver ponds out in the middle. Out beyond the pond, the draw rose sharply in a series of steeply slanted meadows. Directly overhead, almost as if it were leaning over the little basin, the bulky white mass of Glacier Peak rose ponderously, so huge as to be almost unbelievable.

There was a rocked-up spring behind the last tent frame, a sandy-bottomed pocket of icy water about two feet deep and perhaps three feet across. The outflow trickled off along the edge of the trees toward the horse corrals at the lower end of the camp.

None of the trees in the little grove were much more than fifteen feet tall, and they were brushy—spruce mostly. We were within a quarter of a mile of the timberline. There were a lot of low shrubs—heather, Miller said—lying in under the trees, and moss in the open spaces. I noticed a lot of sticks and downed trees lying around.

"Beaver," Miller said. "Greatest firewood collectors around."

McKlearey rode on in and climbed down off his horse. He still kept off to himself.

"Clint'll be along in a few minutes," Miller said. "Let's get a fire goin' so we can have some coffee."

We all moved around picking up firewood, and Miller scraped the debris out of the fire pit. The wood was bone dry, and it only took a few minutes for a good blaze to get started.

Then Clint came in with the pack-string, and we started to unpack. The two-gallon coffee pot and a big iron grill that looked like a chunk of sidewalk grating were the first things to come off. Clint filled the pot from the spring behind the tent frames while Miller piled several big rocks in close to the fire to set the grill on.

"A man can cook with just a fire if he's of a mind," he said, "but this makes things a whole lot simpler." He set the grill in place while Clint dumped several fistfuls of grounds into the water in the pot.

"Don't you use the basket?" Stan asked.

"Lost it a couple years ago," Clint said. "Don't do no good up this high anyway. Water boils at about a hundred and seventy up here. You gotta get the grounds down close to the fire and kinda fry the juice out. Gives you somethin' to chew on in your coffee with them grounds floatin' loose, but that never hurt nobody."

He rummaged around in one of the packs and came up with a sack of salt and dumped a couple pinches in. Then he did something that still makes my hair stand on end. He fished out a dozen eggs, took one and cracked it neatly on a rock. Then he drank it, right out of the shell. I heard Sloane gag slightly. Clint paid no attention to us but crumbled the shell in his fist and dropped it in the pot. Then he clamped on the lid and put the pot down on the grill over the fire.

"I've heard of the salt before, Clint," I said when my stomach settled back down, "but why the eggshell?"

"Damn if I know," he said. "Only thing is, I never tasted coffee fit to drink without it had some eggshell in it."

I didn't ask him why he'd drunk the raw egg. I was pretty sure I didn't want to know.

"We'll have some jerky and cold biscuits with our coffee," Miller said. "That'll tide us till we get camp set up and Clint can fix a real meal."

We all sat around the fire on logs and stumps waiting for the coffee to boil. It boiled over, hissing into the fire with a pungent smell, three times. Each time Clint doused cold water into the pot and let it boil again. Then, the fourth time, he decided it was ready to drink. I'll have to admit that it was damned good coffee. The strips of beef-jerky chewed a bit like old harness leather, but they were good, too, and the cold biscuits with honey set things off just right. I don't think I'd realized just how hungry I was.

Miller brushed the crumbs out of his mustache and filled his coffee mug again. "First thing is to check out the corrals," he said. "We'll need two good ones anyway—that way we won't be stirrin' up the pack animals ever'time we want a saddle horse. Way we'll do it is this: Go around those nearest two corrals and yank real hard on ever' place that's wired. Any place that comes loose, we'll rewire. Balin' wire is looped around that dead tree by the spring. Soon as we get that done, we can unsaddle the stock and turn 'em loose in the corrals. We brought some oats for 'em, but we'll have to picket 'em out to graze in the daytime while you men are up on the ridge. After we get the horses tended to, we'll set up the tents."

"Couldn't some of us start on the tents while the others work on the corrals?" Sloane asked, puffing slightly again.

"I suppose we could," Miller said, "but we'll do 'er the way I said before. Me'n old Clint there was in the Horse-Marines when we was pups, and the first thing we learned was to see to the stock first. Up here a man without a horse is in real trouble. She's a long damn walk back down."

"I see what you mean," Cal said, breathing heavily. He was used to making the decisions, but Miller was in charge, and now we all knew it.

It only took us about fifteen minutes to check out the corrals. Most of the lashings were still tight. Then we unsaddled the horses and turned them into the corrals, laying the saddles over the top rail of a corral we weren't using. Miller dumped oats from a burlap sack into a manger that opened onto both corrals. The horses nuzzled at him and he moved among them. He spoke to them, his voice curiously gentle as he did.

Then we all went up to the fire and had another cup of coffee. The sun was sliding down toward the tops of the peaks above us, and the air was taking on a decided chill. We stood looking at the welter of packs, sleeping bags, and rolled-up tenting that lay in a heap under the tent frames.

"Take a week to get all that squared away," Jack said.

"Hour on the outside," Clint disagreed.

First we put up the tents. They were little six-by-eight jobs that fit neatly over the frames. Miller and Clint showed us how to set them up and pull them tight. We set up five tents and then piled all the packs in the end one.

"Leave the front of that one open and tied back so's I can get in and out easy," Clint said. He showed us where to put the packs to make sure he knew where everything was. Then Miller sent us out to gather moss to pile into the rectangular log bed frames on the ground inside the tents.

"Next to feathers, that's about the softest bed you're gonna find."

"Right now, I could sleep on rocks," I told him.

"No point in that unless you have to." He grinned.

It really took a surprisingly short period of time to set up

camp. Miller and Clint had it all down pat, and McKlearey
was a damned good field soldier. He seemed to be everywhere,
checking tent ropes, ditching around the tents, cleaning dead
leaves out of the spring. His cut hand didn't seem to bother him,
but the bandage was getting pretty used-looking. Miller took to
calling him "Sarge," and Lou responded with "Cap," something
the rest of us didn't have guts enough to try yet. Maybe it was
that they'd both been in the Marines. Lou seemed to be coming
around. He even gave Stan some friendly advice about his bedding, pointing out that the sticks Stan had gathered with the moss
he put in his bed frame might be just a touch lumpy.

Sloane grinned at us all as we hauled in our third load of
moss and began to blow up an air mattress.

"You goddamn candy-ass," Jack said.

"Brains," Sloane said, tapping his forehead. "This ol' massa
ain't *about* to sleep on no col', col' groun'." He went on
blowing into the mattress. He was sitting on the ground near
the fire, and his face kept getting redder and redder. He really
didn't seem to be making much headway with the mattress.
Then he got a funny look on his face and sort of sagged over
sideways until he was lying facedown in the dirt.

"Christ, Sloane!" Jack said sharply. We all jumped to get
him up again.

"Leave 'im be!" Miller barked. He stepped in and rolled
Sloane over onto his back. He felt Sloane's pulse in his throat
and then pulled over a chunk of log to put the big man's feet
up on.

"Altitude," he said shortly. He looked around at us. "His
heart OK?"

"He's never had any trouble I know of," Jack said, "and
I've known him for years."

"That's a break. Get some whiskey."

We all dove for our sacks, but Lou beat all of us. He was
already out. Miller nodded approvingly. He and McKlearey
began working on Sloane, and soon they had him awake.

"Son of a bitch!" Cal said thickly. "That's the first time
that's ever happened."

"Better take 'er easy for a bit," Miller said. "Takes some
men a while to get adjusted to it. You come from sea level to
better'n eight thousand feet in less'n a day."

"I just couldn't seem to get my breath," Cal said.

I picked up his air mattress and blew it up for him. Toward
the end I got a little woozy, too.

"Easy, boy," Clint growled. "We don't need two down."

"Sloane, you dumb shit," Jack said, "why didn't you bring a bicycle pump? You like to scared the piss outa me."

Sloane grinned weakly. "I figured as windy as this bunch is, I wouldn't have any trouble gettin' enough hot air to pump up one little old air mattress."

"Are you sure you're all right?" Stan asked.

"I'll be OK," Cal said. "Just a little soft is all."

"If I was carryin' as much beer as you are," Jack said, "I'd be pooped, too."

"For God's sake, don't die on us," Lou said. "You still owe me three days' pay."

"You're all heart, McKlearey," I said.

He grinned at me. It suddenly occurred to me that he could be a likable son of a bitch when he wanted to be.

We eased Cal onto his air mattress and then stood around watching him breathe.

"We better get to work on the firewood, men," Miller said. "Ol' Sarge here can watch the Big Man." He gathered up the lead-ropes we'd taken off the packhorses. "Slim," he said to Jack, "you and the Professor and the Kid there take these two axes and that bucksaw and go down into that grove of spruce below the corrals. Bust the stuff up into four-or-five-foot lengths and bundle it up with these. Then haul 'em out in the open. We'll drag 'em in with a saddle horse." I guess that was his way. Miller seldom used our names. It was "Sarge" or "Slim" or "Big Man" or "Professor" or "the Kid." I suppose I should have resented that last one, but I didn't.

The three of us grabbed up the tools and headed off down into the spruce grove.

"You think Cal's going to be OK?" I asked Jack.

"Oh, he'll snap out of it." Jack said. "Sloane's a tough bastard."

"I didn't much like the way his eyes rolled back when he passed out," Stan said.

"Did look a little spooky, didn't it?" Jack said. "But don't worry. Soon as he gets his wind back, Sloane'll run the ass off the whole bunch of us."

We spread out, knocking off dead limbs and dragging downed timber out into the open. We started to bundle the stuff up, tying it with the lead-ropes.

"Say, Dan," Stan said after a while, "give me a hand here with that ax."

I went over to where he was working on a pile of dead limbs.

"It'll take me all night with this saw," he said.

I grunted and started knocking limbs off. I could hear Jack chopping away back in the brush.

"It's beautiful up here, isn't it?" Stan said when I stopped to take a breather. I looked around. The sun had just slid down behind the peaks, and deep blue shadows seemed to be rising out of the ground.

"Good country," I said, echoing Miller.

"I wish Monica could see it," he said, zipping up that bright orange jacket. "Maybe she'd understand then."

I sat down and lit a cigarette. "She gave you a pretty rough time about it, didn't she?"

"It wasn't pleasant," he said. "You have to understand Monica though. She's an only child, and her parents were in their forties when she was born. I guess they spoiled her—you know how that could happen under the circumstances. She's always been a strong-willed girl, and nobody's ever done anything she didn't want them to before."

"She's got to learn sometime," I said.

"I've tried to protect her," he went on. "I know she's not much of a wife really. She's spoiled and willful and sometimes spiteful—but that's not her fault, really, is it? When you consider how she was raised?"

"I can see how it could happen," I said.

"But this trip got to be such an issue," he said, "that I just *had* to do it. I couldn't let it go any longer."

"You've got to draw the line someplace, Stan."

"Exactly," he said. "She just had to realize that I was important, too." He was rubbing his hands together, staring at the ground. "I know she'd do anything to get her own way, and I'm just afraid she might have done something stupid."

"Oh?" I got very careful again. Damn it, I hate this walking on eggshells all the time!

"Some of the things McKlearey's been saying the last few days—I don't know."

"I wouldn't pay too much attention to McKlearey," I said.

"If I thought there was anything—I'd kill him—I swear it. So help me God, I'd kill him." He meant it. I knew he meant it. Stan didn't say things like that. His hands were clenched tightly into fists, and he was still staring down at the ground. I knew that one wrong word here would blow the whole thing.

"McKlearey and Monica? Get serious. She wouldn't touch that crude bastard with a ten-foot pole. McKlearey?" I laughed as hard as I could. It may have sounded a little forced, but I had to get him backed off it. It wouldn't take too much for his mind to start ticking off the little series of items as Clydine had done in her little breakdown of the "Hubby-Wifey-Creepy-Jarhead" caper. Once he did, somebody was liable to get killed.

Stan looked off into the distance, not saying anything. I don't think I'd been very convincing. Then Jack came up, dragging a big bundle of limbs.

"Hey, you guys," he said, puffing hard, "I hit a bonanza back in there. I got enough wood to last a month, but I'm gonna need help gettin' it out."

"Sure, buddy," I said with a false heartiness. "Come on, Stan, let's give him a hand." I hoped to get Stan's mind off what he was thinking.

We spent the next half hour dragging piles of wood out from under the trees. The light faded more and more, and it was almost dark when Miller rode down to where we were working.

"I got them other piles you left farther up the line," he said. "Looks like you got into a pretty good batch here."

"There's plenty more back in there," Jack said, "but it's gettin' too goddamn dark to be climbin' over all that stuff."

"We can haul out some more tomorrow," Miller said. "This'll last a while."

He had a rope knotted around his saddle horn with a long end trailing on each side of the horse. We lashed several bundles of the limbs to each end of the rope and followed his horse back toward the campfire and the greenish glow of the Coleman lantern hanging from a tree limb in front of the storage tent. The grass and moss felt springy underfoot, the air was sharp, and the stars had started to come out.

I think we'd all figured that we'd be able to just sit around the fire now that it was dark, but Miller kept us busy. McKlearey was just finishing up a table. It was the damnedest thing I'd ever seen—crossed legs, like a picnic table and a top of five-foot poles laid side by side. The whole thing was lashed together with baling wire. At first glance it looked rickety as hell, but Lou had buried about two feet of the bottom of each leg in the ground. It was solid as a rock.

"Hey, Professor," Lou said to Stan as we came into camp, "you want to bring that bucksaw over here and square off the ends of this thing?" Lou had immediately picked up Miller's nicknames. Stan gritted his teeth a little, but he did as Lou asked.

"Damn!" Clint said, grinning, "this'll make things as easy as workin' in the kitchen back at the ranch." He had pots and pans spread out on the table even before Stan had finished sawing the ends square.

Miller put Jack and me to work chopping the limbs we'd hauled in into foot-and-a-half lengths and piling them up along one side of the storage tent.

"Latrine's over there, men," Lou said importantly, coming up to us and pointing to a trail leading off into the trees. "I dug a slit-trench and put up a kind of a stool." He was getting a kick out of all of this.

"How's Sloane?" Jack asked him.

"Better, better," McKlearey said. "He'll be fine by morning. It was just blowin' up that goddamn air mattress that laid him out."

Jack grunted and went back to chopping wood. We kept at it for about another half hour, and my stomach was starting to talk to me pretty loud.

"Chow," Clint hollered, and we all homed in on the fire and the food.

"Plates and silverware there on the table," Clint said. "Grab 'em and line up."

We had venison steaks from Miller's freezer at the ranch, pork and beans and corn on the cob.

"Better enjoy that corn, men," Clint said. "That's all I brought. I figured we could spread out a little, first night out."

We took our plates back to the logs and stumps on the far side of the fire and began to eat. Sloane was up and about now and seemed to be a little better.

"Damn good," Jack said with his mouth full.

"Yeah, man," Lou said, shoveling food into his mouth.

It took me a little while to get the hang of holding the plate on my knees, but as soon as I got the idea that there was nothing wrong with picking up a steak in my fingers, I had it whipped.

After we finished eating and had cleaned up the dishes, we finally got a chance to sit down and relax. We all had a drink— whiskey and that icy-cold springwater—and sat, staring into the fire.

"Sure is quiet up here," Jack said finally. He'd be the one to notice that.

"Long ways from the roads," Miller said.

We sat quietly again.

Then we heard the horses snort and start to stir around, and a few minutes later a kind of grumbling, muttering chatter and a funny sort of dragging noise came from the woods.

"What's that?" Stan demanded nervously.

"Damn porkypine," Clint said. "Probably comin' over to see what we're up to."

McKlearey stood up, his eyes and teeth glowing sort of red in the reflected light of the fire. He pulled out his pistol.

"What you figgerin' on Sarge?" Miller asked, his voice a little sharp.

"I'll go kill 'im," McKlearey said. "Don't want 'im gettin' into the goddamn chow, do we?"

"No need to do that," Miller said. "He ain't gonna come in here while we're around. Long as we don't figure on eatin' 'im, there's no point in killin' 'im. I'm pretty sure the woods is big enough for us and one porky, more or less." He looked steadily at McKlearey until Lou began to get a little embarrassed.

"Anything you say, Cap," he said finally, holstering the pistol and sitting back down.

"Knew a feller sat on a porky once—" Clint chuckled suddenly.

"No kiddin'?" Jack laughed.

"Never did it again," Clint said. "Matter of fact, he didn't sit on *nothin'* for about three weeks afterward."

"How did he manage to sit on a porcupine?" Stan asked, amused.

"Well sir, me'n him'd been huntin', see," Clint started, "just kinda pokin' through the woods, havin' a little look over the top of the next ridge, like a feller will, and along about ten or so we got tuckered. We found what looked to be a couple old mossy stumps and just set down on 'em. Now the one *I* set on was a real stump, but *his* stump wasn't no stump—it was a big ol' boar porky—"

The story went on, and then there were others. The fire burned lower, popping once in a while as it settled into bright red coals.

McKlearey had several more drinks; but the rest of us had hung it up after the first one.

"I'd go a little easy on that, if it was me, Sarge," Miller said finally, after McKlearey had made his fourth trip back to the spring for cold water. "It'll have to last you the whole time. It's a pretty fair hike back to the liquor store."

We all laughed at that.

"Sure thing, Cap," McKlearey said agreeably and put his bottle away.

"Well," Sloane said finally, "I don't know about the rest of you mighty hunters, but I'm about ready to tap out. Last night was a little shallow on sleep." He was looking a lot better now but tired. I think we all were.

"Might not be a bad idea if we was all to turn in," Miller said. "Not really a whole lot to do in camp after dark, and we might as well get used to rollin' out before daybreak."

We got up, feeling the stiffness already settling in our over-worked muscles. We all said good night and went off to our tents. Miller and Clint were in the one right by the storage tent, Sloane and Stan in the next one, then Jack and I, and finally, in the farthest one up the line, McKlearey in one by himself— it just worked out that way.

Jack and I stripped down to our underwear and hurriedly crawled into our sleeping bags. It was damned chilly in the tent. I fumbled around and got out my flashlight and put it on the ground beside the gun belt near the top of my bed.

"You suppose we oughta close the flap?" he asked after a few minutes.

"Let's see how it works out leaving it open," I said. I was looking out the front of the tent at the dying fire.

"Well"—he chuckled—"I sure wouldn't want to roll over on that porky."

"I don't think that tent-flap would really stop him," I said.

"Probably not," he agreed. "Man, I'm tired. I feel like I've been up for a week."

"You and me both, buddy," I said.

"It's great up here, huh?"

"The greatest."

There was a long silence. The fire popped once.

"Good night, Danny," he said drowsily.

"Night, Jack," I said.

I lay awake staring at the fire, thinking the long thoughts a man can think alone at night when there are no noises to distract him. Once again I wished that somehow my little Bolshevik could be here to see all of this. Maybe then she'd understand. For some reason it was important to me that she did.

I guess I must have drifted off to sleep, because the fire

was completely out when the first scream brought me up fighting.

"What the goddamn hell?" Jack said.

There was another scream. It was a man—right in camp.

I grabbed up the flashlight in one hand and the .45 in the other. I was out the front of the tent when the next scream came. I stubbed my toe on a rock and swore. I could see heads popping out of all the other tents except one. The screams were coming from McKlearey's tent.

I whipped open the front flap of his tent and put the beam of the flash full on him. "Lou! What the hell is it?"

He rolled over quickly and came up, that damned .38 in his right hand. *Son of a bitch,* he moved fast! "Who's there?" he barked.

"Easy, man," I said. "It's me—Dan."

"Danny? What's up?"

"That's what I just asked *you.* You were yelling like somebody was castrating you with a dull knife."

"Oh," he said, rubbing at his face and lowering his gun, "musta been a nightmare."

"What's wrong?" I heard Miller's voice call.

I pulled my head out of the tent. "It's OK," I called back. "Lou just had a nightmare, that's all. He's OK." I stuck my head back in the tent. "You *are* OK, aren't you, Lou?"

His face looked awful. He rubbed his bandaged hand across it again, and his hand was shaking badly. He tucked the gun back under his rolled-up clothes. "Keep the light here a minute, OK?" he said. He rummaged around in his sack and came out with a bottle. He took a long pull at it. I suddenly realized that I was standing there with that silly .45 pointed right at him. It had just kind of automatically followed the light. I lowered it carefully.

"Want one?" he asked, holding out the bottle toward me.

"No thanks. You OK now?"

"Yeah," he said, "just a nightmare. Happens to a lot of guys."

"Sure."

"All the time. Lotsa guys have 'em."

"Sure, Lou."

"That's true, isn't it, Danny?" he said, his voice jittery as if he were shivering. "A lot of guys have nightmares don't they?"

"Hell," I said, "I even have some myself." That seemed to help him.

"Hey, man," I said, "I'm about to freeze my ass off. If you're OK, I'm going back to my nice warm sack."

"Sure, man," he said. "I'm fine now. 'Night, Danny."

"Good night, Lou."

"Oh, hey, man?"

"Yeah?"

"Thanks for comin' in with the light."

"Sure, Lou."

I closed up his tent and hustled back to my sleeping bag. Damn, it was cold out there!

18

WHEN the gun went off I think we all came up in panic. After the screaming in the middle of the night, I for one thought McKlearey had been having another nightmare and had unloaded on whatever it was that was haunting him. It was morning or at least starting to get light outside. I could see Miller standing calmly by the fire with a coffee cup in his hand. He didn't look particularly excited.

"What's up?" I heard Sloane call. "Who's shootin'?"

"Clint," Miller said. "He took a little poke out this mornin' to see if he couldn't scare up some camp-meat. Sounds like he found what he wanted."

"Jesus!" Jack exclaimed. "Sounded like he was right in camp."

"No, he's back down the trail about a quarter mile or so," Miller said.

I jerked on my pants and boots, wincing slightly at their clamminess, grabbed up the rest of my clothes, and hustled on out to the warmth of the fire. I stood shivering in my T-shirt for a few minutes, staring back along the trail that poked back into the still-dark woods.

"Hey, Cap," Clint's voice called in from out there.

"Yeah?" Miller didn't raise his voice too much.

"I got one. Send somebody out with a packhorse and a knife. I clean forgot mine."

"Right, Clint," Miller looked across the fire at me. "You want to go?" he asked.

"Sure." I said. "Let me finish getting dressed." I hauled on my shirt and sat down to lace up the boots.

"No big rush." He grinned at me. "That deer ain't goin' noplace. Ol' Clint don't miss very often. Have yourself a cup of coffee whilst I go throw a packsaddle on one of the horses." He raised his voice again. "Be a few minutes, Clint."

"OK, Cap," Clint's voice came back. "Better send along a shovel, too."

"Right." Miller went off toward the corral, and I poured myself a cup of coffee and finished lacing up the boots. I went back into the tent and picked up my gun belt.

Jack was struggling into his plaid shirt, trying to stay in the sleeping bag as much as possible at the same time. "You goin' out there?" he asked me.

I nodded, buckling on the belt. "Clint wants a horse and a knife," I said. I pulled the smaller of the pair of German knives from the double sheath that hung on the left side of the gun belt and tested the edge with my thumb. It seemed OK. I grabbed my jacket and hat and went on back through the pale light to the fire.

"I'll be along in a little bit," Jack called after me.

There was a bucket of water on the table, and I scooped some out with my hands and doused it in my face. The shock was sharp, and I came up gasping. I raked the hair back out of my face with my fingers and stuffed my hat on. Still shivering, I drank the cup of coffee.

There was a kind of mist or cloud hanging up on the side of the mountain, blotting out the top. I waded down toward the corral through the gray-wet grass. I could see Miller's dark track through it and Clint's angling off toward the woods.

"You bring a knife?" Miller asked, handing me the lead-rope to the sleepy-looking packhorse he'd saddled.

I nodded. Somehow, it didn't seem right to talk too much.

"He's prob'ly 'bout four-five hundred yards down that trail," he said, pointing. "When you get out there a ways, sing out, and he'll talk you in."

"Right."

I led the horse on into the woods. It was still pretty dark

back in there, the silvery light filtering down through the thick spruce limbs. The horse walked very close to me—maybe they get nervous about things, too.

"Clint?" I called after about five minutes.

"Over here," his voice came. "That you, Dan?"

"Yeah." I followed his voice.

"I kinda figgered it might be you," he said. "You bring a knife and a shovel?"

"Yeah," I said. Then I saw him sitting on a log, smoking a cigarette. His .30-30 was leaning against the tree behind him.

"She's right over there," he said, pointing. He got up, and we walked back farther into the dim woods.

The deer, a young mule doe, had fallen on its side in a clump of heather, its sticklike legs protruding awkwardly. A dead deer always looks tiny somehow, not much bigger than a dog. They look big when they're up and moving, but after you shoot them, they seem to kind of shrink in on themselves. A doe looks even smaller, maybe because there aren't any horns."

"This one ought to last us," Clint said. "Give me a hand and we'll drag 'er out in the open."

We each grabbed a hind leg and pulled the deer out of the heather-bed. Her front legs flopped limply and her large-eared head wobbled back and forth as it slid over the branches of the low-lying shrub. I didn't see any blood.

"Ever gutted many deer?" he asked me.

"One," I said. "I didn't do a very good job of it."

"Well, now," he said, "I'll show you how it's done. Hold that leg up and gimme your knife."

I handed him the smaller knife and held the hind leg up for him.

"Now, you start here—" He made a slit through the deer's white belly-fur and continued it back toward the tail, just cutting through the skin.

"Idea is to keep as much hair out of the meat as you can," he told me.

I watched as he sliced the skin from chin to tail.

"You going to cut her throat?" I asked him. "I thought you were supposed to do that."

"Not much point," he said. "We'll have the head off in about five minutes. Carcass'll bleed out good enough from that, I expect." He pushed the point of the knife through the belly-muscles with a hollow, ripping sound, and started to saw up through the ribs.

"Here," I said, handing him the big knife, "use this one."

He grunted, laying the smaller knife aside. He hefted the big one. "Quite a frog-sticker," he said, looking at the ten-inch blade. He bent back over the deer.

I tried not to look too closely at the way the sliced muscles twitched and quivered.

"Hey, where are you guys?" Jack called from back at the trail.

"Over here," I said.

Clint took the big knife and chopped through the pelvis bone, making a sound a lot like somebody chopping wet wood.

"Ooops," Jack said as he came up on us. "I'll just wait till you guys finish up there."

"Squeamish?" Clint asked, his arm sunk up to the elbow inside the deer's body cavity.

"Not really," Jack said, "but—" He shrugged and went back to where McKlearey was coming through the trees. The two of them stood back there, watching.

"Now then," Clint told me, "you just grab hold of the windpipe here and kind of use it as a handle to pull everything right out." He grabbed the severed windpipe and slowly pulled out and down, spilling out the deer's steaming internal organs. Once they were clear of the carcass, he dragged them several feet away and dumped them in a heap. He came back and chopped away the lower half of each leg, the big blade grating sickeningly in the joints.

"No sense haulin' anything back we can't use." he said. Then he turned to the head.

"Where'd you hit her?" I asked, looking into the body cavity. "I don't see any hole."

"Right here," he said, probing a finger into the fur just under the base of the skull.

"Good shot," I said. "What was the range?"

"'Bout forty—maybe fifty yards. If you're quiet you can get pretty close."

He made a slice around the neck with the big knife about where he'd had his finger and then cut the head away. Bone fragments and small gleaming pieces of copper from his bullet were very bright against the dark meat.

"Let's dump 'er out," he said.

We picked up the surprisingly heavy carcass and turned it over to drain.

"Hey, Slim," Clint called to Jack, "why don't you and the

Sarge there get that shovel off the packhorse and dig a hole so's we can bury the guts?"

"Sure," Jack said, going over to the drowsing horse.

"Ordinarily, I'd leave 'em for the coyotes and bobcats," Clint said, "but then I got to thinkin' that maybe we wouldn't want 'em comin' in this close to camp." He went to the steaming gut-pile and cut the liver free of the other organs. "Breakfast," he said shortly. He fished a plastic bag out of his coat pocket and slid the dripping liver inside.

"This deep enough?" McKlearey asked, pointing at their hole. I noticed that he had on a fresh bandage.

"Yeah, that'll do it," Clint answered. "Just kick them guts and hooves and the head in and cover 'em up. We'll pile rocks on top when you're done."

I looked away. It hadn't bothered me so far, but the deer's eyes were still open, and I didn't want to see them kicking dirt in them.

"That's got it," Jack said.

Clint gave me back my knives. "Pretty good set," he said. "Where'd you come by it?"

"In Germany," I said. "Got it when I was in the Army."

"Damn good steel," he said. "Holds the edge real good."

"They're a bitch to sharpen." I grinned at him. Actually, Clydine had sharpened them for me. I don't know where she'd learned how, but she sure could put an edge on a knife.

We piled rocks on the buried remains of the deer, and then the three of us lifted the carcass onto the pack-frame saddle while Clint held the horse's head to keep him from shying at the blood-smell.

Clint picked up his rifle, and we went on back to camp.

"Dry doe," Clint told Miller when we got back to the corral. "Picked 'er up on that little game trail back in there a ways."

"Looks like she'll last us," Miller said.

"Should. I'll skin 'er out after breakfast when you fellers go up on the ridge."

They put a short, heavy stick through the hocks of the hind legs and hung the carcass to a tree limb a ways behind camp.

After they'd unsaddled the packhorse, we all walked back on up to the fire. Clint washed up and started hustling around the cook table McKlearey'd built for him.

"First blood," Sloane said in the kind of gaspy voice he'd developed since we'd gotten up into the high country.

"This one don't really count." Miller chuckled.

"At least there are deer around," Stan said.

"Oh, there's plenty of deer up here, all right," Miller said.

I got the enameled washbasin and filled it with warm water from the big pot on the fire and did a little better job of washing up than I'd managed earlier. Then Clint ran us all away from the fire because we were in his way.

I walked on down to the edge of the beaver pond and looked out over the clear water. It was about four or five feet deep out in the middle, and the bottom was thinly sprinkled with matchstick-sized white twigs. I saw a flicker under the surface about ten feet out and saw a good-sized trout swim slowly past, his angry-looking eye glaring at me with cold suspicion.

"Hey, man, fish in there, huh?" It was McKlearey. I could smell the whiskey on him. Christ Almighty! The sun wasn't even up yet!

"Yeah," I said. "Wonder if anybody thought to bring any gear."

"Doubt it like hell," he said, jamming his hands deeper into his field-jacket pockets.

I squatted down by the water and washed off my knives. The edges were still OK, but I thought I'd touch them up a little that afternoon.

"Sun's comin' up," Lou said.

I looked up. The very tip of the looming, blue-white peak above us was turning bright pink. As I watched, the pink line crept slowly down, more and more of the mountain catching fire. The blue-white was darkly shadowed now by comparison.

"Nice, huh?" Lou said. His face was ruddy from the reflected glow off the snow above us, kind of etched out sharply against the dark trees behind him. "I can think of times when I'd have give my left nut for just one look at snow. It never melts up there. Did you know that? It's always there—summer and winter—always up there. I used to think about that a lot when I was on the Delta. It's always up there. Kinda gives a guy somethin' to hang on to." He snorted with laughter. "Bet it's colder'n a bitch up there," he said.

"If it got too cold you could always think about the Delta, I guess," I said.

"No," he said, still staring at the mountain. "I never think about the Delta. Other places, yeah, but never the Delta."

I nodded. "How's the hand?" I pointed at the bandage.

"Little sore," he said. "It'll be OK."

"Chow!" Clint hollered from camp.

Lou and I walked on back up toward the tents. Maybe there was more to him than I'd realized.

Clint had fried up a bunch of bacon and then had simmered onion slices in the hot grease and had fried up thin strips of fresh deer liver. There were hot biscuits and more coffee. The little old fart could sure whip up a helluva meal on short notice. We fell on the food like a pack of wolves, and for about ten minutes all you could hear was the sound of eating. The altitude does that to you.

After we'd eaten and were lazing over a last cup of coffee, watching the edge of the sunlight creep down the mountain toward us, Miller cleared his throat.

"Soon as you men get your breakfast settled, we'll saddle up and take a little ride on up the ridge there. I want to show you the stands you'll be usin'. You'll need to see 'em in the daylight 'cause it'll still be dark yet when you get up there tomorrow. Then, too, it'll give us a chance to scout around some."

"You think we'll see any deer?" Stan asked.

"We sure should," Miller said. "I've seen five cross that ridge since we set down to breakfast."

We all turned and looked sharply up at the ridge.

"None up there right now though," he said. "Your bucks'll all be up there. Now some of you men may've hunted mule deer before, and some of you've hunted white-tail. These are all mulies up here. They're bigger'n white-tail and they look and act a whole lot different. A mulie's got big ears—that's how he gets his name—and he can hear a pin drop at a half a mile. He's easy to hunt 'cause you can count on him to do two things—run uphill and stop just before he goes over the ridge. He'll always run uphill when he's been spooked—unless, of course, he's just been shot. Then he'll go downhill.

"A white-tail runs kind of flat out, like a horse or a dog, and if you're a fair shot you can hit him on the run. Your mulie, on the other hand, bounces like a damn jackrabbit, and you can't tell from one jump to the next which way he's goin'. Looks funnier'n hell, but it makes him damn hard to hit on the run. You shoot over 'im or under 'im ever' time.

"That's why it's good to know that he's gonna stop. As soon as he gets a ways away from you—and above you—he'll stop and look back to see what you're doin'. Some people say they're curious, and some say they're dumb, but it's just somethin' he'll always do. Wait for it, and you're likely to get a clear, standin' shot."

"What's the range likely to be?" Sloane gasped.

"Anywhere from one hundred to three hundred yards," Miller said, looking closely at Cal. "Much out past that and I wouldn't shoot, if it was me. Too much chance of a gut shot or havin' the deer drop into one of these ravines. He does that and he'll likely bounce and roll for about a mile. Won't be much left when he stops."

He stopped and looked around. It was the longest speech I ever heard him make.

"Let's go get the horses," he said, almost as if he were ashamed of himself for talking so much.

We trooped on down to the corral, and he made each man saddle his own horse. "Might as well learn how to do it now as later," he said.

I approached that knotheaded gray horse of mine with a great deal of caution. He didn't seem particularly tense this morning, but I wasn't going to take any chances with him. I got him saddled and bridled and led him out of the corral. The others all stopped to watch.

"Well, buddy," I said to him as firmly as I could, "how do you want to play it this morning?"

He turned his head and looked inquiringly at me, his long gray face a mask of equine innocence.

"You lyin' son of a bitch," I muttered. I braced myself and climbed on his back. His ears flicked.

"All right," I said grimly, "let's get it over with." I nudged him with my heels and he moved out at a gentle walk with not so much as an instant's hesitation. I walked him out into the bottom, turned him and trotted him back to the corral.

"How about that?" I called to the others. "Just like a pussy-cat."

"You got him all straightened out yesterday," Miller said. "He won't give you no more trouble."

The others mounted, and we rode off down to the lower end of the basin, crossed the creek, and started up the ridge. Clint's horse, alone in the saddle-horse corral, whinnied after us a couple times and then went over to the fence nearest the pack-horses.

I was a little stiff and sore, but it didn't take too long for that to iron itself out.

The ridge moved up in a series of steps with low brush

202   David Eddings

breaking off each side. A little way out we rode into the sunlight.

About a half mile up from camp, Miller stopped.

"This'll be the first stand," he said. "The Big Man'll be
here." It made sense. This was the lowest post, and Sloane
was having trouble with the altitude.

"You want me to wait here now?" Cal asked, disappointment
evident in his voice.

"No need of that," Millder said, "but we'd better look around
a mite so's you can get it all set in your mind. I'll be droppin'
you off by this white rock here." He pointed at a big pale
boulder. "Best place to set is right over there."

We all got off and walked on over. A natural rock platform
jutted out over the deep ravine that ran down the right-hand
side of the ridge. The other, shallower, ravine with its meadows
ran down into the basin where we were camped.

"You see that notch over on the other side?" Miller said,
pointing it out to Sloane.

"Yeah."

"That's a main game trail. They'll be comin' across that
from the next ravine. Then they'll turn and go on down to the
bottom. They'll be in sight all the way."

"How far is it to that notch?" Sloane gasped.

"'Bout a hundred and fifty yards. It's best to let 'em get all
the way to the bottom before you shoot. That way they won't
fall so far and you'll have plenty of time to look 'em over."

"OK," Sloane said.

"Don't get so interested in this trail that you ignore this
draw here that runs on down to camp though. They'll be crossin' there, too—lots of 'em. And they'll be grazin' in those
meadows."

Sloane looked it all over. "I think I've got it located," he
said, taking a deep breath.

Jack's post was on the next step up the ridge. There was a
bit more brush there, but another big game trail cut into the
ravine from the far side.

"Watch your shots over there, Slim," Miller said. "It breaks
off pretty sharp, and a deer'd get busted up pretty bad if it was
to go over that edge."

"Yeah," Jack replied, his eyes narrowing, "I can see that."

Stan was next up the hill, his post much like the two below.

McKlearey's post was down in a notch.

"You'll have to watch yourself in here, Sarge," Miller told

him. "You're right in the middle of a trail here, and you might get yourself stampeded over if they start to runnin'."

"Stomp your ass right into the ground, McKlearey." Jack laughed. "Wouldn't that be a bitch?"

"I'll hold 'em off till you guys get here." Lou grinned. "We'll ambush the little bastards."

My post was the highest on the ridge. The horses scrambled up the rocky trail from McKlearey's notch, their iron-shod hooves sliding and clattering.

"I'm puttin' the Kid up here," Miller explained, "'cause that horse he's ridin' is the biggest and strongest one in the string. This little stretch of trail can be a bitch-kitty in the dark."

"Anybody wanna trade horses?" I asked, not meaning it.

We came out on the rounded knob at the top of the trail and looked around.

"At least you'll have scenery," Jack said. He was right about that. You could literally see for a hundred miles in every direction except where the peak whitely blotted out a quarter of the sky.

We all got down and walked around, looking out at the surrounding mountains.

"Buck!" Miller said, his voice not loud but carrying to us with a sharp urgency.

The deer was above us. I counted him at five points, but that could have been off. He was a hundred and fifty yards away, but he still looked as big as a horse. He watched us, his rack flaring arrogantly above his head like a vast crown. It was probably my imagination, but his face seemed to have an expression of unspeakable contempt on it, an almost royal hauteur that made me feel about two feet tall. None of us moved or made a sound.

Slowly he turned the white patch of his rump to us, flicked his tail twice, then laid his ears back and bounded up the mountainside as if he had springs on his feet. He soared with each jump as though the grip of earth upon him was very light and he could just as easily fly, if he really wanted to.

Far up the rockslide he slowed, stopped, and looked back at us again. Then he walked off around the ridge, picking his way delicately over the rocks, his head up and his antlers carried proudly.

I still felt very small.

19

MILLER split us up then and sent us on back down the ridge by several different trails. He told us to ride slowly and keep a good sharp eye out for any really big bucks.

"Come on, Cal," I said to Sloane, "let's ease on down this way."

Miller glanced at me and nodded once. One of us was going to have to stick pretty close to Calvin from here on out.

"Sure thing," Sloane said with a heartiness that sounded hollow as all hell. He was looking pretty tough again.

We rode off slowly, and I concentrated pretty much on picking as easy a trail as I could find. The sun was well up by now, and the air up there was very clear. Every limb and rock stood out sharply, and the shadows under the bushes were very dark. I could hear the others clattering over rocks now and then above us. After about five minutes Cal called weakly to me.

"Better hold up a minute, Dan." He jumped down off his horse and lurched unsteadily off to the side of the trail. I rolled out of the saddle and caught his bridle before his horse could wander off. I tied both horses to a low bush.

He was vomiting when I got to him, kneeling beside a rock and retching like a man at the end of a three-day drunk.

"You OK?" I asked. A guy always asks such damned stupid questions at a time like that.

He nodded jerkily and then vomited again. He was at it for quite a long time. Finally he got weakly to his feet and stumbled back toward the horses.

"Jesus, Cal," I said, trying to help him.

"Don't tell the others about this," he said hoarsely, waving off my hand.

"Christ, man, you're really sick, aren't you?"

"I'll be OK," he said, hanging onto his saddle horn. "Just don't tell the others, OK?"

"If you say so," I said. "Let's sit down a bit."

"Sure," he agreed.

I led him over to a clear place and went back to get the water bag hanging on my saddle horn. When I brought it back, he drank some and washed off his face. He looked a little better, but his breathing was still very bad, and his face was pale inside the framing fur of his parka hood.

"I just can't seem to get used to it." He gasped. "God damn, I can't. It's like there was a wet blanket over my face all the time."

"You ever have trouble at high altitudes before?" I asked him.

"No more than anybody else, I don't think. Oh sure, I'd get a little woozy and I'd get winded easy, but nothing like this. Of course, I haven't been up in the mountains for five or six years now."

"It'll settle down," I said—not really believing it. "Hell, we've only been up here for a day or so."

"I sure hope so," he said. "I don't know how much more of this I can cut."

"Cal," I said after a minute or so, "if it gets bad—I mean really bad—you'll let me know, won't you? I mean, shit, none of this is worth blowing a coronary over."

"Hell," he said, "my heart's in good shape—it's my fuckin' *lungs*."

"Yeah, I know, but tell me, huh? I mean it."

He looked at me for a moment. "OK, Dan," he said finally, "if it really gets bad."

That was a helluva relief.

"Like you said, though, it'll settle down." His face had a longing on it that was awfully damned exposed.

"I've just *got* to make this one, you know?" he said. "If I don't make it this time, I don't think I ever will."

"I'm not sure I follow you," I said.

"Look, Dan," he said, "let's not kid each other. I know what I am—I'm a big fuckin' kid—that's what I am."

"Hey, man—"

"No, let's not shit each other. I wouldn't say this to any of the others. Hell, they wouldn't understand it. But you're different." He lit a cigarette and then immediately mashed it out. "I sure as shit don't need *those* things."

"I've cut way down, too," I said, wanting to change the subject.

"This whole damn trip," he went on, "it's a kid thing—for

me anyhow. At least it was when it started. It was just another
of the things I do with your brother and Carter and McKlearey
and a whole bunch of other guys—parties, booze, broads, the
whole bit—all kid stuff. I gotta do it though. You see, my
old man was fifty-five when I was born. My old lady was his
second wife. I can't ever remember him when he wasn't an
old man. I get this awful feeling when I get around old people—
like I want to crawl off and hide someplace."

"You're not alone there," I told him. "I ever tell you about
the Dan Alders' curse? With me it's old ladies on buses. Drives
me right up the wall every time."

He grinned at me briefly. He almost looked like the old Cal
again.

"So I hang around with young guys," he went on, "and I
do the stuff they do. Shit, man, I'm forty-two years old, for
Chrissake! Don't you think it's time I grew up? I own four
businesses outright, and I'm a partner in about six more. Let's
face it, I'm what they'd call a man of substance, and here I
am, boozin' and partyin' and shackin' up with cheap floozies
like that goddamn Helen. Jesus H. Christ! Claudia's ten times
the woman and about a million times the lady that pig was on
the best day she ever saw." He shook his head. "I've gotta be
outa my goddamn rabbit-ass mind!"

"We all do funny things now and then," I said, wishing he'd
change the subject.

"I don't know why the hell Claudia puts up with me," he
said. "She knows all about it, of course."

"Oh?"

"Shit yes! Do you think for one minute I could hide anything
from *her*? But she never gives me hell about it, never com-
plains. Hell, she never even mentions it. The goddamn woman's a saint, you know that?"

"She's pretty special," I agreed.

Sloane looked out over what Mike used to call the Big
Lonely.

"God, it's great up here," he said, "if only I could get my
goddamn *wind*!" He pounded his fist on his leg as if angry
with his gross body for having failed him.

"Anyway"—he picked it up again—"like I was sayin', this
started out as just another kid thing—something I was gonna
do with Jack and Carter and some of the guys, right?"

"If you say so," I said. He had me baffled now.

"Only it isn't that anymore. This is *it*, baby. This is where little Calvin grows up. This time I make it over the hump. By God, it's about time, wouldn't you say? Claudia deserves a real husband, and by God I'm gonna see that she's got one when I get back. He looked up at the sky again. "This time I'm gonna make it, I really am." Then he started coughing again, and I started worrying.

After he got straightened around with his breathing apparatus again, we got up and went back to the horses.

"You think I can make it, Dan?" he asked after I'd helped him back on his horse.

I looked at him for a minute. "You already have, Cal," I said. "That was it back there. Anything else is just going to be a souvenir to remember it by." I went over and climbed up on Ned. A guy can say some goddamn foolish things sometimes. But Cal needed it, so I said it—even though we both knew "growing up" doesn't happen like that. It takes a long time—most of your life usually.

Then we heard the other guys yelling farther up the slope. We nudged the horses over to where we could get a clear view of the ravine. We both looked up and down the opposite ridge for a minute and then we saw what they were yelling about.

It was a white deer.

He was a buck, maybe about a seven-pointer, but he wasn't as big as the five-point we'd seen earlier. His coat was a sort of cream-colored, but his antlers were very dark. He stood about a quarter of a mile away on the other ridge, his ears flickering nervously at all the shouting the others were doing. I suppose like most albinos, his eyes weren't really too good.

"Look at that!" Sloane said reverently. "Isn't that the most beautiful goddamn thing you ever saw?" He handed me his binoculars. They brought the thing up pretty close; they were damn good glasses.

The deer's eyes were a deep red, so he was a true albino. You could actually see the pink skin in places where the wind ruffled his fur back. He looked more completely defenseless than any animal I've ever seen. For some reason, when I looked at him, I thought of Clydine.

I gave the glasses back to Sloane and sat on the horse watching until the deer's nerves finally got wound too tight and he bounded off across the other ridge and out of sight.

"Isn't that something?" Cal gasped.

"Never seen one before," I said. "I've seen a lot of deer, but that's the first white one I've ever seen."

"The son of a bitch looked like a ghost, didn't he?"

"Or like Moby Dick," I said, and then I wished I hadn't said it. It was so goddamn obvious.

"Yeah. Moby Dick," Sloane said. "They got him at the end of the book, didn't they?"

"No," I said. "He got *them*—the whole damn bunch. All but Ishmael, of course."

"I never read it," Sloane admitted. "I saw the movie though—first half of it anyway. I was with this girl—"

"I'd rather you didn't mention that name to the others," I said, forgetting Stan for a moment.

"What name?"

"Moby Dick."

"Why not?"

"It's a real bad scene, man. Just say it's a superstititon or something, but don't get Jack and McKlearey started on something like that. Somebody's liable to wind up dead."

"You *are* jumpy," Sloane said. "What's got you all keyed up?"

"Man, I'll tell you, this whole damn trip is like setting up housekeeping on top of a bomb. McKlearey's been playing McKlearey-type games with a couple women we both know. If we don't keep a lid on things, Jack and Stan are going to go off in a corner and start to odd-man to see who gets to shoot the son of a bitch."

"Jesus!" Sloane said.

"Amen, brother, amen. This whole trip could turn to shit right in our faces, so let's not buy trouble by starting any Moby Dick stuff. That son of a bitch sank the whole goddamn boat, and I left my water wings at home."

"Hell," he squawked, "I can't even swim."

Of course the first thing Stan said to me when Sloane and I came trailing into camp was "Call me Ishmael," in a properly dramatic voice.

"I *only* am escaped to tell thee," I grated back at him just as hard and as sharp-pointed as I could make it, hoping to hell he'd get the point.

"What the hell are you two babblin' about?" Jack demanded.

Stan, of course, had to tell him.

We unsaddled the horses, turned them loose in the corral, and then all went on up to the fire where Clint was working on lunch.

"Man"—Jack was still carrying on about the white deer—
"wasn't that the damnedest thing you ever saw?"

"Pretty damn rare," Miller said. "Most likely a stag though."

"Stag?" Sloane asked. "I thought any buck-deer was a stag."

"Well, not really," Miller said. "A stag is kinda like a steer
with cows. Either he's been castrated or had an accident or he
just ain't got the equipment. Most of them freaks are like that—
I don't know why."

They talked about it all the way through lunch. I kept trying
to pour cold water on it, but I could see all the others visualizing
that white head over their mantelpieces or what-not. I began
right about then to hate that damned deer. I wished to hell he'd
fall off a cliff or something.

After lunch we hauled in more firewood and cleaned our
rifles. McKlearey lashed together a kind of rifle rack and put
it in the back of the supply tent. "Keep the scopes from gettin'
knocked around that way," he rasped. His bandage was dirty
again.

The sun went down early—it always would here, right up
against the backside of that peak like we were. The twilight
lasted a long time though. We had venison steak for dinner and
settled down around the fire to watch the last of the daylight
fade out of the sky.

They went back to talking about that damned white deer
again.

I'd been kind of half-assed watching McKlearey. He'd been
making a lot of trips to his tent for one reason or another, and
his eyes were getting a little unfocused. I figured he was hitting
his jug pretty hard again.

I caught Miller's eye, and I knew he'd been counting
McKlearey's trips, too. He didn't look too happy about it.

"Well, I'll sure tell you one thing," Jack was saying, "if
that big white bastard crosses *my* stand, I'll dump 'im right in
his tracks."

"You said it, buddy," McKlearey said, his voice slurring a
little. "How about you, Danny Boy?"

"I came up here to hunt," I said. "I'm not declaring war on
one single deer."

"There's lots of deer up on that mountain," Miller said.
"Lots are bigger'n that one."

"Just like the girls in Hong Kong, huh, Danny?" McKlearey
said, trying to focus his eyes on me.

"I wouldn't know, Lou," I said. "I've never been there, remember?"

"Sure you have, Danny. Me'n you made an R and R there once."

"Not me, Lou. You must have me mixed up with somebody else."

He squinted at me very closely. "Yeah," he said finally, "maybe so. I guess maybe it *was* another guy."

What the hell was *that* all about?

We kept on talking until it got completely dark, and Miller suggested that we all get to bed. I walked on down to McKlearey's slit-trench to unload some coffee. On the way back I met Clint.

"Say, Dan," he said, his voice hushed, "What's the score on old Sarge anyway? Does it seem to you he's actin' a little funny?"

"Lou? I don't know, Clint. I don't really know him all that well. Seems to me he's been acting a little funny ever since I first met him."

"Well," he said, "I know one thing for sure. He hits that bottle about as hard as any man I've ever seen. That ain't good up this high."

"He's used to it," I said.

"Maybe so, but Cap's a little worried about it. He wants this trip to go smooth, and already he's got a sick man and one that's actin' kinda funny. Don't take too much to spoil a trip for ever'body."

"I think it'll work out, Clint. Once we get to hunting, we'll be OK."

"I sure hope so," he said.

"Sure, Clint, it'll all settle down, don't worry." I wished that I could be as sure as I sounded. I walked on back up to the tent.

Jack was already in bed and about half-asleep, so I just undressed and crawled in my sleeping bag.

I lay in my sack, staring out at the fire and remembering the other deer—not the white one—and how he'd soared and bounced up the mountainside. Almost as if he could fly, if he really wanted to. For me, at least, it was going to be a good hunt.

20

"TIME to roll out." Clint's head blotted out the looming white mountain in the doorway of the tent. I was immediately awake. It's funny, in town or anyplace else, I always have a helluva time waking up. When I'm hunting though, I snap awake just like I was a different guy.

I was dressed and out to the fire while Jack was still mumbling around looking for his pants. I washed up and hunkered down by the fire waiting for the coffee to finish boiling. Slowly one by one the others joined me.

"Darker'n hell," Jack said. "What time is it, anyway?"

"Four," I said. We both spoke quietly, our voices hushed by the deep silence around us. Lou came out rubbing down the tape on a fresh bandage. I wondered why he didn't wear a glove or try to keep that hand out of the dirt.

Miller came up from the corral about the same time Stan and then Sloane came out of their tent.

"Cold," Stan said shortly, zipping up his new jacket and getting up close to the fire.

"Mornin', men," Miller said. "Coffee ready?"

"In just a minute or so, Cap," Clint said. He looked around, his battered old cowboy hat pushed back from his face. "You fellers are gonna have to step back from the fire if you want any breakfast."

We all moved obediently back away and he began slapping his pans down on the grill. "Coffee's ready," he said. "Take it over to the table there."

I carried the heavy pot to the table and started pouring coffee into the cups. Then we all stood back in the bunch in front of the tents watching Clint make breakfast.

"We'll get up there well before first light, men," Miller said. "I'll ride all the way up to the top with the Kid here, and then I'll come on back down with the horses. They'd just get restless on you and move around and spook the deer. Besides, they might run off if you happen to get off a shot today."

"It's ready," Clint said. "Come get your plates."

We lined up, and he filled our plates for us. We sat down to eat. Miller continued with his instructions. "I'll bring the horses down and put 'em out to graze in this meadow out here. I'll be back up to get you about ten or so. Isn't likely there'll be much movin' after that. We'll go out again about three thirty or four this afternoon." He bent his face to his plate and scooped in three or four mouthfuls of scrambled eggs. He stared off into the dark while he chewed, his white mustache twitching with each bite.

"I don't know as I'd shoot today," he said. "Just kinda get an idea of the size of the deer. Lots of men bust the first one they see with horns. There's a lot of deer on this mountain. A lot of big ones, so take your time."

He ate some more. By then the rest of us had finished. He looked at his watch. "I guess we'd better saddle up," he said, rising.

The rest of us followed him on down to the corral. The moon was still high over the shoulder of the peak, and it was very bright out from under the shadow of the spruces. I'd had visions of fumbling around with flashlights and lanterns while we saddled the horses, but the moonlight was bright enough to make it almost as easy as doing it in broad daylight.

After we'd saddled the horses, we led them back up to the tents and picked up our rifles.

"How about the signals?" Sloane gasped, patting the butt of his Ruger.

"Oh, yeah," Miller said. He didn't sound very enthusiastic. "How 'bout this? One shot means a down deer. Two shots for one wounded and running. Three shots if you're in trouble—hurt or sick or hangin' off a cliff by one hand. OK?"

"Sure," Sloane said. "Anything'll work as long as we all know what it is."

"You fellers better get movin' if Cap's gonna get them horses back down by shootin' time," Clint said.

We tied our rifles to the saddles and climbed on. Miller led the way, and we strung out behind him single file.

By the time we got to his stand, Cal was breathing hard. Even though the horse was doing all the work, he was puffing as if he'd climbed the hill by himself.

"You OK?" Miller asked him.

"Fine," Sloane gasped. "You gonna take the horse with you now?"

"No. Just tie him to that bush there. I'll be back down in about half an hour or so—before shootin' time anyway. You might as well go on over and get settled now though."

"Right," Cal said, grunting as he slipped off his horse.

"Good luck, Sloane," Jack said. "Try not to bust anything bigger'n a twelve-point."

"Sure," Cal grinned. Then he giggled, and I think that made us all feel better. We waved and moved on up the mountainside.

Jack tied down his horse and faded back into the shadowy bushes with a backward wave.

Stan dismounted stiffly and stood by his horse, watching us as Miller, McKlearey, and I rode on up the ridge.

It was darker than hell in McKlearey's notch. His face was nothing more than a pale blur as he reined in his horse.

"This is as far as I go," he said.

"I'll be back down in a few minutes, Sarge," Miller said.

"I'll be here, Cap. Good luck, Danny boy."

"Same to you, Lou," I answered.

Then Miller and I went slowly on up the steep trail to my post.

The moon was just slipping behind the shoulder of the mountain as we came out on the knob at the top of the ridge.

"Better let my eyes settle into the dark a bit before I start back," Miller said. "Give the horse a rest, too." We both climbed down.

I offered him a cigarette and we squatted down in the darkness, smoking.

"Clint tells me you went to college," Miller said after a while.

"Yeah," I said. "Before I went in the Army."

"Always wished I'd had the chance to go," he said. "Maybe then I wouldn't be finishin' up on a broke-down horse-ranch, scratchin' to make a livin'."

"From the way I see it," I said, "you're one of the lucky ones. You're doing something you like."

"There's that, too," he admitted. "I don't know as it all adds up to all that much though. The work's hard and the pay's pretty slim. A man always wonders if maybe he coulda done better."

"I know a lot of people who'd trade even across with you, Cap," I said.

He chuckled. "I guess there ain't much point worryin' about it at this stage."

I untied my rifle and the water bag from my saddle.

"You got ever'thing, son? All your gear, I mean?"

"Yeah," I said, "I'm all set."

He stood up. Then he scuffed his boot in the thin dirt a couple times. Finally he blurted it out. "What's eatin' on old Sarge, anyway?"

"God, Cap, I don't know. Maybe he's just having trouble reconverting to civilian life. I met him about a month ago, and he's been jumpy as hell all that time. I've about halfway got a hunch he had a pretty rough time in Vietnam—he's out on a medical. Malaria, I think."

"Mean stuff," he said. "Clint gets a touch of it now and then."

"Oh?"

"Puts him flat on his back."

"Yeah. I've heard it's no joke."

"I sure wish ol' Sarge would go a little easier on the liquor though. I can sure tell you that."

"At the rate he's going," I said, "that bottle of his won't last much longer."

"He's got more'n one," Miller said gloomily. "That sack of his clinks and gurgles like a liquor store. I wonder he had room for spare sox."

"Oh, brother," I said.

"Did you talk with the Big Man on the way down yesterday?" he asked, changing the subject.

"Yeah," I said. "He's going to let me know if he gets really bad."

"That's a real good idea. Clint can take him back on down if he gets too sick. Most men start to get their wind before this."

"I think he'll be all right now," I said.

"I sure hope so." He looked around. "Well, I guess I better be gettin' on down."

"Yeah," I said. I glanced at my watch. "About half an hour till shooting time."

"Ought to work out about right, then," he said. "Well, son, good luck."

"Thanks, Cap."

I watched him ride on off down the trail with Ned trailing behind him. Then I slung my rifle and walked on up to the top of the knob. I sat down and lit another cigarette. I'd meant to ask him if the smoke would spook off the deer, but I'd forgotten.

I unslung the rifle and started pulling cartridges for it out of my gun belt and pushing them one by one into the magazine. I eased the last one up the tube with the bolt and then pushed the bolt-handle down. I snapped on the safety and carefully laid the rifle down on a flat rock. Then I loaded the pistol and put it back in the holster. Now what the hell was I supposed to do for the next twenty-five minutes?

I sat down on the rock beside the rifle again and looked off toward the east. I could just make out the faintest hint of light along toward the horizon out there.

I remembered a time in Germany when I'd pulled the four-to-six shift on guard duty and had watched the sun slowly rise over one of those tiny little farming villages with the stone-walled, red-tile-roofed houses huddled together under a church spire. It's a good time for gettings things sorted out in your mind. I wonder how many times other guys have thought the same thing—probably every guy from along about the year one.

One thing was sure—I was a helluva long way from Germany now. I started to try to figure out what time it would be in Wertheim about now, but I lost track somewhere off the east coast. I wondered what Heidi was doing right now. I still felt bad about that. If only she hadn't been so damn trusting. No matter what I'd told her, she'd gone on hoping and believing. It was a bad deal all the way around. She'd gotten hurt, and I'd picked up big fat guilt feelings out of it.

And naturally that got me to thinking about Sue. Oddly enough, it didn't bother me to think about her anymore. For a long time I'd deliberately forced my mind away from it. About the only time I'd thought about her was when I was in the last stages of getting crocked—and that usually wound up getting maudlin. At first, of course, I'd been pretty bitter about it. Now I could see the whole thing in a little better perspective. I'd told a lot of people that it wouldn't have worked out between Sue and me, but that had been a cover-up really. Now I began to see that it was really true—it *wouldn't* have worked out. It wasn't just her old lady either. Sue and I had looked at the world altogether differently. She'd have probably turned into a Monica on me within the first six months.

That made me a little less certain about graduate school. Maybe I'd just gone ahead and made those plans to go back to the campus in Seattle with some vague idea in the back of my mind about possibly getting back together with her again. Or maybe I was just looking for a place to hide—or to postpone things. I was awfully good at postponing things.

The streak of light off along the eastern horizon was spreading now, and the stars were fading. A steel-gray luminosity was beginning to show in the rocks around me. It was still about fifteen minutes until it would be legal to shoot. Once again I found myself wishing my little Bolshevik could see this. Talk about an ambivalent situation, that was really it. I guess I knew she'd been right that night at Sloane's orgy— she and I weren't for keeps. There was no way we could be, but lately I couldn't see anything nice or hear anything or come up with an idea without wanting to share it with her. She was a complete and absolute nut, but I couldn't think of anybody that was more fun to be around.

A deer crossed the brow of the ridge on the far side of the ravine. I think I looked at it for about thirty seconds before I actually realized it was a deer. It was still too dark to tell if it was a buck or a doe. I began to get that tight excitement I get when I'm hunting—a sort of a double aliveness I only get then. I picked up my rifle and tried to see if I could catch the deer in the scope, but by that time it was down in the brush at the bottom of the ravine. Then I started paying attention to what I was doing. I began scoping the ravine and the ridge carefully.

It was getting lighter by the minute. I counted three more deer crossing the ridge—three does and a small buck.

I checked my watch. It was legal to shoot now.

In the next hour, thirty or forty deer crossed the ridge and another dozen or so drifted across the meadow behind me. Most of them were does, of course, and the bucks were all pretty small. I put the scope on each one and watched them carefully. Deer are funny animals, and I got a kick out of watching them. Some would come out of the brush very cautiously, looking around as if the whole world was out to get them. Others just blundered on out as if they owned the woods.

The pink sunlight was slipping down the peak above again, and it was broad daylight by now.

The white deer crossed the ridge above me from the meadow at my back just before the sun got down to the rockfall.

I caught the flicker of his movement out of the corner of my eye and swung the scope on him. He crossed about seventy yards above me, and he completely filled the scope. I think he looked right straight at me several times. I could see his pale eyelashes fluttering as he blinked nearsightedly in my direction.

It never occurred to me to shoot. Maybe if I had, I could have headed off a whole potful of trouble, but it just didn't occur to me—I'm not even sure I *could* have shot. I just wasn't so hungry that I had to kill something unique.

21

"YOU see any with any size?" Miller asked when he came back up about ten thirty.

"One pretty good three-point was all," I told him. I'd decided the less I said about the albino, the better.

"There'll be bigger ones," he said. "The others already went on down." He was looking at me kind of funny.

"I haven't seen anything in the last hour or so," I told him, walking over to Ned. The damn fool horse reached out and nuzzled at me, almost like a puppy. I scratched his ears for him.

"You two sure seem to be gettin' along good." Miller chuck-led.

"I think he's all bluff," I said, tying the rifle to the saddle and hooking the water bag over the horn. I climbed on, and we started down the ridge.

"The Big Man don't seem much better," he said when we got out past McKlearey's notch.

"He'll hold on," I said. "This is awfully important to him." Miller grunted.

It was close to eleven when we got back down to camp.

"What the hell's the matter with your eyes Dan?" Jack demanded as I climbed down at the corral. "That big white bastard damn near walked over the top of you up there—couldn't 'a been more'n thirty yards from you."

"Oh?" I said. I saw Miller watching me closely. "I must have been watching another deer."

"Hell, man, that's the one that counts."

I unsaddled Ned and ran him into the corral.

Jack shook his head disgustedly and stalked back up to the fire. I followed him.

"I'm not shittin' you," he told the others. "Just goddamn near ran right over him. I was watchin' the whole time through my scope."

"Why didn't you shoot?" McKlearey demanded.

"Christ, Lou, he was almost a mile away, and Stan, you, and Dan were all between me and him. I ain't about to get trigger-happy."

"Are you sure it was the same deer?" Stan asked.

"Ain't very likely there's more than one like that on the whole mountain," Jack said. "I still can't see how you missed spottin' him, Dan."

"Coulda been brush or a rise of ground between the Kid and that deer," Miller said, pouring himself a cup of coffee. "That ground can be damn tricky when you get at a different angle."

"Now that's sure the truth," Clint said. "I seen a nine-pointer walk no more'n ten yards in front of ol' Cap here one time. From where I was sittin' it looked like they were right in each other's laps, but when I got down there I seen that deer had been in a kind of shallow draw."

Miller chuckled. "Biggest deer we seen all that year, too."

"I guess that explains it then," Jack said dubiously.

"Where's Sloane?" I asked.

"He's lying down in the tent," Stan said. "He's still not feeling too well."

"Is he asleep?"

"I think he was going to try to sleep a little."

"I won't pester him then," I said. "Any of you guys see any good ones?"

"I seen a four-point," McKlearey said, "but I figure it's early yet."

"That's playin' it smart, Sarge," Miller said. "We got plenty of time left."

"What time you think we oughta go back up?" Jack asked him.

"Oh, 'bout three thirty or so," Miller said. "Evenin' huntin' ain't all that productive this time of year. Deer'll move in the evening, but not near as much as in the mornin'."

We loafed around until lunchtime and then ate some more

venison and beans. We tried to get Sloane to eat, but he said he didn't feel much like it, so we left him alone.

The rest of the guys sacked out after we'd eaten, but I wasn't really sleepy. I was feeling kind of sticky and grimy and thought a bit about maybe trying to swim in the beaver pond, but one hand stuck in there convinced me that it would be an awful mistake. I think that water came right out of a glacier somewhere. I settled for a stand-up bath out of the washbasin and called it good. Then I washed out my shirt and underwear and hung them on limbs to dry. I felt better in clean clothes and with at least the top layer of dirt off.

At three thirty we went down to the corral. Sloane was still feeling pretty rough, and Miller suggested that maybe he ought to just stay in bed so he'd be better tomorrow. Cal didn't give him much of an argument.

"Horses'll be OK to stay with you men," Miller said. "They're a whole lot quieter come evenin'. I'll just ride on up to the top with the Kid here, and we'll come on down end of shootin' time."

We all got on our horses and started up the ridge. It felt a little funny not having Cal along. Each of the others peeled off at their regular stands, and Miller and I scrambled on up to my knob at the top.

We got down and tied the horses securely and went on up to the rock where I'd sat that morning.

Miller lit a cigarette. "Sun's still pretty warm, ain't it?" he said.

"Yeah," I agreed. I could see that something was bothering him.

After a long while he said it. "How come you didn't shoot this mornin'?"

"I didn't see anything I wanted to shoot," I said.

"I was down below watchin' you with my field glasses," he said. "I saw you follow that freak deer with your scope all the way across the ridge. I don't think your brother saw you."

"I don't know, Cap," I said. "I just didn't feel like shooting him."

He nodded. "Maybe I'd feel the same way," he said. "I've seen a few of 'em and I've never shot one."

"I just watched him," I said. "I don't think I even considered pulling the trigger on him."

"In a way I almost wish you had. It woulda put an end to

it. Your brother and ol' Sarge are startin' to get at each other about it."

"I know," I said. "I wish the damn deer would get the hell off this side of the mountain."

"Ain't very likely."

I had a cigarette.

"Doe," Miller said, nodding at the other ridge.

We watched her step daintily down into the ravine. Then something spooked her. She snorted and bounded up the side of the ravine and on over the ridge.

"Picked up somebody's scent," Miller said. "Breeze gets a little tricky this time of evenin'."

We sat in silence, watching several does and a couple of small bucks pick their way on down the ravine. The sun crept slowly down toward the shoulder of the peak, and the shadows of the rocks and bushes grew longer. It was very quiet up there.

The sun slid behind the mountain, and the lucid shadowless twilight settled in. After a while Miller checked his watch.

"I guess that's about it," he said.

We got up and went back to the horses.

"Evenings *are* a little slower, aren't they?" I said.

"Yeah," he agreed, "like I said."

We mounted up and started down. McKlearey was already on his horse waiting for us, but we had to whistle for Stan and Jack. It was almost dark by the time we got down to the corral. We unsaddled and went back up to camp.

"Boy," Jack said, "you weren't kiddin' when you said pickin's were lean at night. I don't think I seen more'n half a dozen."

"You saw more than I did then," Stan said.

"I seen eight or ten," McKlearey said.

"I know some fellers don't even go out in the afternoon, Clint said, "but a man never knows when that big one'll come easin' by. Besides"—he grinned—"it gives me a chance to get supper goin' without havin' all you men under foot."

We got the point and backed away from the fire to give him a little more room.

"I don't mind goin' out," McKlearey said. "That's what we came up here for. I wouldn't want old Whitey gettin' past me."

"Don't be gettin' no wild ideas about *my* deer," Jack said.

"He ain't yours till you get your tag on 'im, Alders."

"I'll tag 'im," Jack said, "don't worry about that."

"Not if I see 'im first, you won't," McKlearey snapped.

"I told you men yesterday," Miller said, "that there's a whole lot of deer up on that mountain. You get your mind all set on just that one, and you're liable to come up empty."

"One of us is bound to get 'im," Jack said.

"Not necessarily," Miller said. "There's a hundred or more trails on that ridge. He could be crossin' on any one of 'em."

"I'm still gonna wait a few days before I fill my tag," Jack said.

I went over to see how Sloane was doing. I'm afraid that about two or three more smart remarks from my brother, and I'd have had to get in on it. Jack could be awfully knot-headed stubborn when he got his back up.

"Hey, Cal," I said, poking my head into his tent. "How's it going?"

"A little better now, Dan," he said from his bed. "I think it's startin' to settle down finally."

"Good deal, Cal. I'm glad to hear it."

"Come on in," he said, "have a blast." He giggled. That made me feel better right there.

"Now there's an idea," I said. I went on into his tent. He fished out his bottle and we each had a small snort.

"I'll tell you, buddy," he said, "it just damn near had me whipped there for a while. About ten this morning it was all I could do to climb up on that horse."

"You been sleeping straight through?" I asked him.

"Dozing," he said. "I feel pretty good now. Except I'm hungrier'n hell."

"Wouldn't be surprised," I said. "We couldn't interest you in lunch."

"I couldn't have eaten lunch if you guys had all held guns on me."

"You about ready to make an appearance?" I asked him.

"Sure thing. Chow about ready?" He sat up, carefully.

"Should be."

"Good." He pulled on his boots and got slowly to his feet. "I ain't about to rush it this time," he said.

"Good thinking."

We went out to join the others, and there were the usual wisecracks about Sloane loafing around camp. He laughed and giggled as if nothing were wrong. I could see the relief in Miller's face. We all felt a helluva lot better. Having a man sick like Cal had been is just like having a heavy weight on top of everybody's head.

"You're lookin' a helluva lot better there, Sullivan," McKlearey said.

"Who?" I asked him.

"Sullivan there." He pointed at Cal with his bandaged hand. I shrugged. Maybe it was some kind of goof-off nickname.

"Come and get it," Clint said, "or I'll feed it to the porky."

"Where is that little bastard anyway?" Jack said as we walked toward the fire.

"Oh, he's still around," Miller said. "Just watch where you set."

We lined up and Clint filled our plates. Then we went over and sat around the fire to eat.

"Hell," McKlearey said suddenly, staring at Cal. "You ain't Sullivan."

"I never said I was." Sloane giggled through a mouthful of beans.

"Hey, Danny," McKlearey said, "where the hell is Sullivan?"

"Sullivan who?" I asked.

"Oh, shit, you know Sullivan as well as I do."

"Sorry, Lou. It doesn't ring a bell."

He looked at me closely. "Oh," he said. "No, I guess it wouldn't. I guess I was thinkin' about somebody else."

"McKlearey," Jack said, "what the hell are you smokin' anyway?"

"Well," Lou said, grinning broadly at him, "I tried a pine-cone this morning."

"How was it?" Sloane giggled. "Did it blow your mind?"

"Aw, hell no," Lou said. "Turned it inside-out a couple times, but it didn't even come close to blowin' it."

Who the hell was Sullivan, for Chrissake?

We finished eating and cleaned up our dishes. Then we all sat down around the fire with a drink.

"Same layout for tomorrow as this morning?" Sloane asked.

"Seems to work out pretty well," Miller said, "and you men all got them posts you're on pretty well located by now."

"God, yes," Jack said. "Let's not switch around now. I'd get lost sure as hell."

"Well, then," Sloane said, polishing off his drink, "if there aren't gonna be any changes, I think I'll hit the sack."

"Christ, Sloane," Jack said, "you been sleepin' all day."

"Man, I need my beauty sleep." Cal giggled.

"Somehow," I said, grinning, "I think it's a little late for that."

"Never hurts to give it a try," he said, getting up.

"I'll call it a day, too," Stan said.

"What a buncha candy asses," McKlearey rasped.

"Four o'clock still comes damned early," Clint growled at the rest of us. It occurred to me that the little old guy had to be up at least a half hour before the rest of us, and he might feel it was bad manners to go to bed before we did.

"Why don't we all hang it up?" I suggested. "Maybe then you mighty hunters won't be so damn rum-dum in the morning."

"I suppose a good night's sleep wouldn't kill me," Jack said. We all got up.

"Man," Lou said, "this is worse than basic training."

"But this is *fun*, Lou," I said.

"Oh, sure"—he grinned at me—"I'd rather do a little sack-time with some high-class broad." He winked knowingly at Stan.

Christ! Was he *trying* to get killed?

Stan's face tightened up, and he went off to his tent without saying anything.

The rest of us said good night and scattered toward our sacks.

"Sloane seems a lot better," Jack said after we'd gotten settled.

"Yeah," I agreed. "That's a helluva relief."

"God, it must be awful—gettin' old like that," he said suddenly.

"What the hell are you talking about?" I asked him. "Sloane isn't old."

"You know what I mean," Jack said. "When your lungs or your legs give out like that."

"Oh, hell. Sloane's got a lot of miles left in him," I said. "He's just a little winded."

"It gives me the creeps, that's all."

"That's a helluva thing to say."

"I know, but I can't help it."

"What's eating at you, Jack?" I asked him, sitting up.

"I'm not gettin' anyplace. It's like I'm standin' still."

"What the hell brought this on?"

"God damn it, I've known Sloane since I was a kid. He's

always been able to handle himself and anything that came along. He's always been the roughest, toughest guy around."

"Jesus, Jack, it's not his fault he gets winded up here. It could happen to anybody."

"That's just it. A couple more years, and it's damn likely to happen to *me.*"

"Oh, bullshit! You're not carrying the gut Sloane is."

"It's not only that," he said, and his voice had an edge of desperation. "It's what I was sayin' before—I'm not gettin' anyplace. Hell, I'm not any further ahead right now than I was five goddamn years ago. I've got a marriage goin' sour. I've got a pissy-ass, two-bit job—hell, I had a better job year before last. Man, I'm just goin' downhill."

What the hell could I say? As far as I could see, he was calling it pretty close.

"It's been just too much booze, too many women, too many different jobs," he went on. "I've just *got* to dig in, goddammit, I've got to!"

"All you have to do is make your mind up, they say." What an asinine thing to say!

"Christ! I wish I could be like you, Dan, you know that? You know where you're goin', what you're gonna be. Me, I'm just floppin' around like a fish outa water. I just can't seem to settle down."

"Man, it's not just exactly as if you were over the hill or anything."

"You know what I mean. I keep hopin' something will click—you know—make it all snap into place so I can get settled down and get started on something. Maybe this trip will do it." He stared gloomily at the fire.

He was *afraid!* Jack had been talking for so long about how he wasn't afraid of anything that I guess I'd almost come to believe it. Now it came as a kind of shock to me. Jack was afraid. I didn't know what to say to him.

"You want a belt?" I asked him.

"Yeah. Maybe it'll help me sleep."

I fished out my bottle and we each had a quick drink. Then we both sat staring out at the dying fire.

We were still awake when McKlearey started screaming again.

"*Sullivan,*" he screamed, "*look out!*" Then there was a lot more I couldn't understand.

By the time I got untangled from my sleeping bag and got

outside the tent, Lou was standing outside, still hollering and waving that goddamn .38 around. I wasn't just exactly sure how to handle it.

"McKlearey!" It was Sloane. He had his head out of his tent, and there was a bark to his voice that I hadn't heard him use very often.

"Huh?" McKlearey blinked and looked around, confused. "What's up, Cal?"

"You're havin' another bad dream," Sloane said. "Settle down and put that goddamn gun away."

"What?" Lou looked down and saw the pistol in his hand. "Jeez!" he said. "Sorry, you guys. I musta had another damn nightmare." He lowered the gun and went back into his tent holding his left hand carefully in front of him to keep from bumping it.

After a minute or so I heard the clink of a bottle in there. What the hell? As long as it kept him quiet.

22

I woke up the next morning before Clint came around to shake us out. I could see the little old guy and Miller standing over by the fire and hear the low murmur of their voices. I got up quietly and went on out of the tent.

"Mornin', Dan," Clint said.

"Clint. Cap," I said.

"Coffee'll be done in just a bit," Clint said.

"Ol' Sarge seems to have got settled down," Miller said, his low voice rumbling. "At least I didn't hear him no more last night."

"I think he's only good for about one of those a night," I said.

"Well," Clint growled, "I don't know about him, but it's about all *I'm* good for."

"Amen," I agreed.

"I better go check the horses," Miller said and went off down toward the corrals.

I finished dressing and asked Clint if I could give him a hand with breakfast.

"Naw, Dan, thanks all the same, but I got 'er just about ready to go on the fire."

"OK," I said and got cleaned up.

"Coffee's done," he said as Miller came back up.

"Thanks, Clint," I said. "It's a little chilly this morning."

"Some," Miller agreed, shaking out his cup.

"I sure hope we don't get any snow," I said.

Miller grinned at me. "You got a thing about snow, son?"

"I went on maneuvers two winters in a row in Germany," I said. "I got a little used up on it."

"We *could* get some," he said, "but it's not very likely. I wouldn't lose no sleep over it."

The three of us had coffee. It was kind of sleepy and quiet— a private sort of time of day. None of us said much. The moon over the top of the peak was very sharp and bright.

"I better roust out the others," Clint said finally.

"I'll get 'em," I said.

"OK. I'll get breakfast on."

I woke up the others and then went back down to the fire. The smell of bacon and frying potatoes was very strong, and I realized I was hungry.

Jack came straggling down to the fire, his unlaced boots flopping loosely on his feet and his baseball cap stuffed down on his scrambled hair. "Son of a bitch!" he said, "it's colder'n a witch's tit."

"You keep company with some mighty strange women," I said, just to be saying something.

Clint doubled over with a wheezy, cackling kind of laugh. Even Miller grinned. I didn't really think it was all that funny myself.

"Always a smart-ass in the crowd," Jack growled. He finished dressing and washed up. By then the others had come out.

Sloane looked a lot better, and we all felt relieved about that.

"This cold'll hold the deer back a little," Miller said as we started to eat. "They're liable to be dribblin' across them ridges most of the mornin', so I won't be back up to get you men till 'bout noon or so." We all nodded. "Clint'll fix you up with some sandwiches to kinda tide you over."

"That's a good idea," Jack said. "I got a little gaunt yesterday."

We finished eating and went down to the corral and saddled up by moonlight again. Then we led the horses back up to camp, got our rifles and sandwiches and started up the ridge.

None of us said very much until after we'd dropped Sloane off. Then Stan dropped back to where I was riding and pulled in beside me.

"Did you hear him last night?" he said, his face tight in the moonlight.

"Who?"

"McKlearey."

"You mean all that screaming? Hell, how could I help it?"

"No," he said. "I mean before we went to bed. That clever little remark he made—about a 'high-class woman.'"

"It didn't mean anything, Stan," I said. "He was just talking."

"Maybe, but I don't think so."

"Oh, come on, Stan. He talks like that all the time. It doesn't mean a thing."

"I wish I could believe that," he said, "but somehow I just can't. I'm about to go out of my mind over this thing."

"You're imagining things." God, he acted so positive!

"Your post, Professor," Miller said from up in front of us. Stan nudged his horse away before I could say anymore.

"He was daydreamin'." McKlearey chuckled raspingly. "He's got a young wife with a wild body on her." He laughed again. Stan didn't turn around, but his back stiffened.

We rode on up the ridge and dropped off McKlearey.

At the top Miller wished me luck and went on back down. He seemed to have something on his mind—probably the same thing the rest of us did.

I sat on my rock waiting for it to get light and trying not to think about it. I didn't want it to spoil the hunting for me.

Once again the sky paled and the stars faded and the deer started to move. I saw one pretty nice four-point about seven or so, but I held off. I still thought I might be able to do a little better. The rest were all either does or smaller bucks.

The sun came up.

By eight thirty I began to feel as if that rock was beginning to grow to my tailbone. I'd swung my scope up and down the ravine so many times I think I knew every branch and leaf on the scrubby, waist-high brush, and there must have been trails out in the meadow behind me from my eyeballs. Nothing had gone by for about fifteen minutes, and frankly I was bored. Sometimes that happens when you're hunting—particularly stand-hunting. Maybe I just don't have the patience for it.

I stood up and walked down the knob a ways. I wondered if I could see any of the others. I made damn sure the safety was on and then ran the scope on down the ridge. I could see the camp a mile and a half or so away. It looked like a toy carelessly dropped at the edge of the spruces. The beaver pond looked like a small bright dime in the middle of the yellow-green meadow.

I was sure I could make out Clint moving around the fire, and I thought I saw Miller among the horses grazing in the lower meadow. I swung the scope up the ridge a ways.

I could see the white boulder that marked Sloane's post, but Cal himself was under the upswelling brow of the next hump. I spotted Jack rather quickly. He was standing up, tracking a doe over in the ravine with his rifle.

I searched the next post for a long time but couldn't locate Stan—which was odd, since his post was all out in plain sight with no obstructions in my line of sight. I thought maybe he was lying under some brush, but that orange jacket of his should have stood out pretty vividly against or even under the yellowing leaves of the sparse brush.

I moved the scope on up to the notch. A lazily rising puff of cigarette smoke pinpointed Lou for me—even though he was the only one of us who wasn't wearing any kind of bright clothing. He'd rigged up a kind of half-assed blind of limbs and brush and was sprawled out behind it, his rifle lying against a limb. He was only about a hundred and fifty yards down the hill. He raised his arm to his face with a glint and a flicker of that white bandage. He had a bottle with him. Maybe that's what had Miller so worried. McKlearey sure didn't seem to be hunting very hard.

I was about ready to go on back up to my rock-roost when I caught a flash of color in the thick brush between Stan's post and McKlearey's notch. I put the scope on it.

It was Stan. He was crawling through the bushes on his hands and knees. His face looked sweaty and very pale. He seemed to be trembling, but I couldn't be sure.

"What the hell is he up to?" I muttered under my breath. I watched him inch forward for about five minutes. When he got to the edge of the notch, he stopped and lay facedown on the ground for several minutes. He was about fifty yards above and behind McKlearey.

I didn't like the looks of it at all, but there wasn't a helluva lot I could do at that point.

Then Stan raised his face, and it was all shiny and very flushed now. He slowly pulled his rifle forward and poked it out over the edge of the bank.

I suddenly was very cold.

Stan got himself squared away. There wasn't any question about what he was aiming at.

"No, Stan!" It came out a croak. I don't think anybody could have heard it more than five feet away from me. Helplessly I put my scope on McKlearey.

Stan's shot kicked up dirt about two feet above Lou's head. McKlearey dove for cover. Instinct, I guess.

I didn't really consciously think about it. I just snapped off the safety, pointed my rifle in the general direction of the other side of the ravine and squeezed the trigger. The sound of my shot mingled and blurred in with the echo of Stan's.

I saw the white blur of his face suddenly turned up toward me for a moment, and then he scrambled back into the brush.

McKlearey was burrowing down under his pile of limbs like a man trying to dig a foxhole with his teeth.

There was something moving on the other side of the ravine. It flickered palely through the bushes, headed down the ridge.

It was the white deer. Apparently the double echo was confusing hell out of it. It ran down past McKlearey and on down the ravine. A couple minutes later I heard several shots from the stands below. Jack and Cal were shooting.

I hoped that they'd missed. The poor white bastard was just an innocent bystander really. He had no business being on that other side just then.

I looked down and saw that my hands were shaking so badly that I could barely hold my rifle. I took several deep breaths and then slowly pulled back the bolt, flipping out the empty in a long, twinkling brass arc. It clinked on a rock and fell in the dirt. I closed the bolt, put the safety back on, and picked up the empty. Then I went back up to my rock and sat down.

23

"Man!" Jack said when I got back down to camp, "the son of a bitch ran right through the whole damn bunch of us!"

"I shot at him five times!" Sloan gasped, his face red. "Five goddamn times and never touched a hair. I think the son of a bitch is a ghost, and we all shot right through 'im." He tried to giggle but wound up coughing and choking.

"You OK?" I asked him.

He tried to nod, still choking and gasping. It took him a minute or so to get settled down.

"Did you shoot, Dan?" Jack asked me.

"Once," I said, taking out the empty cartridge case, "and I think Stan did too, didn't you, Stan?"

He nodded, his face very pale.

"I got off three," Jack said. He turned to Miller. "I thought you said they always ran uphill, Cap."

"Ninety-nine times out of a hundred," Miller said.

"Maybe one of us hit him," Sloan gasped.

Miller shook his head. "He cut back on up over that far ridge when he got past you men. I expect all the shootin' just kept pushin' him on down. I don't imagine he can see too good in broad daylight with them pink eyes of his."

Lou didn't say anything, but his eyes looked a little wild.

We ate lunch and then all of us kind of poked around looking for something to do until time to go back up again.

I wound up wandering down to the pond again. I stood watching the fish swim by and trying not to think about what had happened that morning.

"Why don't you watch where the hell you're shootin'?" It was McKlearey.

I looked at him for a moment. "I know where I was shooting, Lou," I told him.

"Well, one of them damn shots just barely missed me," he said. His hands were shaking.

"Must have been a ricochet," I said.

"I ain't all that sure," he said. He squatted down by the water and began stripping off his bandage.

"I've got no reason to shoot you, Lou. I don't have a wife." I just let it hang there.

He looked at me for a long time, but he didn't answer. Then he finished unwinding his hand. The gash in his palm was red and inflamed-looking, and the whole hand looked a little puffy.

"That's getting infected," I told him. "Clint's got a first-aid kit. You'd better put something on it."

"It's OK," he said. "I been pourin' whiskey in it."

"Iodine's cheaper," I said, "and a helluva lot more dependable."

He stuck the hand into the water, wincing at the chill.

"That's not a good idea either," I said.

"I know what I'm doin'," he said shortly.

I shrugged. It was his hand, after all.

"Danny," he said finally.

"Yeah?"

"You didn't see who shot at me, did you?"

I didn't really want to lie to him, but I was pretty sure Stan wouldn't try it again. He'd looked too sick when we'd gotten back down. "Look, Lou," I said, "with the scopes on all the rifles in camp, if somebody was trying to shoot you, he'd have nailed you to the cross with the first shot. If one came anywhere near you, it was more than likely just what I said—a ricochet."

"Maybe—" he said doubtfully.

"You're just jumpy," I said. "All keyed up. Shit, look at the nightmares you've been having. Maybe you ought to go a little easy on the booze.

"That's why I drink it," he said, staring out across the beaver pond. "If I drink enough, I don't dream at all. I'm OK then."

I was about to ask him what was bothering him, but I was pretty sure he wouldn't tell me. Besides, it was none of my business.

We went back up to camp, and he went into his tent.

We went out at three thirty again, the same as we had the day before.

"I thought you wasn't gonna shoot at that deer," Miller said when we got up to the top.

I couldn't very well tell him why I'd shot, and I didn't want to lie to him. "I was just firing a warning shot," I said. In a way it had been just that.

He looked at me for a minute but didn't say anything. I'm not sure if he believed me.

None of us saw anything worth shooting that evening either, and we were all pretty quiet when we got back down.

"Come on, men," Miller said, trying to cheer us up. "No point in gettin' down in the mouth. It's only a matter of time till you start gettin' the big ones."

"I *know* which one I'm gonna get," Jack said. "I'm gonna bust that white bastard."

"Not if I see 'im first," McKlearey said belligerently, nursing his hand.

They glared at each other.

"All right," Jack said finally, "you remember that bet we got?"

"I remember," Lou said.

"*That* deer is the one then."

"That's fine with me."

"That wasn't the bet," I said flatly.

They both scowled at me.

"Dan's right," Sloan said, gasping heavily. "The original bet was best deer —Boone and Crockett points." His voice sounded pretty wheezy again, but his tone was pretty firm.

"There's still the side bet," Stan said very quietly. I'd forgotten about that one.

McKlearey stared back and forth between the two of them. He looked like he was narrowing down his list of enemies. "All right," he said very softly. It didn't sound at all like him.

"I don't want you men shootin' at that deer when he's up on top of no cliff or somethin'," Miller said. "I seen a couple men after the same deer once—both of 'em so afraid the other was gonna get it that they weren't even thinkin' no more. One of 'em finally shot the deer right off the top of a four-hundred-foot bluff. Wasn't enough left to make a ten-cent hamburger out of it by the time that deer quit bouncin'."

"We'll watch it," Jack said, still staring at McKlearey.

Lou edged around until he had his back to a stump and could keep an eye on both Jack and Stan. His eyes had gone kind of flat and dead. He was sort of holding his bandaged hand up in the air so he wouldn't bump it, and his right hand was in his lap, about six inches from the butt of that .38. He looked like he was wound pretty tight.

We tried talking, but things were pretty nervous.

After a while Stan got up and went back to the latrine. I

waited a couple minutes then followed him. He was leaning against a tree when I found him.

"Stan," I said.

"Yes." He didn't look at me. He knew what I was going to say.

"Be real careful about where you place your shots from now on, OK?"

He took a quick breath but didn't say anything. I waited a minute and then went on down the trail.

When the others got up to go to bed, Miller jerked his head very slightly to me, and he and I sat by the fire until they had all gone into their tents.

"I've got to go check the stock," he said. "You want to come along, son?"

"Sure, Cap," I said. "Stretch some of the kinks out of my legs."

We stood up and walked on down toward the corrals. Once we got away from the fire, the stars were very bright, casting even a faint light on the looming snowfields above us.

Miller leaned his elbows across the top rail of the corral, his mustache silvery in the reflected starlight, and his big cowboy hat shading his eyes. "Them boys seem to be missin' the whole point of what this is all about," he said finally.

"I'm not very proud of any of them myself, about now," I said. "They're acting like a bunch of damn-fool kids."

"I've seen this kinda stuff before, son. It always leads to hard feelin's."

"Maybe I *should* have shot that deer."

"Not if you didn't want to," he said.

"I wouldn't have felt right about it, but it'd sure be better than what's going on right now."

"Oh, a friendly bet's OK. Men do it all the time, but them boys are takin' it a little too serious."

"Well, most of that's just talk," I told him. "They go at each other like that all the time. I wouldn't worry too much about it. I just don't like the idea of it, that's all."

"I don't neither," he said, "and I'll tell you somethin' else I don't much like."

"What's that?"

"The feelin' I keep gettin' that we ain't all gonna finish up this hunt. I've had it from the first day."

I couldn't say much to that.

"I sure wouldn't want one of my hunters gettin' shot on my first trip out." He looked at me and grinned suddenly. "Wouldn't be much of an advertisement, now would it?"

24

SLOANE was much worse the next morning. Much as he tried, he couldn't even get out of the sack. Both Stan and I offered to stay with him, but he insisted that we go ahead on up.

Breakfast was kind of quiet, and none of us talked very much on the way up the ridge.

Miller looked down at me from his saddle after I'd dismounted at the top. "If the Big Man don't get no better," he said, "Clint's gonna have to take him on down. This is the fourth day up here. He just ain't comin' around the way he should."

"I know," I said.

"I like the Big Man," Miller said. "I don't know when I've ever met a better-natured man, but I ain't gonna be doin' him no favors by lettin' him die up here."

I nodded. "I'll talk with him when we get back down to camp," I said.

"I'd sure appreciate it, son," he said. "Good huntin'." He took Ned's reins and went on back down.

It was chilly up there in the darkness, and the stars were still out. I sat hunched up against the cold and tried not to think too much about things. Every now and then the breeze would gust up the ravine, and I could pick up the faint smell of the pine forest far down below the spruces.

The sky began to pale off to the east and the stars got dimmer.

I kind of let my mind drift back to the time before my father died. Once he and I had gone on out to fish on a rainy Sunday morning. The fish had been biting, and we were both catching them as fast as we could bait up. We both got soaked to the skin, and I think we both caught cold from it, but it was still one of the best times I could remember. Neither one of us had said very much, but it had been great. I suddenly felt something I hadn't felt for quite a few years—a sharp, almost unbearable pang of grief for my father.

It was lighter, and that strange, cold, colorless light of early morning began to flow down the side of the mountain.

I quite suddenly remembered a guy I hadn't thought about for years. It had been when I was knocking up and down the coast that year after I'd gotten out of high school. I'd been working on a truck farm in the Salinas Valley in California, mostly cultivating between the mile-long lettuce rows. About ten or so one cloudy morning, I'd seen a train go by. About as far as I was going to go that day was eight or ten rows over in the same field. I walked the cultivator back to the farmhouse and picked up my time. That afternoon I'd jumped into an empty boxcar as the train was pulling out of the yard headed north.

There was an old guy in the car. He wasn't too clean, and he smelled kind of bad, but he was somebody to talk to. We sat in the open doorway looking at the open fields and the woods and the grubby houses and garbage dumps—did you know that people live in garbage dumps? Anyway, we'd talked about this and that, and I'd found out that he had a little pension of some kind, and he just moved up and down the coast, working the crops and riding trains, with those pension checks trailing him from post office to post office. He said that he guessed he could go into almost any post office of any size on the coast, and there'd be at least one of his checks there.

He'd said that he was sixty-eight and his heart and lungs were bad. Then he'd kind of looked off toward the sunset. "One of these days," he'd said, "I'll miss a jump on one of these boxcars and go under the wheels. Or my heart'll give out, or I'll take the pneumonia. They'll find me after I been picked over by a half-dozen other bums. Not much chance there'd be anything left so they could identify me. But I got that all took care of. Look—"

He'd unbuttoned his shirt and showed me his pale, flabby, old man's chest. He had a tattoo.

"My name was Wilmer O. Dugger," it said. "I was born in Wichita, Kansas, on October 4, 1893. I was a Methodist." It was like a tombstone, right on his chest.

He'd buttoned his shirt back up. "I got the same thing on

both arms and both legs," he'd said. "No matter what happens, one of them tattoos is bound to come through it. I used to worry about it—them not bein' able to identify me, I mean. Now I don't worry no more. It's a damn fine thing, you know, not havin' nothin' to worry about."

I think it had been about then that I'd decided to go to college. I'd caught a quick glimpse of myself fifty years later, riding up and down the coast and waiting to miss my jump on a boxcar or for my heart to quit. About the only difference would have been that I don't think I'd have bothered with the tattoos.

The breeze dropped, and it got very still. I straightened up suddenly and picked up my rifle. It felt very smooth and comfortable. Something was going to happen. I eased the bolt back very gently and checked to make sure there was one in the tube. I closed it and slipped the safety back on. I could feel an excitement growing, a kind of quivering tension in the pit of my stomach and down my arms and legs, but my hands were steady. I wasn't shaking or anything.

A doe came out on the far side of the ravine. Very slowly, so as not to startle her, I sprawled out across the rock and got my elbows settled in so I could be absolutely sure of my shot.

The doe sniffed a time or two, looked back once, and then went on down into the ravine.

Another doe came out of the same place. After a minute or so she went on down, too.

Then another doe.

It was absolutely quiet. I could hear the faint *toc-toc-toc* of their hooves moving slowly on down the rocky bottom of the ravine.

I waited. I knew he was there. A minute went by. Then another.

Then there was a very faint movement in the brush, and he stepped softly out into the open.

I didn't really count him until later. I just saw the flaring rack and the calm, almost arrogant look on his face, and I knew that he was the one I wanted. He was big and heavily muscled. He was wary but not frightened or timid. It was his mountain.

He stood broadside to me and seemed to be looking straight across at me, though I don't really think he saw me. Maybe he just knew that I was there, as I had known that he would be.

I put the cross hairs of the scope just behind his front shoulder and slipped off the safety. His ears flicked.

I slowly squeezed the trigger.

I didn't hear the shot or feel the recoil of the rifle. The deer jerked and fell awkwardly. Then he stumbled to his feet and fell again. He got up again slowly and kind of walked on back over the other side of the ridge, his head down. It didn't occur to me to shoot again. I knew it wasn't necessary.

I stood up, listening now to the echo of the shot rolling off down the side of the mountain. I jacked out the empty shell, slipped the safety back on and slung the rifle. Then I started down into the ravine. I could hear the three does scrambling up through the brush on the far side.

The going was pretty rough, and it took me about ten minutes to get to where he'd been standing. I looked around on the ground until I found a blood spot. Then another. I followed them down the other side.

He'd gone about a hundred yards down the easy slope of the far side of the ridge and was lying on his side in a little clump of brush. His head was still raised but wobbling, as I walked carefully up to him. His eyes were not panicky or anything. I stepped behind him, out of range of his hooves, and took out my pistol. I thumbed back the hammer and put the muzzle to the side of his head between his eye and ear. His eye watched me calmly.

"Sorry I took so long to get here, buddy," I said.

Then I pulled the trigger.

The gun made a muffled kind of pop—without any echo to it, and the deer's head dropped heavily, and the life went out of his eye. I knelt beside him and ran my hand over his heavy shoulder. The fur felt coarse but very slick, and it was a kind of dark gray with little white tips shot through it. He smelled musky but not rank or anything.

I stood up, pointed the pistol up toward the top of the mountain, and fired it again. Then I began to wonder if maybe I'd given the wrong signal. I put the pistol back in the holster and slipped the hammer-thong back on. Then I leaned my rifle against a large rock and hauled the deer out in the open. I walked back on up to the ridge and hung my jacket over a bush to mark the spot for whoever came up with a horse.

I went back to the deer and started gutting him out. I wasn't nearly as fast as Clint was, but I managed to get the job done finally. I did seem to get a helluva lot of blood on my clothes though, but that didn't really matter.

I was trying to get him rolled over to drain out when Clint came riding down the ridge, leading Ned and a packhorse.

"Damn nice deer," he said, grinning. "Six-pointer, huh?"

"I didn't count him," I said. I checked the deer. "Yeah, it's six points, all right."

"Have any trouble?" He climbed down.

"No. He came out on the ridge, I shot him, and he kind of staggered down here and fell down. I'm afraid I busted up the liver pretty bad though." I pointed at the shredded organ lying on top of the steaming gut-pile.

"Where'd you take him?" he asked.

"Right behind the shoulder."

"That's dependable," he said. "Here, lemme help you dump 'im out."

We rolled the deer over.

"Heavy bugger, ain't he?" Clint chuckled.

"We're gonna get a rupture getting him on the horse," I said. "Say, how'd you get above me anyway?"

"I come up through the meadows and then across the upper end of the ravine at the foot of the rockslide. Gimme your knife a minute."

I handed it to him.

"Better get these offa here." He cut away two dark, oily-looking patches on the inside of the deer's hind legs, just about the knees. "Musk-glands," he said. "Some fellers say they taint the meat—I don't know about that for sure, but I always cut 'em off on a buck, just to be safe." Then he reached inside the cut I'd made in the deer's throat and sliced one on each side. "Let's turn him so's his head's downhill," he said.

We turned the deer and blood slowly drained out, running in long trickles down over the rocks. There really wasn't very much.

Clint held out his hand. I wiped mine off on my pants, and we shook hands.

"Damn good job, Dan. I figure that you'll do."

It was a little embarrassing. "Hey," I said. "I damn near forgot my coat." I went on up to the ridge-top and got it. The sun was just coming up. I felt good, damned good. I ran back down to where Clint was standing.

"Easy, boy,"—he laughed—"you stumble over somethin' and you'll bounce all the way to Twisp."

"OK," I said, "now, how do we get him on the horse?"

"I got a little trick I'll show you," he said, winking. He took a coil of rope off his saddle and dropped a loop over the deer's horns. We rolled him over onto his back, and Clint towed him over to a huge flat boulder with his horse. The uphill side of the boulder was level with the rest of the hill and the downhill side was about six feet above the slope. Then he led the packhorse over and positioned him below the rock. I held the packhorse's head, and Clint slowly pulled the deer out over the edge.

"Get his front feet on out past the saddle, if you can, Dan," Clint said.

I reached on out and pulled the legs over. When the deer reached the point where he was just balanced, Clint got off his horse and came back up.

"You're taller'n me," he said. "I'll hold the horse, and you just ease the carcass down onto the saddle."

I went around onto the top of the rock and carefully pushed the deer off, holding him back so he wouldn't fall on over. It was really very simple. Once the deer was in place we tied him down and it was all done.

"Pretty clever," I said.

"I don't lift no more'n I absolutely have to." He grinned. "Fastest way I know to get old in a hurry is to start liftin' stuff."

"I'll buy that," I said. "Which way we going back down?"

"Same way I come up," he said. "That way we don't spook the deer for the others. You 'bout ready?"

"Soon as I tie on my rifle," I said. I went back and got it and tied it to the saddle. Ned shied from me a little—the blood-smell, probably.

"Steady, there, knothead," I said. He gave me a hurt look. I climbed on and we rode on up to the top of the ridge. We cut on across the foot of the rockfall and out into the meadows.

"Cap was gonna come up," Clint said, "but somebody oughta stay with the Big Man, and I know these packhorses better'n he does."

I nodded.

We rode on slowly down through the meadows toward camp. I could see the others over on the ridge, standing and watching. I waved a couple times.

"God damn, boy," Miller said, "you got yourself a good

one." He was chuckling, his brown face creased with a big grin.

"Had it all gutted out and ever-thin'," Clint told him.

Sloan came out of his tent. He was still breathing hard, but he looked a little better.

"Hot damn!" he coughed. "That's a beauty."

I climbed down off Ned.

"I fixed up a crossbar," Miller said. "Let's get 'im up to drain out good."

Clint slit the hocks and we slipped a heavy stick through. Then we led the packhorse over to the crossbeam stretched between two trees behind the cook-tent. Miller had hooked up a pulley on the beam. We pulled the deer up by his hind legs and fastened him in place with baling wire.

"Damn," Miller said, "that's one helluva heavy deer. Three hundred pounds or better. Somebody in the bunch might get more horns, but I pretty much doubt if anybody'll get more meat."

We stood around and looked at the deer for a while.

"How 'bout some coffee?" Clint said.

"How 'bout some whiskey?" Cal giggled and then coughed.

"How 'bout some of both?" Miller chuckled. "I think this calls for a little bendin' of the rules, don't you?"

"Soon as I see to my horse." I grinned at them. I walked over toward Ned, and my feet felt like they weren't even touching the ground, I felt so good.

25

I got up at the usual time the next morning and had breakfast with the others. I felt a little left out now. The night before had been fine, with everyone going back to look at the deer and all. Even with the skin off and the carcass in a large mesh game bag to keep the bugs off, it looked pretty impressive. Clint and I had salted the hide and rolled it into a bundle with the head on top. I wasn't sure what I'd do with it, but this way

I'd be able to make the decision later. After the big spiel I'd given Clydine the day I'd left about not being a trophy hunter, I was about half-ashamed to keep the head and all, but I knew I'd have to have it in case of a game check. I thought maybe I could have the hide tanned and made into a vest or gloves or something—maybe a purse for her.

At breakfast I watched Cal carefully. He was coughing pretty badly, but he insisted on going down. I noticed that he didn't eat much breakfast.

We all walked on down to the corral, and I watched the others saddle up. Ned came over and nuzzled at me. I guess he couldn't quite figure out why we weren't going along. I patted him a few times and told him to go back to sleep— that's what I more or less had in mind.

"Go ahead and loaf, you lazy bastard," Jack said.

Miller chuckled. "Don't begrudge him the rest—he's earned it."

"Right," I said, rubbing it in a little bit. "If you guys would get off the dime, you could lay around camp and loaf a little bit, too."

"Of course, all the fun's over for you, Dan," Sloane gasped.

I'd thought of that, too. We went back up to the tents so they could pick up their rifles.

I stood with my back to the campfire watching them ride off into the darkness. The sound of splashing came back as they crossed the little creek down below the beaver dam.

"More coffee, boy?" Clint asked me.

"Yeah, Clint. I think I could stand another cup."

We hunkered down by the fire with our coffee cups.

"Now that you've shown them fellers how, I expect we'll be gettin' a few more deer in camp."

"Yeah," I agreed. "If they'll just get off that damn nonsense about that white deer."

"Oh, I expect they will. I got about half a hunch that all you fellers shootin' at 'im the other day spooked 'im clear outa the territory."

"I sure as hell hope so," I said.

"Knew a feller killed one once," he said. "He gave me some steaks off it. I dunno, but to me they just didn't taste right. The feller give up huntin' a couple years later. I always wondered if maybe that didn't have somethin' to do with it—'course he was gettin' along in years."

I wasn't really sure how much Clint knew about what had happened that day, so I didn't say much.

"What you plannin' on doin' today?" he asked me.

"Oh, I thought I'd give you a hand around camp after a bit," I said.

"You'd just be under foot," he said bluntly.

"We can always use more firewood." He grinned.

"Then I might ride old Ned around a little, too. I wouldn't want him to be getting so much rest that he's got the time to be inventing new tricks."

"Oh, I wouldn't worry none about that. I think you and him got things about all straightened out."

"But the first thing I'm gonna do is go back to bed for a while," I said, grinning at him. "This getting up while it's still dark is plain unhealthy."

"It's good for you." He chuckled. "Kinda gets you back in tune with the sun."

The more I thought about that, the more sense it made. Whatever the reason, when I went back to bed, I rolled and tossed in my sleeping bag for about an hour and a half and then gave it up as a bad job. I got up, had another cup of coffee, and watched the sunrise creep down the side of the mountain.

I finally wound up down by the beaver pond, watching the trout swim by.

"You wanna give 'em a try?" Clint hollered from camp.

"You got any gear?" I yelled back.

"Has a duck got feathers? Come up here, boy."

Miller was sitting by the fire mending a torn place on the skirt of one of the saddles. "Old Clint never goes no place without his fishpole," he said. "He'd pack it along on a trip into a desert—probably come back with fish, too."

The little guy came back out of his tent putting together a jointed, fiber-glass rod. He tossed me a leather reel case. I opened it and took out a beautiful Garcia spinning reel.

"Man," I said, "that's a fine piece of equipment."

"Should be," he growled, "after what I paid for it."

Somehow I'd pictured him as the willow-stick, bent-pin-and-worm kind of fisherman.

"How you wanna fish 'em?" he asked me.

"What do you think'll work best? You know a helluva lot more about this kind of water than I do."

He squinted at the sky. "Wait till about ten or so," he said.

"Sun gets on the water good, you might try a real small spoon—Meppes or Colorado spinner."

"What bait?"

"Single eggs. Or you might try corn."

"Corn?"

"Whole kernel. I'll give you a can of it."

"I've never used it before," I admitted.

"Knocks 'em dead sometimes. Give it a try."

We got the pole rigged up, and I carted it and the gear down to the pond. I'd never used corn before, and it took me a while to figure out how to get it threaded on the hook, but I finally got it down pat. After about ten minutes or so I hooked into a pretty nice one. He tailwalked across the pond and threw the hook. I figured that would spook the others, so I moved on down to the lower pond, down by the corrals.

The lower pond was smaller, deeper, and had more limbs and junk in it. It was trickier fishing.

On about the fourth or fifth cast, a lunker about sixteen inches or so flashed out from under a half-buried limb and grabbed the corn before it even got a chance to sink all the way to the bottom. I set the hook and felt the solid jolt clear to my shoulder. He came up out of the water like an explosion.

I held the rod-tip up and worked him away from the brush. It was tricky playing a fish in there, and it took me a good five minutes to work him over to the edge.

"Does nice work, don't he?" Clint said from right behind me. I damn near jumped across the pond. I hadn't known he was there. When I turned around, they were both there, grinning.

"He'll do," Miller said.

I lifted out the fish and unhooked him.

"Want to try one?" I asked, offering the pole to Clint.

I saw his hands twitch a few times, but he firmly shook his head. "I get started on that," he said, "and nobody'd get no dinner."

"Shall I throw him back?" I asked, holding out the flopping fish.

"Hell, *no!*" Clint said. "Don't *never* do that! If you don't want 'em, don't pester 'em. Put 'im on a stringer and keep 'im in the water. Catch some more like 'im and we'll have fresh trout for lunch—make up for that liver you blew all to hell yesterday."

"Yes, *sir!*" I laughed, throwing him a mock salute.

"Don't *never* pay to waste any kinda food around Clint here," Miller said.

"I went hungry a time or two when I was a kid," Clint said. "I didn't like it much, and I don't figger on doin' it again, if I can help it."

The hollow roar of a rifle shot echoed bouncingly down the ridge.

"Meat in the pot," Clint said.

There were three more shots, raggedly spaced.

"Not so sure," Miller said, squinting up the ridge.

"We going up?" I asked, gathering up the fishing gear.

"Let's see what kind of signal we get," Miller said.

We waited.

There finally came a flat crack of a pistol. After a minute or so there was a second.

"Cripple," Clint said disgustedly.

"It happens," Miller said. "I'll go. This might take some time and—"

"I know," Clint said. "I gotta fix dinner."

"I'll come along," I said.

Miller nodded. "Might not be a bad idea. We might need some help if the deer run off very far."

I took the gear back to camp and then went on down to the corral. "Any idea who it was?" I asked Miller, who was scanning the ridge with his glasses.

"Not yet," he said. "Yesterday we could see you goin' on over the other ridge."

"I got a hunch it was Stan," I said. "That pistol of his has a short barrel."

"Ain't the Big Man or your brother," he said. "I can see both of them, and they ain't movin'."

I waited.

"Yeah, it's the Professor, all right. He's just comin' up out of the gully."

We saddled our horses as well as Stan's horse and the pack-horse.

"We'll cut along the bottom here and go up on the other side," he said.

"All right."

We rode on up to the head of the basin and crossed the ravine just above the tree line. We could see Stan's fluorescent jacket in the brush about a mile up above. We started up.

We found him standing over the deer about a half mile from

the ravine. The deer was bleating and struggling weakly, several loops of intestine protruding from a ragged hole in his belly.

"Why didn't you finish him off?" I demanded, swinging down from the saddle.

"I—I couldn't," he stammered, his face gray. "I tried but I couldn't pull the trigger." He was standing there holding his pistol in a trembling hand.

I pulled out the .45, thumbed the hammer, and shot the deer in the side of the head. He stiffened briefly and then went limp.

I heard Stan gag and saw him hurry unsteadily away into the bushes. We heard him vomiting.

"His first deer?" Miller asked me very softly.

I nodded, putting the .45 away.

"Better go help 'im get settled down. I'll gut it out. Looks a little messed up."

I nodded again. The deer was a three-point. I think we'd all passed up bigger ones.

"Come on, now, Stan," I said, walking over to him. "It's all done now."

"I didn't know they made any noise," he said, gagging again. "I didn't think they *could*."

"It doesn't happen very often," I said. "It's all over now. Don't worry about it."

"I made a mess of it, didn't I?" he asked, looking up at me, His face was slick and kind of yellow.

"It's all right," I said.

"I just wanted to get it over with," he said. "I tried to aim where you said, but my hands were shaking so badly."

"It's OK," I said. "Anybody can get buck-fever."

"No," he said, "it wasn't that at all. It was what happened the other day—when you saw me."

I didn't say anything. I couldn't think of anything to say.

"I know you saw me," he said. "I really wasn't trying to kill him, Dan. You have to believe that. I just had to make him quit talking the way he was—about Monica."

"Sure, Stan. I know."

"But I just had to get it over with. I've got to get away from him. Next time—" He left it.

I glanced over at Miller. He was almost done. He was even faster than Clint. I was sure he couldn't hear us.

"You all right now?" I asked Stan.

"You're pretty disgusted with me, aren't you, Dan?" he asked.

"No," I said. "It's not really your fault. Things just got out of hand for you, that's all. You OK now?"

He nodded.

"Let's go give Miller a hand with the deer," I said.

He stood up and wiped his face with his handkerchief.

"I'm awfully sorry, Mr. Miller," he said when we got back. "I guess I just froze up."

"It happens," Miller said shortly, cleaning off his knife. "Bring that packhorse over here."

I got the horse.

We loaded the deer onto the horse and lashed him down.

"Did you leave any of your gear over on the other side?" Miller asked him.

"No," Stan said, "I brought everything along."

"Well, let's go on down then."

We climbed on the horses and rode on down to the bottom and across the ravine.

"What's the matter with Cal?" Stan said, pointing up the ridge.

I looked up, Sloane was standing up, weakly waving both hands above his head at us.

I looked at Miller quickly.

"Somebody better go see," he said.

I nodded and turned Ned's nose up the hill.

Above me, Sloane fumbled at his belt briefly and then came out with his Ruger. He pointed it at the sky and fired slowly three times, then he sagged back down onto the ground.

I booted Ned into a fast lope, my stomach all tied up in knots.

26

"DAN," Sloan gasped when I got up to him, "I'm sick. I've got to go down." He looked awful.

"Your chest again?" I asked, sliding down out of the saddle. Ned was panting from the run uphill.

Sloan nodded weakly. "It's all I can do to breathe," he said.

"Here," I said, "you get on the horse."

"I can't handle that horse," he said.

"I'll lead him," I said. I tied his rifle and canteen to the saddle and helped him up. Ned didn't care much for being led, but I didn't worry about that.

"How is he?" Miller asked when I got him down.

"Bad," I said, "worse than ever."

"Let's get 'im off the horse."

We got him down and over to the fire.

"Do you want a drink, Cal?" I asked him.

He shook his head. "My goddamn heart's beatin' so fast now it feels like it's gonna jump out of my goddamn chest."

Miller squatted down in front of him and looked him over carefully. "I hate to say this," he told Cal, "but I'm afraid you're gonna have to go on back down. You're gettin' worse instead of better."

Cal nodded.

"I'll refund part of what you paid."

"No," Cal said. "It's not your fault. You took us on in good faith. You don't owe me a dime."

Miller shrugged. "I wish to hell it hadn't happened," he said.

"I was doin' OK there for a while," Cal said, "but it came back this morning worse than ever."

"Well, let's get you laid down for now. That way you can get rested up for the ride."

We got Sloane over to his tent and came back to the fire.

247

"Somebody's gonna have to go out with him," Miller said. "He ain't gonna be able to drive the way he is."

I felt a sudden pang—almost a panic. I didn't want to leave yet. Then I was ashamed of myself for it.

"I'll go," Stan said very quietly. "I rode with him coming over, and besides, I'm all finished up now anyway."

Miller nodded, not saying anything.

"I could just as easily go, Stan," I said, not meaning it.

"There are other reasons, too," he said.

I looked at him. He really wanted to go. "All right, Stan," I said.

Miller looked at me. "You want to go fetch the others down for dinner, son?" he said. "I'll help Clint get things together for the trip down."

"Sure," I said. I went on down to get the horses.

Neither Jack nor McKlearey seemed particularly upset when I told them that Cal and Stan were leaving.

"I didn't figure Sloane would be able to hold out much longer," Jack said. "I've been sayin' all along that he wouldn't get it under control."

That wasn't how I remembered it.

McKlearey had merely grunted.

When we got back down though, the camp was pretty quiet. Stan had packed his and Sloane's gear and had it all laid out by the corral.

After we ate, we all pitched in and helped get things ready.

Clint skinned out Stan's deer and got it in a game bag. "I'll take yours down, too," he told me. "I'll hang it in the icehouse at the place."

"Have you got an icehouse?" I asked him. "I didn't think there were any of those left in the world."

"Well, it ain't really an icehouse. We got a big refrigeration unit in it. We don't keep it set too cold. Works about the same way."

McKlearey came over and looked Stan's deer over. "Ain't very big, is it?" he said.

"I don't see yours hangin' up there yet," Clint said.

McKlearey grunted and walked off.

"I'm gettin' to where I don't much care for ol' Sarge," Clint said.

"You're not the only one," I told him.

"Still," Clint said, squinting at the skinned carcass, "it really ain't much of a deer."

"Better than nothing," I said.

Clint, Stan, and Sloane left about two that afternoon. The rest of us stood around and watched them ride out. We'd tried to joke with Cal a little before he left, but he'd been too sick. His face was very pale, framed in the dark fur of his parka hood. The day seemed pretty warm to me, but I guess he felt cold. Just before they left, he gave Miller his tag.

"If you get a chance"—he gasped—"you might have somebody fill it for me."

"Sure," Miller said, "we'll get one for you."

"I think I'll go on up a little early," McKlearey said after they'd disappeared down the trail.

Jack looked at him narrowly. "Maybe I will, too," he said.

"Not much point," Miller said.

"We can find our way up there," Jack said.

Miller looked at them. Finally he shrugged. "Just don't stay too late," he said.

"We both got watches," McKlearey said, nursing his bandaged hand.

Miller walked away.

I felt like there'd been a funeral in camp. Jack and Lou went on up the hill, and I sat around watching Miller get things squared away for dinner. I offered to help but he said no.

"You take care of that fish?" he asked me.

"Oh, hell." I'd completely forgotten the fish.

"Why don't you see if you can get a few more?" he said.

"Sure." I got Clint's pole and went on down to the pond. It was a little slow, but I managed to get three more before the sun went down. I cleaned them and took them back up to camp.

"Enough to go around." Miller grinned at me. He seemed to be in a better humor now.

"I guess if I was fishing to eat, I wouldn't starve," I said, "but I don't think I'd gain too much weight."

"Not many would," he said. "Clint, maybe, but I sure wouldn't. Maybe I just ain't got the patience."

"Maybe you just can't think like a fish," I told him.

He didn't answer. He was looking on off toward the mountains.

"Weather comin' in," he said.

I looked up. A heavy cloudbank was building up along the tops of the peaks.

"Bad?" I asked him.

"Hard to tell. Rain, most likely."

Lou and Jack came on down about dark, and we ate supper. There weren't enough trout to make a meal of, so we just ate them as a kind of side dish.

With Clint, Stan, and Sloane gone, the group around the fire seemed very small, and it was a whole lot quieter.

"I think I seen 'im today," Lou said finally.

"Where?" Jack asked quickly.

"Up above me. I think I'll move on up to Danny's spot tomorrow."

"You'll have to walk that last bit," Miller said. "That horse of yours ain't that good."

"I can do that, too," Lou told him.

After that, nobody said much.

"Clint coming back tonight?" I asked Miller finally.

"More'n likely," he said. "He'll probably try to beat the weather."

"Think we'll get snow?" Jack asked him.

"Could. Rain more likely."

"What'll that do to the deer?"

"Hold 'em back at first. They'll have to come out eventually though."

I sat staring at the fire. I didn't much like the way Lou and Jack were beginning to push on Miller. The whole situation had changed now. With the others out of camp, things were getting pretty tight. Before, Cal and Stan had been around to kind of serve as a buffer between these two, and, of course, Clint's stories had helped, too. It was a lot grimmer now. I almost began to wish I'd gone down with the others. That would have left Miller right in the middle though, and that wouldn't have been any good. He didn't know what was going on.

"I suppose we might as well bed down," Miller said finally. "I imagine we'll get woke up when Clint comes in."

We all stood up and went off to our tents.

"I wish to hell you and McKlearey would get off this damn thing about that stupid deer," I told Jack after we'd crawled in our sacks.

"You know what's goin' on," he said shortly. "I ain't gonna back away from him like Larkin did."

"Stan didn't back away," I said. "Stan finally got smart."

"How do you figure?"

"Day before yesterday he took a shot at Lou. Sprayed dirt all over him."

"No shit?" Jack sounded surprised.

"Scared the piss out of him."

Jack laughed. "I wish I coulda seen it."

"It's not really that funny," I said. "That's why Stan left camp. He wasn't sure he could make himself miss next time."

"I sure wouldn'ta missed. So Lou was playin' around with Stan's wife, too, huh? I didn't think he was her type."

"He isn't. She got stupid, is all."

"Well, don't get shook. I ain't gonna shoot 'im. I'm just gonna outhunt 'im. I'm gonna get that deer."

I grunted and rolled over to go to sleep.

McKlearey had another nightmare that night, screaming for Sullivan and for some guy named Danny—I knew that it wasn't me. It took us quite a while to get him calmed down this time.

Then about two thirty or so Clint came in, and we all got up again to help him get the horses unsaddled. It had started to drizzle by then, so we had to move all the saddles into the now-empty tent where Stan and Cal had slept.

All in all it was a pretty hectic night.

27

It drizzled rain all the next day. Miller had told Jack and Lou that there was no point in going out in the morning if it were raining, so we all slept late.

Camping out in the rain is perhaps one of the more disagreeable experiences a man can go through. Even with a good tent, everything gets wet and clammy.

Ragged clouds hung in low over the basin, and the ground turned sodden. Clint and Miller moved around slowly in rain-shiny ponchos, their cowboy hats turning darker and darker as they got wetter and wetter. The rest of us sat in our tents staring out glumly.

The fire smoked and smoldered, and what wind there was always seemed to blow the smoke right into the tents.

"Christ, isn't it *ever* gonna let up?" Jack said about ten

o'clock. It was the fourth time he'd said it. I was pretty sure that if he said it again I was going to punch him right in the mouth.

"Piss on it," I said. "I'm going fishing."

"You're outa your tree. You'll get your ass soakin' wet out there."

I shrugged. "I've got plenty of dry clothes," I said and went on out.

"Can I use your pole, Clint?" I asked.

"Sure. See if you can get enough for supper."

"I'll give it a try." I picked up the pole and went on down to the ponds again. I'd kind of halfway thought I'd alternate between the two ponds, giving the fish time to calm down between catches, but I didn't get the chance. The larger, upper pond was so hot I never got away from it. The top of the water was a leaden gray, roughened up with the rain and the little gusts of wind. Maybe it was just obscured enough that the fish couldn't see me, I don't know for sure, but they were biting so fast I couldn't keep my hook baited. I caught seven the first hour.

It slowed down a little after lunch, about the time the rain slackened off, so I hung it up for a while and went on back up to camp. Jack and Lou took off for the ridge, and Clint, Miller, and I hunched up around the fire.

"Should clear off tonight," Clint said. "Weather forecast I caught last night down at the place said so anyway."

"I sure hope so," I said. "With the other two gone down and the rain, it's so damned gloomy around here you can carve it with a knife."

"How many fish you get?" he asked me.

"Nine or ten so far," I said. "I'll go get some more after I dry out a bit."

"There's no rush, son," Miller said. "You're right about missin' the other two though—I mean like you said. When a bunch of men start out on somethin' together, it always kinda upsets things if some of 'em don't make it all the way through." He turned to Clint. "'Member that time the bunch of us went out to log that stretch up by Omak and old Clark got hurt?"

"Yeah," Clint said.

"I don't think old Clark had said more'n about eight words in two months," Miller went on, "and he always went to bed early and stayed off by himself, but it just wasn't the same without him there."

"Yeah, that's right," Clint said.

They started reminiscing about some of the things they'd done and some of the places they'd gone. They'd covered a helluva lot of ground together, one way or the other—particularly after Miller's wife had died about twenty years or so ago.

I listened for a while, but I kind of felt as if I were intruding on something pretty private. I guess they were willing to share it, or they wouldn't have talked about it, but I've never much enjoyed that kind of thing. I'd a whole lot rather take people as I find them and not know too much about their past lives.

"Well," I said, standing up, "I guess I'd better get back to work if we're going to have trout for supper."

"Work?" Clint chuckled. "Who are you tryin' to kid?"

I laughed and went on down to the lower pond.

It was a lot slower now, and the fish seemed sluggish. I let my mind drift. I don't think I intended to. Usually I kept a pretty tight grip on it.

It had been on a day like this that I'd taken off from the Old Lady that time. I could still remember it. I'd gotten a job at one of the canned goods plants when I'd gotten out of high school, and when I came home from work that day, I'd found her in bed with some big slob. I'd yelled at him to get the hell out of the house, but he'd just laughed at me. Then I'd tried to hit him, and he'd beaten the crap out of me.

"Hit the little snot a time or two for me, Fred," my mother had yelled drunkenly.

After he'd finished with me and gone back into the bedroom, I had packed up a few clothes and taken off. I'd only stopped long enough to paint the word "whore" on the side of the house in green letters about five feet high and swipe the distributor cap off Fred's car. Both of my little revenges had been pretty damned petty, but what the hell else can you be at seventeen?

There was a shot up on the ridge. Then another. Then three more from a different rifle. The echoes bounced around a lot, muffled a little by the still lightly falling rain.

I stood waiting for the pistol-shot signal, but one never came. "Trigger-happy bastards," I said and went back to fishing.

I caught three more pretty good-sized ones just before the sun went down, and I cleaned the whole bunch and carted them up to the fire. By then the rain had stopped, and the sky was starting to clear.

"Got a mess, huh?" Miller said.

"Best I could do," I said.

When Lou and Jack came back, they were both soaked and bad-tempered.

"Keep your goddamn shots off my end of the hill, McKlearey," Jack snarled as soon as Lou came in.

"Fuck ya!" McKlearey snapped back.

"That's about enough of that, men," Miller said sternly. "Any more of that kinda talk, and we'll break camp and go down right now."

They both glared at him for a minute, but they shut up.

Clint fried up the trout, and we had venison and beans to go along with them. I was starting to get just a little tired of beans.

McKlearey had taken to sitting off by himself again, and after supper he sat with his back to a stump a ways off from the fire, holding his bandaged hand with the other one and muttering to himself. He hadn't changed the bandage for a couple of days, and it was pretty filthy. Every now and then I'd catch the names "Sullivan" and "Danny," but I wasn't really listening to him.

We all went to bed fairly early.

"Goddammit, Jack," I said, "Miller's not kidding. He and Clint have just about had a gutful of you and McKlearey yapping at each other about that damned white deer. Now I know a helluva lot more about what's happening than they do, and I'm starting to get a little sick of it myself. If you're going to hunt, hunt right. If you're not, let's pack it up and go down the hill."

"Butt out," he said. "This is between that shithead and me."

"That's just the point," I said. "You two are slopping it all over everybody else."

"If you don't like it, why don't you just pack up and go on down? You're all finished anyway."

"Then who the goddamn hell would be around to keep you and McKlearey from killing each other?"

"Who asked you to?"

"I invited myself," I said. "In a lot of ways I don't think much of you, but you're my brother, and I'm a son of a bitch if I want to see you get all shot up or doing about thirty years in the pen for shooting somebody as worthless as McKlearey." Maybe I came down a little hard. Jack's ego was pretty damned tender.

"As soon as they get those saddles out of there," he said, "I'll move over to Sloane's old tent."

"Don't do me any favors," I said. "I'll be all moved out by noon."

"Whichever way you want it," he said.

We both rolled over so our backs were to each other.

28

AFTER he got back from taking Jack and Lou up the hill next morning, Miller came up to where I was sitting by the fire. "Feel like doin' a little huntin', son?" he asked me.

I looked up at him, not understanding what he was talking about.

"Somebody ought to fill the Big Man's tag for him," he said. I'd forgotten that.

"Sure," I said, "I'll get my rifle."

"We'll poke on down the trail a ways and hunt in the timber. That way we won't bother them two up on the hill."

The sky had lightened, and the pale light was beginning to slide back in under the tree trunks.

"Try not to shoot up the liver this time," Clint said, faking a grouchy look.

"OK, Clint." I laughed.

Miller and I got our rifles and went on down to the corral. I saddled Ned and we started on out.

"We'll go on down into the next valley and picket the horses," he said after a while. "Do us a little Indian huntin'."

"You'd better field-strip that for me," I said.

"Put our noses into the wind and walk along kinda slow. See what we can scare up."

"Good," I said. "That's my kind of hunting."

"Get restless sittin' still, is that it, son?"

"I suppose," I said.

"If I'm not bein' nosy, just how old are you?"

"Twenty-five last April," I said.

He nodded. "'Bout what I figured. 'Bout the same age as my boy woulda been."

I didn't push it. He and Clint had said a few things about "the accident" the day before. I hadn't known he'd had any kids.

"Lost him the same time I lost my wife," he said quietly. Then he didn't say any more for quite a while.

We rode on down into the valley and got into the pine trees.

"Creek there," he said. "Wind'll be comin' up the draw this time of day."

"Good little clearing right there for the horses," I said pointing.

"Should work out about right," he said.

We went on, dismounted, and hooked Ned and Miller's big Morgan to a couple of long picket-ropes. We unhooked our rifles and went on down into the creek-bottom. Miller's rifle was an old, well-used bolt-action of some kind with a scope that had been worn shiny in a couple places from being slid in and out of the case so many times. It had obviously been well taken care of.

"I see you brought that hog-leg along," he said, nodding at my pistol belt.

"Starting to be a habit," I said. "Besides, I keep extra rifle cartridges on one side, and my knives are on it," I said. I still felt a little apologetic about the damned thing.

"Can you hit anything with it?" he asked me.

"Not at any kind of range."

"You shootin' high or low?"

"Low."

"You're pushin' into the recoil just before you shoot," he said. "Clint always used to do the same thing."

"How do you mean?"

"Just before you fire. You push your hand forward to brace your arm for the kick." He held out his right forefinger pistol-fashion and showed me.

"Maybe you're right," I said, trying to remember the last time I'd fired it at a target.

"Get somebody to load it for you and leave a couple empty. Then shoot it. You'll be able to spot it right off. Barrel dips like you was tryin' to dig a well with it when you click down on an empty chamber."

"How does a guy get over it?"

"Just knowin' what you're doin' oughta take care of most of it."

I nodded.

"Well, son," he said, grinning at me, "let's you and me go huntin', shall we?"

"Right, Cap," I said.

"You take the left side of the creek, and I'll take the right. We'll just take our time."

I jumped the creek, and we started off down the draw, moving very slowly and looking around.

Miller stopped suddenly, and I froze. Slowly he pointed up the side of the draw and then passed the flat of his hand over the top of his big hat. No horns. Doe.

She stepped out from behind a tree, and I could see her. Miller and I both stood very still until she walked on up out of the draw. Then he motioned, and we went on.

The trees were fairly far apart, and there wasn't much under-brush even this close to the creek. The floor of the forest was thickly covered with pine needles, softened and very quiet after the rain from the day before.

A faint pink glow of sunlight reflected off the snow-fields above began to filter down between the tree trunks. The air was very clean and sharp, cold and pine-scented. I felt good. This was my kind of hunting.

We walked on down the creek-bed for about a half hour or so, spotting seven or eight more deer—all does or small bucks.

We went around a bend, and Miller froze. He poked his chin straight ahead.

I couldn't see the deer. Apparently Cap couldn't either, at least not clearly. He kept moving his head back and forth as if trying to get a clear view between the trees. He lifted his rifle once and then lowered it again. He held out his hand toward me, the fingers fanned out. Five-point.

Then he pointed at me and made a shooting motion with his hand, his forefinger extended and his thumb flipping up and down twice. He wanted me to shoot. Shoot what, for God's sake?

I put my scope on the woods ahead, but I couldn't see a damn thing. Then the buck stepped out into an open spot about a hundred yards away and stood facing me, his ears up and his rack held up proudly. I started doing some quick computations. I leaned the rifle barrel against a tree to be sure it would be steady and drew a very careful aim on a point low in the deer's chest, just between his front legs. I sure didn't want to mess up this shot with Cap watching me.

I slowly squeezed the trigger. When a shot is good and right on, you get a kind of feeling of connection between you and the animal—almost as if you were reaching out and touching him, very gently, kind of pushing on him with your finger. I don't want to get mystic about it, but it's a sort of three-way union—you, the gun, and the deer, all joined in a frozen instant. It's so perfect that I've always kind of regretted the fact that the deer gets killed in the process. Does that make any sense?

The deer went back on his haunches and his front feet went up in the air. Then he fell heavily on one side, his head downhill. The echoes bounced off among the trees.

"Hot damn!" Cap yelled, his face almost chopped in two with his grin. "Damn good shot, son. Damn good!"

I felt about fifteen feet tall.

I jumped the creek again, and the two of us went on up toward the deer.

"Where'd you aim, son?"

"Low in the chest—between the legs."

He frowned slightly.

"I'm sighted an inch high at two hundred," I explained. "I figured it at a hundred yards, so I should have been four to six inches above where I aimed. I wanted to get into the neck above the shoulder line so I wouldn't spoil any meat."

"Or the liver." He chuckled.

"Amen to that. I'd get yelled at something awful if I shot out another liver."

"Old Clint can get just like an old woman about some things." He laughed.

The deer was lying on his side with blood pumping out of his throat. His eyes blinked slowly. I reached for my pistol.

"You cut the big artery," Cap said. "You could just as easy let 'im bleed out."

"I'd rather not," I said.

"Suit yourself," he said.

I shot the deer through the head. The blood stopped pumping like someone had turned off a faucet.

"You always do that, don't you, son?" he said.

I nodded, holstering the pistol. "I figure I owe it to them."

"Maybe you're right," he said thoughtfully.

We stood looking at the deer. He had a perfectly symmetrical five-point rack, and his body was heavy and well-fed.

"Beautiful deer," he said, grinning again. "Let's see how close you figured it. Where'd you aim?"

"About here," I said, pointing.

"Looks like you were about eight inches high," he said. "You took him just under the chin."

"I must have miscalculated," I said. "I'd figured to go about six high."

He nodded. "You was shootin' uphill," he said. "You forgot to allow for that. It was a hundred yards measured flat along the ground—only about seventy yards trajectory though."

"I never thought of that."

He laughed and slapped my shoulder. "I don't think we'll revoke your license over two inches," he said.

"Tell me, Cap," I said, "why didn't *you* shoot 'im?"

"Couldn't get a clear shot," he lied with a perfectly straight face.

"Oh," I said.

"Well, son, let's gut 'im."

"Right."

With two of us working on it, it took only a few minutes to do the job.

"Why don't you go get the horses while I rig up a drag?" Cap said.

"Sure." I leaned my rifle against a tree and took off. We were only a short distance from the horses really, and it took me less than ten minutes to get them. I rode on back, leading Miller's big walnut-colored Morgan.

"You move right out, don't you, son?" Cap said as I rode up.

"Long legs," I said.

"I'm just about done here," he said. He was sawing at a huckleberry bush with his hunting knife. I got off and handed him the big knife. He chopped the bush off close to the ground.

"That's sure a handy thing," he said. "Almost like an ax."

"That's what I figured when I got the set," I said.

He'd rigged up a kind of sled of six or eight of the bushes packed close, side by side, and lashed to a big dead limb across the butts and another holding them together about three feet or so up the trunks. He doubled over a lead-rope and tied it to the limb across the butts. Then we lifted the deer carcass onto the platform and tied it securely with another lead-rope. He tied a long rope to the doubled lead-rope at the front of the drag and fastened it to his saddle horn.

"You want me to hook on, too, Cap?" I asked him.

"Naw," he said. "Trail's too narrow, and old Sam here's big enough to pull the bottom out of a well if you want 'im to."

We stood for a moment beside the place where the deer had fallen.

"Good hunt," he said finally, patting me on the shoulder once. "We'll have to do 'er again some time."

I nodded. "This is the way it ought to be," I said.

"Well," he said, "let's get on back, shall we?"

We mounted and cut across up to the trail.

"Damn nice deer." Clint grinned when we got back to camp.

"Look at that shot," Miller said. "Right under the chin at about seventy or eighty yards uphill. The Kid there could drive nails all day with that rifle of his at about two hundred yards. Made the gun himself, too. Restocked one of them old Spring-fields."

"He fishes OK, too," Clint said, "and it don't seem to me he snores too loud. Reckon we oughta let 'im stay in camp?"

Miller looked at me for a minute. "He'll do," he said. We all grinned at each other.

"How 'bout us all havin' a drink?" Miller said. "I'll buy." He went into his tent and came out with a fifth of Old Grand-dad. He poured liberally into three cups and we stood around sipping at the whiskey.

"I ain't had so much fun in years," Cap said. "It was a real fine hunt."

"I ain't too much for all that walkin' you're partial to," Clint said, slapping one of his crooked legs.

Cap chuckled. "I told you that rodeoin' would catch up to you someday. Any action up there on the hill this mornin'?"

"Heard a couple shots earlier," Clint said. "No signals though."

"Probably missed," Cap said sourly. "Them two are each so worried that the other one's gonna get that damn freak that they can't even shoot anymore."

Just thinking about Jack and Lou almost spoiled the whole thing for me. I tried not to think about them. The morning had been too good for me to let that happen.

29

AT lunchtime I rode up the ridge to pick up Jack and Lou. Jack just grunted when I brought him his horse, and McKlearey took off down the hill ahead of me. They'd both moved uphill a ways, McKlearey onto my old post, and Jack up to Stan's.

I came up to the corral about the time Lou was getting off his horse. Jack was waiting for him.

"Now look, you son of a bitch," he started. "I told you to do your goddamn shootin' in your own territory."

"Fuck ya!"

"I mean it, goddammit! That goddamn deer came out right in front of me, and you were at least five hundred yards away. You didn't have a fuckin' chance of hittin' 'im. You shot just to run 'im off so I couldn't get a clear shot."

"Tough titty, Alders. Don't tell me how to hunt."

"All right, motherfucker, I can see the whole hillside, too, remember. I can play the same game. And even if you dumb-luck out and hit 'im, I'll shoot the son of a bitch to pieces before you can get to 'im. You won't have enough left to be worth bringin' out."

McKlearey glared at Jack, his face white. They were standing about ten feet apart and they were both holding their rifles. Jack's hand was inching toward the butt of his automatic.

"That's just damn well enough of that kinda talk," Miller's voice cracked from behind them.

"This is between him and me," Jack said.

"Not up here, it ain't," Miller said. "Now I don't know what kinda trouble you two got goin' between yourselves back in town, but I told you the first day to leave all that stuff down there. I meant what I said, too."

"We paid you to bring us up here," McKlearey said, "not to wet-nurse us." His eyes were kind of wild, and he was holding his rifle with the muzzle pointed about halfway between Jack and Cap.

261

I'm still not sure why I did it, but I slipped the hammer-thong off my pistol. I think Lou saw me do it because he slowly shifted his rifle until it was tucked up under his right arm so there was no way he could use either of his guns.

Miller had thought over what Lou had said. "I guess maybe we better just pack up and go on back down," he said. He turned his back on them and walked back up to the fire.

"We paid for ten goddamn days!" McKlearey yelled after him.

I hawked and spit on the ground, right between them.

"He can't do that," Jack said.

"Don't make any bets," I said flatly. "You guys made a verbal contract with him that first day. He told you that if there was any trouble in camp, we'd all come out. You agreed to it."

"That wouldn't stand up in court, would it?" Lou asked.

I nodded. "You bet it would. Particularly around here. If you were going to take him to court, it'd be in this county, and the jury'd all be his neighbors." I wasn't that sure, but it sounded pretty good.

"Well, what the hell do we do now?" Jack demanded.

"You might as well go pack your gear," I said. "He meant it about going back down."

"Who needs 'im?" Lou said. "Let 'im go."

"It's twelve miles back to the road, McKlearey," I said, "and he'll take the horses, the tents, and all the cooking equipment with him. Even if you got that damned freak deer, how would you get him out of the woods?"

He hadn't thought of that.

"You sound like you're on his side," Jack accused me.

"How 'bout that?" I said. I walked off down toward the pond. It was a helluva goddamn way to wind up the trip.

I guess both Jack and Lou did a lot of crawfishing, but Miller finally relented. I suppose he really didn't want his first trip as a guide to wind up that way. Anyway, they managed to talk him out of it.

Much as I wanted to stay up there, I still thought Miller was making a mistake. I went back to camp and moved all my gear into the empty tent.

"You don't have to do that, Dan," Jack said quietly as I started to roll up my sleeping bag.

"We'll both have more room this way," I said.

"Christ, Dan, you know how McKlearey can rub a guy raw."

"Yeah," I said, "but you're grown-up now, Jack. You're not some runny-nosed kid playing cowboys and Indians." I stopped in the doorway of the tent. "One other thing, old buddy," I said, "keep your goddamn hand away from that pistol from now on. There's not gonna be any of that shit up here." I went on out of the tent. McKlearey was standing outside. I guess he'd been listening.

"That goes for you, too, shithead," I told him.

Christ! I was right in the middle again. How the hell do I always get myself in that spot?

It took me about fifteen minutes to get settled in, and then we ate lunch. Nobody talked much. Both Jack and Lou went back to their tents after we finished.

"I probably shouldn't have changed my mind," Cap said quietly. "I got a feelin' it was a mistake."

"They've quieted down a bit," I said. "I'll go on up with my brother from now on—maybe I can keep him from getting so hot about things."

"What's got them two at each other that way?" Clint asked me.

"They just don't get along," I said. I knew that if I told them the real story, it would blow the whole trip. "This has been building for quite a while now. I thought they could forget about it while they were up here, but I guess I was wrong."

"Sure makes things jumpy in camp," Miller said shortly.

"It sure does," I agreed.

Jack wasn't too happy about my going up the hill with him, but I don't think he dared to say much about it in front of Miller.

When we got up there, he wouldn't talk to me, so I just let it go.

A good-looking five-point came out just about sunset, but he ignored it. No matter what he might have told Miller, he was still after that freak. After shooting time, we rode back to camp without waiting for Lou.

"That was a nice deer you got for Sloane," Jack said finally. I guess he wanted to make peace.

"Fair." I said. "It was a lot of fun hunting that way."

"How'd you do it?"

"Miller and I just pussyfooted through the woods until we spotted him."

"Sloane'll be pretty tickled with him."

That seemed to exhaust that topic of conversation pretty much.

Supper was lugubrious. Nobody talked to anybody else. Jack stared fixedly into the fire, and McKlearey sat with his back to a stump, watching everybody and holding that filthy bandage out in front of him so he wouldn't bump his hand. I wondered how bad the cut was by now.

I fixed myself a drink and settled back down by the fire.

"Watch yourself, Danny," Lou said suddenly, his eyes very bright. "Same thing might happen to you as happened to Sullivan."

It didn't make any sense, so I didn't answer him. I noticed, though, that after that he concentrated on me. He seemed to flinch just a little bit every time I moved. Did the silly bastard actually think I was going to shoot him?

"Bedtime," he finally said. He got up and went to his tent. Jack waited a few minutes, and then he went to his tent, too.

I talked quietly with Cap and Clint for a while, trying to stir up the good feeling we'd had going that morning, but it didn't quite come off. I think we were all too worried.

I went on back to the latrine. On my way back to my tent I heard a funny slapping kind of noise over in the woods. I stopped and waited for my eyes to adjust to the dark a little more. Then I saw a movement.

It was McKlearey. I guess he'd rolled out under the back of his tent or something, and he was back in the trees practicing his draw.

He was getting pretty good at it.

30

CLINT woke me the next morning, and I rolled out of the sack quickly. It was chilly, and for some reason it seemed darker that morning than usual. Then it dawned on me. The moon had already set. It had been going down earlier and earlier every morning, and now it was setting before we even got up.

Breakfast was as quiet as supper the night before, and we had to take the lantern down to the corral with us when we went to saddle the horses. Miller seemed particularly grim. We mounted up and rode on up the ridge. It was a damned good thing the horses knew the way by now because it was blacker than hell out there.

Miller had insisted that Jack take Sloane's old spot, the lowest on the hill, and that Lou take the very top one. I guess he wanted to get as much distance between the two of them as possible.

As soon as Cap dropped us off, Jack went over to the edge of the ravine. I stayed with the horses until Cap came back from dropping off Lou.

"I sure hope they both fill today," he said. "All the fun's gone out of it now."

"Yeah," I said. "I'll remind Jack that there's only three more days. Maybe that'll bring him to his senses."

"Somethin' is gonna have to. See you about noon, son."

"Right, Cap."

He rode off down into the darkness, and I went over to find Jack.

"See anything?" I asked.

"Still too goddamn dark," he said, and then, "I don't know why I had to get stuck with the bottom of the hill like this."

"Man," I told him, "I got a five-point yesterday four miles below here. They're all over the side of the mountain."

"Not the one *I* want," he said.

"Are you still hung up on that damn thing?"

265

"I said I was gonna get that white one, and I meant it."

"Goddamn it, Jack, there are only three days left after today. You're going to wind up going down empty."

"Don't worry about it," he said, "I know what I'm doin'."

We sat waiting for it to get light.

The sky paled and the shadowy forms of the rocks and bushes began to appear around us. Several does and a couple small bucks went down the ravine below our post.

"They're starting to move," I said.

"Yeah."

I looked at the thin, dark man beside me with the wiry stubble smudging his cheeks and chin. Jack's eyes were hollow, with dark circles under them. The red baseball cap he was wearing was pulled low over his eyebrows, and he was staring fixedly up the gorge. I tried to make out the shadow of the boy I'd grown up with in his face, but it wasn't there anymore. Jack was a stranger to me. I guess I'd been kidding myself all along. He always had been a stranger. The whole business when I'd gotten back to Tacoma had been a fake. I suppose we both knew it, but neither one of us had had the guts or the honesty to admit it.

When the white deer came out, he was on top of that bluff that was opposite Jack's old post. The rock face dropped about forty or fifty feet onto a jumble of rocks and gravel and then fell again into the wash at the bottom of the hill. Maybe Jack wouldn't see him.

"There he is!" Jack hissed.

Damn it!

"What is it?" he demanded, his hands trembling violently. "Two hundred yards?"

"It's pretty far," I said, "and he's right on top of that cliff."

The deer looked around uncertainly, as if he were lost. Somehow he looked more helpless than ever.

Jack was getting squared away for a shot.

"Wait, for Chrissake!" I said. "Let him get away from that goddamn cliff."

"I can't wait. McKlearey'll spot him." His hands were shaking so badly that the end of his gun-barrel looked like the tip of a fishing rod.

"Calm down," I snapped. "You'll never get off a shot that way."

"Shut up!" he snapped and yanked the trigger.

His Mauser barked hollowly. The deer looked around, startled. "Run, you son of a bitch," I muttered under my breath.

Jack was feverishly trying to work the bolt of his gun, his shaking hands unable to handle the simple operation.

"Calm down," I said again.

"He'll get away," Jack said. "Oh, Jesus, he'll get away!" He rammed another shell up the tube. He fired again, not even bothering to aim.

McKlearey's gun barked from up the ridge. He must have been at least six hundred yards from the deer.

"Oh, Jesus!" Jack said, fighting with the bolt again. He stumbled to his feet.

"Jack, for Christ's sake, calm down! You'll never hit anything this way!" I put my hand on his arm.

"Get away from me, you bastard!" he screamed. He spun on me, pointing the rifle at me and still fighting with the bolt.

It was happening—it wasn't exactly the way it had been that day in the pawnshop, but it was close enough.

I thumbed off the hammer-thong and left my hand hanging over my pistol-butt. "Don't close that bolt with that thing pointed at me, Jack," I told him.

Maybe some day you'll be no good, and then I'll shoot you. There it was again.

"I mean it, Jack," I said. "Point that gun-muzzle away from me." I felt very cold inside. I knew he could never close that bolt and get his finger onto the trigger before I got one off. I was only about five feet away from him. There was no way I could miss. I was going to kill my brother. It hung there, an absolute certainty—no fuss, no dramatics, nothing but a mechanical reflex action. I felt disconnected from myself, as if I were standing back, watching something I had no control over. I even began to mourn for my dead brother.

Then his face kind of sank in on itself. He knew it, too.

Then McKlearey fired again.

Jack spun back around and fired at the deer three times in a row from a standing position, his hand very smooth on the bolt now.

The deer had frozen up. I thought I could see him flinch with the sound of each shot.

McKlearey fired.

Jack fired his last round. His hand dove into his jacket pocket and came out jerkily with a handful of shells. He started feverishly shoving them down into the magazine.

McKlearey fired again.

The deer lurched and fell on his side, his sticklike legs scrabbling at the rocks and bushes.

"Aw, no!" Jack said in an agonized voice.

The deer stumbled to his feet, staggered a step or two and, with what looked almost like a deliberate lunge, fell off the cliff.

"Aw, God damn it!" Jack said, his voice breaking oddly.

The deer hit the rock-pile below and bounced high in the air. I could hear his antlers snap off when he hit. His white body plunged into the brush like a leaping trout reentering the water. I heard him bounce again and tumble on down the ravine.

"Aw, goddamn son of a bitch!" Jack sobbed, slamming his rifle down on the ground. He sat down heavily and buried his face in his hands. He was crying.

Up the ridge McKlearey gave a wild yell of triumph followed by a barrage of shots from his pistol. He must have emptied the thing. Maybe, with any kind of luck, one of them would drop back in on him.

31

I went straight on down into the ravine, leaving Jack on the ridge to get himself straightened out. The brush was a little tough at first, but I got the hang of it in a couple minutes. I just bulled on through, hanging onto the limbs to keep from falling—kind of like going down hand over hand.

I could still hear McKlearey screaming and yelling up on the knob at the top of the ridge.

I'd marked the last place where I'd seen the deer, and I hit the bottom a good ways below where that had been. I was pretty sure I was below the carcass.

The wash at the bottom of the ravine was about fifteen feet wide and six to ten feet deep. I imagined that when the snow melted, it was probably a boiling river, but it was bone-dry right now. Most of the sides were steep gravel banks with large rocks jutting out here and there.

I finally found a place where I could get down into the wash. I seemed to remember hearing some gravel sliding after the deer had stopped bouncing. I started up the ravine.

The deer was about a hundred yards from where I'd come down. He was lying huddled at the foot of a gravel bank in a place where the wash made a sharp turn. He was dead, of course.

Only one of his legs was sticking out; the others were all kind of tucked up under him. The protruding leg was at an odd angle.

His head was twisted around as if he were staring back over his shoulder, and a couple of his ribs were poked out through his skin. His fur wasn't really white but rather a cream color. It had smudges and grass stains on it—either from his normal activity or from the fall through the brush.

His antlers were shattered off close to his head, and the one red eye I could see was about half open. There was dirt in it.

A thin dribble of gravel slithered down the steep bank and spilled down across his shoulder. A heavy stick protruded from the bank just above him.

"You poor bastard," I said softly. I nudged at his side with my toe, and I could hear broken bones grating together inside. He was like a sack full of marbles.

"Probably broke every bone in his body," I muttered. I took hold of the leg. It was loose and flopping. I tucked it back up beside the rest of him. Folded up the way he was, he didn't take up much more room than a sack of potatoes. I squatted down beside him.

"Well," I said, "you did it. God knows we ran you off this hill often enough. You just *had* to keep coming back, didn't you?" I reached over and brushed some of the dirt off his face. The eye with the dirt in it looked at me calmly.

"I sure wish I knew what the hell to do now, old buddy," I said. "You're Lou's deer, and I suppose I ought to make him keep you, no matter what shape you're in. Christ only knows, though, what that'll lead to."

How did I always get into these boxes? All I wanted to do was just look out for myself. I had enough trouble doing that without taking on responsibilities for other people as well. I had to try to figure out, very fast, what would be the consequences of about three different courses of action open to me

right now, and no matter what I decided to do, I had no guar-
antees that the whole damn mess wouldn't blow up in my face.
I sure wished that Miller were here.

I could hear McKlearey yelling, but he sounded like he was
coming down the hill now. Whatever I was going to do, I was
going to have to make up my mind in a hurry.

I put my hand on the deer's shoulder. He was still warm.
A kind of muscle spasm or reflex made his eyelid flutter at
me.

"You're a lot of help," I said to the deer. I stood up.

I could hear McKlearey crashing around in the brush several
hundred yards up the ravine.

"Well, piss on it!" I said and pulled on the limb sticking
out of the gravel bank. The whole bank gave way, and I had
to jump back out of the way to keep from getting half-buried
myself. The slide completely covered the carcass. I stood holding the stick for a moment, then I pitched it off into the brush.
I turned around and went on back downstream.

Lou crossed the wash and came down over the rock-pile at
the foot of the cliff. He stopped yelling when he started finding
pieces of antler. He was there for quite awhile, gathering up
all the chunks and fragments he could find. Then he came on
down. I had climbed up out of the wash and was standing up
on the bank when he got to where I was.

"You find 'im, Danny?" he asked me from down in the
wash. His face was shiny with sweat, and his eyes were fever-
ish.

"I came up from down that way," I said. "He must be above
here somewhere." It wasn't exactly a lie.

"No, I came down this creek-bed. He ain't up there."

I shrugged. "Maybe in the brush somewhere—"

"The bastard busted his horns," he said, holding out both
hands full of dark fragments.

"Damn shame," I said.

He began stuffing the pieces into various pockets. "A good
taxidermist oughta be able to glue 'em all back together, don't
you think?"

"I don't know, Lou. I've never heard of anybody doing it
before."

"Sure they can," he said. "But where the hell is the goddamn
deer?"

"It's got to be up above," I said. "Did you get any kind of
blood-trail?"

"Shit! The way that fucker was bouncin'?"

"Maybe if we find one of the places where he hit—"

He'd finally finished stuffing chunks of horn in his pockets, and suddenly his eyes narrowed and he squinted up at me. His face was very cold and hard looking.

"Oh, *now* I get it," he said. "You and your *brother*, huh? You two are tryin' to keep *my* deer."

"You couldn't *give* me that deer after you knocked it off that cliff," I told him flatly.

"That's *my* goddamn deer," he said angrily.

"I never said it wasn't."

"Where the hell is it? Where the hell have you got my deer?" His voice was getting shrill.

"Come on, Lou, get serious."

"Don't do this to me, Danny." His eyes were bulging now.

"Settle down, Lou. Let's go back up and check out the brush."

"Danny? Is that you, Danny?" His face was twitching, and his voice was kind of crooning.

"Come on, Lou," I said, "let's go back up to where he hit."

"You know what I did to Sullivan, don't you, Danny?"

"Come on, Lou," I said.

Now what the hell was going on?

"It wasn't my fault, Danny. It was so fuckin' dark, and Charlie was all around us."

"Lou, snap out of it!"

"It wasn't my fault, Danny. He come sneakin' up on me. He didn't give me no password or nothin'."

"Lou!"

"Nobody knows where he is, Danny. I hid 'im real good. Nobody'll ever know."

I suddenly felt sick to my stomach.

"Don't tell the lieutenant, Danny. Everything will be OK if you just keep your mouth shut about it." His eyes were wild now.

"Come on, Lou, snap out of it. That's all over now." I was starting to get a little jumpy about this. It could get bad in a minute. And I still wasn't over the little session with Jack up on the ridge.

"I'll pay you, Danny. I got five hundred or so saved up for a big R and R. It's all yours. Just for Chrissake, don't say nothin'."

Very slowly I eased off the hammer-thong again. How many times was this going to happen in one day?

"Please, Danny, I'm beggin' ya. They'll *hang* me for God's sake." His rifle was slung over his left shoulder, and his right hand was on his belt, real close to that damned .38. I wondered if he'd remembered to reload it. Knowing McKlearey, he probably had.

"OK, Kid," he said, "if that's the way you want it." The pleading note had gone out of his voice, and his face was pale and very set.

"McKlearey," I said as calmly as I could, "if you make one twitch toward that goddamn pistol, I'll shoot you down in your tracks and you damn well know I can do it. You know I can take you any time I feel like it. Now straighten up and let's go find that deer." I sure hoped that I sounded more convincing than I felt. Frankly, I was scared to death.

"I been practicin'," he said, his face crafty.

"Not enough to make that much difference, Lou," I said.

He stood there looking up at me. I guess it got through to him—even through what had happened on the Delta—that I had him cold. At least I had him cold enough to make the whole thing a bad gamble for him. Finally he shook his head as though coming out of a bad dream.

"You say you came up the creek-bed?" he asked as if nothing had happened.

"Yeah," I said. "The deer's gotta be above us somewhere— maybe off in the brush."

"Maybe if we each took one side," he said. "It sure as hell ain't down in here." He turned and clambered up out of the wash on the other side.

"Danny?" he said from the other side of the wash.

"Yeah?"

"Sullivan and the other Danny are both dead, did you know that? Charlie got 'em. They been dead a long time now."

"Sorry to hear that, Lou."

"Yeah. It was a bad deal. They was my buddies—but Charlie got 'em."

I didn't want to get started on that again. "Work your way up to where you found those pieces of horn, Lou," I said. "I'll go up this side."

"Sure. Fuckin' deer has gotta be here someplace."

I let him lead out. I wasn't about to let him get behind me.

"You find 'im?" Miller called from the ridge.

"Not yet, Cap," I called back.

"Any sign?"

"Lou found some pieces of horn," I said.

"And some fur," Lou called to me. "Tell 'im I found some white fur, too."

"He got some fur, too," I relayed.

"He's gotta be down there then."

"Yeah. I know."

"Did he go off that bluff?"

"Yeah. I saw him fall."

Cap shook his head disgustedly and started to come down into the ravine.

The three of us combed the bottom for about an hour and a half. We passed the collapsed gravel bank about a half dozen times, but neither of them seemed to notice anything peculiar about it.

"It's no good," Miller said finally.

"But he's down here," Lou said. "We all seen 'im fall. I got 'im. I got 'im from way up there." He pointed wildly.

"I ain't doubtin' you shot him," Cap said, "but we ain't gonna find 'im."

"He's *gotta* be here," Lou said frenziedly. "Let's go back just one more time. He's here. He's *gotta* be here."

Miller shook his head. "Face it, Sarge," he said. "He's under a rockslide." He nudged the bank of the wash with the tow of his cowboy boot. A small avalanche resulted. "This whole gully is like this. One little bump brings it right down. There's two dozen places in this stretch we been workin' where the bank has give way just recently. He could be under any one of 'em. Only way you're gonna find that deer is with a shovel—and even then you wouldn't get him till the snow came."

"Maybe he's under a bush," Lou said. "Did we look over there?" He pointed desperately toward a place we'd all checked a half dozen times.

"We ain't gonna find 'im," Miller said.

"I *gotta* find 'im!" Lou screamed. "I gotta!" Then his face fell apart, and he started to cry like a little kid.

Miller stepped up to him and slapped him sharply in the face.

"Come out of that, now, Sergeant!" he barked. "That's an order."

Lou's eyes snapped open. "Sorry," he said. "Sorry, sir. I—I guess I lost my head."

"Let's get on up to the ridge," Miller commanded.

We started climbing. McKlearey coughed now and then—
or maybe he was sobbing, I'm not sure.

I still didn't let him get behind me.

32

I don't think either Jack or Lou said more than ten words the
rest of that day. Miller, Clint, and I were so busy watching
them that we didn't say much either, so it was awfully quiet
in camp. Neither one of them went out that evening, and we
all sat around staring at each other. At least McKlearey had
quit talking to himself.

The next morning they were still pretty quiet, and I got the
idea that they both wanted to finish up and get on back down
the mountain.

I went up on the ridge with Jack again, and almost as soon
as it was legal shooting time, we heard McKlearey's gun bang
off once, and then a minute or so later the flat, single crack
of his pistol.

"Lou got one," I said to Jack. It was pretty obvious, but
the silence was beginning to bug me.

"Yeah," Jack answered indifferently.

We saw Miller going on up, trailing Lou's horse and a pack
animal. About twenty minutes later he went on back down with
Lou and what looked like a pretty damn small deer.

"Shit!" Jack snorted. "The great hunter! I've seen bigger
cats." Maybe he was coming out of it a little—maybe not. I
couldn't tell for sure.

It was almost lunchtime when a fair-sized buck came down
the draw.

"Four-point," I whispered to Jack, who hadn't even been
watching, I don't think.

"Where?"

"Coming down the bottom of the gully."

"Yeah, I see 'im now," he said. His voice was very flat.

"I'll take 'im." He squared himself around into a sitting position, aimed, and fired. The buck dropped without a twitch.

"Good shot!" I said.

He shrugged and cranked out the empty. It clinked against a rock and rolled on down the hill.

"You going to signal?" I asked him.

"Miller'll be up in a few minutes anyway," he said.

"Yeah, but we'll need a packhorse."

"Maybe you're right," he said. He wearily pulled out the automatic, thumbed it, and touched it off in the general direction of the mountain above us. "Let's go gut 'im," he said.

We went down and field-dressed the deer. By the time we were done, Miller was there with the horses and a rope. He tossed us one end, and with a horse pulling from up above and the two of us guiding the carcass, getting the deer up was no trick at all.

"Damn nice deer," Miller said rather unconvincingly.

"It's worth the price of the tag, I guess," Jack said. He seemed pretty uninterested.

We got everything loaded up and went on back down to camp.

Clint and McKlearey had already gone on down. Miller told us that Lou had been all hot to leave, and there weren't really enough packhorses to haul out all of our gear and the deer as well, so Clint had loaded up and they'd gone on down.

"How big a one did he get?" Jack inquired.

"Two-point," Miller said. "Nice enough deer, but I think old Sarge musta made a mistake. He probably shoulda waited till he had a little more light."

Jack didn't say anything.

"Clint won't be back till late again," Miller said, "so we'll go on out tomorrow mornin'. We oughta skin your deer out and let it cool anyway. I tried to tell that to Sarge, too, but he seemed to be in a helluva rush for some reason."

"Probably got a hot date back in Tacoma," Jack said sourly.

Miller let that one go by.

We ate lunch and skinned out Jack's deer, and then Jack went into his tent to lie down for a while. I wandered around a bit and then went on down to the pond to molest the fish. The sun was hot and bright on the water, and the fish weren't moving.

Miller came on down after about a half hour and stood watching me as I fished. "Any action?" he said finally.

"Pretty slow, Cap," I said.

"Usually is this time of day."

"Maybe if I pester 'em enough, they'll bite just to get rid of me."

He chuckled at that.

I made another cast.

"Trip sure turned out funny," he said finally.

"Yeah," I agreed.

"I got a hunch Ol' Sarge oughta see a doctor of some kind. He sure went all to pieces yesterday."

I nodded. "I guess something pretty bad happened to him over in Vietnam," I said. I didn't want to go into too many details. I'd pushed the whole business about Sullivan and Danny—the other one—into the back of my mind, and I was doing my level best not to think about it.

"I kinda thought that might have somethin' to do with it," Cap said. "It's all kinda soured me on this guidin' business though."

"Don't judge everybody by us, Cap," I said. "You run a damn fine camp, and you know this country as well as any man could. None of what happened up here was your fault. This was all going on before we ever got up here."

"I keep thinkin' I shoulda done somethin' to head it all off before it went as far as it did though," he said, squinting up at the mountain. He still looked a lot like God.

"I don't think anybody could have done anything any differently," I told him. "You just got a bad bunch to work with, that's all. Nobody could have known that Cal was going to get sick or that McKlearey was going off the deep end the way he did. It was just the luck of the draw, that's all."

"Maybe," he said doubtfully. "Then, maybe too, I just ain't cut out for it. I can tell you right now that you're the only one of the whole bunch I'd care to go out with again. Maybe if a man's goin' into the business, he can't afford to have them kinda likes and dislikes."

I couldn't say much to that really.

Finally he cleared his throat. "I'm gonna ask you somethin' that ain't really none of my business, so if you don't want to answer, you can just tell me to keep my nose where it belongs, OK?"

"Shoot," I said. I knew what he was going to ask.

"You found that freak deer yesterday, didn't you, son?"

I nodded.

"Thought maybe you had. You're too good a hunter not to have, and you was the closest one to the place where he dropped into that gully."

"He was down in the wash," I said quietly, not looking at him, "all busted up. I dumped one of those gravel banks over on him. I just didn't think he was worth somebody getting killed over."

"Was it really that bad between your brother and the Sarge?" he asked.

"Yeah," I said, looking out over the pond. "It was getting real close. I figured that if neither one of them got the damn thing, it'd cool things down."

"You think pretty fast when you have to, don't you?"

"I was right in the middle," I said. "It was the only thing I could come up with in a hurry to keep the roof from falling in on me. I'm not very proud of it really." That was the truth, too.

"I don't know," he said after a minute, "from where I sit, it makes you look pretty tall."

I didn't understand that at all.

"A man's more important than a deer," he said, hunkering down and dipping his fingers in the water. "Sometimes a man'll forget that when he gets to huntin'. You're just like me, son. You wouldn't never try to take another man's deer or keep 'im from findin' it. It's just somethin' a man don't do. So you figure that what you done was wrong—particularly since it was the Sarge who shot the damn thing, and you don't like him very much. But you'd have done the same thing if it'd been your brother shot 'im. A lot of men wouldn't, but *you* would. Takes a pretty big man to do the right thing in a spot like that."

I felt better. I'd been worrying about it a lot.

"You gonna reel that fish in, or let 'im run around on the end of your line all day?" he said to me.

"What?" I looked at the pole I'd laid down across a log. The tip was whipping wildly. I grabbed the rod before the fish could drag it into the water. I brought him in close to shore, reached down into the water and carefully unhooked him. "Don't tell Clint," I said, shooing the exhausted trout back out into deeper water.

"Wild horses wouldn't get it out of me." He laughed. We went on back up to camp.

After that, things were OK again. Jack kept pretty much to

his tent except for supper, and Cap and I spent the rest of the afternoon getting things squared away so we could break camp the next morning. I moved my gear back into Jack's tent so we could strike the one I'd been sleeping in as well as McKlearey's.

After supper, Jack had a couple of drinks and went back to his tent. Cap and I sat up telling stories and waiting for Clint to get back.

The little guy came in about ten thirty, madder than hell.

"That damn burrhead run off on me, Cap," he growled as he rode up.

"Run off? What do you mean, run off?"

"We got about a half mile from the bottom, and he kicks ol' Red in the slats and took off like a scared rabbit. When I got to the bottom, ol' Red was all lathered up and blowed and wanderin' around not tied to anything, and that burrhead and that pile of nuts and bolts he called a car was gone."

"Didn't he take his deer?" Cap asked.

"He didn't take nothin'! He even left his rifle tied to the saddle."

"He say anything at all?"

"Not a word—not a good-bye, go to hell, kiss my ass, or a damn thing. I figured maybe he'd gone on down to the place. I was gonna have some words with him about runnin' off and leavin' me with all the work, but there wasn't a sign of 'im there neither. He just clean, flat took off. I left all his stuff in the barn. I don't know how the hell we'll get it all back to 'im."

"We'll take it back," I said. "I'll see that he gets it all."

Clint grunted, still pretty steamed.

Cap shook his head. "I sure misjudged *that* one," he said.

"Somebody oughta take a length of two-by-four to 'im," Clint said. "That was a damn-fool kid stunt, runnin' off like that."

"Well," Cap said, "we can't do anything about it tonight. Let's unsaddle the stock and get to bed. And you better cool down a mite. You know what the doctor told you about not losin' your temper so much."

"Hell," Clint said, "I'm all calm and peaceful *now*. 'Bout time I started up the hill, I was mad enough to bite nails and spit rust."

We finally got things squared away and got to bed.

The next morning I was up before the others, so I got the

fire started and got coffee going and then wandered around a
bit, kind of getting the last feel of things. I like to do that with
the good things. The others I kind of just let slide away.

It had been a good hunt—in spite of everything—and I'd
worked out whatever it was that I'd needed to work out. Some
people seem to think that things like that have to be all put
down in a set of neatly stated propositions, but it isn't really
that way at all. A lot of times it's better not to get too specific.
If you feel all right about yourself and the world in general
where you didn't before, then you've solved your problem—
whatever it was. If you don't, you haven't. Verbalizing it isn't
going to change anything. One thing I could verbalize, though,
was the fact that I had a couple of friends I hadn't had before.
Just that by itself made the whole trip worth everything it had
cost.

"Who's the damn early bird?" Clint growled, coming out
of the tent all rumpled and grouchy-looking.

"Me." I grinned at him.

"Mighta known," he said. "You been bustin' your butt to
get your hands on the cookware ever since we got up here."

"I figured I could ruin a pot of coffee just as well as you
could," I said.

"Oh-ho! Pretty smart-alecky for so damn early in the mornin'," he said. "All right, boy, since you went and started it,
we'll just see how much of a camp cook you are. *You* fix
breakfast this mornin'. Anythin' you wanna fix. There's the
cook tent."

"I think I've been had," I said.

"I guess they don't teach you not to volunteer in the Army
no more," he said. "Well, I'm goin' back to bed. You just call
us when you got ever-thin' ready." He chuckled and went on
back into his tent.

"You're a dirty old man," I called after him.

He stuck his head back out, thumbed his nose at me, and
disappeared again.

I rummaged around in the cook-tent and dragged out everything I could think of. I'd fix a breakfast like they'd never seen
before.

Actually, I went a little off the deep end. A prepared biscuit-
flour made biscuits and pancakes pretty easy, but I kind of
bogged down in a mixture of chopped-up venison, grated potatoes and onions, and a few other odds and ends of vegetables.
I wound up adding a can of corned-beef hash to give the whole

mess consistency. I didn't think I could manage a pie or anything, so I settled for canned peaches.

"All right, dammit!" I yelled. "Come and get it or I'll feed
it to porky."

They stumbled out and we dug into it. I'd fried up a bunch
of eggs and bacon to go with it all, and they ate without too
many complaints—except Clint, of course.

"Biscuits are a little underdone," he said first, mildly.

"Can't win 'em all," I told him.

"Bacon could be a mite crisper, too," he said then.

Cap ducked his head over his plate to keep from laughing
out loud. Even Jack grinned.

"Flapjacks seem a little chewey, wouldn't you say?" he
asked me.

I was waiting for him to get to that hash. He tried a forkful
and chewed meditatively.

"Now *this*," he said, pointing at it with the fork, "is the
best whatever-it-is I've ever had." He looked up with a perfectly
straight face. "Of course, I ain't never *had* none of this whatever-it-is before, so that might account for it."

I didn't say anything.

"I ain't gonna ask you what's in it," he said, "'cause I don't
really wanna know till I'm done eatin', but right after breakfast,
I *am* gonna go count the packhorses."

Miller suddenly roared with laughter, and pretty soon we
were all doing it.

After breakfast we struck the rest of the tents and began to
pack up. It didn't really take very long to get everything all
squared away.

A camp you've lived in for a while always looks so empty
when you start to tear it down. We even buried in McKlearey's
slit-trench and covered over Clint's garbage pit.

"Well," Cap said, looking around. "What with that table
and all, I guess we're leavin' the place better'n we found it."

"You bet," Jack said. He seemed to be getting over it all.

We loaded up the packhorses, saddled up, and rode on down
the trail. I looked back once, just before we went into the trees.
I didn't do it again.

"Down there is where Cap and I got the deer for Sloane,"
I told Jack as we passed the place.

"That was a nice deer," Jack said. "You wound up shootin'
the best two deer we got, you know that?"

"I hadn't thought of it," I said.

"That's because you were concentratin' on huntin' instead of all that other shit like the rest of us." Coming from Jack, that was a hell of an admission really.

We didn't say much the rest of the way down.

It was a little after noon when we got back down to where the trucks were. It took us a while to get the gear all off the horses and into the stock-truck and the pickup, but by about one we were on our way back to Miller's ranch. Jack got me off to one side and told me he wanted to ride on down with Cap, if I didn't mind.

"I've got a few things I ought to explain to him," my brother said. "I think I screwed up pretty bad a few times up there, and I'd kinda like a chance to square things, if I can."

"Sure, Jack," I said. I went over and climbed up into the stock-truck with Clint.

Maybe there was some hope for Jack after all.

33

"I don't know how the hell we're gonna get all that stuff in that car of mine," Jack said when we got to Miller's.

"We'll have to put a couple of those deer in the back seat," I said. "If we put them all in the trunk, it's going to overbalance so bad it'll pull the front wheels right up off the ground."

It took some juggling, but we finally managed it all.

"I'm gonna have to go on into Twisp and pick up a few things," Miller said, coming back from turning the horses out to pasture. "I'll call the game warden. He'll give you a note explainin' why you got so many deer. That way you won't have no trouble with any game checks on down the line."

"We'd appreciate it, Cap," I said. I walked with him back up toward the house.

"Your brother told me a few things on the way down," he said.

"Yeah," I said, "he told me he planned to."

"I can see where he had a lot workin' on him," Cap said,

dumping his clothes bag on the back porch.

"He's not as bad as he seemed to be up there," I said.

"He's a lot younger'n you," Cap said.

"No. He's two years older."

"That's not what I meant."

"Oh. Maybe—in some ways anyhow."

"In a lotta ways. I got a feelin' that in a lotta ways your brother ain't never gonna grow up. I started off callin' the wrong man Kid. He's likable enough; he just ain't grown-up."

"Who really ever grows up all the way, Cap?" I asked him.

He grinned at me. "If I ever make it, I'll let you know."

I laughed. "Right," I said.

"You got my address here?" he asked me.

"Yeah," I said.

"Drop me a line once in a while, son. Let me know how you're makin' out."

"I will, Cap. I really will." I meant it, too.

He slapped my shoulder. "We stand here talkin' all afternoon, and you two'll never get home."

We went on back out to the cars. Miller and Clint climbed in the pickup and led out with Jack and me laboring along behind in the overloaded Plymouth.

I saw Ned rolling out in the pasture where the colt had run when we'd first come here. The old boy was acting pretty frisky. Maybe he wasn't really grown-up yet either.

The game warden met us in Twisp and put all the necessary information down on a piece of paper for us.

"Nice bunch of deer," he said. He shook hands around and left.

"Well, men," Cap said, "I don't want to keep you. I know you got a long trip ahead of you."

"Cap, Clint," Jack said, "maybe I didn't show it much, but I enjoyed the trip, and I appreciate all you did for us up there." He shook hands with them both and got back in his car.

I shook hands with Cap and then with Clint.

"Thanks for everything," I said.

"You come back, son," Miller said, "you hear me? Even if it's only to borrow money."

"And don't make yourself obnoxious by not writin' neither," Clint growled, punching my shoulder.

We were all getting a little watery-eyed.

"I'd better go," I said quickly. "I'll keep in touch." I got quickly into the car.

Jack backed out from the curb, we all waved, and then we drove off.

We stopped for a case of beer and then got out onto the highway. The sun was bright and warm, and we drove with the windows rolled down, drinking beer.

"You get all squared away with Cap?" I asked my brother after a few miles.

"I told him a little about what was goin' on," Jack said. "I don't know how much it squared away."

"He probably understood," I said.

"Hey," he said suddenly, "what day is today anyway?"

"Sunday."

"Man, I lost track up there."

I laughed.

We traded off at Cashmere, and I drove on over the pass. The sun went down before we got to the top, and I switched on the headlights.

"Let's make a piss-call at the summit," he said.

"Sure."

We stopped and used the rest rooms and then drove down into the fir trees on the west side.

"Dan," he said after a while.

"Yeah?"

"I'm sorry I threw down on you up there."

"You didn't mean it, Jack. I knew that."

"You'd have shot though, wouldn't you?"

"I only said that to try to jar some sense into you," I told him.

"Bullshit," he said quietly. "You were all squared off and so was I. It came about that close." He held up his thumb and forefinger about an eighth of an inch apart. "You had me cold, too."

I didn't say anything.

"What the hell was goin' on up there anyway?" he said suddenly. "I'd cut off my leg before I'd do anything to hurt you, and I think you feel the same way. What in hell got into us?"

"McKlearey and that goddamned leper of a deer," I said.

"Maybe it's best nobody found the thing," he said. "God only knows what might have happened."

"I *did* find it," I told him bluntly.

"What?"

"You heard me. I found the son of a bitch and buried it before McKlearey got down there."

"No shit?"

"No shit. I wasn't about to get caught in the middle of a pitched gun battle."

"You did that just to keep him from puttin' me down?"

"You weren't listening," I said. "That's not why I did it. I'd have probably buried the damned thing even if *you'd* shot it. All I wanted to do was keep somebody from getting killed— probably me. You two were wound so damned tight you were ready to start shooting at anybody who came near you up there. Do you know that I had to back *both* of you off in the space of less than fifteen minutes?"

"McKlearey, too?"

"Hell, he was all squared away like Billy the Kid. I had to remind him loud and clear that I could take him if I had to. I got so many guns pointed at me that day I thought somebody had opened season on me."

"Jesus, Kid, I'm sorry as hell."

"Let's forget it," I said. "Everybody was all keyed-up."

"Man, McKlearey sure fell apart at the end, didn't he?"

"His hand was pretty badly infected," I said. "He might have been picking up some fever or something from that, I don't know."

"Yeah, he was holdin' it pretty careful all the time. You want another beer?"

"Yeah. I'm a little tired of whiskey for a while."

We had another beer and bored on down through the darkness, following our headlights.

We grabbed a hamburger and switched off again at Snohomish, and Jack drove on the rest of the way to Tacoma. We pulled into the trailer court about ten thirty.

Jack called Clem and got an OK to hang the deer in a garage at the end of the court. Then we unloaded all our gear, said good night, and went to our own trailers. I sat on the couch in my filthy hunting clothes with my feet up and a bottle of beer in my hand. I was bone-tired, and I damn near fell asleep a couple times.

"You look like the wrath of God," she said, coming in. She was still as cute as ever.

"How did you get over here, Clydine?" I asked.

"Joan's folks bought her a car. I've been borrowing it. I've been past here a dozen or so times since Wednesday." She came over and kissed me. "Did you lose your razor?" she asked. Then she sniffed. "*And* your soap?"

"I've been busy."

"All right," she ordered. "Strip and get into that bathroom."

"The *bathroom*?" I laughed. "Not in the *bathroom*!"

"Move it!" she barked.

I grunted, sat up, and started to unlace my boots.

"What a mess," she said, glaring at the pile of gear on the floor. "Are those things loaded?"

"The rifle isn't," I said. "The pistol is, I guess."

She shook her head disgustedly. "What were you doing with a pistol anyway?"

"Trying to stay alive," I said, a little more grimly than necessary.

"*Men!*" she said.

By the time I'd finished showering and shaving, she had everything but the guns put away. She wouldn't touch them. She had fixed me up a big platter of bacon and eggs and toast.

It felt awfully good just having her around.

"Well," she said when I'd finished eating and we'd moved back to the living room, "did you bushwhack Bambi?"

"Two Bambis," I told her.

"Do you feel better now?"

"I feel better, but not because I shot the deer," I said.

"Something happened up there, didn't it?" she asked me. I don't know how, but she saw right through me.

"A lot of things happened," I told her, "some good, some bad."

"Tell me."

"Do you have to get back home tonight?"

"Not really," she said, "but don't get any ideas—it's the wrong time of the month."

"No idea, my little wisteria of the workers," I said. "I'm too tired anyway." I really was.

"I've missed the botanical nick names," she said, wrinkling her nose at me.

"I've missed *you*, Rosebud."

"Really?"

"Really."

She leaned over and kissed me. "Did you unload that damned frog leg?" she asked me.

"The *what*?"

"The frog leg. The pistol—isn't that what they call it?"

"That's *hog*leg, love."

"Hog-frog, whatever. Get it empty. I'm not going to sleep in a house with a loaded gun."

I reached over and took it out. She watched it the way some people watch snakes. I slipped the hammer and dropped the shells out one by one.

"It's a hideous thing." She shuddered.

"It saved my life a couple times up there," I told her. I was overdramatizing it, I knew that.

"That's the second time you've made noises like John Wayne," she said. "Are you going to tell me what happened or not?"

"I'll tell you in bed," I said. "It's a very long, very involved story, and we're both liable to tap out before I get halfway through it."

"Did it turn out like a bad Western, after all?" she asked.

"Pretty close," I said.

We went to bed, and I held her very tightly and told her what had happened—all of it.

I wasn't sure she was really awake when I finished the story. ". . . and that's it," I said, winding it up.

"Was he really white?" she asked drowsily.

"Kind of cream-colored."

"He must have been beautiful."

"At first he was," I said. "After a while, though, I got to hate him."

"It wasn't *his* fault."

"No, but I hated him anyway."

"You don't make sense."

"I never pretended to make sense."

"Danny?"

"Yes, love?"

"Do you think Cap and Clint would like me?"

"I think they'd love you, Blossom."

She nuzzled my neck. "You say the nicest things sometimes," she said, her voice blurry and on the edge of dropping off.

"Go to sleep, Little Flower," I said.

She nestled down obediently and went to sleep quickly, like a child.

I lay staring into the darkness, and when I did go to sleep, I dreamed of the white deer. It got all mixed up with a dream about a dog until none of it made too much sense, but I guess dreams never really do, do they?

The Parting

34

AFTER she left for class the next morning I called Mike at work to see how Betty was.

"She seems to be coming out of it OK," he said. "She's home now, but she's got to take it pretty damned easy."

"I'm glad to hear she's better," I said.

"Sloane and Larkin both called me after they came down—say, how sick was old Cal anyway? He says one thing, and Stan says another."

"He was pretty damn sick," I said.

"Yeah, I kind of thought he might have been. How was the hunt?" His voice sounded wistful.

"The *hunt* was pretty good," I said. "Things got a little hairy a time or two though."

"McKlearey?"

"Yeah."

"I figured Miller'd be able to keep him in line."

"He did OK, but things still got a little woolly a time or two."

"Did anybody get that white deer Sloane told me about?"

"McKlearey shot him and he fell off a cliff. We never found him."

"Too bad—say, Dan, I gotta get back to work. Gimme a buzz tonight, OK?"

"Sure, Mike. After supper, OK?"

"Right. Bye now."

I guess his boss had been standing over him. I called the pawnshop. Sloane answered. His voice sounded a little puny, but otherwise he seemed OK.

"How are you feeling, Cal?" I asked him.

"Hell," he said, "I'm OK now. I was startin' to come out of it by the time we got back down the hill."

"You see a doctor?"

"Yeah." He giggled. "Claudia was on me about it as soon

291

as I got back. He says it happens to guys my age some times. He's got me takin' it kinda easy for a couple of weeks."

"Good idea," I said. "Oh, we got your deer for you."

"Hey, great, man—how big?"

"Five-point. He's in prime condition."

"Thanks a lot, Dan. Who shot 'im?"

"I did. Miller and I went out and found him."

"Shoot out the liver?" He giggled.

"Not a chance," I said. "Old Clint was threatening to burn me at the stake if I did."

He told me he'd call a processing plant to take care of the deer, and I said I'd drop the hide and horns by later that morning after I'd cleaned my guns.

After I hung up I sorted out all my hunting clothes and took them over to the washhouse. Then I went back and cleaned my guns and McKlearey's rifle. Then I bundled up Lou's gear and the two deer hides and drove on over to the shop.

"Come on in, Dan," Cal called as I pushed my way on in with a big armload of gear.

"I brought Lou's stuff on over," I said.

Cal wanted to know where Lou was. He hadn't shown up for work that morning. I told him that I didn't know and filled him in on the way Lou'd taken off from Clint.

"God," Sloane said, "that doesn't sound like Lou. He's pretty irresponsible sometimes, but he's never gone *that* far before."

"He was pretty badly shook up," I said. "I don't think he was thinking straight toward the end." I told him about McKlearey's shooting the white deer and then not being able to find it.

"God damn," Cal said, "you say he took that .38 along with him?"

"That's what Clint said."

"Christ," he said, his face darkening, "that damn gun's on the record as being here in the shop. If he's gone off the deep end or something and does something stupid with it, it could get my ass in a helluva lotta trouble."

"Shit," I said, "I hadn't thought of that."

"Now what the hell do I do? I don't want to report the gun stolen—that'd get him in all kinds of trouble. I wish I knew where the hell he was."

"Beats me, Cal. He didn't even say good-bye when he left."

Sloane shook his head. "I'll figure something out," he said.
"You want a drink?"

"Sure."

"Come on back." He jerked his head, and we went on into
the back room. I dumped Lou's gear in a corner and Cal reached
down the bottle and handed it to me.

I took a belt and handed it back to him. He capped it up
and put it away.

"Doctor said I oughta back off for a while," he said. "I'm
cuttin' way down on my smoking, too—and I'm on a diet."

"Jesus, Sloane, you're going whole hog, aren't you?"

"Let me tell you, man," he said seriously, "I could feel the
buzzards snappin' at my ass up there. The doctor told me I
came about that close to havin' a coronary." He measured off
a fraction of an inch with his fingers. "Goddamn heart was
workin' doubletime to make up for the lack of oxygen. About
one more day and I wouldn't of made it back down. He says
I gotta quit smokin', cut way back on the booze, lose fifty
pounds, and get ten hours sleep a night. Christ, I feel just like
a goddamn invalid."

"Jesus," I said, "you were sicker'n any of us figured then."

"I was sicker'n *I* figured even," he said. "That damned
doctor like to scared the piss outa me."

"You're going to be OK, aren't you?"

"Oh, I'll come out of it OK. He said there wasn't any
permanent damage, but little Calvin's gonna walk the straight
and narrow for a while."

"Not a bad idea," I said, lighting a cigarette. I saw the
hungry look in his eyes and mashed it out quickly. "Sorry,
Cal," I said.

"It's a little tough, right at first," he said.

We went on back out to the shop.

"You know," he said, "it's funny."

"What?"

"You remember that day up there when I told you I was
gonna buckle down after the trip—maybe grow up a little?"

"Yeah," I said, "I remember."

"Looks like I'm gonna have to do just exactly that." He
giggled, suddenly sounding like the Cal I'd always known.
"This ain't exactly what I had in mind though."

"Somebody once said that a guy shouldn't make promises
to himself," I told him. "He winds up having to keep them."

"Boy, that's sure as hell the truth," he said.

He gave me the address of the packing plant where they'd
process the deer for him, and I told him that Jack and I would
get it over there for him that afternoon.

About noon, Claudia came in.

"Hello, Dan," she said in her deep voice.

"Claudia," I said. She still gave me goose bumps.

"How many cigarettes, Calvin?" She wasn't badgering; she
was just asking.

He mutely held up three fingers.

"Truth?" she asked.

"Ask Dan," he said.

"He's only had one since I got here about ten thirty," I said.
"Cross my heart and hope to turn green all over."

She laughed, and her hand touched my arm affectionately.

"And how many nips from your hide-out bottle?" she asked
him.

"What bottle?"

"The one on the top shelf in the storeroom."

"How'd you find out about *that*?"

"I've always known about it," she said.

He stared at her for a minute and then started laughing. "I
give up," he said. "What the hell's the use anyway?"

"How many?" she repeated.

"Not one. I gave Dan a belt, but I haven't touched a drop."

"Good," she said. "I'm not nagging you, Calvin. This is
for your own good."

"I know, dear," he said. It was the first time I'd ever heard
him use any term of endearment to her.

"You'd better run on along home now," she said. "I put a
big bowl of salad in the refrigerator for you."

"I'm startin' to feel like a damn rabbit," he complained. "I
got lettuce comin' out of my ears."

"But you've lost weight, haven't you?" she said.

"Yeah, I guess so," he said grudgingly.

"And take your nap this time," she commanded.

"Yes, ma'am."

I said good-bye to him, and he went on out. I'd been ready
to leave, too, but Claudia had given me a quick signal to stick
around. After he left she turned to me, her face serious.

"Just how bad was he up there, Dan?" she asked me.

"He was pretty sick," I told her. "He couldn't seem to get
his breath, and there were a couple times when he couldn't

keep anything down. We all figured he'd snap out of it, but he just couldn't seem to get adjusted."

"Why didn't you send him down earlier?" she asked.

"I don't think any of us really knew how sick he really was," I told her. "A couple times it seemed like he was getting better. He'd go on out hunting and things seemed to be coming along fine, but then he'd conk out again. We were all watching him pretty closely, but he kept telling us that he'd be all right in just a little bit."

She shook her head. "Men!" she said. "You're all just a bunch of overgrown children."

"I've been finding that out," I told her.

"I'd die if I lost him, Dan."

Sloane?

I guess it must have shown on my face.

"You don't understand, do you, Dan?"

"It's none of my business really," I told her.

"I know," she said, "but I want to tell you anyway."

Why me, for God's sake? Why always me?

"I think I'm as happy now as I've ever been in my life," she said, looking out the window. "For the first time, Calvin needs *me*—not just the fact that I can keep his books or pick out furniture or any of that. He needs *me*. When he came home, he was frightened—terribly frightened. He came to me for the first time without making it some kind of deal—you know, 'I'll do this for you if you'll do that for me.' It was the first time he didn't try to buy me. You have no idea what that means to a woman."

"I think I do," I said quietly.

"I suppose maybe you would," she said. "You seem to see a lot of things that other people don't." She looked steadily up at me for a minute. "You see, Dan," she said finally, "I can't have any children. I did something pretty stupid when I was about seventeen, and I had an abortion. It wasn't even a doctor who did it, and of course I went septic. I wound up losing everything." She passed her hand across her lower abdomen. "Calvin and I decided not to adopt children—I suppose we could have, but we just decided not to. So *Calvin* is my baby. That's the way it's always been."

I nodded.

"But this is the first time he's ever turned to me this way. Maybe it really isn't much of a basis for a good marriage but—" she shrugged.

"It's probably as good as any," I said, "and better than a lot of them."

She smiled at me. "Thank you," she said, "I thought you'd understand."

We talked a while longer, and then I took off. She was one helluva woman.

I picked up Clydine after her last class, and we went on back to my place. She'd told me quite emphatically that morning that she was going to spend every spare minute with me until I left for Seattle. I wasn't really about to argue with her.

35

I didn't see Stan until the next weekend. I'm not sure why, but I think I was avoiding him. When I called to make sure he was home, I got the distinct impression that he'd have preferred to keep it that way, but it was too late then.

He was growing a mustache, and it made his face look dirty. Stan didn't have the kind of face you'd want to put a mustache on. And instead of one of the usual sober-colored, conservative sport shirts I'd always seen him in, he was wearing a loud checkered wool shirt—outdoorsy as all hell, and on him about as phony as a nine-dollar bill.

"Well, Dan," he said with a nervous joviality, "how the hell have you been?" As if he hadn't seen me in ten years, for God's sake.

"Fair, Stan. Just fair."

We went on into his tidy little living room.

"How's old Cal?"

"He's coming along. His doctor's got him on a short schedule and cut him off on booze and cigarettes."

"He gave me a damn bad scare up there, the poor bastard."

What the hell was all this?

He fidgeted around a little, and our conversation was pretty sketchy. I wasn't sure what this he-man role he was playing was all about, but I desperately wanted to tell him that it wasn't coming off very well.

"Oh," he said, "I've been fixing up the den. I wanted you to see it." He led me back to the room he'd identified as the study the last time I'd been there.

He'd redone the place in early musket ball. The rifle and his shotgun were hanging on the wall where they could collect dust, and there were hunting prints hanging all over the place. I could see copies of *Field and Stream* and *The American Rifleman* scattered around with a studied carelessness. The place looked like a goddamn movie set.

"I'm having that buck's head mounted," he said. "How do you think it would look right there?" He pointed to a place that had obviously been left empty for the trophy.

"Ought to be OK, Stan," I told him.

We went back into the living room and I listened to him come on like the reincarnation of Ernest Hemingway for about a half hour or so.

Then Monica came in and suddenly it all fell into place.

"Did you pick up the beer like I asked you to?" he said to her, his voice cocked like a gun.

"Yes, Stan," she said—rather meekly, I thought.

"Why don't you open a couple for Dan and me?"

"Of course," she said and went on back out to the kitchen.

I watched Stan, who had never smoked, light a cigar. I wanted to tell him that he was overplaying it, but I wasn't sure how to go about it.

I sat around for another half hour or so, listening to him swear and give Monica orders, and then I'd had a gutful of the whole thing. I made an excuse and got away from them.

I suppose that what made the whole thing so pathetic was the fact that it was all so completely unnecessary. After her little misjudgment with McKlearey, Monica would have been pretty docile even without his big hairy-chested routine. Stan was saddling himself with the necessity of playing a role for the rest of his life. He'd get better at it as time went on. In a few years he might even get to the point where he believed it himself, but I don't think he'd ever really be comfortable with it.

I picked up Clydine and told her about it as we drove back on across town to my place.

"What are you going to do about it?"

"I can't do a damn thing," I said. "I sure as hell can't tell him that McKlearey got to Monica, and that's the only way I could convince him that this act of his isn't the thing that put him in the driver's seat."

"But if this is so unnatural for him," she objected, "he's really no better off than he was before, is he?"

"No," I said, "he isn't. He's still in a box—it's just a different box, that's all."

"But you ought to be able to do something," she said.

"Hell, Rosebud," I said, "I didn't hire on as God. Last time I tried to walk on water, I got wetter than hell."

She crossed her arms and glowered straight ahead. "I still think there's *something* you could do," she said. "It's just awful to think about what they'll have to go through for all the rest of their lives."

"Well," I said in my best Hemingway manner, "don't think about it then."

She didn't catch the allusion, and so she was angry with me for being an insensitive clod. You can't win.

When we got to my place, she was still steamed, so we sat around listening to records and not talking to each other. She sure could be stubborn when she wanted to be.

Then Cal called. "Dan," he said, "I just got a call from one of the bartenders on the Avenue, and he said he just saw McKlearey."

"No shit? I thought he'd blown town."

"I really don't much give a damn what he does," Cal said, "but I sure as hell want to get that goddamn pistol back from him. I could write it off on the three days' pay I owe him from the car lot, but the paper has got to be straightened out."

"Yeah," I said, "I see what you mean."

"Are you busy right now? I tried to get hold of Jack, but he's out delivering a camper trailer."

"What do you need?" I asked him, glancing at Clydine. She still wasn't looking at me.

"Somebody's gonna have to run him down—somebody who knows the score. I can't get away until later, and I'm afraid he'll go back in his hole before then."

"You want me to find him?"

"Right. Just tell him to come by the shop. I want him to pick up all this shit of his anyway—and tell me what he wants done with his goddamn deer."

"Which way was he going?"

"God, I really don't know."

"I'll just have to hunt him down then, I guess," I said.

"Thanks a lot, Dan."

"Sure, Cal."

I hung up and went back to the dinky little living room.

"Do you want to play private detective?" I asked her.

She brooded for a minute or so, probably trying to decide whether it would be more fun to keep sulking or to find out what I was talking about. I couldn't quite make up my mind whether I wanted to give her a good solid spanking or a big kiss right on the end of her little snoot.

"What do you have in mind?" she finally asked, not really wanting to give up the good pout she had going.

"We've got to go find McKlearey," I told her.

"Old Creepy-Jarhead himself?"

"That's our man," I told her. "He's got a hot gun, and we've gotta get to him before the fuzz do or before he pulls a caper with it. Our client would find that pretty embarrassing." I lit a cigarette and squinted at her through the smoke.

"Have you been watching television?" She laughed, unable to help it.

"It's a big case, baby," I said, putting the Bogart accent on even more thickly. "Every shamus in town would give his eyeteeth to get a piece of the action."

"OK, Knuckles," she said toughly, standing up and hitching up her blue jeans. "Let's go run down the subject. We gonna rub 'im out when we find 'im?"

"Not unless we have to," I said. "You got your .38 handy?"

She took a deep breath, cocked one eyebrow at me, and gave me a long stare over her upthrusting frontage. "I've always got *my* 38 handy," she said.

"You nut," I laughed. "Let's go."

We went out to my car and began bar hopping back down the Avenue toward town. Some of the bartenders knew McKlearey and some didn't, so it was pretty hit and miss. I still wasn't sure which way Lou was going, and I couldn't be sure if he was still on the Avenue or if he'd cut on over toward Parkland or what.

"We'll try the Patio, and then I'll do what I should have done in the first place," I said.

"What's that, Knucks?" she said.

"Go back to my place and use the phone and the yellow pages."

"Clever," she said. "I can see how you got your rep as the best private nose in the business."

"Eye, baby. It's private eye—not nose."

"Whatever," she said and then laughed. I guess she'd gotten over her mad.

Lou was at the Patio. He was sitting in a booth alone, with a pitcher of beer in front of him. His left arm was in a sling, and his hand had a professional-looking bandage on it.

"Hey, there, Lou," I said with a heartiness I didn't really feel. "How the hell have you been?"

He looked up at me, his eyes kind of flat, as always.

I introduced him to Clydine, and he invited us to join him. He had that gun on him. I didn't see it, but I could almost smell it on him. I wished to hell I hadn't brought my little Bolshevik along.

"Where in hell have you been, Lou?" I asked him after the bartender brought the pitcher I'd ordered. "Nobody's seen you since the hunt."

Something happened back behind his flat, empty eyes. Suddenly he was all buddy-buddy, friendly as a pup.

"Christ, man," he said, "I been in the goddamn *hospital*." He waved his bandaged hand at me. "I picked up a damn good case of blood poisoning in this thing."

"No shit?" I said. "I knew it was giving you some trouble, but I never even thought about blood poisoning."

"Hell," he said, "I had a red streak an inch wide goin' up my arm all the way to the armpit. Man, I was flat outa my head by the time I got to that VA hospital up in Seattle."

"So *that's* why you took off so fast," I said, helping him along.

"Shit, yes, man," he said. "I was about halfway outa my skull even up there—with the fever and all. I knew damn well I was gonna have to get to a doctor in a hurry."

"Christ, Lou," I said, "you should have said something."

"I didn't think it was that bad at first."

Clydine was watching him closely, not saying anything. I think she was trying to fit Lou into all the things I'd told her about him.

I passed Sloane's message on to him, and he said he'd take care of it.

"Hell," he said, "as far as that deer goes, you guys can just go ahead and split it up. I don't care that much about venison myself."

"I suppose we could give it to Carter," I said. "After all, he didn't get to go."

"Hey, there's a good idea. Why don't you just give it to Carter?"

"Tell Sloane when you drop by the shop," I told him, nailing down that point again. I wasn't sure how much it was going to take to separate Lou from that gun. "Oh, Cal says to tell you he'll let you have the pistol for what he owes you from the lot, but he's gotta get the paper on it straightened out."

That seemed to make Lou feel even better. He got positively expansive.

After about a half hour Clydine had to make a run to the ladies' room.

"I bet I acted pretty fuckin' funny up there, huh?" Lou said while she was gone.

"You weren't raving or anything," I said carefully, "but sometimes you didn't make too much sense."

"It was the fuckin' fever," he said. "You know, from the blood poisoning. I can only remember about half of what went on up there."

"Hell," I said, "it's lucky you were even able to walk, as sick as you were."

"Yeah," he agreed. "I was pretty far gone, all right. I bet I *said* a lotta wild stuff, too, huh?"

"Most of it was pretty garbled," I said. I was walking right on the edge and about all I had to defend myself with was a ballpoint pen.

"Guy'll say fuckin' near *anything* when he's out of his head like that, won't he?"

"Hell, man," I said, "you were having screaming nightmares, and you were talking to yourself and everything. I'm not kidding, old buddy, we thought you were cracking up."

He laughed. "I'll bet it scared the piss outa you guys, huh?"

"Shit! We were waiting for you to start frothing at the mouth and biting trees."

"Yeah, I was really gone," he said. "Did I ever say anything about the Delta?" He asked it very casually—too casually.

"Nothing that made any sense," I said. "You said something about how you used to think about snow when you were out there."

"Yeah," he said, "I remember that—not too well, of course, but I remember it. Did I mention any names while I was out my head?"

"I think so," I said, "but I didn't really catch them."

Clydine came back.

"I'm gonna blow this town," Lou said. "Winter's comin' and the rain bugs me."

"Yeah," I said, "it can get pretty gloomy around here."

"And I gotta work outside, too. I can't cut bein' penned up inside. I think I'll cut out for Texas or Florida or someplace. I just came back today to get my gear together."

"Be nice down South this time of year," I agreed. "Make sure you see Sloane before you go though, huh? He's pretty worried about it."

"Sure," he said, emptying his glass. "Hey, tell Jack I'm sorry about givin' 'im such a hard time up there, huh? Chances are I won't get a chance to see 'im before I take off."

"Sure, Lou,"

"I probably won't ever be comin' back up here again," he said. "That probably ain't gonna hurt some guys' feelin's."

"Oh," I lied, "you haven't been all *that* bad, Lou."

He laughed, the same harsh raspy laugh as always. "Look," he said, "I'm gonna have to take off—if I'm gonna see Sloane and all. Just forget anything I said up there, huh—about the Delta or anything, OK?"

"What Delta?" I said.

He grinned at me. "You're OK, Danny—too bad we didn't get to know each other better." He stood up quickly. I could see the bulge of the gun under his jacket. "I gotta run. You take care now, huh?"

"So long, Lou," I said.

He waved, winked at Clydine, and started out. Then he stopped and came back, his face flat again.

"Hey," he said, "I owe you five, don't I?"

I'd forgotten about it.

"Here." He pulled out his billfold and fumbled awkwardly in it. He was carrying quite a wad of cash. He dropped a five on the table. "We're all square now, right?"

"Good enough, Lou," I said.

He poked a finger at me pistol-fashion by way of farewell, turned, and went out.

"Wow," Clydine said in a shuddery voice, "I don't want to play cops and robbers anymore."

"I shouldn't have brought you along," I said.

"I wouldn't have missed it for the world," she said. "He's a real starker, isn't he?"

"He's got all the makings," I said, picking up the five-dollar bill. I looked it over carefully.

"What's the matter?" she said. "You think it may be counterfeit?"

"Nobody counterfeits fives," I said.

"What are you looking for then? Blood?"

"I don't know," I told her. "I think he was pretty close to broke when he came out of the woods, though."

"Maybe he went to the bank."

"That's what worries me," I said, still looking at the bill.

"OK, Knucks," she said, "I told you I didn't want to play cops and robbers anymore. What's on for the afternoon?"

"Let's go to Seattle."

"Why?"

"I'm going to have to go house hunting."

"Oh," she said. I don't think either of us liked the reminder that I'd be leaving soon.

36

ON the first of October I moved to Seattle and began the tedious process of getting enrolled for classes and so forth. I'd found a little place the landlord referred to as a cottage but for which the word "shack" might have been more appropriate. Even when compared to the shabby little trailer I'd been living in, the place was tiny. The fold-down couch that made into a bed was perhaps the most uncomfortable thing I've ever slept in, but the place was close enough to the university to compensate for its other drawbacks.

Even though Clydine and I had both been convinced that my move to Seattle would more or less terminate what some people chose to call our relationship, it didn't work out that way. I kept coming across reasons why I just *had* to make a quick trip to Tacoma, and I think she made seven shopping jaunts to Seattle during my first month up there.

I guess when you get right down to it, I got out of Tacoma

just in time to miss the big messy bust-up between Jack and
Marg—or maybe Jack just held off until I left town, though
that was a kind of delicacy you just didn't expect from my
brother.

About ten o'clock on a drizzly Saturday morning I came
down the steps of the library with a whole dreary weekend
staring me in the face. The bibliographical study for Introduc-
tion to Graduate Studies that I'd assumed would take from
twelve to fourteen hours had, in fact, been polished off in just
a shade under forty-five minutes. I spent another half hour
trying to figure out what I'd done wrong. As far as I could
see, the job was complete, so I left the library feeling definitely
let down and vaguely cheated somehow.

I had absolutely nothing to do with myself, so I decided,
naturally, to bag on down to Tacoma. At least down there I
should be able to find somebody I knew to drink with.

The highway was dreary, but it didn't really bother me.
Without even thinking, I swung on over to Clydine's place.
Who the hell was I trying to kid? There was only one reason
I'd come down to Tacoma, and it sure wasn't to find somebody
to drink with.

I went up the stairs two at a time and knocked at the door.
Her folks were there.

"Danny," she said in surprise when she opened the door, "I
thought you had to work this weekend." She was wearing a
dress and her hair was done up.

"I finished up sooner than I thought," I said.

"Well, come on in," she said. "Meet my folks." She gave
me one of those smark-alecky grimaces that conveyed a world
of condescension, sophomoric superiority, and juvenile intol-
erance. It irritated the piss out of me for some reason, and I
made a special effort to be polite to them.

Her father was a little bald-headed guy with a nervous laugh.
I think he was in the plumbing supply business, or maybe
hardware. Her mother was short and plump and kind of bubbly.
I think they liked me because of my haircut. Some of Clydine's
friends must have looked pretty shaggy to them.

I could see my little leftist smoldering in the corner as I
talked about fishing with her father and Europe with her mother.
I knew that about all I was doing was mildewing the sheets
between the little nut and me and breeding a helluva family
squabble which would probably start as soon as I left. I told

them I had to run across town and see my brother and then left as gracefully as I could.

I snooped around the Avenue a bit, but I really didn't feel like seeing Jack yet, and the pawnshop had a whole platoon of guys lined up inside, so I took a chance and drove on over to Parkland to see Mike. Surprisingly, he was home, and the two of us went into his living room and sprawled out in a couple of chairs and drank beer and watched it rain.

"Damn shame about Jack and Marg," he said.

"Yeah, but it was bound to happen, Mike. It was just a question of time really."

"I've never really been able to figure out what it is about Jack," he said thoughtfully. "I *like* him—hell, everybody *likes* the son of a bitch, but he just can't seem to hang in there the way most guys do."

"I think maybe Cap Miller came closer to Jack's problem than anybody else really," I said.

"Oh?"

"He said that the way he saw it Jack isn't ever really going to grow up. Maybe that's it."

"Not much gets by old Miller," Mike commented.

"It's funny, too," I said. "It's the one thing Jack's been obsessed with ever since I can remember—growing up. He used to think about that more than anybody I ever knew."

"Maybe he tried too hard."

"I think he tried too soon, Mike. Have you ever seen one of these girls who start going out on dates when they're eleven—lipstick, high heels, the whole bit?"

"Yeah, but what's the connection?"

"Have you ever known one of them that ever really grew up? I mean one who wasn't still pretty damned juvenile even when she got to be twenty-three or twenty-four?"

"I always thought that kind of girl was just stupid."

"Maybe that enters into it," I said, "but there's a kind of immaturity there, too."

He shrugged. "I still don't get the connection."

"Well," I said, "I've got a hunch that the patterns we set up when we first start doing something are usually going to be the patterns we're going to follow for the rest of our lives. Now, if you start out trying to be grown-up—or adult, if you prefer that term—while you're still physically and mentally a child, you're going to start the whole business all wrong. You'll start a pattern of *playing* grown-up. You'll contaminate all of your adulthood with that juvenile pattern. I think that's what happens to the little girl with her gunked-on makeup and wobbly high heels. She spends the rest of her life *playing* grown-up. I sort of think that the same thing happened to Jack."

"You mean he's just playing?"

"The worst part of it is that he doesn't know he's playing," I said. "He just doesn't know the difference. He's impatient, he's flighty, he's self-centered, he's intolerant—he's got all the classic traits of immaturity."

"Shit, man"—Mike laughed—"you've just described about three-quarters of the people in the whole damn country."

"Including you and me, probably," I said. "That's another thing Old Cap said. I asked him when *anybody* really grows up, and he told me that if he ever made it, he'd let me know."

"Sounds like you and old Cap got along pretty well," he said.

"I don't think I've ever met a man I liked or respected more," I said, "except maybe my old man."

"He kinda hits a guy that way, doesn't he?"

I nodded. "Say, how's Sloane doing? I was going to stop by the shop, but the place was mobbed."

"Christ"—Mike laughed—"you wouldn't recognize the old fart. He's lost thirty pounds and gone teetotaler on us. He doesn't even drink beer anymore."

"He got a pretty good scare up there, I guess."

"It musta been pretty hairy."

"You know it, buddy. Between him and McKlearey it was a real nervous trip."

"Lou took off, you know."

"Yeah. He told me he was going to."

"That damned trip sure changed a lot of things around here," Mike said.

"I guess it was sort of a watershed. Maybe we were all due for a change of some kind, and the trip just brought it all to a head."

"I sure wish I could have gone along," he said wistfully.

"So do I, Mike."

We talked for another hour or so, and then Betty wanted Mike to take her to the grocery store, so I took off.

I went on by the trailer court, but Jack's trailer was gone. That's always kind of a jolt. The damn things look sort of permanent when they're set down on a lot with fences and grass around them, so you forget that they've got wheels on them.

I dropped down to the trailer sales lot and Jack was sitting in the grubby, cigarette-stinking office with his muddy feet up on the desk.

"Yeah," he said, grinning tightly at me. "I moved Sandy in with me, and I didn't want Marg to pick up on that with the divorce comin' on and all."

"Oh?"

"Yeah," he said, lighting a cigarette. "We got things all kinda hammered out to where I don't get nicked too bad for support money, and I don't want her gettin' the idea that she's the aggrieviated party in this little clambake. I'm not about to get screwed into the wall with alimony payments."

"Where'd you move to?"

"I'm in a court out toward Madrona."

"Where'd Marg go?" I asked.

"She got an apartment out in Lakewood. Not a bad place. I found it for her."

"Sounds pretty civilized," I said.

He shrugged. "I didn't want her gettin' the idea she had any kinda claim on my trailer. I guess her lawyer was pissed-off as hell about it. I got her all moved out before he got the chance to tell her to stay put. Now that *she* abandoned *me*, it kinda cuts down on her share of the community property."

"You figure all the angles, don't you, Jack?"

"I been through it all before," he said. "If a guy uses his head, he don't have to get skinned alive in divorce court. Hey, you want a drink?"

"Sure." I didn't care much for that particular conversation anyway.

"Come on." He got up, hauled on a coat and led me across the soggy lot to a fairly new trailer. "Try to look like a customer," he said, leading the way inside. The trailer was clammy, but it was a little more private than the office. Jack went into the little utility room and pulled a fifth of cheap vodka out of one of the heating ducts.

"The boss can't smell this on me," he explained. "I have a coke afterward, and I'm pure as the driven snow." He laughed flatly.

We each had a couple of pulls from the bottle and then sat around in the chilly living room talking.

"Did McKlearey get that business with the gun straightened out with Sloane before he took off?"

"Yeah," Jack said, "he and Sloane dummied up the paper work and got it all squared away with the police department."

"Did you see him before he took off?"

"Naw, I got a gutful of that motherfucker up in the woods."

"The silly bastard had blood poisoning in that hand," I said. "He claims he was out of his head with the fever and the damned infection."

"I wouldn't bet on that. I think he just plain flipped out."

"It's possible," I said. "He was carrying that .38 when I saw him. Had it tucked under his belt."

"That silly bastard! He's just stupid enough to try to use it, too. He'll get about half in the bag some night and try to knock over a liquor store or a tavern. I hope somebody shoots him."

"At least he's out of *our* hair," I said.

"Yeah."

Somehow Jack and I didn't really seem to have much to talk about. I guess we never had really. I got the feeling that splitting up with Marg had hit him a lot harder than he was willing to admit to me.

"Hey," he said suddenly, "you wanna do me a favor?"

"Sure."

"When I moved the trailer, I found a bunch of stuff that belongs to the kids. I got it all in a box in the trunk of my car. You think you could run it on over to Marg's place for me? I think it's better if I stay away from there for a while."

"Sure, Jack."

"I'll give her a call and let her know you're comin'."

We went over to his car and transferred the box from his trunk to mine.

"Hey, Dan, look at this." He popped open his glove compartment. That stupid .45 automatic was in there.

"Shit, Jack," I said, "you'll get your ass in a sling if they catch you carrying that thing in your car that way without a permit."

He shrugged. "I got kinda stuck on it up in the brush, you know? Shit, a man oughta own himself a pistol—home protection and all that bullshit."

"Maybe so," I said, "but you sure as hell shouldn't be carting it around in your glove box."

"Maybe," I said. We went back in the office and he called Marg.

"She'll be there," he said after he hung up. He gave me the address and I took off again.

It took me a while to find the place. It was one of those older houses that had had the second floor remodeled into a self-contained apartment that you reached by way of an outside staircase. I went on up and knocked.

"Hi, Dan," she said, smiling blearily at me. She smelled pretty strongly of whiskey. "Come on in."

"I can only stay a minute," I said, carting in the box.

"Just set that down," she told me. "The girls are asleep. How about a drink?" She didn't wait for any answer but whipped me up a whiskey and Seven-Up almost before I got the box put down. "Come on in the living room," she said.

I pulled off my wet jacket, and we went on in and I sat on the couch. She sat in the armchair just opposite me and crossed her legs, flashing an unnecessary amount of thigh at me. "How's school?" she asked.

I shrugged. "Takes a while to get back into it," I said. "I think I'm doing OK."

"That's swell."

"I wish I'd gotten here sooner," I said. "I'd have liked to get a chance to see the kids."

"They'll be up in an hour or so," she said, leaning back to stretch her arms. She was wearing a sleeveless blouse, cotton, I think, and when she pulled it tight like that, her nipples stood out pretty obviously. Margaret was too big a girl to run around without a bra.

"Sure has been lonesome around here lately," she said.

"You have any plans—I mean for after—" I left it up there. Under the circumstances it was kind of a touchy subject really.

"Oh," she said, polishing off her drink in two gulps, "nothing definite yet. I'm not worried." She got up, went into the kitchen and came out with a fresh drink.

"You got any special plans for the rest of the day?" she asked, sitting on the couch beside me.

"I've got to get back across town before too long," I lied, ostentatiously checking my watch.

She didn't even bother with subtlety. Maybe she was too drunk or maybe the years with my brother had eroded any subtlety out of her. She simply reached out, grabbed my head and kissed me. Her tongue started probing immediately. I felt her hand fumbling at the front of her blouse and then the warm mashing of her bare breasts against me.

"You wouldn't run off and leave a girl all alone like this, would you?" she murmured in my ear.

"Margaret," I said, trying to untangle her arms from around my neck, "this is no good."

"Oh, come on, Danny," she coaxed. "What difference does it make?"

"I'm sorry, Margaret," I said.

She sat back, not bothering to cover herself. Her nipples were very large and darkly pigmented and not very pretty. "What's the matter?" she demanded. "Has Jack been telling you stories about me?"

"No," I said, "that's not it at all. I just don't think that under the circumstances it would be a good idea." I stood up quickly and gulped down the drink. "I've really got to run anyway."

"Boy," she said bitterly, "you're just not with it at all, are you?"

"I've got to run, Marg," I said. "Tell the kids I said hello."

"I sure never figured you for a square," she said.

"I'm sorry, Margaret," I said. I went out very quickly. Hell let's be honest, I ran like a scared rabbit.

I stopped at the Patio and had a beer to give myself a chance to calm down.

Clydine's folks had left when I got back to her place, and she tore into me for being nice to them.

All in all, I got the feeling that I'd have been away to hell and gone out in front to have just spent the whole day in bed.

37

DEAR CAP AND CLINT,

I've been so busy I kind of got behind in my letter writing. I guess I'm doing OK in school—at least they haven't kicked me out yet.

I was down to Tacoma a couple weeks ago and saw most of the others. Sloane has gone off his diet a little, but he hasn't started putting any weight back on yet. At least he'll have a beer with the rest of us once in a while, if we all get together

*and twist his arm. His doctor is sure now that there wasn't
any permanent damage, so you can quit worrying about that.*

*My brother's divorce should be final about the end of Feb.,
and I think he'll be making himself kind of scarce around here
for a while after that. He'll probably want to go someplace
else for a while to get himself straightened out.*

*Nobody has had any word about McKlearey. We don't even
know where he went. It's probably just as well, I suppose. He
wasn't just the most popular guy around here anyway. I can't
really say that any of us miss him.*

*I haven't seen Stan Larkin for a couple months now, but the
last time he was still playing that same silly game I told you
about before. It's kind of sad, really, because it's all so unnatural for him.*

*I guess we were a pretty odd bunch, weren't we? I'm glad
you changed your mind about giving up guiding. You just happened to get a bunch of screwballs the first time out.*

*My girlfriend and I made up again. I think that's about the
fourth or fifth time since school started. She's a 24-karat nut,
but I think you'd like her.*

*Well, you fellows have a merry Christmas now, and don't
let the snow pile up so deep that it won't melt off in time for
me to get through when fishing season starts.*

> *Well, Merry Christmas again.*
> *So long for now,*
>
> Dan

I write a lousy letter, I always have. I knew that if I read
it over, I'd tear it up and then write another one just damn near
like it, so I stuck it in an envelope and sealed it up in a hurry.

It was Wednesday night, and my seminar paper on Faulkner's *The Sound and the Fury* was due on Friday, but I just
couldn't seem to get it to all fit together. I went back and tried
to plow my way through the Benjy section again. I knew that
what I needed was buried in there someplace, but I was damned
if I could dig it out.

I kept losing track of the time sequence and finally wound
up heaving the book across the room in frustration.

I wondered what the hell Clydine was up to. Lately I'd taken
to listening to the news and buying newspapers to check on
any demonstrations or the like in Tacoma. I think my most
recurrent nightmare was of some big cop belting her in the

head with a nightstick—not that she might not have deserved it now and then.

Maybe that was why I couldn't really concentrate. I was spend ng about half my time worrying about her. God damn it, as harebrained as she was about some things, she needed a fulltime ke per just to keep her out of trouble.

I leaned back and thought about that for a while. I thought about some of the creeps she hung around with and decided that most of them needed keepers a whole lot worse than she did.

I guess it really took me quite a while to come to the realization that I really didn't want just anybody looking out for her. As a matter of fact, I didn't want it to be anybody but me, when I got right down to it. I knew finally what that meant. Of all the stupid, inappropriate, completely out of the question things to get involved in at this particular time! I was still running down the long list of reasons why the whole idea was crazy as I reached for the telephone.

"Hello?"

"Hi, Joan. Is Rosebud there?"

"Yeah, Danny. Just a minute—Clydine!" I wished to hell she wouldn't yell across the open mouthpiece like that.

"Hello." Damn, it was good to hear her voice.

"I want you to listen to me very carefully, Flower Child. I don't want to have to repeat myself."

"My, aren't we authoritarian tonight."

"Don't get smart. This is serious."

"OK. Shoot."

"I want you to transfer up here next quarter."

"Are you drunk?"

"No, I'm stone sober."

"Why the hell would I want to do a dumb thing like that? This isn't much of a school, I'll admit, but it's sure a lot better than that processing plant up there."

"Education is what you make of it," I said inanely. "I want you up here."

"All my friends are down here."

"Not *all* of them, Clydine."

"Well, it's terribly sweet, but it's just completely out of the question."

"Dear," I said pointedly, "I didn't *ask* you."

"Oh, now we're giving orders, huh?"

"Goddammit! I can't get any work done. I'm spending every damn minute worrying about you."

"I can take care of myself very nicely, thank you," she said hotly.

"Bullshit! You haven't got sense enough to come in out of the rain."

"Now you look here, Danny Alders. I'm getting just damned sick and tired of everybody just automatically assuming that I'm a child just because I'm not eight feet tall."

"That has nothing to do with it."

"I'm going to hang up," she said.

"Good," I said. "I'm going to be down there in an hour anyway."

"Don't bother. I won't let you in."

"Don't be funny. I'll kick your goddamn door down if you try that."

"I'll call the police if you do," she yelled at me.

"The *fuzz*? *You*? Oh, get serious! I'll be there in an hour." I slammed down the receiver.

As a matter of fact, I made it in less than an hour. I saw Joan scuttling down the steps as I climbed out of my car.

"Good luck," she called. "I'm heading for the nearest bomb shelter."

"She pretty steamed?" I asked.

"Don't forget to duck."

"Thanks a lot, Joan. You're all heart."

I went on up the stairs. She didn't have the door locked, but she did try to hold it shut against me. I pushed my way on through and we got down to business.

It was a glorious fight—the whole bit. We yelled and screamed at each other, and she slammed doors and threw books at me. I insulted her intelligence and her maturity, and she screamed like a fishwife.

Then she tried to hit me, and I held her arms so she couldn't, so she kicked my shins for a while—barefoot of course.

I'm sure we both knew we were behaving like a couple of twelve-year-olds, but we were having such a good time with the whole thing that we just went ahead and let it all hang out.

Finally she ran crying into the bedroom, slamming the door behind her. I went right on in after her. She was lying across the bed, sobbing as if her heart were about to break.

"Come on, Blossom," I said soothingly, sitting down beside her.

"You—you said such aw—*awful things*," she sobbed.

"Come on, now. You know damn well I didn't mean any of it."

"No, I *don't*," she wailed. "First that awful phone call and now you come down here yelling, and calling me names, and ordering me around, and grabbing me, and—oh, Danny, why?"

"Because I'm in love with you, you little knothead," I said. I hadn't really meant to say it, but it was pretty damned obvious by then.

She rolled over very quickly and looked up at me, her face shocked. "What?" she demanded.

"You heard me."

"Say it again."

I did, and then she was all over me like a fur coat. She tasted pretty salty from all the crying, but I didn't mind. I kissed her soundly about the head and shoulders for ten minutes or so—as I said before, it was a glorious kind of fight.

"You're going to transfer up to the U next quarter," I said firmly.

"All right, Danny," she said meekly. "I know it's stupid, but I can't fight you and me both."

"You knew damn well you were going to do it anyway," I said kissing her again. "Why did we have to go through all of this?"

"I just wanted you to say it, that's all," she said, nestling down in my arms.

"You knew that was what it was all about, for God's sake. You're not dense."

"A girl likes to be told," she said stubbornly.

Women!

38

AND SO, after the holidays, Clydine Stewart, the terror of Pacific Avenue, transferred to the University of Washington. I'm not exactly sure what she'd threatened her parents with to get them to go along with a switch like that in the middle of her junior year, when the loss of credits probably set her back almost two full semesters, but somehow she managed to pull it off.

She rented a sleeping room down the block from my shack—primarily for the sake of appearances and to have a place to store her spare clothes and her empty luggage. She slept there on an average of about once a month.

I suppose that if a man lives with a woman long enough, he gets used to the damp hand-laundry hanging in the bathroom and the bristly hair-curler that he steps on barefoot in the middle of the night, but I wouldn't bet on it.

"You don't put your hair up," I said one morning, as calmly as I could, "so why in the name of God do I keep stepping on these damned things?" I held out a well-mashed curler.

"A girl never knows when she might want to," she said, as if explaining to a child.

We were horribly crowded, and our books and records got hopelessly jumbled, and we were always stumbling over each other. We argued continually about who was going to use the desk and who got firsties on the bathroom in the morning. All in all, it was a pretty normal sort of arrangement. We even wound up sharing the same toothbrush after she lost hers and always kept forgetting to buy a new one.

She even read my mail, which bugged me a little at first, but I couldn't see much point in making an issue out of it since we read all our letters to each other anyway.

"Hey," she said one afternoon as I came in, "you got a letter from Cap Miller."

"Where are you?"

"In the bathtub."

I went on in. She'd gotten over *that* little hang-up.

"Where is it?"

"On the desk."

I bent over and kissed her and then dabbled foam on the end of her nose.

"Rat," she said.

"Are we going to have to go to the store this afternoon?" I asked her, going on back out to the living room-bedroom-study-reception hall-gymnasium.

"We'd better, if you want any supper tonight. Why?"

"Just wondering, that's all."

"Did you get any word on that fellowship yet?"

I picked up Cap's letter.

"Yeah," I said. "I got it." I tried to sound casual about it.

She squealed and came charging, suds and all, out of the bathroom. I got very wetly kissed, and then she saw that the shades were up and scampered back to the tub. What a nut!

I unfolded the letter. It was in pencil.

DEAR DAN,

I have been meaning to write a letter to you ever since we got your fine letter just before X-mas. I was real glad to hear about the big man. I have been awful worried about him ever since the trip last fall.

I was awful sorry to hear that your brother and his Mrs. broke up. That's always a real shame.

The snow here is pretty deep this time of year, but you don't need to worry about being able to get through come spring. Clint says he'll carry you piggyback from Twisp if need be. Ha-ha.

We are all wintering pretty well considering our ages. Clint has a little trouble with his legs that he broke so many times when the weather turns cold. And I have a little trouble getting started out of a morning myself, but otherwise we don't have no complaints to speak of.

Well, Dan, it's about time I went down and fed the stock. Old Ned is resting up so he'll be all full of p—— & vinegar when you come up. I knew you'd like to know that. Ha-ha. I have been going on here about long enough. Next thing you know I'll be turning into one of them book writers your learning about at college. So long till next time.

> *Your friend,*
> CAP

Oh. Clint says to say hello for him, too.

I could see him laboring over the letter with that stub-pencil of his, the sweat trickling down the outer edges of his white mustache.

"He isn't very well educated, is he?" she called from the bathroom.

"He's one of the smartest men I know," I said.

"That's not the same thing."

"I know."

"You can see how hard he worked on that letter," she said. "I kept trying to see through all that stiffness to the real man."

"You have to meet him to see that," I said.

"I hope I get the chance," she said.

"You will," I promised her.

Somebody knocked at the door, and I put Cap's letter down, swung the bathroom door shut and answered it.

It was my mother.

"Danny, baby," she said, her mouth kind of loose and her tongue a little thick.

I couldn't say anything. Just seeing her was like having somebody grab me by the stomach with an ice-cold hand. I know that sounds literary, but that's the only way to describe it. I held the door open and let her in. My hands started to shake.

The years on booze had not been very kind to my mother. Her hair was ratty and gray, and not very clean, and her hat was kind of squashed down on top of it. She'd tried to put on some makeup and had done a rotten job of it. Her coat was shabby, and she had a large hole in one of her stockings.

She stood uncertainly in the middle of the room, waiting for me to say something.

"Sit down, Mother," I said, pointing at the couch.

"Thank you, Danny," she said and perched uneasily on the edge of the couch.

"How have you been, Mother?" I asked her.

"Oh," she said tremulously, "not too bad, Danny. I've got a pretty good job down in Portland. I'm in maintenance." She pronounced it "maintain-ance." "It is with the company that owns this big office building. I work nights."

I nodded. It was about what I'd expected.

"I got a week off," she said. "I heard about poor Jackie's marriage going on the rocks. You heard about that, didn't you?"

"Yes, Mother."

"Well, quick as a shot I went to my boss and I told him I was going to have to have a few days off so I could come up to Tacoma and see if I couldn't help him maybe patch things up. Poor Jackie. He's had such bad luck with his marriages."

"Yeah," I said.

"But he told me it was too late for that, and I was just so awful sorry. Then he told me you'd gone back to school up here, so I just had to come up here and see you. I mean, you *are* my baby and all, and we haven't seen each other in just years and years, have we?"

"It's been a long time, Mother," I agreed.

She was nervously trying to light a cigarette, and finally I fired up my lighter for her. Her hands were shaking as badly as mine were.

"Would you like a drink, Mother?" I asked her.

She raised her face quickly, and the sudden look of anguish cut right through me. She thought I was being snotty.

"No games, Mother," I said. "I'm going to have one, and I just thought you might like one too, that's all."

"Well," she said hesitantly, "maybe just a little one. I've been cutting way down, you know."

"Mixer? Water? It's bourbon."

"Just a little ice, Danny, if you got any."

I fixed us a couple, and I could see by the way her hands were shaking that she needed one pretty badly.

We both drank them off, and I refilled the glasses without saying anything. I think we both felt better then.

"I'm so proud of you Danny, baby," she said. "I mean your college and all. I never told you that, did I? There's so many things I never got the chance to tell you. You and Jackie both seemed to grow up so fast. It just seems like I no more than turned around and you were both gone. First Jackie in the Navy, and then your father passing away, and then you leaving like you did. It just all happened so fast."

"It's like that sometimes, Mother," I said. "Nothing ever stays the same."

"I can still remember you two when you were little," she

said. "Jackie always so lively and full of fun, and you always so quiet and serious. Just like day and night, you two. And now poor Jackie getting divorced again." She dug out a hand-kerchief and held it to her face. She wasn't crying; she was just getting ready.

"He's a big boy now, Mother," I said.

"It's just all so rotten," she said. "You're the smart one. Don't ever get married, Danny. Women are just no good. We're all bitches."

"Now, Mother."

"No, it's true." The tears were running down her face now, smearing her makeup. "Your father was a good man—a fine man, and look what I did to him. He didn't understand me, but that didn't give me the right to hound him the way I did. I tried to be a good wife, but I just couldn't help myself."

"It's all right now, Mother. Just try not to let it get you down."

She finished her drink and mutely held out the glass. I doubt if she was even aware that she was doing it. I filled it again. She was making a good-sized dent in my bourbon, but what the hell?

"I'm pretty much a failure, do you know that, Danny? I failed your father, and I failed you boys." She was crying openly now, the wet, slobbering, let-it-all-go kind of crying you see once in a while in an old wino.

"I'm so sorry, Danny. I'm so sorry."

"It's all right, Mother. It was all a long time ago." How could I get her off it?

"Please forgive me, Danny, baby."

"Come on, Mother." That was too much.

"You've got to forgive me," she said. She looked at me, her eyes pleading and her face a ruin.

"Mother."

"I'm begging you to forgive me, Danny," she said. "I'll get down on my knees to you." She moved before I could stop her. She slid off the edge of the couch and dropped heavily to her knees on the floor.

"Come on, Mother," I said, trying to lift her back to the couch, "get up."

"Not until you forgive me, Danny."

This was silly. "All right, Mother, I forgive you. It wasn't your fault."

"Really, Danny? Really?"

"Yes, Mother. Come on now. Get up."

She let me haul her to her feet, and then she insisted on giving me a kiss. Then she kind of halfway repaired her face. She seemed a little calmer after that. She talked for a few minutes and then got ready to leave.

"I've got just enough time to make connections for the Portland bus," she said.

"Have you got your ticket?" I asked her.

"Oh, yes," she said brightly. "I'm just fine."

"Do you need any money—for a bite to eat or anything?"

"No, Danny, I'm just fine, really." She stood up. "I've really got to go now." She went over to the door. "I feel so much better now that we've had the chance to get things straightened out like this. I've worried about it for the longest time."

"It was good to see you, Mother."

"I'm so proud of you, baby." She patted my cheek and went out quickly. I watched through the window as she carefully made her way around the house in front. Her hat was on lopsided, and her dark coat had a large dusty patch on one shoulder where she'd stumbled against something. She went on out of sight.

"Oh, Danny," Clydine said. "Oh, Danny, I'm so sorry." She was standing behind me, wrapped in a bath towel, huge tears bright in her eyes.

"Oh, it's all right, Blossom. She's been like this for as long as I can remember. You get used to it after a while."

"It must have been *awful*."

"I don't even hold any grudges anymore," I said. "I thought I did, but I really don't. I really forgave her, do you know that? I didn't think I ever could, but I did. I wasn't just saying it." It surprised me, but I meant it. "I just wish she could quit drinking, is all," I added.

39

IT was a Thursday morning several weeks after Mother's visit and Clydine had just got up. I was still lying in bed. She stood nude in front of the full-length mirror that was bolted to the bathroom door. She cupped her hands under her breasts.

"Danny," she said thoughtfully, hefting them a couple times.

"Yes, love?"

"Do you think I ought to start wearing a bra? I'm pretty chesty, and I wouldn't want to start to droop."

I howled with laughter.

"Well," she said, "I *wouldn't*! I don't see what's so goddamn funny."

She was absolutely adorable. Sometimes I'd catch myself laughing for no reason, just being around her. I loved her, not with that grand, aching, tragic passion that I'd pretty well burned out on Susan, but rather with a continual delight in her, a joy just in her presence. Believe me, there's a lot to be said for joy as opposed to tragic passion. For one thing, it's a helluva lot less exhausting in the long run.

Anyhow, nothing would do but our cutting classes and my taking her out immediately so she could buy herself some new bras.

We got back about eleven, and she modeled them for me.

"What do you think?" she said doubtfully.

"It's different," I said.

"You don't like it."

"I didn't say that. I just said it's different. How does it feel?"

"Like a darn straitjacket," she admitted. Then she sighed deeply. "Oh, well, I guess it's just another one of the curses of being a woman."

"Poor Blossom." I laughed.

She stuck her tongue out at me. I'd noticed, but hadn't mentioned, the fact that she'd backed way off on the truck-driver vocabulary and hadn't really gotten much involved with

the militants up here. She'd told me that she disagreed ideo-
logically with the main thrust of the university militants, but I
suspected that she'd just plain outgrown them. At least I didn't
have to worry about her getting her cute little fanny chucked
into jail every weekend. That was something anyway.

After lunch she had a couple of classes, so I had a chance
to get some concentrated work done. I was tackling the possibility that Melville's *Billy Budd* was not a simple hymn of
praise to the natural man, but rather a much more complex
parable of the struggle of good and evil—represented by Billy
and Claggart—for the soul of Captain Vere. I'd landed on it
by way of the chance discovery that Melville had practically
camped on the New York Public Library copy of Milton's
Paradise Regained all during the time he was writing *Billy
Budd*.

I was deep in the mystic mumblings of the Old Dansker
when Jack showed up.

He looked awful. He hadn't shaved for several days, and
his eyes looked like the proverbial two burned holes in a blanket.

"Jesus, man," I said, holding the door open for him, "what
the hell happened to you?"

"I just got out of jail," he said.

"Jail?"

He nodded grimly and collapsed into the armchair by the
door. "You got anything to drink?"

I got him a water glass and poured it half-full of whiskey.
His hands were shaking so badly that it was all he could do to
get a good solid slug of bourbon down.

"What the hell happened, Jack?" I demanded.

"You know that .45 I bought from Sloane?"

"Yeah."

"Well, Sandy stuck the damn thing in her mouth and blew
her brains all over the ceiling of my bathroom."

"Oh, Jesus!"

"The cops held me on suspicion of murder for three days
in the Tacoma jail until they finally decided that she did it
herself. They had the inquest this morning."

"Christ, man, why didn't you get in touch with me?"

"I thought you knew. It's been in all the newspapers and on
the radio and TV."

"We've been pretty busy, and I just haven't paid any attention to the news for a while. God, Jack, I'm sorry as hell. I should have been there."

"Nothin' you coulda done." He shrugged. "They were just playin' games is all. Who the hell ever murders anybody by stickin' a gun in their mouth?"

"When did it happen?"

"Monday night. I'd been out—just kinda pokin' up and down the Avenue, you know. Anyhow, when I got back, there she was all sprawled out over the toilet stool with blood and hair and all that other gunk splattered all over the ceiling. Christ, Dan, I can still see it." He covered his eyes with one trembling hand.

"Finish your drink," I said, holding out the bottle to refill his glass.

He nodded and drank off the whiskey, shuddering as it went down. I filled his glass again.

"Look at that," he said, holding out his hands. They were trembling violently. "I can't stop *shakin'*. I been shakin' ever since I found her. My hands shake all the time."

"Come on, Jack, settle down," I said. He was in tough shape. I should have warned him about it. God damn it, I should have warned him!

"Christ, Dan, I can't. My nerves are all shot. I feel like somebody just kicked all my guts out."

"Was she acting funny or anything before it happened? I mean, did she give you any kind of warning at all?"

"Hell no," he said. "She always was kinda strange—you know, kinda quiet—but she wasn't any different at all. Christ, the last thing she said when I left was, 'See you when you get back.' God, Dan, that sure as hell don't sound like somebody who's gonna kill theirself, does it?"

"No way," I said.

"We was gettin' along just fine. Hell, no beefs, no trouble, nothin'. And then she just ups and kills herself."

"Did she leave a note or anything?"

"Nothin'. I think that's why the cops put the arm on me. She even cleaned the place all up before she did it."

"They got it all straightened out at the inquest, didn't they? I mean, they didn't leave the case open or anything?"

"No. It's all settled. They had a lotta medical experts in and all. Angle of the bullet and all that shit. I was there because I found the body and called the cops. I got to hear the whole thing. Couple guys she'd gone with before I met her got called in, and they both said she'd talked about it when they knew her. Anyway, they finally ruled it 'death by suicide,' and the cops had to let me go. The bastards sure as hell didn't *want* to, I'll tell you that. Once those motherfuckers get their hands on you, they hate like hell to have to turn you loose."

"Yeah," I agreed.

"God," he said, "I couldn't even go back inside my trailer."

"What'd they do, padlock it all up?"

"No, nothin' like that. I just couldn't make myself do it. I went on out there, but I just couldn't go inside. Ain't that a helluva note?"

"You want to bunk in here for a few days?" It wouldn't set too well with the Little Flower, but this was an emergency.

"No, Dan, thanks anyway, but I gotta get outa the area for a while. I'm goin' down to Portland. Maybe stay with the Old Lady or something."

"You're welcome to stay here," I said.

"It's too close, man. I gotta get away. I was just wonderin' if you could maybe come back down with me and get some of my clothes and stuff out of the trailer for me. I can't make myself go back in there. I just can't do it." He sat hunched over, holding both hands around his glass.

"Sure, Jack," I said, "I'll leave a note for my roommate."

"How is she?" he asked.

"She's fine," I said. I scribbled a quick note to her and we took off. I followed his Plymouth on down to Tacoma and on out toward Madrona. It was cloudy and calm that day, and the trailer court seemed kind of shadowy, tucked back in under a bunch of big old pine trees.

I got out and went over to where he'd parked his car. "What do you need, Jack?" I asked him.

"Grab my clothes and some shoes and stuff," he said, not looking at the trailer. "Oh, get my transistor radio, too, huh? It's in the bedroom."

"Sure, Jack."

"Don't go in the bathroom, man. It's awful."

"I'll have to," I said. "You'll need your razor and all."

"Oh," he said.

"It'll be OK," I told him. I went on into the trailer. It took me about twenty minutes to pack up all his clothes. I didn't go into the bathroom until I'd got everything else squared away.

Actually, it wasn't as bad as I'd expected. Most of the mess was in a dried pool between the toilet and the tub. I gathered

up Jack's stuff and took it on out to the living room. I tucked
it all in various places in his suitcases and then hauled them
on out to his car. On my last trip I carried out his radio and
his shotgun.

"No, man," he said, his face turning a kind of pasty color,
"leave that fuckin' gun here!"

"You can't leave it here," I told him. "Somebody might
swipe it."

"*You* keep it then. I can't stand to look at the goddamn thing.
I told you, Danny, my nerves are all shot."

I took the gun over and put it in my car.

"Did you lock up?" he asked me.

I shook my head. "I'll slip the latch when I leave. I'll clean
up that mess in there."

"You don't have to do that."

I shrugged. "Somebody has to."

"Thanks, Danny," he said in a shaking voice. "I don't think
I'm ever gonna be able to go in there again."

"You probably ought to sell it," I told him.

He nodded. "Hey," he said suddenly, "I think there's some
beer in the refrig. Why don't we sit out here and have a couple?
I need something."

"Sure, Jack." I went on back in and carted out the six-pack.

"I'll make arrangements with Clem to pick up the trailer,"
he said as I got into the front seat with him. He started the car.

"Where we going?" I asked him.

"Just down the road a ways. I can't stand to look at that
damn trailer is all."

"OK."

We drove on out to the highway and then pulled off into a
little roadside park.

"God, man," he said, opening a can of beer, "I'm just
completely wiped out. It was all I could do to keep from tossin'
my cookies when you hauled out my shotgun."

"It'll probably take you a while to get over this," I told him,
popping open a can for myself.

"I don't know if I *ever* will," he said. "Danny, my *hands*
shake all the time. I'm *afraid*, and I don't know what the hell
it is I'm afraid of—maybe everything. Shit, I'm afraid of guns,
the trailer, bathrooms, blood—Christ, anything at all, and I
just come all apart."

"You'll be all right, Jack. It's just going to take you some
time, that's all."

He sat at the wheel, staring moodily out at the murky day. "I don't know if you remember or not, but I had an argument with the Old Man once when I was a kid. I said that when a guy grew up, he wasn't afraid of anything anymore."

"I remember," I said.

"He tried to tell me I was all wet, but I wouldn't listen to him. I know what he meant now."

We sat drinking beer and not saying much.

"You fixed OK for money?" I asked him.

"Christ, I don't know. I don't think Old Clem'll spring loose with my check until Saturday. I hadn't thought about that."

"I can give you twenty," I said.

"Hell," he said, "I could always tap Sloane."

"I'd rather give it to you myself," I said.

"Shit," he said, "you already done more than enough."

I shrugged. "You're my brother, Jack. That's what it's all about." I gave him a twenty.

"Thanks, Kid," he said. "I'll get it back to you."

"No rush," I said.

"I suppose I ought to get goin'," he said. "I'd like to make it to Portland before too late."

"Sure, Jack. Just drop me at the gate of the trailer court, OK?"

"Right."

We drove on back and stopped outside the court.

He held out his hand and we shook.

"I probably won't see you for a while," he said, "but I'll keep in touch."

"Sure, Jack."

"It's been a wild six months or so, hasn't it?"

"Far out," I said.

"At least we got to go huntin' together," he said. "That's somethin' anyway."

"It was the best of it," I told him.

He nodded and I opened the door.

"You know somethin', Danny? What I was sayin' about a guy bein' afraid of things—that argument me and the Old Man had?"

"Yeah?"

"He was right, you know that?"

"He usually was, Jack."

"Yeah. Well, I'll tell you somethin', and this is the straight stuff. Maybe I hide it pretty good, but to tell you the honest-

to-God truth, I been afraid all my life. It just took somethin'
like this to make me realize it."

"Everybody's afraid, Jack, not just you. That's what Dad
was trying to tell you. You've just got to learn to live with it."

He nodded. "Well," he said, "take care now."

"You too, Jack."

We shook hands again, and I got out.

I stood at the side of the road watching his battered Plymouth
until it disappeared around a corner about a half mile down the
highway.

That evening I told Clydine about it.

"I told you a long time ago that it was going to happen,"
she said.

"Yeah," I said. "How did you know, anyhow?"

"I just knew, that's all."

"That sure isn't much help," I said. "I mean, if I were to
suddenly go into the business of suicide prevention, it wouldn't
give me much to go on, would it?"

"I don't know," she said thoughtfully, "the girl just seemed
to think of herself in the past tense somehow. Even that creepy
Helen talked about what she planned to do next week or next
year. Sandy just never did. She didn't have any future. A
woman *always* thinks about the future—always. When you
find one who doesn't, watch out."

"As simple as that?"

She nodded. "Along with a good healthy gut-feel for it.
Being around her was like being at a funeral. It wasn't anything
recent, because she had gotten pretty well used to it by then.
She was just waiting for the right time."

"I should have warned Jack," I said.

"He couldn't have stopped her."

"That's not what I meant. He got tangled up in it, and it's
tearing him all up inside."

"He'll come out of it," she said. "He's too much of an egomaniac not to."

"Why, you heartless little witch!" I said.

"Oo, poo," she said.

"Poo?"

"All right then, *shit*!" she snapped. "Your brother's got all
the sensitivity of a telephone pole, and about as much compassion as a meat grinder. He'll make out."

There was no point pushing the issue. She didn't like Jack,
and she wasn't about to waste any sympathy on him.

That night I had the dream again. I caught flashes of a sad-eyed old dog rolling over and over in the snow and of the white deer lying huddled at the foot of that gravel bank, the masculinity of his antlers sheared off by his fall and his deep red eye gazing reproachfully at me through the film of dust that powdered it. And Sandy was there, too, standing nude by the sink in that house out in Milton, her nudity sexless—even meaningless, and her voice echoing back to me:

"It doesn't matter. It's only for a little while, just a little while."

Epilogue

I didn't get the chance to get back up to the Methow Valley that spring. The money ran short on me. I wrote to Cap, of course, telling him how sorry I was, and through the stiff formality of his letters, I could sense his disappointment as well.

I guess I had talked up the high country to my little Bolshevik to the point that she finally got a bellyful of hearing about it because she finally put her foot down.

"This is it," she said in early July, delivering her non-negotiable demands. "We are both going to take two weeks off and go up there. I'm going to meet the great Cap Miller and his crotchety but lovable sidekick Clint. I am also going up to look at that damned Valhalla of yours."

"We can't afford it."

"Chicken-pucky we can't. We've both got a steady income during the school year and good steady jobs this summer. The office I work in shuts down for the first two weeks in August so that all the regular people can take their vacations, and that crazy Swede boat builder you work for is so convinced that you're the greatest thing since sliced bread that he'll probably give you the two weeks with pay."

"Chicken-pucky?"

"Oh, shut up!"

We argued about it for a week or so, but my heart wasn't really in it.

When I approached Norstrom, my boss, he screamed for twenty minutes about how he couldn't possibly spare me and wound up trying to convince me that I ought to go fishing up the inside passage instead.

I had to lie a little in my letter to Cap, and I didn't like that at all. Though I knew he wouldn't have said anything, I also knew that he probably wouldn't have approved of the irregularity of Clydine and myself going off into the hill without benefit of clergy, as it were. I told him we were going to elope,

331

and that this was going to be our honeymoon. It was a big
mistake because he insisted on furnishing everything for our
trip at no charge. I felt like a real shitheel about it.

Anyway, on the third of August, Blossom and I were batting
along on the highway north to Lake Chelan, headed for Twisp.
It was about eight o'clock in the morning and we were both a
little sleepy.

"I don't see why we couldn't have slept a little later," she
complained. We'd spent the night at a motel in Cashmere.

"It takes a good long while to get up there," I said. "It's
not exactly a roadside campground, Tulip."

"Couldn't we at least stop someplace? I'm starved."

"We'll be there in another hour," I told her. "You'll need
all the appetite you can muster to get even partway around the
kind of breakfast Clint cooks up."

She grunted and curled back up in the seat.

I woke her when we got to Twisp, and she insisted on
stopping at a gas station. I fidgeted around for the twenty
minutes or so that she was in the rest room with her overnight
bag, wondering what she was up to.

When she came out, she looked like a different girl. She'd
put in her contact lenses, caught her hair in a loose coil at the
back of her neck, and she was wearing a white blouse and
tailored slacks. She'd even put on lipstick, for God's sake!

"Wow," I said.

"Oh, be quiet."

"You're gorgeous, Rosebud. I mean it."

She looked at me to see if I were kidding her, and when
she saw that I wasn't, she actually blushed.

"All right," she said, "let's go meet your family."

What she'd said didn't really register on me until we were
a ways out of town.

"Why did you say that?" I asked her.

"Say what?"

"About meeting my family?"

"Just a bad joke," she said. "Forget it."

We drove along the twisting, narrow road out toward Miller's place. The road looked different with the poplar leaves all
green instead of the gold I'd remembered from the preceding
autumn, but the whole stretch of road was still breathtaking.

"It's really beautiful, isn't it?" she said finally, touching
nervously at her hair.

"Wait till we get up higher," I said. "It gets even better."

I slowed the car and turned into Miller's driveway. The colt was a yearling now, but he still loved to run. He galloped alongside us, tossing his head.

"I didn't know horses chased cars, too," she said.

I laughed. I hadn't thought of it that way.

"Oh, dear," she said, her voice faltering.

Cap was waiting for us out in the yard, and he looked even more rugged than I remembered him. Then he grinned and it was like the sun coming up.

The two of them almost fell all over themselves charming each other, and I got a helluva big lump in my throat watching the two people in the world I cared most about getting along so well. Then Clint came out, and the party really got started.

Finally we went on into the big, musty old dining room and sat down to breakfast. Miller bowed his head and said grace, probably in Clydine's honor, just a few simple words, but it moved me pretty profoundly.

"My wife always used to like havin' grace before a meal," he said. "Me and Clint kinda got out of the habit since we take a lot of our meals standin' up."

"Let's eat it before it gets cold," Clint said gruffly. He'd outdone himself on the whole meal. I knew damned well he'd been at it since about four that morning. He'd even shaved in her honor.

"I'm real sorry, Dan," he said with his eyes sparkling at me, "but I just couldn't manage to whip up a big mess of that whatever-it-was you fixed for us that time. I just never got around to gettin' the recipe from you."

"All right, smart-aleck," I said.

"Besides," he said, "we're runnin' a little short of pack-horses."

"What's this?" Clydine asked.

They told her.

"What was in it?" she asked me.

I explained how I'd made it.

"No wonder it tasted like stewed packhorse," she commented blandly.

I thought Cap and Clint were going to fall off their chairs laughing.

After breakfast we went on back outside.

"I figured Old Dusty would be about the best horse for the little lady," Cap said. "That's the one the Professor rode up there. He's pretty easygoin', and he's good and dependable."

I nodded.

"We knew you'd want Old Ned again." He grinned.

"You're all heart, Cap."

He laughed and slapped me on the shoulder.

We loaded the horses in the stock-truck and the camping gear and saddles in the pickup and drove on down the driveway again, Cap in front in the pickup, then Clydine and me in my car and Clint bringing up the rear in the stock-truck.

"Oh, Danny," she said, nestling up beside me, "I just love them both. They're wonderful."

I nodded happily.

"Do you think they liked me at all?"

"They loved you, dear."

"That's just because of you," she said.

"No," I said. "They can't do that. Not either one of them. They don't know how."

"I guess they couldn't, could they?"

"No way."

"You love them two old men, too, don't you?" she said suddenly.

I nodded. I probably wouldn't have put it exactly that way, but that's what it boiled down to.

The sun was very bright and the sky very blue. The whole world seemed as if it had been washed clean just that morning.

We turned off the highway and started up the long gravel road toward the beginning of the trail. When we came around that corner and caught the first full glimpse of Glacier Park looming white above us, she gasped.

"Pretty impressive, huh?" I said.

"Wow!" was all she could say.

We all stopped when we got to the road-end and went through the ritual of unloading the packhorses first again.

"Boy, did *you* get lucky," Clint said as we climbed up into the truck after Dusty.

"How's that?"

"That wife of yours. Now, I just *know* you ain't been good enough to deserve somebody like her. You ain't got it in you."

I laughed and the little old guy grinned at me.

We led Dusty out and saddled him.

"Just ride 'im up and down the road kinda easy like, honey," Cap told Clydine after he'd helped her get aboard.

The three of us watched her amble the patient old horse on down the road.

"She sets a saddle well, too," Cap said approvingly. "I think you got yourself a good one, son."

"She'll do," I agreed happily.

Then Clint and I got Ned out.

The big gray glared at me with suspicion and then sniffed at me a couple times. I scratched his ears.

"I think the damned old fool remembers you," Clint said.

"We'll find out in a minute or so," I said, swinging the saddle up on Ned's back. I cinched it good and tight and then climbed on.

"Just how big a head of steam have you two let him build up?" I asked them.

Then they really started to laugh.

"Hell, boy," Cap said, still laughing, "we worked him every day this week. We weren't about to let him break one of your legs for you on your honeymoon."

"Everybody's a comedian these days," I said dryly and rode off down the road to catch up with Clydine.

"Did you see his face?" I heard Clint howl from behind me.

Just before we left, she jumped down off her horse and kissed the two surprised old men and then hopped back up into the saddle. We rode off on up the trail towing a pair of pack-horses, leaving the two of them blushing and scuffing their boots in the dust like a pair of schoolboys.

When we stopped at the top of the first ridge to let the horses blow a little, we could see their tiny figures still standing down by the parked vehicles. We all waved back and forth for a while, and then Clydine and I rode on down into the next valley.

It was about three thirty in the afternoon when we came on down into the little basin. In spite of Cap's assurances, I'd been about halfway worried that we might find about a thousand sheep and a couple herders up there, but the camp was empty.

She sat in her saddle, looking around, not saying anything.

"Well?" I said.

She nodded slowly. "I see what you meant," she said simply.

"Let's get to work," I said. "We've got a lot to do before the sun goes down."

We got down from our horses and checked the corrals. They were still sound. I unsaddled the horses and turned them loose in the corrals and then we went on up to the tent frames. It took us a while to get the two tents up, but we finally got them squared away. The moss we'd all gathered the year before was gone—deer or something, I suppose—so we got to work and hauled in fresh stuff.

Miller or Clint—one or the other—had substituted, with some delicacy, a pair of sleeping bags that zipped together into a double for the mismatched pair that we'd brought, so I modified the log bunk frames in our tent to accommodate the double bag.

The beaver had scattered our firewood, but it didn't take long to get together enough for the night at least.

"I don't know about you, Bwana," she said finally, "but I'm starved again."

I kissed her nose for her. "I'll get right on it," I said. I dug out the big iron grill and got a fired started.

"Clint said he had supper all packed up for us," she said.

"Yeah," I told her, "it's that big sack right at the top of the food pack."

She fished around in the cook tent and came out with the big sack. She carried it over to McKlearey's table and opened it.

"Oh, wow!" she said. "Look at this." She ripped down the side of the sack. "There's a banquet in here. How am I supposed to cook all of this over an open fire? They even put in a bottle of champagne, for cryin' out loud."

"Oh, for Christ's sake," I said.

"What a pair of old sweeties," she said.

Clint had included a note, the first of a dozen or so we found tucked away in various places among the packs. It gave very specific instructions on how to fix supper.

"Well," she said, pulling up the sleeves of the sweatshirt she'd changed into as soon as we'd gotten into camp, "now we find out if I know how to cook out in the woods."

"I'll drop the booze in the spring," I said.

"Then see what you can do in the way of some chairs," she said.

"Chairs?"

"*You* may plan to eat standing up or all squatted down like a savage of some kind, but *I* sure don't."

Women!

I examined the construction of Lou's table and managed to fix up a kind of rickety bench. It was a lot more solid when I dug it into the ground.

"There's a tablecloth in that bag over there," she told me.

"A *tablecloth*?"

"Of course."

The sun had gone down and I built up the fire and cranked up the Coleman lantern to give us light enough to eat by.

We had steak and baked potatoes and all kinds of other little surprises.

"Well?" she said, after I'd taken several bites. "Do I pass?"

"You'll do, Blossom, you'll do."

"Is *that* all?"

"That's enough, kid." I kissed her noisily.

"Tomorrow night you get a big plate of whatever-it-was."

"Oh, God," I said, "anything but that."

We saved the champagne until it was good and cold. Then we sat by the fire and drank it from tin cups. We both got a little fuzzy from it—maybe it was the altitude.

"Danny," she said drowsily after we'd finished the bottle.

"Yes, Rosebud?"

"Let's go to bed and make love."

"What brought that on?"

"Well, damn it, it *is* my honeymoon, isn't it?"

And so we did that.

The days drifted along goldenly. The biting chill of autumn had not yet moved onto the high meadows and, though the nights were cool, by ten in the morning the sun was very warm. As soon as she found out that there wasn't a soul for ten miles or more in any direction, my flower child turned nudist on me. Her skin soaked in the high sunlight, and she started to tan deliciously. All I managed was a sunburn.

She even tried swimming in the beaver pond, but only once. She was almost blue when she came out. I was just as happy about that, all things considered, since I had designs on the trout.

We hiked around a bit and went horseback riding and laid around in the sun and made love at odd intervals. It was strange, seeing her walking around in her pink, innocent nudity in the places where so many other things had happened.

One night, in our cozy double sleeping bag, it got down to confession time.

"Danny?" she said tentatively.

"Yes?"

"You remember that first night—the time when you picked up Joan and me at the theater?"

"Of course I do."

"I knew," she said in a small voice.

"You knew what, dear?"

"I knew you'd never been to prison."

"Oh? How was that?"

"You don't have any tattoos," she said, tracing designs on my chest with her finger. "Everybody who's ever been to prison has tattoos—even if it's only a few spots or something."

I hadn't thought about that. "Why didn't you just blow the whistle on me then?"

"I wasn't really sure until I got your clothes off," she said.

"You sure could have brought it all to a halt at that point," I said.

"I know," she said, her voice even tinier.

"Why didn't you?"

She buried her face in her arms. "I didn't want to," she said.

I kissed her on the ear. "I won't tell anybody if you won't," I said.

"There's something else," she said, her face still buried in her arms.

"Oh? I'm not sure how much truth I can take in one day."

"You remember how I used to talk—about orgies and all that kind of thing?"

"Yes."

"Well," she said, "I was kind of exaggerating. There was only one other boy really."

I didn't say anything. I'd more or less figured that out for myself.

"Are you mad at me?"

"For not being promiscuous?"

"No, dum-dum, for lying to you."

"Well," I said, "it's pretty awful."

She looked up, stricken, until she saw that I was grinning at her.

"You rat!" she said suddenly, pounding on my chest as I laughed at her. "You absolute, unspeakable rat."

I folded her up in my arms and kissed her soundly. It was one of the better nights.

I suppose I'd been putting it off, but I knew that sooner or later I was going to have to go up there. I'd brought the damned pistol belt along—I'd told myself it was for coyotes or something, but I knew that wasn't really it. I had to duplicate as closely as possible what it had been like, so the gun had to go along.

"I've got to go up on the ridge today," I told her as I came out of the tent that morning.

"Oh? I'll go along," she said.

"I don't think you should really," I said.

"Why not?"

"I'm going to see if I can find that deer," I told her.

"Whatever for? Won't it be all—well—"

"Probably."

"Then why on earth do you want to mess around with it?"

"It's not that I want to," I told her.

"I don't suppose there's any point trying to talk you out of it?"

"Not really."

"Well," she said, "have fun."

"That's not why I'm doing it."

"*Men!*" she snorted. We'd both taken to doing that a lot lately.

After breakfast I saddled Ned and came back up to camp. I went in and strapped on the pistol.

"Wow," she said, "if it isn't Pancho Villa himself."

"Lay off," I said. "I shouldn't be too long."

"Take your time," she said, stretching. "I'm going back to bed myself." She went on back to the tent.

I nudged Ned on around and on down to the lower end of the basin and across the creek. "Come on, buddy," I told him. "You know the way as well as I do."

He flicked his ears, and we started up the ridge. Even after this short a period of time, the ridge looked different. I couldn't be really sure if it was the fact that the leaves hadn't started to turn or what, but it took me quite a while to find Stan's old post. I figured that would be about the best place to go down. I tied Ned to a bush and climbed on down to the wash at the bottom of the draw.

I covered the wash from the place where I'd entered it that day the year before to the cliff where the deer had fallen. Apparently, there'd been a helluva run-off that spring, because the whole shape of the thing was different. I'd have sworn that I could have gone straight to the spot, but once I got down there, I couldn't find any recognizable landmarks.

I finally settled on a place that had to have been pretty close, but the shape of the banks was all wrong.

It was gone. There was no way I'd ever be able to verify for myself whether it had ever really been there or not. I suppose

I'd dreamed about the damned thing so often that I'd begun to almost doubt my own memory of it.

Now, with the wash so changed from the way I remembered it, I was less sure than ever. And so the pale flicker in the brush that I remembered would always be a doubtful phantom for me. There in the shadows at the bottom of the wash, I felt a sudden chill. I climbed back up to the ridge and untied Ned.

"Struck out, old buddy," I said, climbing up into the saddle.

He flickered his ears at me, and we went on back down.

That evening, as the sun was going down, Clydine and I were sitting on a log near the edge of the beaver pond.

"It's just lovely up here, Danny," she said. "I think it's the most beautiful place in the whole world."

I nodded. I don't think I'd said more than three words to her since I'd come back down the ridge.

I suppose I'd been building up to the question for several months. I knew that it was inevitable that sooner or later I should ask it despite all its obvious banality under the circumstances. Even so, it surprised me when I heard myself say it— for one thing, it was badly phrased. You kind of halfway expect something a little more polished from somebody with my background.

"Don't you think it's about time we got married?" I asked her.

Just as I had known I was going to ask her, so she had known she was going to be asked. I guess every girl knows that even before the man has actually made up his mind. And so it was that she'd had plenty of time to devise an answer that would let me know how she felt and at the same time assert her independence.

She looked up at me, smiled, and squeezed my arm.

"Why not?" she said.